TWINS
OF A
GAZELLE

MARGARET CULLINGFORD

AN IONIAN
AFFAIR

For "Cubsie"

CONTENTS

CHAPTER ONE

'Marry in haste I get to spend the evening with a dog.' Calista Blake entered the side-lobby of The Old Rectory, wrinkled her nose at the smell, spaniel, rubber boots and waders. A liver-and-white Springer, yawning and stretching, wagged his tail.

He followed her through the heart of the house and its pulsating silence into her study, bagged his favourite spot to lie stretched out along the window seat. Taking a brief from her document case, Calista dropped it with a thwack on the desk's leather surface, not urgent, nothing else to do. She strode over to the window almost the height of the room not for the first time questioning why she had agreed to move to a Leicestershire village with neither pub, nor shop. Tucking strands of hair behind each ear, her gaze wandered towards a distant ridge becoming shrouded in early-evening violet, the spaniel upright now all eager attention. Never having been keen on dogs – smelly beasts with disgusting habits – she appreciated the irony.

'Married women are allowed men friends, Beppo.' - About to leave Chambers Calista had been tempted by a male colleague's invitation to go for a drink. He was between relationships, and she . . . Unwise, there was that time she and Matt had been more than friends - 'Tonight I must make do with you. Come on, let's go.'

A clear May evening, but, she had no intention of going farther than the lawn, did not bother to change out of her lawyer's black. Beppo would have to be content with retrieving his stuffed toy-rabbit again

1

and again. At the bottom of the terrace steps, she bowled over arm. The rabbit arched across the sweep of grass almost reaching the ha-ha at the far end. Beppo waited, pointing till she commanded, 'Fetch.'

No one could accuse her of being hasty in marrying Adam Burgess. For a couple of years previous to their low-key wedding, knowing him in the biblical sense, knowing a lot about him, she assumed she knew him.

The dog returned, tail wagging, dropped his rabbit at her feet, and sat. As she picked up the toy, Calista spoke her thoughts.

'Took me a while, duhh, I don't know him at all.' Beppo cocked his head to one side as though understanding. 'I'd pop down to London to spend the night there with him. He was married to someone else at the time.'

The spaniel gave a low whine as though sympathetic to her mood.

'Stop pretending. You want me to throw this.' She gauged the distance so it landed again just short of the ha-ha. The palaver when it came to rest in the meadow beyond. 'Fetch.'

She was not proud of herself for being the reason for Adam's marriage break-up. She had never thought for one moment he would divorce Annabel on her account. And, no consolation discovering to her cost she preferred being a mistress rather than a wife.

Again, obedient, pleased with himself, Beppo came back and demanded her attention. Patient, he sat waiting, gazing at her with his soulful eyes.

'Not just Annabel left on her own, she's been left to cope with two teenage daughters.'

Again the dog whined to remind her he was waiting. Choosing her spot, she lobbed his toy over the high yew hedge. He waggled round the half-open lych-gate into the spinney.

Calista made her way to the gate. Too late for her conscience to torment her about Annabel and her children. In any case, she doubted Annabel could feel any lonelier than she did now. But for Beppo . . . She indulged him. By the time she was finished, he might prove a useless gun dog. Serve Adam right.

She stopped just inside the coppice, whistled. The dog woofed in response, he did not appear.

'Here boy.'

No Beppo. The ground soggy underfoot, she squelched in the direction of his bark. In subdued evening light, for the first time taking in her surroundings, trees, their new leaves too fresh-green almost translucent to form a canopy, rustled in a light breeze, mass of bluebells beneath, subtle perfume wafted over her. A blackbird's serenade she no sooner heard than he stopped.

The dog waited beside a hazel, his rabbit caught up in it, a few remaining lamb's tails trembling among the leaves. She shook the shrub. Even though light was fading she could see the toy had landed next to a clump of purple-pink flowers contrasting with the blue. She squatted on her haunches the better to see them.

'We've got early purple orchids in our spinney,' she said, not caring her pumps were sopping, tights snagged beyond redemption. 'More often than not, Beppo, it's the small, unexpected pleasures that make life worth living.' She was talking to the trees. Beppo had gone off through the undergrowth out of hearing, out of sight.

She straightened up ready to retrace the path. When Adam was away, the thought gnawed. Did he subscribe to the premise, marry your mistress, you create a vacancy? Despite being no more than she deserved, if she ever discovered he did, no way would she put up with being cheated on.

In the stillness, the rasping caw of crows in the tall ash trees over the other side of the lane – *Light thickens; and the crow makes wing to the rooky wood* - words from the Scottish play. Calista began to hurry, was startled by one of the ominous birds flapping its wings as it took off in front of her, something dead or alive in its beak – *Whiles night's black agents to their prey do rouse.*

'Beppo, here boy,' she called to no avail.

Once back in the house she would phone Adam for a chat. 'Maybe I'll be able to sense if he's with a woman,' she said to the night air.

Adam Burgess waited by a leaden Thames near the Girl and Dolphin Fountain on St Katharine's Way. He watched Sheena Jardine open the Louis Vuitton to pay for her cab. Like the 22 carat gold hoops glistening in her ears, he had given her the bag, maybe salve to his conscience, though he should not feel any particular responsibility towards her. She was well enough rewarded. Three years now since they had been introduced at one of Sonja's 'soirees'. Ever since, for an enhanced booking fee, he had requested Sheena be exclusive to him to attend his needs.

With an anticipatory frisson of pleasure, he observed her unhurried approach.

'Have you been waiting long?' She said.

'Sheena.' He kissed her on both cheeks. 'You look terrific.' And she did, classy, in black designer jeans, her ox-blood-red leather bomber jacket unbuttoned over a softly-draped top hinted at her body's perfection, straightened hair scraped into a coil emphasised the symmetry of her oval face.

Adam suggested they take a stroll around the quays, and started off at an easy pace. They would receive the occasional stare, he middle-aged, long-boned, Anglo Saxon, traditionally-suited by Saville Row, she, easily twenty five years younger, the daughter of a Jamaican father and Liverpool-Irish mother. That much he did know about her courtesy of Sonja. Always choosing to stay in the nearby Tower Hotel, he didn't expect to meet anyone he knew. If he did, Sheena was his PA.

They had not gone far when she stopped. He turned to look at her.

'You seem tense,' she said. 'Why don't we go straight to your room?'

'Wouldn't you like dinner?'

'Are you hungry?' She said.

'If you don't want to eat, I'll get something from Room Service, but I would like to walk a little farther.'

Oh, no Miss, he thought, I'm in no hurry, half the pleasure is in the anticipation. She hardly ever ate with him. He knew why, all the more reason to postpone gratification. She was a discreet user, but not so much fun if she were still torpid from her last fix.

The phone on the bedside table trilled.

'Who the hell . . .' Adam swung his legs off the bed, answered, sitting with his back to Sheena.

'Hello darling. Nothing wrong, is there?'

Cal feeling like having a chat, a first, usually when he called last thing she was content with a short, good-night exchange. Twisting round briefly he looked at Sheena. He never knew, or wanted to know what she was thinking, 'My wife' he mouthed silently and turned his back on her again.

'My mobile's turned off,' he said. 'I've been working.'

Cal was telling him about playing with the dog, nothing vital or particularly interesting for God's sake.

'Orchids in the spinney, you'll have to show me. Look, darling, I really do have something I must finish so . . . '

Now she was apologizing for interrupting him.

'That's okay, darling. See you tomorrow.'

He listened to her farewell.

'Night, night, Cal.'

He stood, put on the bathrobe provided by the hotel.

'You can go now, Sheena.' He gave a wry smile, 'thanks to my wife.'

He was sure he had given Calista no grounds to mistrust him, hoped she would not call him whenever the whim took her. He would emphasize, if his mobile was off, then he was working, interruptions unwelcome. She could always text. As soon as Sheena left, he would smooch her over the phone. That should allay any suspicions she might have. Nothing must jeopardize his scheme.

CHAPTER TWO

Friday - Ithaca

Breathing air astringent with herbs and shrubs, PJ Wood knew how Odysseus must have felt returning to Ithaca. PJ had been away only weeks not decades. He strode up the familiar valley between groves of olives, paused to listen to finches invisible among the trees, to watch the swallows swoop ahead. A goldfinch, scarlet face ringed white and black, flash of yellow on its wing, fluttered on top of the seeded head of a thistle. No matter the sky was overcast, the humidity making him sweat, he always liked to travel the final couple of miles on foot.

His parents had stumbled on the ruin of the old stone house when they were on a hike to the supposed site of Homer's Arethousa spring. His father had the building restored in response to his mother's yen, and in the nine years since her retirement, she had made the Villa Petrinos her permanent home.

'Ma, I'm here.' He pushed open the door.

Putting down his bags, he wandered into the airy living room, its rustic, rough-plastered walls white painted, the perfect backdrop for simple, wooden furniture, couches and chairs covered with vibrant throws. The room, unusually, was ultra-tidy, no newspapers lying around, not a book, not a thing out of place. The kitchen area too was immaculate.

He bounded up to a gallery. 'Ma?' A gentle tap, he opened her bed-room door. Shutters flung back, her bed was smooth, empty, plumped pillows, made ready to climb in. Silence hung heavy.

Returning to the entrance, he retrieved his backpack and equipment, and descended the narrow spiral stair to the cool shadows of his lair, where once was a wine press. He sat on the end of his bed.

For as long as he could remember there had been just him and Ma, his father only ever a fleeting, if welcome intruder. He did not want to imagine what it would mean, his mother not there. He had phoned her just four days ago, unable to say exactly when he would be home. She had sounded chirpy, said she'd expect him when she saw him. If she had been taken to hospital, someone would have got a message to him. Anxiety began to gnaw his stomach. Crossing the room, he flung open the glazed double doors to let in sunshine and air.

Stepping on to the lower terrace, he heard a hoe scratching stony soil. He leapt down steps leading to the vegetable patch, two at a time. Expecting to see their gardener, he stopped. The spare, diminutive figure of his mother dressed in a loose cotton frock and floppy hat, back bent was intent on attacking weeds growing between two rows of beans. The pile of shrivelling greenery, the freshly raked soil between rows of courgettes, aubergines, peppers, told him she had been labouring for quite a while.

'Ma, what the hell do you think you're doing?'

She straightened to look at him with eyes he had inherited, candid, blue as bright as the wild delphiniums which grew in the mountains of Greece. Perspiration trickled down each flushed cheek. Leaning on the hoe, she took a deep breath.

'Start again.' She deepened her voice, 'Hello Ma, great to see you looking so fit and well.' She continued in her own lighter tone. 'What a surprise, PJ. I wasn't expecting you today.' She paused. 'What the hell does it look like I'm doing?'

She had reason to be vexed. He had been away more than a month, incommunicado till his phone call.

'I'm sorry, I . . .'

She came over, a small triangle of face smiling up at him from under the brim of her hat, the lightest touch on his arm, 'Coffee?' She climbed the steps ahead of him using the hoe as a staff.

As usual they sat opposite each other at the small round table on the top terrace shaded by a gnarled old olive tree, in unison taking sips of treacly-sweet Greek coffee. A breeze had got up, that and the ascending sun sweeping away earlier cloud. The leaves of the surrounding grove shimmered silver in white light.

'As always, you look shattered.' Ma softened her observation with one of her puckish smiles. 'How long will you be staying this time?'

'How soon will you be rid of me, you mean?' He returned her smile.

'You do know don't you,' she said, 'you've inherited Hutch's smile.'

'After all these years, you still miss him.'

'Yes and no, you see Hutch watches over me, often giving that sardonic smile when he thinks I'm up to no good. I sense him especially when I'm here, why I could never settle back in England.'

'As long as you keep fit and well,' PJ said.

'Nearly three years since my scare, and last time, my consultant told me she wouldn't need to see me for another six months.' Ma banged the palm of her hand on the table. 'And you know very well you can stay as long as you like. I wish I could celebrate your safe return with a cigarette.'

'Thelma Wood don't even think about it.'

'Hutch used to nag me rotten about smoking.' She gave a deep sigh. 'But eh, let's not get maudlin. I must've known you were coming, cos I baked a cake.' She guffawed, offering him another slice of his favourite walnut cake.

'Thanks, this is really good.'

'Now don't eat too much and spoil your lunch.'

'Ma, you're impossible,' his mouth full of cake. 'What day is it tomorrow?'

'Here, one day's much like another,' Ma said.

'Saturday,' PJ said, 'and the date?'

'Don't ask me.'

'The seventh of May, your birthday.'

'PJ when you're my age, best pretend birthdays aren't happening.'

'Thought we might go sailing, if you feel up to it,' he said.

'Yes please. Nothing I would rather do, birthday or not.'

'We'll invite Evangelos, shall we?' He could not resist a cheeky grin.

'He's very useful on a yacht,' Ma conceded. 'But promise you won't tell him it's my birthday.'

'Why ever not?'

'He'll want to know how old I am.'

'So, we could lie. How old is he?'

'Sixty two, I think.'

'A toy boy, naughty, naughty, Ma.'

'Don't be silly, PJ. We're friends.'

'Good friends?' Smiling, he raised a knowing eyebrow.

'You're not too old for a slap, young man.' Ma gathered their pots and the remains of the cake. 'Now I must begin to think about lunch.'

PJ followed her into the house. Before she could start on her task, he held her by the shoulders so that she had no option but to face him.

'Seriously, Ma, baking, gardening, the house immaculate, don't you think you might be overdoing it?' His voice was soft as he tried not to show his anxiety.

'I had help with the spring cleaning.'

'You didn't do it on my account?'

'I did it for myself,' Ma said.

They looked at each other, so much unspoken. 'The beast's in remission.' Ma too spoke softly the way she used to when he was a small boy. 'I just want to get on with living.'

He kissed her on the forehead before letting go. He, an unplanned child, proof of his parents' indiscretion, was forty years younger than her, yet he often felt he was the more responsible one.

'See anyone interesting in London?' She smiled up at him.

'A woman, you mean.' Now he could smile too. 'I was only there a couple of days, just long enough to talk to the people at the agency.' He made for the stairs down to his room. 'A shower before lunch, I think.'

Ma followed him, called after him. 'PJ you're thirty three. How are you going to meet your significant other if you keep rushing back here to see me? I want to see you settled before I die.'

He turned to look up at her looming above. 'My line of work doesn't really fit 'settled', does it? I am what I do, Ma. Take someone really special to put up with me. Hope springs eternal, but I haven't come across her yet.' About to leap down the last two steps, he shouted up, 'And don't you dare die till you're at least a hundred.'

'Do my best,' she called back then chuckled. 'Don't hold your breath.'

She always did have to have the last word.

CHAPTER THREE

Visitors

N ow is the summer of my contentment about to be made drearily winter by these daughters of Adam,' Calista declaimed, as she walked Beppo over nearby fields. Not only expected to put up with Adam's absences, and exercise his dog, she was now required to entertain Helena and Sasha during their half-term break. At least Beppo, unlike Adam, never left her side, not for long anyway. Having followed the scent of who-knew-what, he came back, rear shimmying, looking for a pat on the head, to be told he was a good boy. She obliged.

Adam fetched his blonde-haired girls from their Dorset boarding school on the Friday before the Spring Bank Holiday weekend. At the cattle-grid's rattle, mindful of her closest friend's counsel, Calista was outside to greet them, Beppo in support.

Sasha, the younger one, leapt from the back of the Jaguar before Adam had turned off the engine.

'Your old home was better, Dad.' she said as he got out. 'Ultra-modern, like you see in magazines.'

The Old Rectory had been built in the late Eighteenth Century, not exactly her choice, even so Calista felt her trademark flush and reminded herself, Sasha was only just fourteen.

Squatting in front of the spaniel, Sasha pulled his ears. 'You're absolutely gorgeous, you are.'

'Hello, Calista.' Helena looked embarrassed. 'Don't be so rude, Sash. This is the first time we've been here.'

Calista felt a stab of conscience. She and Adam had moved in seven months ago, yet the girls had not visited before.

'Let me show you round,' she said 'You might like the grounds.' She was tempted to add *not only a garden, grounds, more extensive than yours at Woodhouse*. That would be descending to Sasha's level.

'Hi,' Sasha said as she straightened up.

If nothing else, the ha-ha was a hit. Wicked according to the girls. They leapt from the top into the meadow only to discover it was not so easy to clamber back. Calista offered a hand to each expecting to be pulled down. The three of them fell into a giggling heap among the buttercups. Beppo's alarm alerted Adam.

'You might've broken something.' The old fusspot loomed above them making them laugh even more.

Helena's verdict house and garden were fantastic on atmosphere, like a set for Pride and Prejudice. Only the swimming pool was out of character.

'You never mentioned the pool.' Sasha accused her father.

'Wanted to surprise you.'

'Pity it's out of doors. Still like our house better.'

'Actually,' Calista said, 'thinking about Jane Austen, a ha-ha features in her novel Mansfield Park.' Her observation wasted, Adam and the girls had already trailed through the courtyard and open French doors into the kitchen'

Their first dinner together began rather well. A special occasion, they were to eat in the elegant dining room with its huge rounded bay. Like the rest of the house, it smelt of lavender-wax.

After consultation with Adam, Calista chose refreshing melon for starters followed by roast duck *aux cerises*, one of the girls' favourites. He assured her they were not faddy eaters. Their housekeeper cooked the meal for them before leaving. All Calista had to do was dish up.

If they were allowed, Calista suggested the girls might like a glass of wine.

'We are. We are. Aren't we Dad?' Sasha.

Dad had already thought of it and produced champagne, Bollinger naturally.

'I'd be the envy of Leicestershire, if people could see me,' Adam said as they chinked glasses, 'having dinner with three gorgeous blondes. You could be sisters.'

'People say that when we're with Mum,' Sasha said. 'How old are you, Calista?'

They were sitting two and two each side of the antique mahogany table. Sasha was beside her. Adam, across the table, raised his eyebrows, gave her an apologetic smile.

'I'm thirty three.' She wasn't ashamed of her age.

'Not all that younger then. Mum's thirty six. And you're thinner. You can be too thin, you know.'

She did know. Feeling her face flush yet again, she pushed her hair behind her ears. She had lost seven kilos since she got married.

'Thirty seven next month.' Adam was sharp. 'Your mother's put on weight.'

'Gross, Dad, the thought of you and Calista . . . Yuck.' Insouciance personified, Sasha concentrated on cutting up a piece of duck breast. 'Incest, if Calista were our sister, that is.'

Adam's expression was tenebrous.

'Darling, a drop more champers would be lovely.' Calista held up her glass. Turning to Sasha, 'When you're older, you'll notice men tend to go for the same physical type. There's an old Marilyn Monroe film, *Gentlemen Prefer Blondes*.'

Adam brought round the magnum, topped up her glass. 'I don't always go for blondes.'

'I did say gentlemen', which made them all laugh, even Adam.

'You're a good cook, Calista,' Helena said.

'Our housekeeper, Pam, you mean. But you'll get a chance to sample my efforts. Over half-term, Pam's taking time off to look after her grand-children.'

'And I love this room,' Helena said. 'The deep-rose walls, the big window, the marble fireplace.'

'Needs pictures,' Sasha, who else.

'I wish I'd brought my sketchbook. And my watercolours and pastels. The house, the lane, the church.' Helena's enthusiasm overflowed.

'No problem,' Calista said. 'First thing tomorrow I'll take you into town. We'll buy what you need.'

'For God's sake, Cal.' Adam sounded annoyed. 'Don't encourage her. Tell her what a great time you had up at Oxford.'

'Unlike you by all accounts, I was a bit of a swot,' which made Helena smile and Sasha giggle. 'I have to say, my time there was the most intense, the most satisfying, and the most exhilarating of my whole life. Still seems like yesterday.'

'Dad wants me to read PPE, Philosophy perhaps, but Politics and Economics.'

'You could combine Philosophy with other subjects, English Literature, maybe,' Calista said.

'I don't want to go to Oxford. I'm not going to Oxford. I'm going to do my best to get into Art School.' Helen spoke quietly but no mistaking she meant what she said.

'Len's really good,' Sasha said. 'Last year, she won the Art Prize, and she got an 'A' in her GCSE.'

'And 'As' in all other subjects,' Adam said. 'Art School, a waste of her intelligence.'

'Not if she has talent, and that's what she passionately wants to do.' She could not believe he was so dismissive of his daughter's ambition.

'This is something Len and I will have to discuss some other time.' His tone angry.

Calista got to her feet. 'Pudding, anyone? Chocolate mousse?'

The girls had seconds, whilst Adam scorned her pudding in favour of ripe Stilton and celery, the remainder of dinnertime being spent on less controversial subjects like what the girls might like to do over the break.

'Nothing special, Dad,' Sasha said. 'We just want to chill, don't we, Len?'

'That's the idea.' Helena gave Calista a smile, 'and for us and Calista to get to know one another.'

'S'pose,' Sasha unenthusiastic.

Calista did not need reminding that was Adam's plan. Just go with the flow, another bit of salutary advice from her laid-back friend, Esther.

First thing Saturday morning, she and Helena went shopping for art materials.

'Thanks for saying what you did about Art School,' Helena said.

'It's what I think.'

'Mum's on my side, too.'

'He'll think we're ganging up on him.'

'Sometimes you have to with Dad.' a throw-away line which made Calista uneasy.

Over the holiday, the late-May sun excelled, and sheltered by high stone walls, they all enjoyed the heated pool, particularly Adam and Sasha who seemed to spend most of the time attempting to drown each other, not necessarily as part of a game, Calista sensed. And there was croquet, a hit with both girls if she pardoned herself the pun.

Meals were the main focus for Sasha's fault finding, on Calista's lasagne, not nearly as yummy as Mum's. Blame Marks and Sparks, Calista told her. Dad's Sunday lunch was nowhere near as good as the lunches he used to produce at home.

'Did Calista choose this really naff house?' She heard Sasha say.

'I did.' Adam flicked his wet towel at her. 'Left to Cal, we'd still be living in an apartment in Leicester city centre, and there'd be no room for you and Len to visit.' He spoke deliberately, punctuating each word with a flick which made contact despite Sasha's efforts to avoid them.

'Ouch!'

'You're not too old to feel my belt across the back of your legs.' Adam hovered over her.

'You wouldn't.' Sasha's face was white. 'Not in front of Calista.' She fled.

'Adam, I should hope you haven't ever done that. It's assault.'

He kissed her lightly on the lips, 'Never come between father and daughter if she needs chastising. Besides, you should've met my nanny and her vicious hair-brush. She used to spank me on my bare bottom. Never did me any harm.' He jumped back into the pool.

By the end of the visit, she and Helena were on Cal and Len terms. Helena was a self-contained, self-reliant girl who spent hours on her own sketching and painting around the grounds and in the village. On the last evening, the two of them in the study, Helena sat, feet up, along the window seat, she in her club chair, both reading. She had left Adam and Sasha watching a DVD in the sitting room, Adam's arm around Sasha who was curled up beside him, her head resting on his chest. She was sucking her thumb.

'Cal?'

She looked up. Helena put aside her book.

'I know Sash is a pain, but she really misses Dad, even though he . . . Not that I don't miss him. But, I realized what was going on long before Sash did.'

For a few moments, Calista was speechless, then 'She must resent me dreadfully, if not hate me. You both must.'

'Not nearly as much as she does Bradley. Bradley's okay, I like him . . . '

'Bradley?'

'Mum's new chap. We knew about him long before Dad did. Came as a shock, I think, when Mum told Dad she wanted a divorce. Lucky Dad found you.'

Calista felt her neck redden. A knot formed in her stomach. She pushed her hair behind her ears.

'Your father and I have known each other quite some time.' Managing to keep her voice even, 'How long has your mother known Bradley?'

'Not sure, about four years maybe, he was Mum's secret for a while.' Helena shrugged. 'Stuff happens. Mum's so much happier, and Dad's obviously okay with you.'

'And all's right with the world.' She had beaten herself up for something that was not her fault.

'You do love Dad, don't you?'

She had to admit, physical attraction, lust, if you got down and dirty, had played a major role in their relationship. When he was around, Adam was also an entertaining companion. When he proposed, the last thing she expected, she was wrong-footed. She played for time. He persisted. She gave in. Not the first time he had overcome her scruples.

Going over to Helena, she took hold her hands.

'Len, your Dad and I, we're fine.'

Except devious old Adam had never mentioned Bradley. Mind racing, she went over to her desk ostensibly to straighten it. Back to Helena, papers rustled as she shuffled, tap-tapped as she tidied.

When Adam told her he and Annabel were divorcing, she assumed he was the prime mover, not the biter bit. She wondered if he had chosen to marry her to save face. If Adam could be less than transparent then so could she. For the time being, she would keep schtum.

She looked down at three neat stacks. Tomorrow she would not be able to find a thing. She returned to her chair.

'So your mother has remarried?'

'Around the same time Dad married you. Bit before, I think. Did he not say?'

'I only met your mother once.'

They were silent for a while, both gazing out of the window.

'Cal?' Helena sounded diffident.

'What is it?'

'Thank you for inviting us to stay.'

'This is your father's home. You're welcome any time.' A relief, Annabel having someone else,

'Mum's so much happier,' Len's words echoed in her ears.

Next morning, as Calista was seeing them off, Sasha came over to her before getting in the car.

'Thank you for having me, Calista.' She looked apprehensive.

'You're welcome anytime, Sasha.' Not too often, though, she thought, immediately feeling mean.

CHAPTER FOUR

Sisters under the skin

Calista watched the Jag disappear, then climbed the steps through the rockery opposite the front of the house, Beppo following. They led onto a terrace farther up the hill. Like the garden above the ha-ha, then the terrace and house, this was a man-made plateau where fruit trees had been planted and replaced over a two-hundred-year period. The plum and cherry blossom had been the first to drop, sprinkling pink confetti, followed by pear blossom falling like snow. Now only delicate pink-white apple blossom lingered on trees. She took a deep breath in, good to be outdoors enveloped in the scent of growing things. Maybe she could yet get to like living in the country.

While Beppo sniffed around and re-marked his territory, she sat on a wooden bench beneath a gnarled old crab apple decked out in abundant white. She took her iPhone from the pocket of her jeans to send a text to Tess, her closest friend – *They've gone, thank God. C u 11.30ish, xx.*

Calista had known Esther Mahoney since her Oxford days. Esther Purslow-Onajole she had been then, and still was professionally, daughter of an English mother, and Nigerian father. In October 1996, she and Tess had both gone up to St Hilda's, the one remaining all-women's college. They were Hildabeasts and proud of it. Assigned adjacent rooms, she and Tess had become friends, agreeing, as this was Oxford and they were a mere stone's throw from the Cherwell, they would give rowing a go. The nicknames they were given came from a song title later voted the tenth worst song of all time, Ebony and Ivory.

'Oh so original', their retort pointing out that Calista was no more as pallid as ivory as Esther was as dark as . . . as . . . 'a raven's wing' some future diplomat interjected.

'What made you choose St Hilda's?' She and Tess would be asked. 'Don't you like men?'

No secret, bets had been made, which man would succeed in splitting them up.

'Let's keep 'em guessing.' Exchanging impish smiles, they agreed playing their part. May be more than friends.

Then along came the joker, Mike Mahoney, spare frame, sinewy, not over tall, roguish, curly hair almost black. The Public School types called him 'The Gipsy'. Mike's eyes were denim blue, his looks, his bravado belied his sensitivity, his soft heart.

Twenty minutes before Esther's e.t.a. Calista got up from her desk after re-organizing and putting in order the papers and files she had stacked unseeing after Helena's bombshell. Beppo, lying along the window seat, raised his head.

'Come on.' She gestured towards the door. 'Let's go and meet Tess.'

At the cattle-grid, Calista picked up the dog, no lightweight, and carried him across. She clipped on his leash and turned to go down to the road which passed by their village, along which Esther should be arriving in her VW Golf. She paused as she often did to survey the church opposite. One day, if, when it was open, she would have a look inside. The church, fittingly, was higher up the hill than the rectory. She ran her musings past the dog. 'Our house is rather grand for a humble curate, don't you think?' When the Old Rectory was built, Calista could not imagine anyone more exalted being responsible for the modest village church, but what did she know? Her knowledge of clergy was based on what she read in Trollope's novels. Anthony's not Joanna's, though she enjoyed those too.

A warm, sunny-cloudy day, the spaniel trotting a short leash-length in front, she bounced downhill.

'Wasn't so great in January, was it?' Again she addressed an unresponsive Beppo forging ahead with gusto as only dogs knew how.

They had reached the road. She turned right reigning Beppo in closer and took out her mobile to check. 'Auntie Tess will be here any time now.' If Tess heard her she would think she was barking – she was becoming like her dad, making puns. 'Our secret, eh Beppo?' She stage whispered.

The farther Esther Mahoney drove from home the more relaxed she had become. East Leicestershire, definitely Hobbit country Esther decided. She loved her children beyond reason, but, at Melton Mowbray taking this minor road south through verdant, undulating Middle Earth, a relief not to be distracted by their usual bickering over some electronic game. She had just passed a turning to Carlton Curlieu, lovely name; and she kept half expecting to meet Bilbo Baggins walking towards her along the verge rampant with cow parsley. Now, unerring, a left onto an even more minor road, she had eventually reached the right fork below a hill. Only another mile to go after that, Cal had said. Esther couldn't remember the last time they had spent time together, just the two of them, and she was curious, what would the Old Rectory be like for real.

She eased her foot off the accelerator, slowed down and came to a halt, not by Bilbo, but Calista, and a spaniel. She pressed down the passenger-door window and said, 'Wanna lift, missus, you an' yer dog?'

Smiling, Calista leaned in. 'Are you sure you don't mind having Beppo in the car?'

'Cal, what are a few dog fleas between friends?'

'Esther Mahoney, how dare you impugn my dog?' Laughing now, Calista let the spaniel into the back, then slid into the front passenger seat.

They turned to each other, and despite the impediment of the steering wheel, managed a kind of hug, saying in unison 'It's so good to see you.'

Esther started the engine. 'You never let on you had a dog.'

'He's Adam's gun dog really, but . . .' Calista twisted round to peer between the two seats. 'You keep me company don't you Beppo?'

'Calista Blake, how un-cool is that?' Esther chortled.

'What? If you had a dog, betcha you'd talk to him.' Calista leaned back in her seat.

'Might get more of a response than I do out of Mike,' came out before she gave herself time to think. She hoped she had not sounded as bitter as she felt.

'That broth of a boy, Mike Mahoney, uncommunicative, to be sure, is he unwell?' Calista sounded mock concerned.

They had come to Calista's village straggling up the hill to their left. 'Now, you told me second left, the turn beyond the row of ironstone cottages. Here we go then.'

The Golf snaked up a narrow tunnel formed by tall trees and hawthorn hedges till on the right hand side of a bend veering left they came to an open, five-barred, metal gate on its middle bar clearly signing, The Old Rectory. Esther swung the car through the opening, wheels grumbling over a grid. She brought it to a halt opposite what she assumed was the main door of the house, at the end of the drive, and at right-angles to the house, what looked like a two-story stable block. She, Calista and the spaniel got out of the car. Esther stood for a moment examining the house's symmetrical late-Eighteenth Century white-stone facade.

'Well' she said, 'not the sort of place a hobbit would live in even though it is on the side of a hill.'

'Tess, I can safely say neither I nor Adam is a hobbit.' Calista ushered her towards the heavy, oak double door between stone columns. 'As it's your first visit, I thought we should make a grand entrance.' Up three shallow steps, she unlocked and flung open both leaves.

They crossed the threshold into austere classicism, a curving stairway climbing to a galleried landing.

'Wow, I'm in the wrong branch of the Law.' Esther was amazed.

'Silly.' Calista put her arm round her shoulders and gave her a squeeze. 'Adam bought the house, not me.' She opened one of an array of white, panelled doors. 'This is my lair, the study. Take a peek, me and Beppo spend a lot of time in here.' To prove Calista's point the dog followed them into the room and leapt onto the window seat.

'Just one thing, Cal, are you sure you've enough book shelves?' She gestured towards the floor-to-high-ceiling light-oak shelving covering one whole wall filled with all kinds of books, not the sort you buy by the yard; and there were more shelves on either side of the door they had come through.

She and Calista looked at each other and laughed, then hugged, a proper one this time. When they broke away, Esther said, 'You've lost an awful lot of weight. Are you okay?' Then, seeing the expression on Calista's face, wished she had not.

Light and space smelling of lavender surrounding her, Esther was drawn to the tall window.

'Not a bad view,' she said. 'Are there steps down to the meadow?'

'No, a ha-ha. Adam's girls were well-impressed by that if nothing else.'

On one side of the lawn, a high clipped-yew hedge, on the left, mellow sandstone latticed by espalier provided the backdrop for an herbaceous border. Esther wondered where the door in the wall led.

'Amazing, straight out of Jane Austen.' she said.

'Have you and Len been exchanging notes?' Calista stood beside her.

'Len?'

'Short for Helena, Adam's older girl. Tell you about the visit later.'

Esther turned to look at her friend who was biting her lip. A mischievous, thought, 'Now you've finally netted your Mr Darcy, will you be having his children? I'm thinking the old biological hickory-dickory-dock.'

'Jesus, I hope not.' Calista's creamy complexion became paler.

'Only teasing darling.' She brushed Calista's cheek with the back of her hand. 'You never were that keen on little ones. Remember when they were babies, I would ask you to hold Fran or Tom while I did something. You didn't like it one bit.'

'I was scared I might drop them. They were gorgeous, still are. Next time you must bring them, and Mike. You must come for the weekend.'

'The kids would love that. Fran especially, she thinks you're awesome. Can't speak for Mike though.'

'What,' mock indignation in Calista's voice, 'you're saying Mike doesn't think I am.'

'Used to one time, didn't he?' Thinking back to their Oxford days, Esther heard the smile in her voice. 'I mean about coming for the weekend, as you well know.' She took a deep breath but feelings got the better of her. 'Bastard let us down last weekend, didn't he?' Calista looked dismayed. 'Don't look so worried, darling. We're a long way from the Divorce Court. Just not on great terms at the moment. One of those proverbial bad patches all marriages go through, I guess. Now, let's enjoy your beautiful house.'

'Come on then,' Calista said.

They walked towards the door, the dog jumped down and followed. 'First off you probably need the loo, then a coffee. Before lunch I'll show you round the house. We've a rather grand drawing room we only use when Adam has business acquaintances to stay, but there's a cosy sitting room too, and a games' room in the under-croft. Maybe a pre-lunch aperitif, and if it's warm enough we can eat . . . Then, I'll give you a tour of the grounds, the orchard, the swimming pool, the coppice . . . '

'Cal, please slow down.' She paused, turned to her.

'Oh Tess, sorry, sorry, I'm so pleased to see you. Can hardly believe you're here at last, and, the icing on the cake, we'll have a whole afternoon all to ourselves.'

Esther was touched, and concerned by the tears glinting in Calista's eyes.

'Cal, darling, I don't have to be back all that early. I can stay till Adam gets back, if you'd like me to.'

'He's not coming back till tomorrow. After he's dropped the girls off, he's going up to London on business.'

Then Calista burst into tears.

CHAPTER FIVE

Confidences

Esther's arms around her, Calista rested her cheek against the soft cotton of her friend's shirt, breathed in her familiar Coco Chanel scent.

'So . . . glad . . . you're . . . here.'

'There, there, darling.' Esther stroked her back.

'What . . . have . . . I . . . done?' Calista croaked through gulping sobs.

'Tell me.' Esther caressed her hair.

She took a deep breath, then another, pulled away just far enough to look Esther in the face. 'Sorry.' Another couple of breaths. 'Stupid cow . . . I . . . I'm okay. Really.'

'Umm.' Looking thoughtful, Esther held her at arms' length. 'Darling, you're amazingly clever, but . . . You'll maybe not like what I'm going to say.' She shook her head, pursed her lips. 'When it comes to people, men in particular, you are incredibly naïve.'

'Cos I'm like my brother. Why I specialize in Company Law, not . . .' Calista shrugged.

'Unlike Stephen, you don't have Asperger's.' Esther stroked her cheek. 'Just one thing.' Looking deadpan, 'The nearest loo?'

'This way.' Smiling, Calista took her hand. 'Esther Purslow-Onajole-Mahoney, how come you have this gift of cheering me up?'

'With a moniker like that, s'nough to make the dog laugh.' Esther said.

By the time Esther joined her in the kitchen, she had done what she always did, had her feelings in check, and busied herself slicing an orange and cucumber. 'Would you like coffee, or shall we start straightaway on this?' She held up a bottle of Pimms.

'Ummm.' Esther pointed to the Pimms.

Calista quarter-filled a crystal water jug with the alcohol, held up a bottle of lemonade, 'Made with real lemons, allegedly.' She added it to the Pimms leaving just enough room for the sliced orange and cucumber plus strawberries, leaves of mint and borage. A couple of ice cubes and fancy straw into two tall crystal glasses, they were ready to go. 'Shall we?' She indicated the open French doors into the courtyard where a wall-fountain murmured.

In cushioned garden chairs they sat either side of a small table shaded by a pergola covered in mauve Wisteria. Calista dispensed drinks. They both took sips.

'Lovely.' Esther smacked her lips.

'You must come more often,' Calista said' 'We could make a habit of this.'

'This house kind'a lends itself to Pimms before lunch.' Esther fished a strawberry from her glass. 'Ours is more your bottle-of-Becks-type.'

'Rubbish, the part of Edwalton you live in is lovely, large houses, not cheek by jowl like in some suburbs.'

'Can't imagine you in Suburbia, Cal. That said never saw you as lady-of-the-manor complete with gun-dog.'

'Surely the parson's wife?' Calista guffawed. 'Adam, a vicar, I don't think so, nothing short of a bishop him.'

'Do you plan to keep horses?' Esther pointed to the stable block.

'The ground floor's the garage, the upper one's fitted out as Adam's office, the theory, he wouldn't need to go up to the City so often. That's what sold me on moving here.' Calista gave a derisive harrumph. ''Scuse me, is that a flying pig?'

Esther put down her glass, moved her chair so as to face her. 'Are you going to tell me why you sobbed your socks off?'

Calista bit her bottom lip hard. 'You'll say, I told you so.'

'Tell me.'

'It's . . . I should say nothing.'

'You're my closest friend. We've known each other half our lives. Not even Mike came between us. If you can't tell me who can you tell? Except Adam, maybe.'

'God, not him.'

Esther looked taken aback.

'I shouldn't say.' Again she bit her bottom lip, then swallowed. 'Not out loud.' She would not break down, not again.

Esther leaned forward. 'Calista Blake, do I have to shake it out of you?'

Unblinking, they stared at each other.

'Tess.' She hesitated.

'Go on.'

'I wish . . . I wish . . . '

'What?'

'Adam, I wish . . . I wish I'd never married him.' She sighed out the deepest of deep breaths.

Esther's expression was inscrutable. Calista wondered if her relief at voicing her feelings showed on her face. And, hallelujah, she no longer needed to cry.

Esther broke the silence. 'I didn't believe he'd ever leave his wife.'

'You've never approved of him . . .'

'Cal.' Esther looked flustered. 'I hardly know him. Though I did used to think . . . I saw him, after a while, moving on. Maybe to someone younger.'

'Esther Mahoney, you call yourself my friend.' Calista feigned indignation, then laughed. Tess looked so embarrassed. 'Thought the same myself. Seriously, though right from the start, he was clear his daughters were his priority.' Calista drained her glass. 'And no one could accuse him of dumping Annabel for some bimbo. I met her once. A party at their house, before, you know . . .' - Adam's solicitor took her because Adam had asked him to. - 'She's quite quirky, artistic.' She held Esther's gaze. 'He was so persistent, and . . . I was attracted to him, thought it'd only be a fling.' Another rueful smile, 'I'm not that naïve, Tess. You must've noticed my aversion to commitment, but I am human.'

Esther nodded, smiling, then looked thoughtful. 'Adam is exceptionally charming. I'll give you that, a real smooth operator.'

'A lot like Mike then.' Bugger that sounded bitchy. Esther's response was a shrug, an enigmatic smile. 'I was stunned when Adam said he and Annabel were divorcing. Not quite so terrible, I thought, now the girls are older. Except. . .'

'Except?' Esther raised a questioning eyebrow.

'Sasha, the fourteen-year-old, she's . . .'

'Insecure?' Esther suggested.

'S'pose. Disturbed is perhaps too strong a word'

'Out with it Cal.'

'I know nothing about children or parenting, but . . . Sasha and Adam, they seem to have this love-hate relationship. She was doing her best to have a go at me - without succeeding in needling me, I hasten to add. She's just a kid for God's sake – I sensed it was Adam she was trying to get at.' Calista had been disturbed when Adam threatened to lash Sasha's calves. Tess would be appalled if she told her that.

'Daughters,' Esther said, 'when they're teenagers, it's usually their mothers they have it in for. I remember I did. Poor Mina, she says I put her through hell. Can't help thinking she's looking forward to when Fran will do the same to me.'

'Same with me and my mother, I recall.' Calista gave a contrite smile.

'Is that why you wish you'd not married? The added bonus of a couple of teenage step-daughters.' Esther said.

An emphatic shake of her head, she pointed to Esther's half-empty glass, then picked up the jug. 'Drink up. Let's finish this. Technically, of course, they are my stepdaughters. Their visit broke the ice, not that I'd been aware of any, ice that is.' - Esther raised both eyebrows, and rolled her eyes. - 'Sasha did thank me for having her. They both did. Won't be seeing much of them, don't suppose.' Although they had livened the old place up, she thought.

'What's the seventeen-year-old like?'

'Len's a lot like Adam, self-possessed . . .'

'Or self-obsessed.' Esther snorted.

'Determined.' Calista continued. 'Despite her natural charm, you suspect an inner core of steel. Sufficient-unto-herself, I suppose you could say.'

'A lot like you then.' Esther smiled. 'The sufficient-unto-herself bit.'

'Think Adam may be knocking that out of me.'

Looking alarmed, Esther sat forward. 'He doesn't knock you about, does he?'

'Good God, no.'

'Sorry, Cal, I do specialize in Divorce.' She leaned back in her chair.

'Len and I, we got along just fine. She's artistic like Annabel, much to Adam's annoyance. I got up his nose too. Took her to buy paints. She wants to go to art school. Adam is insisting she goes up to Oxford. Be interesting to see who wins. Odds even at the moment.'

'She should meet my mother.' Esther said. 'Mina still teaches part-time at St Martins.'

Silence, except for the fountain and twitter of finches in nearby shrubbery, as they concentrated on appreciating their Pimms, Calista wondering how she might bring about a meeting between Len and Mina Purslow, Esther's mother. She was first to drink up. 'I feel so much better, thanks to you.'

'And this, no doubt.' Esther drained her glass, and sat forward in her chair. 'From what little I've seen so far, you're living in a fabulous house with a man you were unable to resist, so why do you wish you'd never married him?'

'Put like that . . .' Calista grimaced. 'Tess, I've never been so lonely in my life. If it wasn't for Beppo . . .' Hearing his name, the spaniel got up and rested his head on her knee. Yet again, she was on the verge of tears. Ridiculous being sentimental about a dog. She fondled his ears.

'Is Adam away a lot?'

'S'not that. I thought I knew him. Now I realize I don't. Never did. And after what Len told me . . . Makes so much sense.'

'What does?'

'Annabel asked Adam for a divorce. Wasn't the other way about.'

'What?'

She told Esther what Helena had told her about Annabel and her Bradley.

'And Adam never mentioned it?' Esther said. Calista shook her head. 'Leaving you to assume . . . Devious bastard. If you'd known what you know now . . .'

'Too late, Tess. And really, when he's in the mood . . .' a heartfelt sigh, 'have to face it. He is my husband. But, not the love of my life. So far, I haven't managed to meet him. If he exists. Come on, lunchtime.' Calista got to her feet. 'Afterwards, I'll show you my domain, and if you want to, you can tell me what's with Mike. We're having grilled brown trout with hollandaise sauce and salad. Adam caught the fish in a local reservoir. He is good for something. And a well-stocked wine cellar. I've a bottle of Sancerre chilling in the fridge.'

'Steady, Cal, I don't relish negotiating Hobbit country half-cut.'

'You must know you're welcome to stay over, except, I suppose . . .'

'Don't tempt me, Cal. Bugger all to go home for. Mum's not bringing Fran and Tom back till tomorrow afternoon. As for Mike, if he does deign to fly in this evening . . . serve him bloody right if no one's home.'

'I'm sure I could find you a spare toothbrush . . .'

They looked at each other and laughed.

As Esther followed her into the kitchen, 'You'll confront Adam, of course, about what Len told you,' she said.

'At the right moment. I can be devious too.'

'Ah, that an inner core of steel.' Esther chuckled. 'God help him.'

Later, both of them lounged nude by the pool soaking up the sun after a swim. 'My kids would love it here,' Esther said. 'So much to explore, and a dog to boot.' She giggled. 'Sorry Beppo, didn't mean that the way it sounded. And there's this. If you'd told me, I would've brought my cozzie.'

'Then we wouldn't have had an excuse to skinny dip. I repeat, you must all come over one weekend, nudity not obligatory. We'll make a date.' Calista leaned over and stroked her cheek. 'I'm so glad you've decided to stay the night Tess.'

'Me too.' Thinking *Cal, darling Cal, lately I've been lonely too*, she gave an involuntary sigh, then said. 'Disastrous.'

'What is?'

'The way you feel. Look around you, Cal. On the surface you've got it all, brilliant career, fantastic house, rich and charming husband, no children admittedly . . .' Esther swung her legs off the lounger to sit sideways the better to observe her friend. 'Are you sure you didn't marry Adam because, deep down, you would like a child of your own.'

'Bloody hell, Tess.' Calista shot up to sit facing her. 'No, really, A. I'm aiming for Silk remember. B. what if he/she was like my autistic brother Stephen, and C. in any case I'm not yet past it. My mother was nearly forty when she had me.'

'Ummm.' Esther held her gaze. 'You want to make QC. Excuse A, I understand. C's a bit of a giveaway. You've obviously not totally closed your mind to children. And, I know you, you'd love your child beyond reason no matter what. Is the problem Adam, maybe?'

Calista swung her legs back up onto her recliner and relaxed into it. 'Come on, Tess, lighten up. Let's enjoy the sun's blessed rays while we can.'

Esther too relaxed back into her chair believing she had touched a nerve.

'I very much doubt Adam wants any more children,' Calista said. 'He is forty seven. Can't imagine him changing dirty nappies. Actually I can.' She laughed. 'A sight to behold.' Then serious, 'Adam, the father of my child . . . No, Tess, then I'd be well and truly trapped.'

CHAPTER SIX

What's with Mike?

That evening, Calista made up a second jug of Pimms which they drank while preparing dinner together.

'Sorry, it's a scratch meal.' She had found minced beef in the freezer and the other ingredients for their one-time, student stand-by, spag-bog. 'Didn't think for one moment you'd be able to stay over.'

'This is great,' Esther said. 'Reminds me of our Oxford days. This is a bigger, better, cleaner kitchen though.' The opposite side of the island unit, Esther was dressing a bowl of salad.

'Happy days.' Calista, busy chopping onion, smiled at the memory. In their final year they had shared a house with four others' Calista held up a generous handful of spaghetti. 'One of these each?'

'Half as much again, should be enough. Have you added plenty of salt and a dash of oil?' Esther said. 'And remember to stir the sauce occasionally.'

'Just about to stir, thank-you. I'm not a totally useless cook.'

'Ooo-er Missus, no need to be tetchy.' Esther guffawed. 'You used to give a pretty good impression of hopelessness.'

'Just for that you can stand over this hot Aga while I raid the cellar for a bottle of Chianti.'

They ate companionably in the kitchen, were tempted by but resisted a second bottle of wine.

'Shall we withdraw to the sitting room?' Calista said. 'I'll make coffee. 'I'm good at that.'

'I'll call Mina,' Esther said. 'Tell her I'm staying over, say "Night, Night" to Tom and Fran.'

'Please give them my love,' Calista said. 'And you might mention to Mina I'd like her to meet my artistic step-daughter.'

As evening deepened into night they sat side-by-side in easy chairs in front of the sitting room's partially open French window, watched the changing light play over the patchwork of arable fields and lush meadows carpeting the valley.

Esther breathed a euphoric 'Aaahh'. 'I could really get used to this. And this brandy.' She held up her glass.

'Adam's best Armagnac. Good isn't it?' Calista said.

'If you're not careful I'll be moving in permanently.'

'If you fall out with Mike big time . . . Can't remember the last time I enjoyed myself so much. I'd have to get rid of Adam. Maybe not. I can just imagine him revelling in a threesome. Talking of threesome's . . .' Calista chuckled.

'Poor Mike, we really wound him up . . .' a smile in Esther's voice.

'Does he ever mention it? He's not forgotten.' Calista said.

'Doubt it.' Esther laughed. 'The look on his face when we cornered him, told him we weren't going to fall out with each other over any man, certainly not him, that we'd found the perfect solution. A threesome, endless fun. Didn't know which way to turn, did he?'

'What sluts. Testimony to how madly in love he was, he didn't scarper screaming.' Calista said.

'Because, I suspect, for a nanosecond he contemplated . . .' Esther tut-tutted. 'We'll never know. You let him off the hook. What did you say? You never told me. Neither has he.'

'Trust me, leave it there.'

'Wasn't because of Mike you never . . .'

'Tess darling, I've already told you, I've yet to meet the love of my life. Mike wasn't him, and I'm ashamed to admit neither is Adam.' She got to her feet, held up the bottle of Armagnac. 'I'm in the mood for just one more. How about you?'

Esther offered up her empty glass.

Calista switched on the lamp on a sofa-table on the other side of the room, then pulled up a footstool to sit opposite her friend. Esther's face was in shadow, what light there was shone on her.

'Now, are you going to tell me what's with you and Mike? What happened last weekend?'

'You know he's been commuting to Amsterdam a lot these past couple of months. Last weekend he was supposed to be joining me and the children in Hampstead to spend the Bank Holiday with Mum. Always managed to get home before. Admittedly he grovelled, apologetic, said he couldn't make it. Fran and Tom were so disappointed. We were supposed to be having a family fun weekend, going to the zoo. Still did, but the kids really miss him when he's away.'

Calista leaned forward, separated Esther's hands clasped tight together in her lap and held them in hers. 'Tess, darling, Mike's a stonking good dad who adores his children. I'm sure he . . . '

'That's what Mum said. Must've been something important to keep him away. He doesn't let on. I know this project he's involved with is stressing him. Cal, lately he's so closed in.'

'He won't talk to you?' She let go Esther's hands, and picking up her brandy, took a sip.

'As soon as Fran and Tom break up, we're off for a couple of escapist weeks on Corfu. Mike's sworn he won't renege, so maybe then . . .'

'Parts of Corfu are lovely,' Calista said. 'Some resorts are a bit tacky though. All sun, sex and ouzo.'

'Sounds great. Too bad Mike will be there, so sex may not be an option.' Esther too picked up her glass, and took a sip of her drink. 'Don't look so concerned, Cal. Our resort sounds ideal for families. You and Adam off to Ithaca again, first leg, I bet, private jet to Cephalonia? And will your villa be ready by then?'

'Tess, you're changing the subject.'

'Not really. At the moment nothing more to tell, so let's sit back and enjoy Adam's excellent Armagnac.'

'Okay, your call. Don't want to spoil our evening.' Calista moved back into her easy chair.

'I'll second that.' Esther held up her glass.

They both took an appreciative mouthful of brandy. 'In answer to your questions,' Calista said. 'Yes, we're off to Ithaca, and no, the villa isn't ready, not quite, much to Adam's annoyance. So far, I've resisted the temptation to say, I told you so.'

Looking out into the night, for a while they sat in silence.

'Tess, is there any chance Mike might be playing away?'

'He's a man, Cal, so yes, but I'm not sure. For the moment I'm giving him the benefit of the doubt.'

'I didn't mean to upset you.'

'Cal, I am a realist.'

'That's something else that gnaws at me about Adam. Now he's married his mistress, me, is he busy filling the vacancy?'

'What makes you think that?' Esther sounded concerned.

'Nothing tangible, just . . .' Calista drained her glass, pushed open one of the French doors. 'Come on, Beppo, time for your final pee. Before we turn in, we take a stroll. You stay here and finish your brandy.'

'Wait for me.' Esther drank up. 'Don't want to miss out walking beneath such a beautiful star-filled sky, something you rarely notice in Suburbia with all its lights. If I didn't now know differently, I'd say, how lucky, you are, Cal.'

'I do say that to myself. Often. I've made my bed, so . . .'

'You could always unmake it,' Esther said. 'I know a good divorce lawyer.'

They looked at each other, gave rueful smiles'

CHAPTER SEVEN

Friday, 10 June in Vondelpark

Louise van de Velde, his PR pundit's idea, a picnic in Vondelpark. In all his trips to Amsterdam, Mike Mahoney had never been. 'You'll like it,' she said. 'A bit like Hyde Park.'

What he liked were the shady, tree-lined avenues. Arching branches formed high, Gothic naves, tracery of leaves not yet summer-tired shimmering in sunlight. A pity, even in such a potential haven you had to be on the alert for whirring, two-wheeled machines. What everyone said about Amsterdam was true. Everywhere, everything and everybody had to make way for bicycles.

Louise had brought crusty baguettes, a chunk of Edam, thinly sliced ham, apricots and bananas, still mineral water to drink.

'Well, Michael, what do you think?'

They were lolling on a brightly squared travelling rug. Of the food laid out between them, only a few apricots and a banana remained. For all too short a while he was relaxed. His mirror image, she was stretched out opposite, arm crooked, her head cupped in the palm of her hand. What did he think? About her? The food? The park? The plush apartment on Prinsengracht they had viewed earlier?

'Very healthy,' he said. We certainly won't get fat on it.'

She smiled, honey-tanned cheeks dimpling. Her eyes were deep viola blue. 'Silly, I mean Vondelpark. If you are still hungry, you can have the apricots.' She reached over. 'The banana is mine.'

She moved to sit with crossed ankles, her ecru linen skirt designed to show her shapely legs to maximum advantage. He glimpsed a flash of virginal-white, lace-clad crotch. Impish, her gaze locking his, she peeled back the skin of the banana with a delicate touch. Slow, as though savouring every millimetre, she fed its flesh between the puckered 0 of her lips. A mischievous glint in her eyes, she bit sharply through. He almost winced, then smiled.

'No wonder you got yourself into trouble.' Thoughtless, tactless, he rolled over onto his stomach facing toward the nearby thicket, concentrated on plucking at blades of grass. '*Het park is aardig.*' he said. Among other things, she was supposed to teach him to speak Dutch

She finished her banana. '*Aardig? Niet mooi?*' Pretty, not beautiful. She sounded disappointed. 'It is nice to be able to walk here from the apartment, don't you think?' she said. 'Jos and Zoe de Vries are really pleased you will rent it.'

The de Vries's, friends of her elder sister and brother-in-law would not have let their home to just anybody, she told him. That was why it was reasonable. The right tenant was beyond price.

'The communal garden's great,' he said. 'From the front, you'd never know it was there.' Esther would have loved the way the place was furnished, but most of all the garden, quirky sculpture in hidden corners among potted plants and shrubbery.

Louise scooped up the remaining apricots and rolled over to lie beside him on her stomach, too close for comfort. He would concede defeat if he hotched away. She brought her head so close to his, he felt her breath against his cheek, smelt her musk. Pressing an apricot to his lips, 'Let's finish these off,' she said.

He took the fruit from her, pushed on to his knees then sat with them bent up. She remained where she was.

'Michael, will you please stop fidgeting. Enjoy the beautiful day in the beautiful park. There is no more to be done until I catch my train, and you your flight.'

He sucked out the stone of the last apricot, threw it toward the thicket, and clasped his legs just below the knee to hold himself still. 'I can't believe everything's done with the setting up. Only the fine-tuning now. That's down to Willem not me.'

'And the reception is organized. We had to issue invitations months in advance to make sure all the right people could attend.'

'Jesus, these glad-handing shindigs, I hate 'em.'

'It is important to do these things,' she said. Louise pushed herself up to sit with ankles crossed again. Until she was settled, he gazed into the distance watching a group of young people play with a Frisbee.

'I know.' What was the use of trying to explain? When he married Esther, she made him believe he could conquer the world. Tess, Tess, what was to become of them?

'You do not think your wife will attend?'

'She's one of the partners in a firm of solicitors. She can't just drop everything, and there are my children, Fran and Tom to consider.' He chewed his bottom lip, spoke his thoughts wishing immediately he hadn't. 'She hasn't been very pleased with me lately.'

'Why not?'

What could he say? Because I helped you, and let her down. A matter of life and death, Louise had told him. Even before, Tess had been uptight. Their sex life had been shot through for a while now. The company MO assured him he could find no physical reason for his not getting an erection. If Tess . . . He couldn't put it all on to Tess and he couldn't, wouldn't, confide in Louise. That old chestnut, my-wife-doesn't-understand-me. What if he said to Louise, right now, more than anything, I would like us to make love? Try to. What if? He grinned, hoping his face didn't look as though rigor had set in.

'I don't know for sure. When you've been married, or lived with someone as long as Esther and I have, you'll probably find from time to time you're not exactly flavour of the month. Eventually, the situation resolves itself, especially when you've children. Either you drift back to normality, or what's bugging you simmers for a while before igniting into a flaming row. Like thunder and lightning, that usually clears the air. The last scenario is best.'

'What if you, or your wife fell in love with someone else?'

This time he laughed. 'Neither of us has the time or the opportunity.' Except, lately, he had wondered. Could Tess be having an affair? Might explain her edginess. 'We're going on holiday end of July. She'll be able to relax. Perhaps she'll tell me what's wrong. I'm looking forward to going away, spending time with her and my children. Setting things up over here has taken more out of me that I realized.'

'Where are you going?'

'Corfu. We usually spend our summer holidays in Ireland with my parents. They retired to Bantry a few years back. This year Esther wanted to go somewhere sunshine is guaranteed.'

'Won't your parents be upset?'

'We'll catch up with them later.'

Louise stretched out her legs and leaned back on her elbows. Her skirt lay taught against every slightest mound of her body, her jacket fell open revealing how tightly her top clung to her breasts. He looked away.

'My mother and father would be very upset if my sister and my brother and their families did not spend the holidays with them,' Louise said.

He assumed this would be on their farm somewhere in North Brabant. She had shown him a photograph of the farmhouse, so-called, peacocks on the gravel path in front of what looked like a late-Seventeenth Century manor house. 'I suppose their children love staying on the farm,' he said.

'They do not go on holiday there. In August we all go to our villa on Lake Como.'

'Who looks after the farm?' He would have thought August was one of the worst times to leave it.

'Our Estate Manager, of course.'

Silly question. Fuck her? No chance. He would be totally out of his depth.

'With everything done and dusted, I doubt I'll be seeing you again,' he said.

She sat up, wriggled along the blanket to sit close, her legs bent sideways so that she could lean her arms on his knees. He felt her breast brush his clasped hands.

'In September, you will.' She lent her cheek on her arms, no longer looking directly at him, her shoulder-length blonde hair falling over her face. 'Will you miss me? I shall miss you. We have been friends, not just colleagues, have we not Michael?'

'You'll be enjoying yourself far too much to miss me. I have to say though, my job over here was made easier because of you. We work well together.'

Pushing on his knees, she got to her feet, smoothed down her skirt, said, 'Nothing I have done for you could repay your kindness when I needed help. I . . . I needed to keep my problem secret . . . and . . . '

'Look on me as an honorary uncle.' Keeping his hands clasped, he stretched his arms above his head, his legs while holding them a few inches above the ground.

'You are too young to be my uncle.'

Feeling the life coming back into his legs and arms, he crouched for a moment. 'Big brother then.' He stood so quickly, he was light-headed. He put his arm around her shoulders, gave her a squeeze.

She buried her face in his chest. 'I do wish you were not married, Michael.'

He gripped her shoulders, held her away from him. 'You just feel grateful because I saved your bacon.'

He reminded himself, he liked being married. He loved Tess, loved Fran and Tom. He let go of her, looked at his watch. A couple of hours more to kill before he had to go for his plane. He put on his jacket, checked his wallet and passport hadn't fallen out of the inside pocket. Louise collected what little debris they had left into a plastic bag, folded the rug. He took it from her to carry. She too checked the time.

She tugged at his free arm. 'We have plenty of time. Back to my place. We can have coffee and I know there is some delicious chocolate cake. Mara bought it but she will not mind if we eat it.'

She lived only minutes from where they had picnicked. Linking her arm in his, she propelled him along. He had little choice.

CHAPTER EIGHT

Friday, 10 June, Edwalton

He drew up the Windsor carver and sat where Esther had set a place for him. The kitchen somehow worked at both a functional and emotional level. He preferred to work and read at the scrubbed-pine table rather than at his desk in the study. Behind him, an old Welsh dresser where Esther displayed some of the collection of antique Willow Pattern she had inherited from her maternal grandmother. Thank God they never used it. He remembered the first time he went to Sunday lunch at Gramma and Gramps's anxious to make a good impression – 'Love the plates,' he said, 'Are they Wedgewood?' 'As a matter of fact,' Gramma replied, 'Minton. They've belonged to my family since the early Eighteen Hundreds, or so my grandmother told me.' His response made her laugh, 'Whoops, perhaps I won't offer to dry after all.' They had got along fine ever after. Early Nineteenth Century gold-rimmed Minton, God knows what dishes his ancestors in south west Ireland had eaten their praties off at that time.

Esther plonked an individual bowl of salad in front of him.

'Tom took a while to settle,' he said as an opener. 'He kept wanting another story. I shall be glad when he can read himself to sleep.'

'He can read. He wanted to have you all to himself. You let Fran monopolise you.'

'She was fast asleep when I went in to kiss her.' He picked at his salad. 'She looked like an angel.'

'Well, she isn't.' Her back to him, Esther fiddled with the microwave.

Opposite him, a built in oven and grill, ceramic hob and hood, modern units and overhead cupboards, Esther had decided the Aga must go when they moved in ten years ago. Facing him, she leaned against the worktop.

'You must be tired,' she said, 'after a long day, chasing about playing hide-and-seek. Why did you let them drag you out into the garden soon as you walked through the front door? And look at the state of your trousers. The whole suit will have to go to the cleaners.'

'Please don't nag, Pudding. I am tired.' What if he said, *As soon as we've eaten let's go to bed?* 'They seemed so pleased to see me. I do miss them.' *I miss you too.*

The microwave pinged. The medium sized pizza she placed on a cooler plate had some vegetarian concoction as a topping. She peered at it. 'Doesn't look much. Maybe there's ham in the fridge.' She unwrapped a couples of thin slices, sniffed. 'Perhaps not,' and binned them. She rummaged some more to produce a piece of dried-up Edam. 'Looks like I must do a shop,' she said.

Once upon a time after working away, knowing he would have been satiated with hotel restaurant fare, she would cook him one of his favour-ites, sausages and mash with onion gravy, or nutty-tasting cabbage, not over-boiled, then fried in bacon fat from thick rashers she would grill to go with the cabbage.

'Aren't you going to eat with me?'

'I had beans on toast with Tom and Fran.' Perhaps you'd like some wine.'

'Only if you'll have a glass with me.'

'Better not. Things to do in the garden.'

She pulled out a chair to sit opposite him, rested her hands on the table, interlocked her fingers. He noticed her press her thumb-pads together, move them apart, press them together, again and again. 'I was at Hart's today. Had to meet a client. He bought me lunch.'

'Did he now?'

'Really, Mike, there was no hidden agenda. I bumped into Charles Pennington.'

'CP.' Mike said, 'our illustrious Chairman.'

'Apparently, the company's Netherlands' expansion would not have gone so well without your hard work,' Esther said. 'He thanked me profusely for sparing you.'

'Good old CP knows how to squeeze every last micro-litre out of you, tells all and sundry what a marvellous fellow you are. God help you if you don't live up to the hype.'

'He's always championed you against the opposition, those weaselling Public School types on the Board. No need for that chip on your shoulder, Mike. You may have gone to a north London Comprehensive, but you did go up to Oxford, whereas . . .'

'And I married you, Pudding. You made me believe in myself. As for sparing me, what's new? Just happens to be Amsterdam this time, not Newcastle, or Bristol, or . . .'

She looked down at her hands. 'Seems to have taken more out of you this time.' She got to her feet. 'His parting shot was, not long now till September the first, as though I should be excited.'

'Oh that.' He pushed his plate away, leaving a third of the uninspiring pizza.

'I expect you had a good lunch too,' she said.

He felt his face flush. 'Lunch? Yes, I ate lunch.'

He pushed back his chair and stood, binned the remains of the pizza, carried his dirty pots into the butler's pantry and put them in the sink. He had lost count of the times he'd been told the kitchen sink was for preparing vegetables. Esther followed him as far as the doorway.

'You can leave them. I was waiting for you to finish before I put on the dishwasher.' She stood her ground. 'So what is so special about September the first?'

'One of those glad-handing dos to announce the company's official arrival in the Netherlands. Everybody who's supposedly somebody will be there. The sort of thing I detest. Wives are expected . . . only . . .'

'You don't want me there.'

'Don't be absurd.'

She came right into the room opened up the dishwasher, bending over to peer inside. She was wearing her housewife gear, legging jeans which stretched over her enticing butt. Once upon a time he would have taken advantage of her pose. Giggling, she would have rubbed her bottom against his groin until . . . Arms folded, he remained where he was leaning against the sink. She came and stood in front of him, close enough for him to smell her perfume, Coco Chanel, to notice the dark shadows of her nipples where her breasts, bra-less, undulated beneath a white T-shirt.

'When were you going to tell me,' she said. 'I can't just drop every-thing at a moment's notice. And there's Fran and Tom.'

What if he did what he might have done in a previous life, pull her to him, hold her, tell her, Relax Pudding, stop getting your knickers in a twist, begin to . . . He kept his arms folded.

'Honestly, Pudding, I did intend to tell you soon.'

Her face clouded. She bit her bottom lip as though irritated, and moved round him to collect the washing up.

'I shall be based here until September,' he said, 'though I'd better warn you, come the autumn, for a while I shall have to spend a fair bit more time over in Amsterdam.'

'And shall we notice any difference?' Her voice dripped sarcasm.

He watched as she re-arranged the dishwasher clattering its contents wondering how many pots would remain intact once scalding water hit them.

'Pudding.'

'What now?'

'It is next weekend we're off to Cal's, isn't it? I was wondering, how about going on a picnic this Sunday?'

'You've promised to be home in time to set off early next Friday even-ing, remember. A picnic, where?'

'No problem being home early. As I said, I shall be based here till September. I thought a picnic in some nice parkland,' he said.

'Where we'll find everyman and his wife, his children, and his dog have the same idea. 'We have a perfectly good garden all to ourselves here.'

'Just a thought, more fun for Fran and Tom.' He was defeated.

She stood upright, slammed the door shut, and switched on the machine.

'There is something you could do for me, Mike.'

'What's that Pudding?'

She made for the doorway and turned. 'For Christ's sake stop calling me Pudding.'

'Sorry. What is it you want me to do?'

'That's it.'

'You're not a bit like one. You know that. Just a . . .'

'Past its sell-by date,' she said. 'In case you hadn't noticed, I was last pregnant seven years ago.'

He saluted. 'Yes Ms Purslow-Onajole.' She always lightened up when he used her professional handle.

She wheeled round. 'If you have anything further you've omitted to tell me, or any more bright ideas. I shall be gardening.'

Absolutely shattered, he remained leaning against the sink. A relaxing shower beckoned, followed by a bit of mindless TV, anything to stop him dwelling on that afternoon and . . .

Almost ten o'clock and still a glimmer of daylight when Esther returned from whatever she had been doing outside. Brought up in a Camden Council flat, gardens were outside his brief. Sprawled in his favourite armchair, too tired to concentrate, and thank God, too fagged even to dwell on the events of the day, he had no idea what rubbish he was watching.

'I've locked up,' Tess said, then still hovering in the doorway of the sitting room. 'Maybe on Sunday we could go out to Rutland Water for a picnic. We could hire bikes. Tom and Fran would like that.'

'Brilliant.' He almost leapt up and kissed her. He hadn't ridden a bike since Oxford. Useful to get the hang of it again for Amsterdam.

'I'm whacked,' she said. 'Good night.'

'Night, night. Shan't be long.'

He fell asleep looking forward to seeing Calista Blake, couldn't remember the last time they'd met up. He hoped she was happy with this Burgess fellow. Tess didn't think much of him. One thing in his favour, pots of money. Dear Cal, he owed her. She probably didn't realize how much. Oxford had been a nightmare till he met her. But for her . . . and Tess, of course . . .

Nearly two o'clock when he came to, the telly rattling away. Better be careful not to wake Tess.

CHAPTER NINE

Tuesday, 21 June

After dark, Calista was always vigilant. On the main street couples, or small groups, one or two loners, on the way home from the pub, making for the chippy, By the cashpoint no one passed close. She retraced her steps into the side-street, the car-locks clunked as she pointed the key.

'Nice motor.'

Parked with the driver's side next to the pavement, she was poised to open the door, and slide in. Drawing herself up, the youth was a head shorter, no muscle man. Under the street light, his face looked thin, pasty. She braced herself ready to take him on. Someone behind her, he tugged at the clutch bag tucked under her arm. She clung on to it. Wheeled round, car key clenched in her other hand. She was ready. A blow across number two mugger's head. Pasty caught her arm. She lashed out with her feet. One-to-one, she could have prevailed. The three of them were too much for her. Bag yanked from her, she was floored, car key wrenched from her hand. Pain split her head. She passed out.

The lightest touch.

'Miss? Miss? Can you hear me?'

She can open her eyes. See every shade of grey. Smell the musty pavement.

Again the voice. 'You've had a fall, mi duck. Must'a knocked you out.'

Didn't fall. Pushed. Must get up. Moving, agony. Is that whimper her?
'Don't move, luv.'

Something soft, warm, is placed over her, tucked round her.

'What's yer name, me duck?' His face, close to hers, shadowy.

'Cal,' she whispered tasting blood. She must think.

'I'm going for 'elp, Cal. Nip'll stay with you.'

Feet in large, lace-up men's shoes, colour indistinct. Then she remembers scruffy trainers coming at her. She begins to shiver. She can't stop.

'Stay. Good Girl. Stay.'

She can raise her head, just a little. Jesus, it throbs. All she can hear. The glistening eyes of a small dog. Adam said don't look a dog in the eye. He feels threatened. She closes hers. Opens them.

Adam. God, no. They took Adam's second Jag, his convertible. Must sort it. Mentally she's on her feet. The state she's in, how will she get home? She begins to cry. Like the shivering, she can't stop herself.

The dog stretches. Wagging its rear as it gets up.

The shoes again. Their wearer crouches down.

'Cal, don't cry. Ambulance will be here. Nip and me'll wait with you'

And then she'd be on her own.

At the hospital, she was sequestered in a cubicle on an unyielding cot to be kept in overnight for observation.

'Thank God it's only bruising.' Adam's voice.

Only bruising, the whole of her being throbbed. Someone was stroking her cheek. She struggled to open her eyes. In his light-weight summer suit Adam looked as fresh as when he left for London at seven the previous morning.

'You could've been knifed.'

She didn't remember a knife. Happened so quickly. One of them went for the bag. She resisted. Thrown to the ground. One of them a girl, 'Rich bitch! Then she put the boot in. That was all she could tell the policeman.

'How did you know I was here?' She tried to smile.

'You told the paramedic where I was.' He pulled up a chair, took her hand, and brushed her fingers with his lips.

'They phoned the hotel?'

'Who else, would they contact? Your parents in Spain. Your brother in California.'

'Were you asleep?'

'I came straight away.'

'The last train . . .'

'Limousine service.' He stood. 'Now try to sleep.'

'Adam.'

He bent over her.

'Sorry about the car.' She had taken the favourite of his Jags for the fun of it.

'So am I.' He kissed her lightly on the lips and was gone.

Arriving home later that Wednesday, Adam carried her upstairs. He ran a relaxing rose-scented bath and bathed her like a baby, before tucking her up in their huge, soft bed. Pam prepared lightly grilled sole with button mushrooms, and creamy mashed potatoes, easy to eat, easy to digest. Under Adam's attentive eye, she cleared her plate. Putting the tray to one side, he took her hand in both of his.

'Are you going to tell me what you were doing out on your own gone eleven o'clock?'

She explained, discovering she didn't have enough cash to pay the young woman who helped Pam she had driven over to Harborough to a cash-point. 'Harborough of all places.' She was beginning to feel angry, and tearful. 'Your beautiful car.'

'What was wrong with yours?' He raised a questioning eyebrow, looking severe. 'At least you're all in one piece.' Then, he smiled. 'A fright, but . . .'

Adam was as solicitous as a mother hen, making sure she had titbits to tempt her, and plenty of rest. He insisted she shouldn't think of going into chambers until after the weekend. The way she felt, she doubted she would ever leave home again. Waking in the night, whimpering from a bad dream, Adam caressed her, and whispered reassurances until she went back to sleep.

Next day, determined not to let the trauma of the mugging grind her down, she phoned her colleague Matt Wakeham first thing. She would not put her casework on hold. Going into her study to wait for him she discovered an arrangement of sunshine yellow roses filling the empty hearth, from Adam. Then Matt arrived with half a dozen perfectly sculpted, white lilies. Pam ushered him in.

'What have those bastards done to you?' He held her lightly, kissing each battered cheek.

'Lucky her two mates were intent on nicking the Jag, or she would've kicked my head in.'

'A she?'

She nodded. 'Thank God we're on holiday in a few weeks.'

When Adam arrived home, late-afternoon, she clung to him, thanking him for the lovely roses. Holding her away, he glanced at the lilies, elegant in a tall square glass vase on her desk.

'Where did you get those?'

'Matt Wakeham'

'Rather funereal, don't you think.' Letting her go, he turned away

She and Matt had been friends since Bar School, for a while lovers. He once said the lily's your flower, Cal, pellucid, and straight as a die. Tears streamed down her cheeks. She began to cry like a child. She couldn't stop herself. At once, Adam's arms were around her.

'Don't, please don't.'

'Can't . . . stop.'

'You must rest before dinner.' He held her, comforting her whilst she sobbed till she could sob no more. His shirt front was soaked.

In the dressing room, out of habit, Calista stood in front of the cheval glass before taking off her clothes. She put a hand to her cheek. But for the kick, she might not look quite such a gargoyle. A lump on her left temple where her head hit the pavement. She shuddered to think what several kicks would have achieved. As it was her face was stiff and swollen, her right eye black and blue, her bottom lip split. Lucky the car was parked driver's side to the kerb. If she had fallen on the road, those punks might have run over her.

Unbuttoning her simple cotton frock she shrugged it off letting it fall at her feet leaving her standing in the skimpiest pair of silk briefs. As soon as they were upstairs, Adam had shed his business suit and gone for a shower. He said he would walk Beppo while she rested. She started. He was standing behind her, naked except for a towel sarong.

'Lisa,' she said to his reflection.

'No, darling.' He stroked the bruises on her left side where she had borne the brunt of her fall. 'Me, Adam, you, Cal.'

'The girl who kicked me, I remember now, *leave it, Lisa*. One of the lads pulled her away. The other was starting the car.'

He was covering her aching shoulder with kisses, his lips soft and caressing, the scent of him reminding her of a walk in woods refreshed by rain. His hold was firm but gentle as he scooped her up.

'Bed for you, my girl.'

Putting her down, uncovered, on the cool sheet, he sat on the side of the bed.

'Did you know you've the prettiest nipples?' He nuzzled each in turn. 'Strawberry-flavour, definitely.'

Despite her aches, enjoying the sensation, she giggled. 'My breasts aren't very sexy.' Flatter than ever, as she lay on her back.

He brushed each nipple with his thumb. 'Pert and to the point, when I do this.' He ran his hand over her stomach concave between protruding hip-bones.

'And I'm too thin.'

'I don't like matronly women.'

Easing down her pants, he lifted her buttocks placing a pillow under them, 'To cushion your bruises.' His smile was dreamy.

He walked to the other side of the bed to lie, propped up on one elbow, beside her. He slipped his free hand between her thighs, probing with cool firm fingers. Already aroused by his caresses, sighing with pleasure, she opened her legs, and closed her eyes. Then anxious opened them, 'I look such a fright.'

'Your bruises excite me.' He nuzzled her ear, then kissed her eyes, her cheeks, the tip of her nose, caressing her split lip with his tongue.

'Now, let's see where else you need kissing better.'

He ran his lips and tongue down the length of her body, lingering over her breasts, her navel, on down between her legs. Her aches forgotten, she squealed with pleasure. Penetrating her, he took his time. She thought she was going to die. Climaxing, he gave his customary satisfied groan, rolled on to his back and reached for her hand.

'If this is what your being mugged does for us . . .'

She shuddered.

'Eh.' He leaned over and kissed her cheek. 'A joke in bad taste. You always liked it in the afternoon.'

'You did all those nice things you always used to.' Ages and ages since he had taken so much trouble. Since they were married, she had come to the conclusion Adam looked on a wife as mere convenience. Nowadays, on those occasions when he was home, and more rarely, felt the urge, his manoeuvring her onto all fours was routine, their coupling basic, functional, concise.

'I was a better lover than I am a husband, you're saying.' - She felt her neck go red. 'Can't have you seeking consolation elsewhere.' He ran the palm of his hand over her body. She winced when, lingering on her bruises, he pressed down on them.

'You know I wouldn't do that. I really wouldn't.'

Then he dug in hard with his fingertips.

'Adam, you're hurting me.'

He brushed her cheek with his lips, and rolled off the bed. 'Do try and rest now. I'm off for a swim.

What about poor Beppo's walk came into her head as she fell asleep.

CHAPTER TEN

Saturday, 30 July

Secure in her capsule in the high blue yonder, Calista viewed dust-mouse-like clouds scuttling along the jagged ridges of arid karst. Albania, where were the clustered shelters of human life on that stony ground, she wondered. Kristina, the maid at their rented villa last year was from there. She was pleased Kristina had married her Yiorgos, a Cinderella story. Before Yiorgos fell in love with her, Kristina must have been lonely living far away from her family. Yet in the face of hardship, she had seemed able to maintain an air of cheery stoicism. Calista admired her, she should follow her example, and not let the mugging grind her down. She still suffered flashbacks, no longer walked out late, except in the garden with Beppo. Even then she was nervous as a cat, the slightest rustle, imagining intruders, but she would not give in.

She switched her attention to the sea, pure ultramarine below.

'I think that's Corfu. Tess and Mike must be a week into their holiday.'

How close Corfu's north-eastern promontory was to the Albanian mainland. In the Nineties the Greeks had trouble with Albanian pirates. She hoped Tess and Co were not beset by brigands. Remembering her Shakespeare, *What country, friends, is this? Illyria, lady.* In *Twelfth Night* Viola disguised herself as a man because Illyria was noted for the lawless profession of piracy. Albanians were probably the descendants of Ancient Illyrians. She loved this corner of the world, its ancient history, its mythology. As for Corfu, *The Tempest*'s witching isle. With luck, there Tess and Mike would become re-enchanted with each other. Maybe on

Ithaca she would with Adam.

Adam too gazed out of the window. Deep in thought, he hardly registered the scene below. He smiled across at his wife. Super-clever, aloof, you'll get no joy out of Miss Iceberg, his solicitor Taylor Dando warned. But, at his request Dando had been happy enough to bring her along to his party, Does one's reputation no harm, old boy, to be seen with Calista Blake.

When he and Dando consulted her on some labyrinthine contractual problem he didn't want to run past the rest of his partners, he was bowled over by her intelligence, her professionalism. That she was a timeless classical blonde was his undoing. He had to have her. Needless to say, she wasn't a virgin, unsophisticated though, considering her age. Pity she had jibbed at going as far as he would like, why he needed Sheena Jardine. The new jargon for time-honoured practices, BDSM had a ring to it - bondage, dominance, sadomasochism, though even if Calista had been game, he would still have need of Sheena's services. Variety, the spice of life, as the saying goes. The thought of Sheena's sultry compliance . . . Best not dwell on pleasures he wouldn't enjoy for at least a month.

He should never have married Annabel, had realized his mistake immediately. Len and Sash were his compensation. A shock, Annie's announcement she was in love with someone else. Her lack of enthusiasm for having sex on those sporadic occasions he felt duty-bound to perform should have warned him, except it turned him on, made his taking of her all the more enjoyable. In tears that last time, 'I want a divorce.' She verged on hysteria. He argued against, as much for her sake as for his girls. The chap she had fallen for was some academic, without tenure at that. As long as she was discreet, he could tolerate her affair, told her as much, no angel himself. He offered her a quid pro quo. She turned him down, pleading I want the chance to be happy before I'm too old.

His affair with Cal had lasted longer than anticipated. She never questioned his assertion he and Annabel stayed together for the sake of his girls. A boon, Cal being ambitious, not bothered about a conventional relationship. When he proposed he promised he would put no demands on her that would interfere with her career. A relief when she accepted. Now he could provide an alternative home for the girls complete with stepmother of impeccable reputation. Cal showed no signs of wanting children herself. So many women around her age became broody. He used to think she would drift away, set up shop with someone like Wakeham to produce a sprog. Wakeham, always sniffing around, none of his relationships lasted. In love with Cal, no question. What might have been disaster turned out rather well. The girls liked Cal, she liked them well enough, and he had checked Wakeham's endgame. All was right with his world.

Their private charter descended over the sheer cliffs and sandy coves of the western coast of Cephalonia ready to land at the airport on a narrow spit of land on the edge of the Ionian Sea. They seemed to skim the ripples of glinting sapphire. A soft landing, Adam, content, anticipated Ithaca.

As their taxi climbed up into the mountains through pine forests and hillside villages to descend to the port of Sami and the ferry to Ithaca, Cal sat mute beside him holding his hand. He enjoyed the scenery. The herds of goats epitomised eternal Greece, their nifty footwork on sheer hillsides sent cascades of stones and rocks on to the road, not, as he had once thought, disgruntled locals laying traps for scooter-riding tourists. He squeezed Cal's hand. She remained silent.

Not until they were on the ferry standing at the rail, the craggy limestone mass of Ithaca looming ahead quite out of the blue, she said, 'Do you think Tess and Mike will be okay?'

'Tess and Mike?'

'She met him through me. I'll hate myself if their relationship goes belly up.'

'They seemed perfectly okay the weekend they spent with us.'

'Fran and Tom had a great time, and Tess and Mike did both say, and separately, how much they'd enjoyed themselves,' Calista said.

'I should hope so. We were perfect hosts. Good food, good wine, swimming, croquet, country walks. We must invite them again. Next time Mike and I may be able to fit in a round of golf. I'd like to know more about his company and its expansion. I do hope they're not over-reaching themselves.'

'If they are, daresay your conglomerate might take an interest.' Calista said.

'That would depend. Anyway, to get back to what you said, their problems are nothing whatsoever to do with you.'

'But for me, they might not have got to know each other.'

'But for Taylor Dando, neither would we. Can just imagine him feeling responsible for any marital difficulties we might have.'

'Me, Tess and Mike, we've got history. I got to know Mike first. Through me he got to know Tess. Then if you can remember what it was like at that age, though they tried not to show it, became obvious Mike and Tess . . . '

'So?' He shrugged. He really didn't want to hear Cal's adolescent reminiscences.

'He was so good looking, with that cheeky smile, yet he never came on to you. You never felt . . . pressurized, I suppose. The opposite of you.'

'Thanks.'

'You know what I mean. He's dark and roguish. You're fair and aloof. Loads of girls had the hots for him. I was surprised and really chuffed when he asked me for a date. We got on really well, and, we were young and . . . He was the one I did it with first, have sex.' - Adam gave a quick glance at two small boys hanging over the rail nearby, probably unable to hear Cal for the continuous drum of the ship's engine. - 'He was a virgin too, in his second year would you believe, so . . . I think we both felt maybe we should . . . Everybody else seemed to be . . .'

'At it,' Adam said. 'I knew there was a reason I ought not to like him. Now I know.' Thankfully, the boys were being dragged off the rail by their father before they fell overboard. Adam put his arm round her shoulders. 'Only kidding.'

'Do you know, the very first time, he was so nervous, he came before . . . He was so embarrassed, poor love.'

'Poor bastard.'

'Oh, we soon got it right.'

Adam looked round to make doubly sure no one was eavesdropping. A dozen or so family groups, Greek mostly, he guessed, the children restless, noisily excited. Most of the tourists were in couples like him and Cal, mature, thirty-something and upwards. An elderly quartet sat silently, some distance away, definitely British, probably, come evening, liking nothing better than a vituperative game of bridge. About to point them out, Cal was still talking about the Mahoneys. Great. What with that and the judder and oily smell of the engine, he was in danger of getting a headache.

'We were never jealous of each other, me and Tess.'

He put his arm around his wife's shoulders and gave her a squeeze. 'Is Tess having a similar problem with him? If you were exchanging girly confidences, I hope my performance relative to his wasn't in the frame. Though come to think of it, you may have forgotten how well I do it. You've been most off-putting of late. I hope you'll be more obliging while we're on holiday. Or, I may look elsewhere.'

'You can be an absolute shit.'

'Cal, Tess and Mike must sort themselves out. You can't do it for them. Besides, Tess is the one who specializes in divorce, not you.'

She pulled him round to face her.

'What I'm trying to say is, but for me, she might never have married him, and now it's all gone pear-shaped. She's so fed up and unhappy. They don't make love anymore.'

'Jesus wept. *Cherchez l'autre femme*.' There were men who couldn't cope with more than one woman at a time, but to give up on Tess Mahoney. Uncanny her resemblance to Sheena Jardine.

'You think so too? If he has someone else, she'll have just cause. Make things easy, a quick divorce.'

'No matter what, it isn't easy, especially when there are children.'

'I'm so sorry, Adam.' She took his hand.

He turned the better to look into her eyes. 'There's no need for you to be.' Pulling her to his side, he slipped his arm around her waist. 'This business with Tess and Mike sounds serious. But what made you think of it, here of all places?'

'Flying over Corfu.'

Calista rested her head on his shoulder. She was nearly twenty nine when he met her. Lucky she stuck with him as long as she did. She wouldn't understand his need to unwind with Sheena. He looked on it as a cabbalistic ritual, whether performed privately in a hotel room, or at one of Sonja's renowned soirees. One thing for sure, Cal, like Annabel, must never find out.

Passengers were already queuing to disembark as they chugged through the narrow neck between two headlands which almost enclosed the bay where Vathi's quay-side tavernas and colourful buildings stood glowing in afternoon sun, ochre and white against olive- and pine-green slopes. Their imminent arrival was being announced first in Greek then English. The boat passed the islet of Lazaretto surrounded by a luminous band of silver and emerald, reflections on still blue water.

'Fabulous.' She turned to him smiling.

Adam pushed the bedroom shutters back against the wall and stood at the balcony rail. On the narrow road that twisted along the isthmus their taxi had got stuck behind a juddering old pick up, complete with two children bouncing around in the back, obligatory in rural Greece. They had been constrained by the pick-up's turn of speed all the way north.

He took in a deep breath of pine-scented air. The eerie light was magical. All around soft grey-greens and blues shaded to indigo. Tomorrow all this would come alive in golden sun, emerald and sapphire. Swallows would swoop overhead, and the cicadas' chorus would be deafening. The sun had disappeared completely behind the tree-covered hillside. On either side of their villa, named Erato after the muse of erotic poetry, groves of olive and groups of cypresses cascaded down to the sea. The villa stood on a vine-covered terrace cut into the slope, thirty feet above a shingle cove. Once the site of a goatherd's hut, the present shelter could not be more different. He heard Cal's step on the spiral staircase connecting the upper to the lower floor.

'Let's go down to the sea,' she said.

'Any chance of something to eat. I don't fancy the walk into the village.'

They dined on the terrace, ate their first Greek salad of the year, thanks to their new maid, Kristina's replacement. It was always the best for the intensity of taste and smell, tomatoes flavoured by the hot sun, cucumber, crunchily refreshing, slices of sweet red onion, succulent olives and green peppers topped by a slab of creamy-sharp *feta* sprinkled with basil. Calista drizzled dark olive oil with a dash of wine vinegar over the green, red and white. The bread, stale by evening, they dunked in pools of oil left in the salad bowl. There was yoghurt and honey, peaches, nectarines. They drank white wine tasting of crisp green fruit.

While Calista went up to unpack, he cleared the table, then returned to the terrace to linger over a final glass amid the scents of wild herbs and pine, the sound of the sea rippling over pebbles in the cove below. When he estimated she would have finished her task, revived by the food, he anticipated sex. Barefoot, silent as a stalking lion, he climbed the spiral stair.

He stood in the doorway of their room. Calista was bent over, forearms resting on the balcony rail. Half prepared for bed, he assumed, she wore only a narrow-strapped, T-shirt. Her legs tantalizingly apart, her naked buttocks enticed him. He undid his belt – if she were Sheena . . . – and unzipped his chinos. Careful to make no noise, he liberated himself from them and his boxers. So immersed in her own world, she did not notice his approach. He rested his hands on her hips, rubbed his erection against her.

'No Adam, please no.'

'Yes, Cal, yes.' With his left hand he gripped her by the scruff, his forearm resting on her back, pinning her down.

'Please.' She struggled. 'I'm sorry . . . So sorry, I . . .'

'No excuses. Your period ended on Thursday.' Then he whispered in her ear. 'Thank you, darling. You know I love to play rough.'

None too gentle, with the first two fingers of his right hand he probed her sex, but to no avail. If that was how she was determined to play it . . .

'No . . . please . . . no . . . Let me ex . . .'

She sounded as though she was having difficulty breathing. He entered her, felt her resistance, which made his resolve to have her all the stronger.

He heard her swallow. 'Adam, please, I've forgotten to bring my pills.'

He hesitated, to play her, half withdrew. His tone even, 'That was careless, darling.' Then, injecting incredulity, 'Were you thinking we should remain celibate for the duration of our holiday?' Finally, with menace, 'I think not.'

He thrust into her with full force. She gasped, stifled what sounded like a sob. He guessed not with pleasure. Too bad. To prolong his, and whatever she was feeling, in his head, he recited his six through to twelve times' tables, an old trick, achieving an uncertain rhythm. He remembered the whack from his nanny's hairbrush for every one he got wrong, which served to make his momentum stronger. Satisfied at last, he ejaculated onto the small of her back.

He stood away. 'There darling, I've been ultra-careful, just in case.' He gave her a playful slap on her bottom. 'Better go and clean ourselves up.'

Slow, with the help of the balcony rail, she stood up straight, turned to him, tears in her eyes. 'Did you have to be such a brute? You've really hurt me.'

'You shouldn't have tried to freeze me out. Let that be a lesson.' He pulled her to him, kissed her on the forehead. 'Trouble is, you've such an alluring arse. Soon as I can, I'll get us a supply of condoms.'

Taking her by the wrist, he pulled her into their bathroom and turned on the shower.

CHAPTER ELEVEN

Sunday

When Calista woke up, Adam lay on his side looking at her, smiling. 'Feeling better this morning?' he said.

She held her breath, dreading he would roll her over on her stomach, the signal he wanted sex. 'Still sore,' she said.

'Sea water will put an end to that.' He sat up, swung himself off the bed. 'I'll go down and make tea.'

The previous night, he had showered with her, sponged her back, and between her legs while she sobbed. She could not stop herself. She cried for the months of loneliness she had endured, the misgivings she tried to deny, not for the physical pain he had just inflicted.

'Eh, can't be that bad.' He wrapped her in a towel, held her to him. 'A while since you were a virgin, darling.' He carried her to their bed, lay her on it, and sat on the edge his arms braced either side of her looking down at her face. 'I know what we can do.'

He returned with a small plastic bowl of water, found cotton wool balls in her make-up bag. 'I've dissolved table salt in the water,' he said. 'Now open your legs and let me swab you.'

Too exhausted, too overwrought to face any more beastliness, she did as he asked. He tended her with such care and gentleness, at any other time he might have turned her on.

'There, there,' he said. 'You'll be fit for further service in no time.' He pulled the top sheet over her. 'You must go to sleep before you tempt me into being a bad boy again.'

That morning, he brought her up a mug of Earl Grey, no milk, no sugar. 'You have a lie in, while I go down to the village for bread.'

In shorts and T-shirt ready to go, he hovered in the bedroom doorway. 'I'm sorry I hurt you, Cal. Last night, here in this wonderful spot . . . I . . . I . . .' He sighed. 'I so looked forward to the release having sex always brings. Can we put what happened behind us, is what I'm trying to say. Enjoy the rest of our holiday.'

He seemed genuinely contrite, and she had set so much store on Ithaca working her magic on their ailing relationship.

'I would like nothing better,' she said.

His look of relief, she was sure, was genuine too. 'Thank you, darling. Thank you.'

They lingered over breakfast on the terrace, early sunshine flickering through vines covering the pergola, wafts of jasmine scent teasing on the warm breeze. An appetizer of fresh orange juice was followed by Adam's bread, lashings of butter so more-ish, a whole crusty loaf was in danger of disappearing.

'Better leave some for lunchtime,' she said. And, from the fridge, ham, and cheese, a fresh egg each if they could have been bothered to cook, and apricot jam, and fruit. 'Wonder what the new maid's like. You wouldn't know it wasn't Kristina who has done the shopping.'

This was the third consecutive year they had rented the Erato. The previous year, learning from the first when they had stayed only one illicit week, they had engaged Kristina to lay in stocks beforehand, and to arrive early to prepare breakfast Monday to Saturday when she came to service the villa. When they discovered their own place would not be finished in time, and Kristina married with a baby . . . 'No problem,' Yiorgos had informed Adam, 'Kristina will arrange everything with your new maid.'

As was their custom to stir them into action, they had finished breakfast with a cup of good strong coffee. '*Ena nes*' as the Greeks said, bore absolutely no resemblance to the instant coffee you got back home.

Then down to their secluded cove where, for the past hour, lulled by the schurr-schurr of waves rippling over pebbles, they lay naked side by side on sunbeds, he on his stomach, she on her back. They had chosen to relax, not be tempted to inspect their unfinished villa. In any case, Calista preferred the Erato's location, and was not thinking about very much at all, though she doubted the same could be said of Adam. One thing she had discovered, when he seemed most content that was when his brain was most active.

'This is the best,' she said.

'Absolutely.' Adam said.

'What are your thinking?' she asked.

A long drawn out sigh in reply. Stay calm, she told herself, don't probe.

'Fancy a swim?' He dug her in the ribs with his elbow.

'I was nearly asleep.'

'Thought so.' He swung his legs round and stood up. Then laughing, tipped her off her bed. 'Come on, lazybones.'

'Sadist.' She pushed herself up onto her feet. She was laughing too.

Holding hands, at first they paddled in the shallows, then they began splashing each other. Wading deeper, to her squeals of delight, they plunged in, weaving and diving around and under each other like dolphins. Eventually, exhausted, cushioned by water like silk, they floated on their backs toes-to-toes, eyes closed, faces toward the sun.

They ended the morning snorkelling, shadowed myriads of small and not so small fish playing tag among weed and rocks embellished with sea urchins. Just before two, they climbed back up to the Erato for a light lunch. Afterwards, a siesta in the cool of their shuttered room high among the pines, serenaded by a cacophony of cicadas,.

'Shall we find out if all that sea water has done the trick, darling?' Propped up on one elbow, he stroked her cheek.

She lay on her back, relaxed, drowsy, and replete with food and wine. In her head, a quick calculation. She was unlikely to get pregnant so near to the end of her last period. In any case . . .

Before she could respond, 'I'll take that as a yes.'

His hand was cool between her thighs as his probing fingers worked their magic. She drew up her knees, opened her legs, and threw her arms back either side her head. He manoeuvred himself between her legs. Instead of bracing himself to penetrate her, to her surprise he said, 'To be absolutely sure, I think I should kiss her better, don't you?' Kneeling, gentle, he caressed her breasts with his lips, tickled her navel with his tongue. Finally, holding her thighs apart, he nuzzled her sex bringing her to orgasm with his lips and tongue.

'Better now, darling?' He sat back on his heels.

'Yes.' She smiled up at him, stretched her legs either side of him.

'Would you return the compliment? Take me in your mouth.' He indicated his erection. 'I'll be a gentleman, withdraw in the nick of time. No unpleasant aftertaste, promise.'

He had tried so hard to make amends. She really did not feel she could refuse.

No Erato day would be complete without a trip in the villa's small boat. Back down to the beach after their sensuous afternoon, she helped Adam push it into the waves till it floated clear. He leapt in and lowered the outboard, she scrambled into the prow. Lowering sun washed all the colour out of the sea and sky, where one ended and the other began indistinguishable. They might putter on and on into infinity through the easy swell, as romantic as Calista remembered.

Eyes closed, lolling on cushions, listening to the phut, phut of the outboard, she told herself she was silly to have misgivings. So what if Annabel had been the prime mover in their divorce. Adam had not been obliged to ask her to be his second wife. Since the mugging, when he was home, he was considerate, attentive, seemed to accept she did not always feel like having sex when he did. As for his absences, unnecessary commuting was a tiring waste of time, and the tranquillity of the Old Rectory was growing on her. She was beginning to think of it as home. She opened her eyes.

'Must make the most of absolutely everything.' She leaned over the side to gaze down into the translucent water.

'Just what we are doing,' Adam said.

'Things change.' An involuntary shudder, paradise on earth could, would never last.

'No avoiding Fate,' he said.

CHAPTER TWELVE

Monday, Tuesday, Wednesday

Monday, so as not to be labelled 'slug-a-bed', Calista showered in the bathroom of the spare room whilst Adam used theirs. A pareo draped over a bikini, she was the first downstairs and out onto the terrace in time to hear a car engine switch off at the end of the track. Women's voices, two by the sound of them, speaking a language she didn't recognize. Then Kristina appeared, her slight build eclipsed by a taller young woman with the assured walk of a fashion model in shorts revealing long tanned legs, a strappy T-shirt, perfect breasts. The clothes, Calista could tell, not from any run-of-the-mill department store. She held a full plastic carrier as though it were a Louis Vuitton.

'Kristina.' Calista rushed over, took both her hands – dear Kristina with her strong work-roughened hands – and kissed her on each cheek. 'You're looking well. Marriage must suit you.'

Kristina blushed. 'Mrs Burr . . .'

'What did I tell you last year?'

'Cal.' Then her sharp-features and brown eyes seeming huge in her thin face were transformed, as always, by the most radiant of smiles. 'I am very happy.' Then, sounding hesitant. 'I will never be able to thank you.'

'You're obviously content, that's thanks enough.' And fingers crossed, Calista thought, this relationship I interfered in won't go pear-shape like Tess and Mike's. 'Where's this baby of yours? Have you not brought him to see me?'

'I promise I will. Yiorgo's mama is looking after him. I came with Ledi,' – Kristina gestured towards Miss Stunning – 'to show her how you and Mr Burgess like things done. Ledi is the wife of my brother.'

Ledi put the shopping down on a chair, and held out her hand. Calista took it, cool and satin smooth. They exchanged smiles. Calista's gaze was drawn to Ledi's unusual amber eyes.

'Ledia Halili-Kavathi, pleased to meet you Mrs Burgess.' She spoke English with a hint of East Coast American.

'And to meet you, Ledia.' Calista wondered why she was working as a maid. She turned to Kristina. 'I understand now, you were speaking *Shquip* to each other.'

Another of Kristina's smiles. 'You remembered, yes we were speaking Albanian.'

'Who was?' Adam had appeared on the terrace, urbane in ecru linen slacks and sky-blue, short-sleeved shirt. 'Kristina.' He too took her hands and kissed her on each cheek, 'How's young Dhionysios? No longer giving you sleepless nights I hope.' Then, as though he had not noticed her before, 'And you are?' Smiling, he held out his hand for Ledia to take.

Calista felt a stab of unease as she observed his appraisal of Ledia's strawberry-blonde hair scraped back into a coil, her regular features, and on down the contours of her body to her painted toenails peeping from leather gladiators.

'Darling, this is Ledia,' Calista said, 'our maid, and Kristina's sister-in-law.'

'Delighted to meet you, Ledia.'

Calista watched as Adam held Ledia's hand in both of his longer than was absolutely necessary for politeness' sake. Kristina had told her about the tendency of Albanian men, her brother Nik in particular, to be jealous with menace. For all her savoir-faire, Ledia blushed. Her hand released, she picked up the carrier bag.

'Tina,' she said, then something in *Shquip* as she went indoors, smiling.

Kristina called after her, the only words Calista understood, 'Mr Burgess' and 'Cal', her tone disapproving.

Kristina turned to her. 'Breakfast will not be long, now', and followed Ledia in.

'Well,' Calista said, 'Ledia has made an excellent first impression, I gather.'

'Not your average Greek cleaning lady,' Adam said.

She wondered if she ought to warn him about jealous Albanian husbands.

Whilst they ate, Adam not so leisurely as the previous day, he announced Kristina would be giving him a lift over to their villa's site to meet Yiorgos and the builder.

'There's so little left to do. Last time I was over I was sure we'd . . .' His frustration was palpable. 'With luck I'll see it more or less finished before we go home.'

'That explains the hurry, why you aren't dressed for the beach.' All she had seen of Adam's project, a more ambitious build than the Erato, and with a pool, were the original plans, photographs in various stages of development, a computer simulation of how it was supposed to look when it was finished. 'Can I come too?'

'Not today,' he said.

'I am supposed to be having some say in how it's furnished, aren't I?' She wasn't that bothered. Adam had consulted her on the kitchen and the bathroom fixtures and fittings, and, as she had done at the Old Rectory, she would employ an interior designer to do the donkey work.

'Yiorgos may have to take me over to Vathi to sign just one more form.'

Or bung someone or other a backhander, Calista thought.

'Okay,' she said. A relaxing morning on the beach beckoned. 'Have you any idea when you'll be back.'

Pulling an apologetic face, Adam shrugged.

After he and Kristina had left, she lingered over her coffee. Time to get to know the help. Ledia came out with an empty tray. Calista noted her rubber gloves.

'Would you like me to get you anything more, Mrs Burgess? If not, I will clear the table, if I may.'

Smiling, Calista gestured she could go ahead. 'Where did you learn English, Ledia?'

'Tirana.' She didn't pause from loading dirty pots.

'I wondered. Your English is very good,' Calista had no wish to upset her, 'but you speak with a slight American accent.'

'My teacher at the language school was American. I used to think, one day I should like to go to the United States.'

'Maybe you will,' Calista said.

Ledia compressed her lips, shook her head, a flash of resentment in her expression. 'I do not think so, not now.'

'When we first met,' Calista said. 'Kristina told me she was learning English because she wanted to go to England. She seems happy enough living here.'

The table cleared, Ledia lodged the piled-up tray on the edge of it. Her expression softened. 'I am pleased Kristina is happy, and Yiorgos. They are kind. And Dhionysius is beautiful. I wish I had a baby like him.' Her fleeting look of anguish put a stop to Calista suggesting one day she might. Ledia and the tray went indoors.

Calista drained her cup, picked up the saucer and followed her through to the kitchen. 'Are you and your husband also happy here in Kioni? You probably know we're building a holiday villa on land leased from Yiorgos's parents. We love it here.'

'Yes, many people like to come here on vacation.' Ledia took the pots from her. 'When it is finished I think you will like your villa very much.' Back towards her, Ledia filled the sink with hot water ready to do the washing up. 'Please excuse me, Mrs Burgess, I must get on. I have three other places to clean today, and I would like to be home by lunchtime.'

'But of course. See you tomorrow.'

'Ciao, Mrs Burgess,' She did not turn round.

Alone, Calista was comfortable enough sunbathing topless with her cover-up near at hand. Beneath a cloudless sky, her sunbed raked so that she could sit up, she was content to be charmed by all-shades of blue, from aquamarine through turquoise and sapphire to ultramarine, to feel the warmth of the sun on her body, to listen to the water's schurr schurr, breath in the scent of herbs and the pines. Almost perfection, she missed Beppo. He would love doggy paddling in the sea. 'But you'll be fine, old boy.' She spoke her thoughts aloud. Adam had been furious when she refused to have him put into kennels for three whole weeks. She told him of her fait accompli, 'Pam's as fond of him as I am. She's going to look after him while I'm away.' 'For heaven's sake, Cal, he's a dog, not a child.' A small enough victory, one up to her nevertheless.

She let down the back of her bed so that she could lie on her stomach for a while, started her book, became engrossed, turned over onto her back, read some more. She stretched, sat up, took a swig from the bottle beside her bed. The once cool mineral water was unpleasantly lukewarm. Never tiring of contemplating the tranquil scene, she sat for a while, then delved into her beach bag to check her phone, just gone one o'clock. Time for a leisurely swim before lunch.

She ate alone.

Afterwards she returned to the beach to read. At this rate she would get through Stieg Larsson's Millennium Trilogy easily within the first week. Matt Wakeham had lent her all three volumes– 'I got completely hooked,' Matt said. 'Read them one after another. And you'll love Lisbeth Salander.' She was so absorbed, she didn't hear Adam until he was only a few steps away.

'I'm so sorry darling.' Still in the clothes he wore that morning, he flopped on the nearby vacant sunbed. 'I could spit. We were, are so nearly there. I did have to go over to Vathi with Yiorgos. We followed the builder to his yard, problems with some of the bathroom fittings. The sunken bath for our en suite wasn't to the specified measurements, and the crates containing two of the lavatory pans and two of the sink units were so badly damaged their contents were smashed. The builder was anxious I authorised and was willing to pay for replacements.'

'Did you see the damaged items, the wrong-size bath?'

'Only the bath. It'll look great when we get the right size. I didn't see the other stuff. Yiorgos has assured me, I can trust the builder. After all, he did recommend him, and though construction took longer than I hoped, this is the first time something like this has happened. Sufficient to say, money has changed hands and delivery of undamaged and correct sized goods, fingers crossed, guaranteed. But yet another delay.' He sighed. 'Never mind, with a bit of luck . . .'

'What's going to happen to the wrong-sized bath?'

'As it had already been paid for, Yiorgos insisted the builder brought it to the site.' Adam chuckled. 'Perhaps I'll give it to Yiorgos. We popped up to the villa when we got back. Ledia came with us. I think she'd like a sunken bath.' He swung his legs round, stood up, and began to strip off his clothes. 'Fancy a swim? Too late, now, to go out in the boat.'

Hand in hand they waded into the water.

Except for Ledia bringing fresh bread and serving breakfast which included a hardboiled egg each, and no sex in the afternoon, nor later for that matter, Tuesday was a repeat of Sunday.

'If you don't mind,' Adam said, 'I don't want to go anywhere today, not until we go down to the village for dinner.'

'Fine by me.' She was at least two-thirds through *The Girl with the Dragon Tattoo*, could hardly wait to get back to it, then felt a twinge of guilt. She ought to be more enthusiastic about Adam's villa.

Wednesday followed the same pattern as Tuesday. Still no sex, even though she had now noticed a packet of condoms in Adam's wash bag. He must have got them in Vathi. She was content enough. What holidays were all about, relaxing together, enjoying each other's company. Long may it last, she could only hope

CHAPTER THIRTEEN

Reflections

On Wednesday evening, Calista and Adam sat at the same table as on Sunday, Monday, Tuesday which Marcos, the brother of the owner of their villa reserved for them at his taverna. As always the tempting aroma of marinated fish, or meat seared over charcoal sharpened their appetites. At their feet, the sea lapped the harbour wall, lights reflecting on dark water, silver and copper. Work-a-day fishing boats and flotilla yachts rode at anchor side by side under a star-lit sky, blue-black above, the conversation from other diners a background murmur. They were content to sit in companionable silence enjoying the evening, which, like the warmth of a scented bath calmed body and mind.

She took a sip of wine, glancing across at him. She wondered if her un-quietness, her discontent earlier in the summer was nothing whatever to do with what he did, or left undone, but all to do with her inability to adapt to her new role as wife. She smiled across the table.

'What are you smiling at? You look like a cat that's filched a sea-bass.'

'Right now, maybe that's how I feel.'

He did not ask her to elaborate. Both finished eating, he excused himself. She took sips of wine as her gaze wandered towards the picture made by the boats, the patterns of light on the inky wash of sea. She thought back remembering her and Adam's second encounter.

Happenstance, Friday of the week following her conference with Adam Burgess and Taylor Dando she sank, red-faced from running, into the nearest remaining First Class seat as the Sheffield train pulled out of St Pancras. The suit hiding behind the Evening Standard opposite had probably thought he was safe from invasion at a two-seater table.

'You only just made it, Miss Blake.' Folding his newspaper, Adam Burgess smiled across at her.

She hadn't registered the colour of his eyes before, hazel, not blue as she assumed. Warmth crept up her neck. With a bit of luck he would think it was because she had rushed. She tucked her hair behind her ears.

'Mr Burgess.' She returned his smile. 'Thank God for air conditioning.' She waved her hand in front of her face.

'A warm day, certainly, let's hope the good weather lasts the weekend.' She was glad he allowed her to settle before, 'Are you often in London?'

A Friday evening, the regular travellers were actually talking to each other and no danger of her and Adam Burgess's conversation echoing the length of a hushed carriage. She explained she was assisting a Q.C. currently involved in a case before the Chancery Division of the High Court.

'I'm impressed.'

She felt that tell-tale warmth again.

'Sorry, that sounds so self-important.' But you see, being asked to assist means he has faith in my abilities and I have to make absolutely certain I don't screw up.'

'Ambitious rather than self-important, I'd say.' He looked thoughtful. 'You'd get my vote any day, and Dando's, that I can tell you.'

While they talked, the train glided out of London under graffiti daubed bridges, through deep, grime-encrusted cuttings, buddleia, and willow-herb maintaining a tenuous hold in the walls. Kentish Town, West Hampstead, Cricklewood flashed by. As it outpaced north-bound motor traffic running parallel at the bottom of the M1, an attendant asked if they would like a drink.

'Please let me buy you one,' Adam said, 'though I doubt the dry white wine can be recommended.'

Bristling a little at his assumption, 'Actually, I'm dying for a G.&T.'

'A woman after my own heart.' He bought both of them doubles. 'Now we can sit back and enjoy the start of the weekend. Are you planning to do anything exciting, Miss Blake?'

'Not exciting exactly, but I'm looking forward to it.' She told him she was going over to Nottingham to keep a friend from her Oxford-days company. Tess, a Saturday golf-widow lived in Edwalton in a house with a big garden, great to relax in when the weather was good, that Tess had a little girl and a younger boy who tended to keep them occupied.

'And you Mr Burgess?'

'Only if you count a round of golf.' He laughed. They were both leaning forward, arms on the table, the better to hear each other. He was married as she guessed, though he wore no ring, and mentioned his wife only in passing. 'Like your friend, Annabel's a Saturday golf-widow.'

The archetypical proud father, he told her all about his daughters, Helena thirteen, and Sasha, ten. He frequently stayed up in London during the week so liked to devote Sundays to them.

'You're fond of children, Miss Blake?'

She had to admit she was ambivalent about them. Tess's two were cute, but she really didn't see herself as a mother.

'When I see poor Tess worn to a frazzle, despite the *au pair*.'

'You're a dedicated career woman then?'

She smiled in reply. He stretched his legs, which, firm and warm, came to rest either side of hers, touching, but not pressing. Her whole being glowed, not just her neck and face. He had her trapped, whether unconsciously, or with mischievous intent, the hammer-beat of her heart told her she couldn't be sure. Either way she couldn't move. The wings of a dozen frantic moths fluttered in the pit of her stomach. If his action were deliberate . . . Again she combed her hair behind her ears with her fingertips, then took a gulp of gin.

'And what do you do for fun? You do have fun, Miss . . . This is ridiculous. May I call you Calista? And for God's sake, call me Adam.'

'Please, not Calista, everyone calls me Cal,' she said.

She was jolted back to the present and Kioni harbour by someone getting up at the next table and knocking the back of her chair. Adam was a long time. Must have been waylaid on his way back from the loo.

'Sorry,' He kissed the top of her head before sitting down.

'Where have you been?'

'Talking to Yiorgos. You don't mind if I go fishing, do you?'

She delayed the length of a sigh's silent exhalation. No idyll endured.

'When are you going?'

Thursday, they dined earlier than usual. Adam was going out in Yiorgos's fishing boat, and wouldn't be back until dawn. No way was she going to return to the Erato right then. Not even the promise of starting *The Girl Who Played with Fire* could entice her to sit around on her own until time for her solitary bed.

'May I sit here Marco?'

She indicated an empty table next to the taverna entrance set a little back from the rest. When Marcos's friends dropped by, they usually sat there. Tucked away, she would feel happier about being alone.

'Please.' He gestured with open palm. 'May I get you something?'

She ordered a carafe of cool white wine which Marcos brought her himself, plus *mezedhes*, olives, squares of goat's cheese, pieces of octopus, tiny spicy meat balls, cucumber, tomato. As darkness fell, relaxing to be surrounded by the buzz of conversation without having to make the effort to participate, to observe, from her new perspective, the world and his wife, his friends.

Most tables were lively with chatter, a couple of larger parties raucous with laughter. One couple sat reading which, as it grew darker could not be easy. The lights strung along the quay and around the taverna were not over bright. She guessed neither the man nor the woman could be more than thirty. He had finished eating, and was intent on yesterday's *Times*. She had propped her book against the oil and vinegar, absentmindedly forking in mouthfuls between turning pages. Those with no souls could be found everywhere.

She knew Adam's restlessness was not because he was soul-less. Obvious, he adored this place as much as she did. Once she got used to doing nothing, she was content. Adam wanted to be up and doing, planning the next project. Only now was she getting to know him. Romantic meals, snatched afternoons of love, intense weekends in glamorous places, Paris, Venice, were no preparation for everyday married life.

She took a sip of wine. Tess was right. She really did have it all, except for children, but that was a bonus. Look at her, poor darling. Depressed and stressed out when she had been stuck at home with Fran and Tom. Anxious and exhausted when she tried balancing a career against domestic obligations. Adam hadn't so much as hinted he wanted her to have children. She guessed his less than easy-going daughters were enough.

Her thoughts were disrupted.

'PJ' Marcos bellowed, right next to her.

He had been standing in the doorway without her realizing. She looked up, followed his gaze. A spare man, average height, no trend-setter, in faded navy polo shirt and khaki shorts, his skin bordering on chestnut, his dark hair, close-cropped reminiscent of her brother's old Action Man toy made his way towards them. Marcos moved out of the doorway, his back half turned to her. She still had a view of the stranger. When he smiled, a vertical crease appeared in each cheek, giving him an air of sardonic amusement. The two men astonished her by hugging and kissing each other on each cheek.

'When did you get back?' Marcos spoke English.

'Sunday night. Done practically nothing but sleep since.'

'Your mother, is she okay?'

'Fine.' Raising his hands, he crossed his fingers. 'Wouldn't be here otherwise. God, Marco. It's great to be back, if only for a while.' About to draw a chair out from the table, he recoiled. 'I'm so sorry.' That smile so unapologetic. 'I didn't know Marcos was already entertaining a friend.'

She felt her neck redden.

'This lady and her husband are staying at the Erato,' Marcos said. 'Mr Burgess has gone fishing with Yiorgos.'

He scanned the tables in front of the taverna, and those which lined the harbour across the narrow road. All were taken.

'Marco, if your friend doesn't mind sharing with me.' She was conscious that on any other evening that particular table would have been free.

'I shall be delighted to have company,' Mr Sardonic said.

CHAPTER FOURTEEN

PJ Wood

'PJ Wood.' She took the hand he extended. Not used to callouses her turn to recoil except she didn't. 'Everyone calls me PJ. Not even my mother has the courage of her convictions.' He spoke clear, educated English with just a hint of mid-Atlantic. She refused to ask why he was known by his initials.

'Calista Blake. I mean Burgess.'

He took the chair opposite. Whilst he discussed with Marcos what he would eat and drink, she could observe him without seeming rude. Beneath his polo shirt, he was lean and sinewy, the ideal shape for a long-distance runner. She wondered how he earned his living.

'Are you eating?' He smiled across the table. His fact lit by light from inside the taverna, his eyes startled her. They were the deepest lobelia-blue.

'I've already eaten.' Not very much, her insides had been a tangle of knots. The thought of spending the night up at the villa alone . . . Anyone would think she was not used to being on her own, and Kioni was the least threatening of places.

'Only a salad,' Marcos said. 'Why don't I get Petros to prepare you the mixed fish dish for two? PJ would like that.'

He agreed he would.

She was tempted. The wine had helped her relax and the *mezedhes* had given her an appetite. A meal would prolong the time she could spend in company. Her eyes met PJ's, his look as guarded as she felt.

'That would be lovely, Marco.'

Marcos seeming pleased with his salesmanship went inside.

'Do you come here often?' Too late, she heard what she said. This time, their eyes meeting, they burst into laughter.

'Shouldn't that be my line, Mrs Burgess, or may I call you Calista?'

'Cal, please. Everyone calls me Cal.'

They were interrupted by Marcos bringing PJ a beer and more *mezedhes*. She looked longingly at the meat balls. Her glass nearly empty, Marcos poured the last of the wine from the carafe.

'Unusual name.' PJ drank half the contents of his glass. He put it down only to re-fill it with what beer remained in the bottle. 'What does it mean?'

He offered her some of the appetizers. She took just a few olives and a piece of cheese.

'My father told me it's from the Greek.' Although she was wearing a low-cut, strappy dress, it was quite dark now, and with only the dim lights strung around the taverna, she hoped he didn't notice the flush of self-consciousness suffusing her neck and chest. 'The feminine version of Calisto.' She hesitated. 'Something to do with good?'

'*Kallistos.*' His face lit up in recognition. 'Ancient Greek meaning Most Beautiful.'

She was sure her neck and chest must be crimson. 'Did you learn Greek at school?' A man with roughened hands, a classical scholar, he must be an archaeologist.

'My father was keen that I should.' He took a sip of beer. 'To answer your question, when I'm out on my boat, I usually drop in. And you?'

Perhaps his smile was not really mocking. Maybe he was a contented, good-humoured man. She told him this was the third year running she and Adam were staying at the Villa Erato, that in the evening they invariably walked down to the harbour to eat at Marcos's taverna. She told him how much they enjoyed going out in the villa's small boat.

'Whereabouts do you stay?' She imagined him pottering around in a similar boat.

'We have a house just outside Vathi.'

'Quite a way to come.'

She noted the 'we'. He must have a wife or partner too but why was he here alone.

'Not in my sloop. I'm on my way to Fiskardo to meet up with a couple of people. We plan some serious sailing.'

A sloop sounded very grand. Embarrassed, she looked away. The flame of a single romantic candle flickered on every table except theirs. She was disappointed, until Marcos preceding a waiter bearing an enormous platter of fish, brought them their very own candle.

She and PJ complimented him on the selection of fishes: sea-bass, sardines the size of large pilchards, calamari, red mullet, a few shrimps the size of small lobsters, pieces of swordfish, and a bowl of olive oil, lemon and herb dressing to spoon over. The waiter whisked away her empty carafe and glass, and brought a bottle and two fresh wine glasses, filling each a third full of deep pink wine.

'Sorry, perhaps you'd prefer white. I usually drink rose in summer.'

She loved rose. Adam dismissed it, a woman's tipple. She was beginning to enjoy herself, like a schoolgirl playing truant. The couple who had spent the whole of their meal reading, looked as though they were about to leave. The man stood first, and, unspeaking, waited by his chair. Calista couldn't resist telling PJ about them. He turned to get a better look, just as the woman, unspeaking, unsmiling, closed her book, got to her feet, and followed the man through the tables.

'Off for a night of unbridled passion, I bet.' PJ grinned. She laughed.

Everyone was talking, laughing to a background of lyrical Ionian *kantadhes* spilling from the speakers.

She and PJ helped themselves careful not to take more than the other, the calamari crisply fried, the other fish brushed with oil, oregano and seasoning and char-grilled, a simple tomato and cucumber salad the ideal accompaniment. PJ, like her, she noted with relief, had no time for refined knife-and-fork etiquette, surrendering to the satisfaction of using fingers to pull away every last morsel of flesh from bony skeletons, to hold shrimp-shells and suck out their contents, to dunk bread and mop up olive-oil dressing and juices. Licking her fingers, before using her finger bowl, she became aware of his gaze, and that smile.

'You're remarkably slim, considering . . .' She felt herself bristle even before he added, 'An appetite for food, always a good sign in a woman.'

She was aware of the maxim a woman who enjoys food also enjoys sex. Only since coming to Ithaca, had she got back her appetite for food.

'So, what do you do, Cal, other than being Mrs Burgess? Anything slightly more interesting?'

She shook her head, disbelieving, wondering about the hapless one he had left at home.

'What if I asked what do you do, anything slightly more interesting than being Mr Wood? Always assuming there's someone foolish enough to be Mrs Wood.'

'A woman with attitude.' He had the gall to laugh. 'I misread you. I had you down as . . .' He hesitated. 'My guess is your husband is . . . a rich man.' He shrugged. 'But you haven't been married long.'

'I'll have you know I'm thirty three, a barrister who specializes in company law - that sort of thing - and for the past seven years, have kept myself, more than adequately, and would be perfectly able to do so now, and in the future.' She paused, thinking, I must never forget that. 'For professional purposes, I am, and always will be, Calista Blake.'

As he topped up both their glasses, she noticed he was trying not to smile. She began to laugh. 'That was so pompous.'

'Emphatic, as though you needed to remind yourself, as well as put me in my place.' Another of his mischievous grins. 'You may be blonde, but decidedly not dumb.'

She refused the bait this time.

'Did you always want to be a lawyer?' The intensity of those eyes compelled her to answer. Before she could speak, 'I bet you were a clever little girl.'

He looked thoughtful. She realized, he didn't mean to sound condescending.

'No cleverer than a boy who learnt Ancient Greek. My father was a solicitor. I used to love going to his office. So much going on, and as soon as I was old enough, I used to sit in on court cases.'

'And you went one better. He must be proud of you.'

'He says so.' She hesitated.

'But?'

She told him, a stranger, what weighed on her conscience. Her great-grandfather had established the firm, Arthur Blake, Son & Partners in Northampton, back in the 1880s, and her father hadn't retired till he was seventy, she suspected, though he never said, waiting for her to take over.

'But you see I went up to Oxford, read Jurisprudence, got interested in what I'm doing now. Arthur Blake, Son & Partners still exists. Sadly there are no Blakes any longer.'

'You rebelled.'

'Some rebel, me.'

'The potential's there.' He appraised her, not critically as Adam did, as though he wanted to understand. Perhaps he was a psychologist, not an archaeologist. Before she could ask, 'We'll divide up the rest of the fish.' He shared what remained between them. 'You're an only child?' came out of the blue.

'I've a brother, twelve years older.' She told him about Stephen being difficult. 'He has Asperger's.' Her parents hadn't planned on having more children. 'I was an accident. My mother was nearly forty when she had me.'

'Snap! Except my mother was single and forty, and I'm her only child. I do have a half-brother, Brian, but he's a lot older, twenty years. I'm meeting him and Paul, his partner in Fiskardo.'

The enigmatic look he gave her. He must realize she was not the sort of person to be shocked by his illegitimacy, or his half-brother's sexual orientation. She took a sip of wine, and before she could respond,

'I'm thirty three too. When's your birthday?'

'Sixth of October. And yours?'

The evening had taken on the flavour of a blind date. Inevitable, unless they were just going to sit there stoically stuffing their faces.

'February, the eighth,' he said.

'I'm older than you.' Absurd she felt it an advantage.

'Umm.' He regarded her deadpan. A couple of beats, 'I've a weakness for older women. Especially when, they're intelligent and wealthy.'

She almost choked on a piece of mullet she had saved till last. Pouring water from the jug, he handed her the glass. 'Do I annoy you?'

Drinking, she shook her head. The correct answer would be yes and no. The waiter hovered, clearing the table. They had only just finished. While taking their time, eating, drinking, talking, the other tables had emptied, the second waiter busy removing all the cloths, and the seat-pads from the chairs. She and PJ were the last, except for a couple by the waterfront, who, as soon as she noticed them, stood to leave.

'You seem to have the knack of making me laugh when I shouldn't,' she said.

'Better than making you cry.'

She would have accused him of being psychic, if she believed in such nonsense. Marcos appeared, placing a tot of *raki* in front of PJ.

'May I bring you a Metaxa, or a liqueur, Mrs Burgess? On the house.'

She had drunk too much already, hence her loquacity, and refused politely. A disbelieving glance at her watch. Gone midnight.

'I must be getting back to the Erato.' She was dreading the walk all alone. Only because of that damned mugging. Pushing back her chair, she stood, 'But first, if you'll excuse me . . .'

When she returned, PJ wasn't there. If he too had gone to the loo, she would have heard him next door.

'Where's PJ?'

'Gone to check his boat, perhaps.' Marcos shrugged.

Disappointment displaced apprehension about the walk home. She was crushed. He had left without saying 'Good-bye'.

CHAPTER FIFTEEN

Mind the bugs don't bite

'**M**arco, what do I owe you?'

'Been taken care of, Mrs Burgess.'

If she paid half, Marcos could reimburse PJ the next time he saw him, she thought. Then PJ reappeared.

'You must let me pay my share.'

'Indulge me.'

He would expect her to argue. 'Well, thank-you. It has been lovely.' She meant it. 'For a moment I thought you'd run out on me without saying "Goodnight".'

'I'm lots of things, Cal, but I try not to be a boor. That's B O O R though you may think I'm a B O R E', his signature smile.

She also smiled, shook her head.

'Just wanted to check *Thelma Jane* was as she should be,' he said.

'Who's Thelma-Jane?' His daughter, she should remonstrate with him for leaving her alone.

'My yacht. My insurance doesn't cover sloppy seamanship.'

Whilst they had been talking, Marcos had turned off the lights, was about to lock the taverna door.

'I think now's the time to say 'Kali nichta,' she said.

'Not so fast Calista Blake. It's late. I'm walking you home.'

Marcos obviously knew him well, liked him, which was some recommendation, and she was not looking forward to walking alone through the olive grove gone midnight. She could think of nothing to say, except

Thank you, then added, 'But on one condition, you show me your sloop before we go.'

'Okay,' he said.

They wished Marcos 'Good night'. PJ's hand in the small of her back he steered her onto the road, their direction towards the mole at the far end of the harbour, the other tavernas like Marcos's, and the kafeneions along the way in darkness, the light from a couple of widely spaced street lamps minimal. They heard the rasp of Marcos's scooter as he left for home, then only the sea lapping the harbour wall, boats riding moorings. They would have to double back to take the route to the Erato.

Thelma Jane was the first craft, or last depending which end you started, tied up a couple or so boat-widths from the next. Its mast creaked eerily as they approached. PJ climbed into the well at the back, then helped her down. There were an awful lot of ropes. Her nose wrinkled at the smell of engine oil, and what she thought of as sacking.

'Why does it smell of engine, when it's a sailing boat?'

'It's a she,' he said. 'A Bermudan sloop, a Contessa 32,' and, as he switched on lights in the cabin, talked of length, beam, and draught-size, which meant nothing to her. He explained she had an engine housed under the cockpit, and showed Calista the navigation area, the saloon, the galley. All shipshape and Bristol fashion came to mind.

'And in the bow,' he gestured to a doorway where the saloon tapered, 'there's another berth, a shower, and the head.'– Whatever the head was. She did not want to show her ignorance. - 'What do you think of her?'

'I'm impressed,' she said. 'I've never actually been on a yacht before. She's not as big as I imagined, though.'

'Big enough when I'm the only crew, but trust me, Cal, there's nothing quite like scudding along alone through the swell, the sound of the wind in her sails.'

'Umm, the romance of the seas.' She imagined just the two of them . . .

'Glad you think that,' he said. 'Come on, I've thought of a shortcut.' Which was to take an inflatable across the bay instead of walk round by the road. Gliding beneath the stars over dark water to the swish of oars, the approaching headland a looming mass was eerie, preternatural. With PJ she felt safe.

He beached the dinghy, produced a pocket torch.

'I've got one too,' she said. 'I used to be afraid of the dark.'

'You aren't now?'

'When I was little, silly.' And now out of doors, if she were honest, unless Beppo was with her.

'When I was little,' he said, 'and my mother went out for the evening, I used to lie awake afraid she might not come back.'

'How awful.' She meant it.

Once they began walking, they did not talk much, she trying to work out what was with this stranger. She had spent only a few hours in his company, yet it was as though she had known him all her life. Not a breath of air, as they went along the track through the olive grove, the stillness heavy with dark expectation, the scent of herbs and dried grasses almost suffocating.

'What's that overpowering smell?'

'Wormwood, I think,' PJ said.

As they approached the Erato, she felt her breath quicken. 'Would you mind coming in with me?'

In her bag, she fumbled for the key. Taking it from her, he opened the door, and went in first, switching on lights, illuminating the whole of the open-plan ground-floor. He climbed the stairs, and came down again.

'Everything's fine.'

'Would you like a coffee, tea, anything?' She said.

'A glass of water would hit the spot.'

He followed her into the kitchen area, leant against the sink. She poured them still mineral water, cold from the fridge.

'You're nervous of being here on your own,' he said.

She told him she knew she was being absurd. 'A year ago, I would've thought nothing of it,' and found herself telling him all about the mugging.

'How about I kip here? Till dawn, that is.' He indicated the banquette in the sitting area.

She felt her eyes widen, her heart beat faster, her breathing become shorter. She put her glass down. Her hand was shaking.

'You know I mean you no harm.'

The only time he had touched her was to help her in and out of the tender, on and off *Thelma Jane*.

'No need to sleep on that uncomfortable old thing.' She gestured towards the banquette. 'You probably checked the other bedroom.'

At the top of the stairs, 'Night, night, Calista Blake.' He spoke softly.

'Night, night, PJ Wood.' Nameless dread that had threatened to overwhelm her lifted. 'Sleep tight.'

'Mind the bugs don't bite.' He finished for her.

Neither moved. As though spellbound, silent, they held each other's gaze, his eyes almost level with hers. The step each took brought them close enough for him to run his fingers through her hair. Gentle, he held her head while he kissed her, she responding lips parted, tasting him, her tongue seeking his. Her arms wrapped around him, she felt his body firm against hers. They came up for air. He took her by the hand, opened the door to the spare room, and led her inside.

At arms' length, lit only by the light from the landing, they looked at each other, the ache between her thighs, the physical longing for him overwhelming her. He cupped her face, brushed her lips with his thumbs. Silent, she felt for the waistband of his shorts, undid the fastener and the zip. He too unspeaking let go of her to step out of them, his erection proud. He heeled off his canvas shoes. Then holding her by the waist, walked her backwards to the bed, eased her onto it, crosswise. He pushed up her skirt, tugged off her briefs, pulled off her ballerinas. No preliminaries, she bent her knees, opened her legs, threw her arms either side of her head. He braced himself over her, entered her. She entwined her legs around his waist, her arms around his neck. A fleeting awareness of the bed frame protesting to their rhythm, she closed her eyes, cried out again and again, giving way to elation beyond bearing. She could die.

He climaxed with a deep-throated growl, sank down onto her, his cheek pressed to hers. She liked his not pulling away as soon as he came, flexed her muscles encouraging him to stay as long as possible. And so they lay, unspeaking, their breathing sounding as though they had run a race. He began to weigh heavy, she, happy to endure drank in his musk. Then, muffled, near her ear, 'Calista Blake, what have we done?'

Before she could think what to say, he levered himself up. She let her arms fall back either side of her head. He reached over, switched on the nearest bedside light, propped himself on his forearms still covering her body with his, looked into her eyes, gave one of his smiles. 'We're like a couple of hot teenagers, not two thirty-something sophisticates.'

True, and she didn't care, though she didn't want him to think badly of her.

'I don't normally do anything remotely like this,' she said.

'Would never dream you did.' He kissed her on the lips. 'Neither do

I.' Serious, 'You do believe me, don't you?'

She nodded. She just knew.

He pushed himself into a standing position. Naked from the waist down, he looked . . . vulnerable. She began to pull the front of her skirt down over her legs. He took hold of her hands.

'Let me help you take off your dress.' He looked sheepish. 'There's a bit of a mess on the skirt.' He pulled her to her feet, then grinned. 'Guess the noise you were making means you might think it was worth it.'

She swivelled round so that he could unzip her. 'Something else I don't often do.'

Unencumbered by a bra, she wriggled her arms out of the straps to let her dress fall to her feet. He put his arms around her, cushioning her breasts, pressed, his front to her back, kissed the nape of her neck. The touch of his lips sent shivers down her spine. He turned her to face him, then stepped back, and looked.

'I'm too thin,' she said.

'I see a beautiful woman, Calista Blake.'

She felt heat suffuse her chest, her neck, her face. 'Let's see you in all your glory.' She went to pull at the hem of his polo shirt.

Laughing, he evaded her, reached up to take hold of the back of its collar, and pulled the whole thing off. Her turn to look. No more than a couple of inches taller than her, an all-over tan, not a spare ounce of flesh, toned, not muscle-bound.

'I see a beautiful man, PJ Wood.'

He blushed. 'A man in need of a shower if we're going to share the same bed.' Then he looked uncertain. 'I hope we are.'

A step towards him, she stroked his cheek, ran the palm of her hand over his chest, his stomach, moist with sweat. 'I'll scrub your back if you scrub mine.'

They sponged each other, followed by exploring every contour of each other's body with the palm of their hand, their fingertips. With soft towels they patted each other dry. Crouching on her heels in front of him, she caressed his sex with her lips, got the response she hoped for.

'Calista Blake, now look what you've done.'

Before the inevitable conclusion, laughing he pulled her to her feet, wrapped her towel around her, picked her up like a baby, and took her to place her down on the bed, her head on a pillow. He kissed her on the lips, her throat, breasts. Delicate, his fingers cool, he probed between her legs. She opened them. His tongue caressed her, she not succeeding in suppressing squeals of utter bliss.

When he needed to come up for air, she made to sit up. 'Your turn now.'

He pinned her down. 'My choose,' his smile dreamy as he entered her.

This time he didn't hurry. Each time she gave a climactic cry of pleasure, he withdrew, kissed her eyelids, her lips, and began again. She didn't, couldn't complain when he came giving his growl of blissful satisfaction.

'I'm squashing you,' he said.

'S'okay.' She had done her best to encourage him to stay.

He rolled off to lay beside her. Then propping himself on his side, 'Cal, you should try and sleep now.'

'What about you?'

'I'm here to guard you, remember.' He leaned over, took his Omega sailor's watch from the bedside table and put it on. 'Gone half past three.' He pulled the top sheet over them, switched off the light, and drew her to him, her back to his front, spoons. 'Come on, be a good girl. Bee byes.'

'PJ?'

'What?'

'Sometimes you can be so irritating.'

'And you never?' She heard the smile in his voice. He nuzzled her neck. 'Best stint of guard duty I've ever been asked to do.'

His body next to hers like being wrapped in a blanket, she wanted to savour every last minute. Guard duty? Maybe he wasn't an archaeologist, maybe he was a proper sailor, PJ Wood, RN, the last thing she remembered.

Cal asleep, PJ eased himself onto his back. He couldn't afford to nod off in case he slept in too long. Hands behind his head, he gazed through the open window at a starlit sky, took in deep breaths of pine-scented air. A long, long time since a woman had come close to stirring his emotions. Sian Jones in his early twenties, they might have been married and divorced by now. He had never got to grips with the concept of one-night stands, didn't expect a girl to sleep with him until he got to know her. He had no qualms about paying for top-class relief when he felt the need, an arrangement of mutual advantage to both parties, although for the most part, celibacy was not too much of a problem, so long as he concentrated on the job he loved.

Calista Blake, he had stood in shadow observing her. Side-lit from the doorway of the taverna, a study in monochrome, her aura of melancholy arrested him. He determined to share her table, and after only a few hours, like the old song, she had gotten under his skin,

She's married, remember. If she were happy, she would never have . . . What had he done? Was this night their beginning? And their end? God forbid.

CHAPTER SIXTEEN

Next Day

Not properly awake, Calista reached out. No Adam. Pushing herself into a sitting position, she massaged her eyelids with her fingertips. With a start, she remembered, opened her eyes. No PJ. Not a sound from the bathroom. She swung her legs off the bed and stood, stomach churning, heart aflutter, breathing in shallow bursts. She draped the top sheet around her. Her watch on the bedside table said 7.10. Adam had said he would be back around dawn, any time soon. She picked up her briefs and crumpled dress to stash with other clothes which needed washing. No sign of PJ's discarded garments. She went downstairs.

'PJ?'

He wasn't in the kitchen or living area, or out on the terrace. A sense of loss took hold. She went back up to their room, a scrap of paper on his pillow next to hers. 'Dearest Cal, I shall never ever forget our night together. Carry on being emphatic. Hope we meet again one day. PJ'

She folded it to the size of an over-large postage stamp. Holding it tight, she lay down on the bed, buried her face in his pillow. A slight astringency combined with spice, his smell. 'You could've woken me.' Now, she would never know what PJ signified, whether he was an archaeologist or in the Royal Navy, if he was married with a child at the house in Vathy. She fell asleep revisiting their magical night.

'Cal, wake up.' Adam was shaking her. 'Ledia's getting breakfast.'

She turned over on her back, opened her eyes.

'What are you doing, sleeping in here wearing a sheet?'

Clutching PJ's note tight in her fist, feeling guilty about not feeling guilty, she smiled up at him, asked if he'd had a good time.

'Fantastic. Would've been back earlier, but Yiorgos was showing me how to get the fish out of the net, how you fold them without getting them into a tangle. The nets, I mean. Couldn't very well just leave him to it.' He sat down on the bed. 'God, I'm whacked.'

As she pushed herself up, she contrived to sit on the note, suggested Adam go and shower. She would bring him breakfast in bed, and afterwards he could sleep.

'Not to worry, darling, I've arranged with Ledia to bring me my breakfast.'

So full of his fishing trip, he asked no questions about how she had spent the rest of her evening. Neither did he press her on why she was in the spare room. He yawned, making a noise about it.

'Excuse me.' He stood ready to leave. 'I really am exceptionally tired. If you don't mind, I think I will turn in.'

She did not mind a bit.

His back turned as he made for the door, she hid the note under her pillow, then swung herself off the bed. 'I'll just collect some clothes,' she said.

Showered, dressed in shorts, a halter top and sneakers, her precious note palmed, she went downstairs, and hid it in the bottom of her handbag before having a word with Ledia to say the sheets and towels in the spare room would need laundering because she had slept there the previous night.

'No problem.' Ledia, her impassive self, insisted she would take up Mr Burgess's breakfast saving Calista the trouble.

She would have liked to be a fly on the wall when Miss Stunning walked in with the tray.

As always, rays of sunshine filtering through the vines, the scent of jasmine, the terrace was the perfect place for breakfast. Far from tranquil herself, she nevertheless managed to eat some bread and the egg Ledia had boiled leaving the yolk runny without being yucky as instructed on her second day. And this morning for both her and Adam, tea not coffee, Earl Grey more refreshing than coffee. Like some lovesick girl, she lingered at the table reliving every moment of the evening and night she had spent with PJ Wood.

She wandered into the kitchen for a refill of tea. No sign of Ledia who was probably changing the bedclothes in the spare room. Come to think of it, a stroll down to the village beckoned. There she would have a coffee, see if she could find something different for lunch. Adam would probably be asleep by now.

Before she did any shopping she walked around the harbour to the mole. No sign of *Thelma Jane*. She called in at Marcos's for a coffee.

Feigning nonchalance, 'PJ obviously got off okay.'

'Bright and early,' Marcos said. 'I met him in the bakery buying bread and doughnuts.'

She felt her trademark flush. 'Good of him to buy me dinner. I hope one day Adam and I may be able to do the same for him.'

'He often comes here,' Marcos said, then smiled. 'I have something to show you Mrs Burgess.' He disappeared inside, then emerged with a platter of fish the size of smallish herring, except she didn't think herring lived in the Ionian Sea.

'What are they?'

'Sardines. Yiorgos and your husband caught them last night.'

She just couldn't resist, 'How big were the ones that got away?'

Marcos looked nonplussed, then laughed. 'Tonight Petros will cook them for you.'

'They'll be delicious, Marco.' She drained her cup. 'Better go. Have to drop in at the shop.'

She bought a packet of pasta, a tin of tomatoes, onion, courgettes, an aubergine, a green pepper, some Parmesan-like cheese. As a surprise, she would make a vegie sauce for the pasta with shavings of cheese on top. Her way of trying to make amends, perhaps. She knew to the depths of her soul, given the chance, she would do what she had done all over again.

Unhurried, she followed the track through the olive grove to the Erato she and PJ had taken in the middle of the night, 'He often comes here', Marcos's words tantalized. So . . . Half way home, she was surprised to see Ledia on her moped puttering towards her. Ledia appeared equally taken aback. She came to a halt.

'Mrs Burgess.' She looked flustered.

'Ledia, has there been a problem? You're leaving much later than usual.'

'No problem. Mr Burgess kept me talking. We thought you must have gone to the beach. Better go, or I shall be very late.'

As she walked on, "talking", Calista mused. One of Granny's came to mind, 'While the cat's away . . .'

CHAPTER SEVENTEEN

Saturday, Sunday, Monday

Saturday evening, about to leave their usual harbour-side table, she and Adam noticed Kristina and Yiorgos were sitting by the taverna entrance. Calista began to doubt she had sat there with PJ only two nights ago, more like a dream than real life. Best stay that way, Calista thought, especially if PJ were married, maybe even had a child, children, and yet, and yet . . . She did not and never would regret that night.

She and Adam went over to say hello.

'How long have you two been here?' Adam asked.

'We have only just arrived.' Yiorgos got to his feet. 'Please, join us. A drink before you go?'

'That would be lovely,' Calista said. If they stayed a while, by the time they got back to the Erato Adam might be too tired to want to bother with sex. The past couple of days she had managed to side-step that eventuality. Unrealistic to expect to be able to divert him for much longer. She just needed more time to . . . Adam was her husband, dammit. She ought to be racked with guilt.

'Darling, aren't you going to sit down?' Adam, who was already, touched her arm. 'Yiorgos has got you a chair.'

'Sorry, I was daydreaming.' She sat down on Kristina's right Adam's left, not in exactly the same place as Thursday thank God, although that would be difficult with four of them around this particular table only meant for two. 'Is Dhionysius inside asleep in his buggy? I haven't seen him yet. May I take a peep?'

'Ledi is baby-sitting,' Kristina smiled. 'She is always happy to look after him. Poor Ledi.'

'Ledia doesn't strike me as poor despite . . .'

'She would love a baby of her own.' Kristina sighed.

'Maybe one day she will have one.'

'I do not think that is possible now,' Kristina said.

Calista remembered the look of pain on Ledia's face when they talked about Dhionysius. None of her business. Nor why a young woman who wore by-no-means cheap clothes worked as a maid.

The two men were talking about Adam's villa. She always thought of it as Adam's. She supposed she should say 'ours'. The memory of the small rustic house his grandiose project had by now replaced filled her with sadness. Irrational perhaps, she would have liked to see the old incorporated into the new. 'Don't be absurd,' Adam told her. 'It's a hovel, good for nothing but demolition'. She wondered how Kristina felt about that. As soon she got the chance she would ask.

'Cal hasn't got round to having a look,' Adam was telling Yiorgos. 'She might as well wait until the bathrooms are done. You say the pipework has been completed, and the replacement units will arrive on Monday.'

'The builder tells me they will be installed next week,' Yiorgos said.

Marcos arrived and asked what they would all like to drink. She, Adam and Yiorgos ordered in English. Before Kristina could speak, Marcos leant over and spoke to her at length in Greek. After he had gone inside. Calista noticed Kristina turn her head to look to her left. Calista followed her gaze. Except for a party of Greeks who had arrived around ten thirty, Marcos's clientele had thinned. For some reason Kristina's attention was drawn to two men sitting at a table second row in from the harbour wall. The light was just bright enough for Calista to see the elder, at a guess nearer fifty than forty, portly, round faced, his close cropped dark hair flecked with silver, the taller, athletic-looking man, perhaps not even thirty, had dark hair worn not quite collar length. With a nose like an eagle's beak, he had a handsome arrogance about him. Both wore expensive-looking casual shirts. Calista noticed Yiorgos reach for Kristina's hands entwined on the table. He gave them a squeeze, left his large hand covering hers.

Marcos returned with their order, plus a bowl of cashews in their shells, and one of potato chips Greek-style. As he placed each drink in front of them he said their name, Mrs Burgess, Mr Burgess, Yiorgo, and last, Kristina with a question mark. Kristina shook her head, then said 'Ochi' [No]. The rest was all Greek to Calista, but she did not sound best pleased that much Calista did understand. She wondered what it had been all about.

She saw Yiorgos give Kristina's hand one last squeeze, then tender 'Drink your nice milk-shake, Tina.' Protective, he rested his right arm along the back of her chair, used his left hand to raise his glass of Metaxa. They all clinked glasses. 'Stin Iyasoo!'

'Just this once, I wish I could have a Metaxa.' Kristina sounded despondent.

Yiorgos kissed her on the cheek. 'As soon as Dhionysius no longer needs your milk, I will buy you a whole bottle,' he said. 'As long as you do not drink it all at once.'

'Only tonight do I feel like drinking, Yiorgo.'

'Try not to worry. Your little brother is twenty nine years old.' Yiorgos turned to Adam. 'When you bring Mrs Burgess to look at the villa, you must come by our house so that she can see our boy.'

'Oh dear, I'm not sure about that, Yiorgo.' Adam laughed. 'When she sees him she might want one of her own.'

Calista felt heat rise on her neck, her face. 'I would love to come and see him if that's okay with you, Kristina,' she said. 'While Kristina and I coo over him, and have a nice long gossip, you can take my husband to the kafeneion, Yiorgo. Do manly things. Drink raki, play backgammon, ogle the young girls who walk by.'

Yiorgos laughed. 'You have observed Greek men well, Mrs Burgess. In the home it is the woman, especially the mother, who is the boss.'

'Same where I come from,' Adam said.

Calista wondered how Kristina got on with Yiorgos's mother. She had been relieved when Adam's mother had died before it was necessary for them to be introduced. Despicable of her, but.

A pleasant half hour passed. Back at the Erato, as she had hoped, Adam's head no sooner rested on his pillow than he was asleep.

On Sunday, she could tell, Adam was restless. A change of routine, they chugged along in their little boat in the morning instead of late afternoon. Comfortable lounging on cushions in the prow, inescapable her thoughts would dwell on PJ Wood. She wondered what Tess would say when she told her about him. She had to tell someone, and only Tess would do. Now she did have a twinge of conscience. Days since she had given Tess and her ailing marriage a second thought. She believed Tess and Co were due home that day. Fingers crossed Corfu had worked some kind of magic.

'How about a trip to Cephalonia?' Adam broke into her reverie.

'Not now, silly. And certainly not in this boat,' he said in answer to her comment.

'I was being frivolous,' she said.

'Just a couple of days or so,' he said. 'Last year we did say one day we might take a look.'

Back at the villa, they got out the guide book and map to plan an itinerary.

Monday morning, breakfast was brief. Down in the village, whilst Adam went about the business of making arrangements for their tour of the neighbouring island, she sat by the harbour watching fishermen unloading their catch, a flotilla party preparing to put to sea.

When Adam joined her, 'See that sinister-looking boat,' she said. 'Who do you think it belongs to? Drug smugglers?'

The only motor yacht in port, stooped crone-like black amongst the gaiety of blue and white fishing boats, the fretwork of tall masts of sailing cruisers. Relieved only by a silver flash along her sides, the darkened glass of her portholes and cabin windows looked like a myriad of baleful eyes.

'If I were a serious drug smuggler, I wouldn't choose a craft that so dramatically drew attention to me.' Adam said. 'Probably some Italian tycoon who likes his privacy. See the chap in the stern?'

A portly chap with a tan, his stomach over-hanging his swimming trunks, sat engrossed in a copy of the Financial Times, his face hidden by shades and a floppy sun hat.

'I think he might have been at Marcos's on Saturday night,' Calista said. 'Why do you say Italian when he's reading the F.T?'

'She's flying the Greek and Italian flags.'

A younger man, definitely the one at Marcos's on Saturday night - she told Adam she recognized him by his distinctive nose - dressed in shorts and T-shirt, came out of the cabin with two mugs. The older man folded his paper and took one. The young man sat down beside him and the two of them began to talk.

'Come darling, let's stroll along the quay. Get a little closer.' Adam said.

As they passed the motor yacht, he put his arm around her shoulders as though whispering sweet nothings. 'I was right. They're speaking Italian.'

A deck-hand was making ready to cast off. As the boat was being manoeuvred out of her mooring by another sailor at the helm, they could see she was called Nephititi registered in Trieste.

'Let's get back to the Erato before the day-trippers start to arrive,' she said.

As they passed Marcos's taverna he was standing in the doorway's shadow so intent on watching the Nephititi put to sea, he hadn't noticed them until they both piped up together, 'Kalimera Marco'.

Surprised, 'Kalimera and bye-bye Mafiosi.' He gestured toward the departing Nephititi.

She and Adam exchanged glances.

'What makes you think they're Mafia?' she said.

'I didn't like the way they persisted with their questions. The two of them ate here on Saturday evening. I told them I couldn't help, which is true, but what a surprise. What brings you to the village at this time of day? Would you like a coffee?'

Declining his invitation, they told him about their planned excursion to Cephalonia.

'Much busier than Ithaca,' Marcos said.

On the hot and sticky drag back to their villa, they made up stories about the Nephititi and the mysterious duo who had asked Marcos questions he either could not or would not answer.

On Tuesday morning she and Adam caught the ferry from nearby Frikes to Fiskardo where they were to pick up a hire car for their tour of Cephalonia. Fiskardo where PJ said he was making for. Maybe . . . but no, Friday to Tuesday, he would be long gone 'scudding along through the swell, the sound of the wind in her sails'.

CHAPTER EIGHTEEN

Thursday, 11 August – Esther and Mike

Bliss, music from one of her favourite old CDs, *Jazz Night and Day* now downloaded onto her iPod was playing through their Zeppelin Air just loud enough to be heard through the open French window, Coltrane's unmistakable sax well into 'Nancy with the Laughing Face'. Dinner over, she and Mike were on the patio chilling. Mike, bare feet, bare legs, in shorts and singlet-T-shirt, sexy Mike. A bottle of Prosecco, still half full, was strategically placed between them in the ice bucket. Esther caressed nearby fronds of lavender, its pungency overwhelming the still air.

Tom and Fran and the others should have landed in Ireland by now. About an hour and a half Cork to Bantry Mike had told her. Mike's sister had collected them early yesterday, the kids beside themselves with excitement looking forward to their first time ever over at Gramps and Nan's when their three cousins would also be there. Great for her in-laws, as she and Mike probably would not have been able to take them over just yet. A strange feeling waving them off in Kath's car. She had to hold back tears. 'They'll be okay, won't they?'

'They'll be grand. You'll see.' Mike had rested his hand on her hip, stroked her to calm her, something he always used to do when she got uptight. Smelling early morning fresh from his shower, she had been tempted to put her arms round his neck, nuzzle into him. Corfu had been a success as far as they as a family were concerned. No making love, even so she and Mike had been more relaxed with each other.

'I'll make fresh coffee,' he said. 'Then I really must pop into the office.'
He had promised he wouldn't be late home. He wasn't.

'Tess, we really must talk.'

He seemed laid back about it. Yet ice chased through her being. She stopped stroking the lavender, gripped the arm of the lounger, gulped a mouthful of fizz from the champagne flute she held in her other hand.

'We've got to face up to it Tess, we haven't been getting on. Been on my mind a lot.'

Silent herself, she listened to Peggy Lee, 'Gee Baby Aint I Good to You'.

He started again. 'I've been trying to pinpoint when things may have . . . well . . . when they seemed to begin to fray at the edges.' – *That's right, Mike, wheel out the clichés why don't you.* – 'Maybe as far back as when Tom was born. I know he wasn't planned, but you did want him, didn't you?'

Fran not quite fourteen months, then along came Tom, not as she had programmed. Perhaps exactly as Mike had, or so she had suspected. Heart racing. Deep breaths. Be still.

'How could you even begin to think that?'

'I think that's when you began to . . . to withdraw from me,' Mike said.

Coltrane again, with the Duke this time, 'In a Sentimental Mood'.

'I withdrew from you?' Her voice soft. *She didn't intend to quarrel. The children away, they had time to get used to there being just the two of them again. He was her husband, no more selfish or neglectful than the next. In Corfu he had been attentive, considerate.*

'You've become more and more aloof,' he said. 'You freeze me out.' - *For a while, after Tom. Among all sorts of other things going on in her head, she was afraid of getting pregnant a third time. And now. She felt her whole being charge with dread. He must have someone else. Why then, she wondered, had he gone on holiday with them.* - 'If you think back, Tess, you must remember after Tom was born we went through days when we hardly spoke. We never had a laugh like we used to, let alone make love.'

So unfair, nothing particularly amusing about spending most of her waking hours shovelling food into one end of a baby and a toddler, then dealing with the residue at the other. Unrelenting, she had put her head down, got on with it. Nevertheless, she had delighted in her amazing daughter, her gorgeous son.

'Correct me if I'm wrong,' she said, 'but you were the one who spent his nights on the study divan. And you accuse me of withdrawing from you.'

'You sent me away. No point in both of us having sleepless nights, you said.'

Silence, except for 'Mood Indigo' wafting out through the patio door. Almost dark, lights began to shine from neighbouring detached houses, homes redolent of privacy, secrets concealed behind thick privet and hawthorn. Unless voices were raised in anger outside, or excitement, their owners could be neither seen nor heard.

'I used to tell you what was happing in the company,' Mike said. 'Changes and chances, I tried to discuss what I was hoping to do. You were so interested you used to fall asleep.' A pause, she said nothing. Silence except for the music. 'I was working bloody hard. Had to stay sharp, watch my back. I haven't been to one of your Public Schools.'

For Christ's sake, Mike, she wanted to say. Get over it. You didn't need to, you're doing fine. Zoot Sims and the Al Cohn Quintet were playing 'Two Funky People'. She poured herself more Prosecco. *If they were talking times past.* 'After we had Fran, I would've liked you to spend more time at home, and certainly after we had Tom.' – *His turn not to respond apparently.* – 'When you were home, you were usually working on something. All day Saturday, playing golf.'

'You had Fran and Tom.'

The old grievance burbled to the surface. 'I would've given anything for some help.' She heard herself. Plaintive. Pathetic.

'Whatshername used to come and clean like . . . whoever it is now.'

'Okay, emotional support then,' she said, 'like your being home in time to help me bathe them, settle them for the night. Once in a while get up and see to Tom.'

He said nothing. A female artist she did not recognize was singing something she did not know, 'Don't weep for the lady'. The singer had a deep rich voice. A slow, sad song, not self-pitying. Stoical. She listened through to the end.

'I was so alone, cut-off,' she said. 'And you were too much up your own arse to be bothered with my insignificant woes.' *Shut up. He was the one who wanted to talk.*

'No Tess, I wasn't up it. I was working it off for you and Fran and Tom.'

Maybe that's what he kidded himself he was doing it for. He was a competitor. She doubted she would have fallen for him if he hadn't been.

Carmen McRae was singing 'Summer Time', one of her all-time favourites. She used to sing it to Fran and Tom to get them to sleep. Mike launched himself from his lounger and into the sitting room. He turned the music off, raised his voice, 'Christ, Tess, what is this anodyne crap?'

No more than you might expect from someone whose all-time favourite was Pulp's 'Different Class'.

She remained still. He didn't come out again. Silence snarled. She got up and followed him indoors, pulled to the French window. He sat in a corner of the Chesterfield, arms folded, one leg stretched along the seat, the other flexing furiously to a silent rhythm transmitted through the pumping ball of his foot. She perched on the edge of an armchair at right angles to where he sat. She was almost facing him. She leaned forward, cupped the bowl of her champagne flute in both hands, arms resting on her knees. The only light was from a lamp next to the Zeppelin Air on the far side of the room. Silenced hammered inside her head.

'I thought once we had a family you'd . . .' – *More history* – 'When Fran came along, you said you would stay home, look after her yourself.' – *Not until she went to university* – 'I always imagined us with four kids.' His leg stopped pumping. His arms unfolded. His hands came to rest on his thighs. 'Too late now.'

She had told him no more babies after Tom. He was trying to say everything was her fault. If he had ever really loved her, he would have understood. She wanted to shake him, scream, I thought I was going mad. Suffocating silence. Deep breaths. No good crunched up. She sat back. Slowly in. Slowly out. Better. Stay calm.

'Then your fait accompli cooked up with Burroughs. Chris is delighted I'm going back, you told me. Pompous prick, always had the hots for you. Where you're getting it now perhaps. One thing's for sure, it's not from me.' - *How dare he suggest she was the unfaithful one when he was screwing some Dutch girl* – 'Only going back part-time, you said. Your hours crept up, then you got your precious partnership. No wonder you're stressed out. No wonder we've not made love since God knows.'

'Nothing to do with your not being able to get it up, then? Not with me anyway. Who is she Mike? Your bit of Dutch. Isn't that what you're coming round to telling me? That Bank Holiday weekend you were supposed to come with us to Mum's, you were with her.'

She was going to cry. Through a mist she saw him sit forward, elbows on knees, his head in his hands. Then he sat up, shook his head. She couldn't speak. She blinked, trying to control her stupid tears. He got up, came over to her. Balancing himself, he squatted in front of her. Her frock had ridden up. She felt at a disadvantage. She waited for him to say, you're right.

'Tess, listen.' Head resting against the chair back, she closed her eyes. She didn't want him to have the satisfaction of seeing her tears. He put his hands on her knees and shook her, not hard. 'Please listen. I did start to tell you. I remember one evening saying, come autumn I would have to spend more time in Amsterdam. So will we notice a difference, you said. No curiosity, no regret that I might be away more than ever. You had better things to do in the garden than talk to me.'

She could scarcely catch her breath. Now his hands were resting on her thighs, burning into her. She kept her eyes tight shut.

'Thing is, from the beginning of September, I shall be based over there. The Board decided they wanted me to stay on for a while after setting things up. Means a full Executive Directorship.' - *Questions, so many. Her throat was too tight. She opened her eyes. His seemed directed at a spot just above her cleavage. He looked tense.* - 'Came completely out of the blue. I thought it would go to Willem Langmeijer. I had to accept.'

She found her voice. 'You're going to walk out on Fran and Tom.'

His thumbs dug into the flesh. 'Don't exaggerate. I've been really worried about them, and about you. You don't realize how flaky you've been. Haven't you noticed how subdued they are sometimes. Corfu did us all good, but we can't spend our lives on permanent holiday. - *Silence subsiding into soft whispers.* – 'I did think about Tom and Fran. They're not yet at a critical stage at school. The Netherlands wouldn't be a bad place for them to spend some time. Not that that's at issue. I shall be back most weekends. I hardly see them during the week anyway.'

She opened her eyes wide. She had the sensation of watching herself raise the glass she held firmly rooted by its base on the arm of the chair. Then flung it hard as she could across the room. The Waterford crystal, part of a set they had been given as a wedding present, shattered against the opposite wall, fragments clattering on the polished wood below. She clenched her fists to smash them into his face. He was too quick for her. He caught her wrists. Pulling her forward, she felt his wine-scented breath.

'Admit it,' he said, 'If I'd told you when the Board made the offer, you would've kyboshed the deal. The next time something exciting was in the pipeline, I wouldn't have got a look in. I know the Board. No point in offering this to Mahoney, turned the Netherlands down. I'd have been stuck, unless I quit, or more likely been eased out. I had no choice. Accept or quit.'

Panting with anger, she tried to free her wrists. His grip was too strong. Her frock had ridden up even further. 'Bastard. Bastard. You could've told me. I'm not such an unreasonable bitch.' Using all her strength, she kicked out with both feet, caught him fair and square in the groin. Not deliberate, she just wanted him to get away from her. He let her go, his face white. He rolled onto his side, curled into a ball. She pulled her dress over her knees, clasped them to her chest as great gulping sobs welled from the depths of her soul. Rocking back and forth in her chair, she took a deep breath in. Slowly let it out. She took another, and another. 'I hope you hurt like hell.' She spat the words. 'You underhand, deceitful, double-dealing shit.'

She watched him as he pulled himself on to the Chesterfield. He lay back against the cushions eyes closed. 'I . . . wanted . . . to . . . tell . . . you.'

She stood up. 'What you really want is a divorce, I suppose. Wouldn't want to cramp your style with all that Dutch tottie on offer.'

She walked out of the room and up the stairs. Once in their room, heart and bladder fit to burst, she made for their bathroom. Then lay on the bed just as she was, tears prickling her eyes. She began to cry. She sobbed and sobbed. He should have had the guts to tell the truth.

CHAPTER NINETEEN

Mike

Right then he couldn't have gone after her even if he had wanted to. At last the throbbing began to subside. Cautious, he felt his genitals. Everything where it ought to be as far as he could tell. Lucky Tess was barefoot. Cautious, he got to his feet. He could do with a beer.

Sitting at the kitchen table, he tilted his glass and poured the Kronenberg, took a mouthful. 'That went rather well, don't you think, Cal?' He spoke the words aloud as though she were sitting opposite.

On their visit to the Old Rectory, late Saturday night Cal had engineered the two of them stayed down to finish their brandies, the sitting room cosy for a heart-to-heart. She told him what was obvious to him. Tess was unhappy and dissatisfied in their marriage. He told Cal he hoped the holiday in Corfu might help. A relief to discover Tess had the same idea. 'Whatever's got into you guys?' Cal had said. 'You still love each other. Mike, you need to talk to her.' He had promised he would, and now he had.

That weekend away had been great for Fran and Tom, and for him and Tess. At home Burgess was laid back, a host whose only aim seemed to be making sure they all enjoyed themselves. Who wouldn't staying somewhere like a bijou hotel, a swimming pool, and all that space for the kids to rampage? On the Saturday, so as to give Tess and Cal a bit of time together, he, Burgess, Fran and Tom had taken a stroll along the lane to the next village, two to three miles there and back. A pint before lunch. No moans from the kids about it being too far. They took the dog with them. 'Dad, can we have a dog?' Fran said. 'Pretty please.' How to explain to an eight-year-old, our life-style wouldn't suit a dog.

Cal might be Tess's closest friend. Yet, against the odds, she was his mate as well. He remembered the first time he spoke to her, seen her around, who could miss her, or Tess, always the two together. Cal, long-legged blonde, athletic without seeming butch, Tess, blue-black hair, 'a woman of colour' as Halle Berry had famously called herself. He could think of no better way to describe Tess. Like him, Cal and Tess were reading Jurisprudence, except they were in their first year, he his second. Oxford, still alien as far as he was concerned, his parents so proud, nothing he could do except keep his head down and study. And then he met Cal. Cal rowed, so did Tess. He didn't, not big and beefy enough. One of his Merton friends, Big Dave from Nottingham did. Like him, Dave had been to a State Comprehensive. 1997, the spring term, or Hilary if you like, a Saturday night, the end of Torpids, he was with Dave in the pub crowded with oarsmen, so was Cal. Dave didn't really need to point her out. 'She rows for St Hilda's, and her mate Tess, but she's not here. Let's go and have a word. The Hooray Henrys think they're a couple of Lesbo's. Me, I think it's a wind-up on Tess and Cal's part.' In answer to Dave's question about Tess's absence, turned out she had a rotten cold.

Despite being what Da called Posh Tottie, right from the start he got along fine with easy-to-talk-to Cal. As soon as Dave introduced him, 'I've seen you around,' she said, Next thing he knew, Dave was patting him on the shoulder. 'Leave you two to chat. Just seen . . . Uhh . . .' and he was gone. 'Wonder who Uhh is?' Cal gave an impish smile. 'Some girl,' he told her. 'Big Dave's amazingly popular.' He must have revealed the touch of envy in his voice. 'And you're not?' Cal sounded surprised. He felt himself colour, then, 'Think the clue's in the "Big". Cal chuckled. 'I really wouldn't know about that, Mike.' If he hadn't felt at ease with her, he would never have revealed the speculation as to what Dave owed his success.

'Your glass is empty,' Cal had said. 'So is mine. Shall we . . . ?' She pointed towards the bar. Since she seemed happy enough to spend time with him, no way was he going to run out on her. He discovered, like him, Cal was into films. By the end of the evening, they had arranged to meet again to see 'Portrait of a Lady'. 'Jane Campion's the director,'

Cal said. 'Mission Impossible' was more him, but anything with Nicole Kidman was okay.

Dating Cal made Oxford so much more bearable, and one in the eye for the Henrys who were running a book on which one of them would succeed first with either Cal or Tess, unless the rumour was true that is. When Dave had asked him how it was going, 'Wicked,' he replied, 'she's so easy going.' Dave raised an eyebrow, 'Easy?' He had felt himself go red, 'We're good mates, s'all.' 'You do realize,' Dave said, 'Cal asked me to introduce her to my dark-haired friend with the roguish smile. Get in there. What's stopping you?'

Their first time was almost a disaster. He was so nervous . . . Nothing for it but to apologize, and fess up. Twenty years old, more than half way through his second year and . . . 'You've never done it before,' Cal said. 'Mike Mahoney I was counting on you. Neither have I.' Then with one of her mischievous smiles, she sat astride him, sex to sex. 'We'll just have to keep trying till we get it right.' Didn't take them long. They liked each other, were attracted to each other, they had fun whether out and about or in bed. Through Cal he got to know Tess.

He had tried to play down this 'thing' he sensed between them. Out-wardly both Cal and Tess seemed two cool chicks, except once he got to know her he realized Tess wasn't anywhere near as self-reliant as Cal, nor, deep down, as confident. If only he had met Tess first . . . Almost the end of the Michaelmas Term of his third year, life was no longer that much fun.

Cal and Tess in their second year were sharing a student house with some others. 'We're cooking a special dinner,' Cal said, 'and you're in-vited.' When he arrived, only Cal and Tess were home.

The three of them at the kitchen table rather like the one he sat at now, except then delicious smells came from the oven. Roast duck prepared by Tess as it turned out. They had manoeuvred him into sitting at the head, Cal and Tess either side. Tess had poured them each a Manzanilla sherry – very Oxford, very posh. 'We've a proposition for you,' Cal said with one of her impish grins. They had suggested they make a threesome. 'I believe the old-fashioned term is 'daisy chain',' Cal said. He went hot and cold, tried to second guess how he should respond. Before he could, Tess had left the room.

'Don't look so worried,' Cal said. 'You and Tess, I'm neither unaware, nor blind. Lately, you've been careful to avoid each other when before you'd been so matey. Let's face it, Mikey, you've not been my laughing-boy for quite a while. Neither has Tess been herself lately. And there were other signs like . . .' a shrug. 'You seem to have had an awful lot of tutorials to prepare for, essays to write which somehow got in the way of . . . well you know what. ' She had leaned over and stroked his cheek. 'My suspicions aroused, I asked Tess if you'd upset her. With my advocate's hat on, I suggested we might invoke the Law of Torts for any wrong you'd done. Poor Tess admitted she was upset because of the wrong she felt she had done me. She had fallen in love with my boyfriend. She said I know I don't stand a chance. But, she does, doesn't she, Mike?'

'I don't want to hurt you, Cal.'

'Mike, you may come across as a bit of a scally, as my old gran used to say, you're just a big softie at heart. I can't be responsible for my two best-est mates being miserable, can I?'

'I feel so guilty, Cal,' he had told her. 'I . . . You were . . .'

'Mike Mahoney, we were both virgins, okay. Do I seem the type to settle down with the first person I slept with, have his kids? Kids, yuck, not till I'm at least thirty. And no way will I turn into a slapper just because you picked my cherry. I was nineteen already, a late starter by today's reckoning. Now shall we call Tess back in?' She went towards the door. Before opening it, she turned. 'Promise me one thing, the two of us can still be mates? Tess and I hope to be and . . . Not that I shan't miss bedding you.' One of her beguiling, full-of-mischief smiles.

A threesome? No that would be unethical. 'Don't see how we can't be mates,' he said. 'I like you too much to . . .' Cal might be self-assured, self-centred she was not.

Cal called to Tess to come back in, and, as the saying goes, the rest was history. Till now that is.

Mike drained the last of the Kronenberg. 'Cal, I talked and I blew it. I know, I know, should've waited a couple of days. Got us both used to being on our own, then . . .'

As he and Cal had kissed 'goodnight' on the landing, that Saturday night, by then Burgess, Tess, Tom and Fran asleep, Cal's parting shot, 'Greater love hath no woman, than she give up her lover for a friend.' For a moment she had him wondering. Then a flash of the old Cal – she had been somewhat subdued, he thought, and she was thinner than she used to be – 'Just teasing.' and that impish grin. 'Sort it, Mike. Please.'

Not as easy as Cal might think. His brain ached, all the stuff Tess had spewed out, and the things he'd said, picking at old sores. No way did he want a divorce. Whatever put that idea into her head? He needed his bed. If Tess were still awake, he might have to kip on the study divan. Cautious, he opened their bedroom door. The bedside lamp still on, Tess was asleep lying on top of the duvet. He went over and looked at her, felt an absolute shithead. Obvious she had cried herself to sleep. He fetched a throw from the study to cover her, then slipped under beside her. As he put out the light, 'I love you Tess Mahoney, but, that could change if you're going to make a habit of kicking me in the balls.' Tess stirred in her sleep. He held his breath. She didn't wake. Thank God, enough raw emoting for one night.

CHAPTER TWENTY

An Ionian Sunday Afternoon

A pleasurable end to another lazy afternoon, Adam wished he could paint, sea-jade, sapphire, fir-green, brilliant white, Cal an ideal model. He wished he could paint like Matisse. Cal confined only by the briefest bikini lolled among cushions like an odalisque in the prow of the boat. Since they had been on Ithaca her creamy skin had deepened to tawny gold. Her sleek cap of hair, bleached lighter by the sun, caught the afternoon light. Her eyes were closed. She arched her neck throwing back her head.

'Glad we made the effort to make our trip,' she said, 'but it's good to be back.'

He too would love to close his eyes, to drowse in the heat-hazy, late afternoon, lulled to sleep by the boat's movement, the concentrated warmth on his body. The scent of earth-rooted herbs from the rocky shoreline was intense, an invisible umbilical cord connecting them to their Earth Mother.

They had returned from Cephalonia yesterday, a day later than intended, in time for lunch at the villa, and a siesta, the only disappointment Cal's immediately falling asleep. No opportunity for siestas on Cephalonia, too busy sightseeing, and by the time they got to bed, no sex, he was exhausted. He needed Calista to be relaxed and satisfied. He had yet to tell her about Len and Sash, something he must do before they went home. No way was he going to allow them to live in the States with Annabel and Bradley Brown, even though Boston was comparatively civilised. They could visit their mother as often as they liked, but he wasn't going to have their education disrupted. Cal would just have to get used to the idea of his girls making their home with them.

Phut, phut, phut, their little boat puttered joyfully. Cal opened her eyes and looked around.

'We've come a long way today. I bet that's Mavronas Point.'

He threw back his head and laughed. 'I don't think so.'

'Do you know what I think would be absolutely fantastic?' - Right then, he would have denied her nothing, almost. - 'If we had a beautiful boat like one of those, a sloop perhaps.' She pointed to one of the distant white triangles scudding across sapphire blue sea' 'We could go for miles and miles with only the sound of the wind in our sails. We wouldn't have to listen to a noisy old outboard.'

'Neither of us can sail.'

Despite Cal's scathing remarks, the outboard continued to propel them merrily along and for a while, silence except for the phut, phut of the engine. Conscious of Calista's eyes upon him, he tightened his stomach muscles. She closed her eyes again, arched her back, and stretched spreading her legs. He searched along the shoreline for signs of a secret and secluded cove, where wooded precipice of land tumbled into the sea. Riding safely anchored he would make love to her in the boat. On reflection, perhaps not.

'Look over there, below the cliff,' he said. 'Some kind of patrol boat.'

She sat up and turned, kneeling for a better view.

'What do you think they're doing?'

'Waiting to pounce on tourists offending public decency. We'd better start back, unless you want to carry on round to Frikes. Maybe the Nephititi which fascinates you so much has put in there.'

'When we saw it moored in Argostoli I was curious,' she said.

'Just two chaps on holiday meeting up with another mate. What made you take a photo of them and their yacht? If Marcos was right, we might've ended up dead meat.'

'They didn't notice me. Too busy arguing.'

She turned away and knelt upright, a figurehead. By the time he had steered in an arc to retrace their route, they had overshot the patrol boat. Closer to land going back, there was no other vessel except theirs and the anchored boat.

'Whatever they're looking for, I think they've found it,' he said.

They were re-passing the patrol at just the wrong moment. A black rubber head bobbed up by the stern. A burly figure with impressive epaulettes knelt on the platform. Joined by another policeman, the two of them dragged something quite large on to it.

'Have they saved him?' Cal, anxious, horrified, turned her head to look at him.

The body flopped in the prone position. Adam averted his eyes. Neither Epaulettes, nor his assistant, were making any attempt at resuscitation. How he wished they could go faster, get the hell out of it, but the little boat was already at full throttle. Epaulettes got to his feet.

'*Ela, ela*!' The shout rang clear across the water as he beckoned them closer.

They were in no position to cut and run. Cal slumped back on to the cushions. Despite her tan, she was a lighter shade of pale. He felt the blood drain from his face as soon as he saw the body.

'What does he want with us?' Cal said.

He tried, unsuccessfully, not to let his eyes stray from the officer, inscrutable in mirror shades. He was at pains to manoeuvre their boat so that Cal couldn't see the corpse. Drawing up alongside, he saw himself reflected in the policeman's glasses. Letting the outboard idle, he prayed it wouldn't die on him.

'English?' the policeman said.

He nodded.

'Please. I am Sergeant Mastorantonakis. You come here every day?'

'This is the first time.'

Phuuut, phuuut, the outboard sighed. The gentle slap of sea against the side of both boats was louder than the sound of the small engine. Unable to see the policeman's eyes, dressed only in swimming trunks, he felt vulnerable. The engine phuttered and stopped. He was conscious of Cal looking at him, not at the policeman.

Questioned, he said they were staying at the Villa Erato in Kioni, just starting their third and final week.

'We've been on Cephalonia. Came back yesterday morning.'

Nodding, the policeman turned away, shouting something in Greek. The sergeant faced him again.

'Is he from the island?'

The policeman shrugged. His assistant appeared carrying two small plastic cups. He offered them one each.

'Drink.' He indicated the contents should be knocked back. 'It has not been nice for you or Madama.'

Raki. He was glad of the shot.

'A formality, you understand. I must take your names.'

His assistant produced a notebook. Adam spelt them out. His superior added their Kioni address.

'Thank you, Mr Burgess, Madama.' The policeman nodded their dismissal.

The outboard spluttered into life, first try. Adam looked across at Cal. Tears in her eyes, she was curled foetal-like on her cushions. He heard the more powerful engine of the patrol boat start up. As it overtook them, the Sergeant half saluted.

'Sit by me.' He beckoned Cal over.

'That poor man,' she said.

CHAPTER TWENTY ONE

Sunday, 14, August – England

Saturday evening, around midnight his mother-in-law, Mina called. 'You might be mustard at what you do, Mike. You're rubbish when it comes to handling my daughter. Get your arse up here pdq.'

Sunday morning, the late-summer sunrise burnt up haze overlaying fields and woods as fast as he burnt up the miles down the M1. He played Mozart as he drove, one of the piano concertos, and, he didn't know why, the *Requiem*. He arrived around half past seven. At the gate, about to buzz the security intercom, his gorgeous mother-in-law – slim, almost as tall as him, cap of fair hair flecked silver -- emerged with her two whippet rescue dogs. They exchanged kisses. She suggested he join her for a walk. Tess was still asleep.

'Awake till almost dawn, I suspect,' Mina said.

They strolled down Millfield Lane to get onto Hampstead Heath along the path through Highgate Ponds remarking only on what a glorious morning it was. Finches and other small birds twittering in the shrubbery, N6, Mina's London postcode had the feel of being out in the sticks. Others enjoying the morning were joggers or fellow dog-walkers. Most of them seemed to know his mother-in-law and the whippets. They began to climb. Mina said she wanted him to herself to hear his side of things. Tess had spent the two nights she had stayed crying into her pillow, the guest room TV on mute, picture flickering. 'Best save our breath till we reach the top.'

Just below the summit of Parliament Hill they found a seat where they could sit with London's landmarks spread in front of them, except he sat hunched forward, forearms resting on his thighs, hands clasped between his knees looking at the brown cracked earth where feet had scuffed away the grass. The dogs, couchant like heraldic beasts at her feet, Mina at one end of the bench half turned towards him, he was conscious she was giving him all her attention. She understood him, would hear him out. He told her everything.

'Really hurt accusing me of not helping enough when Fran and Tom were babies. I missed out, I know. What could I do? So much going on in the company. She need never have gone back to work, Mina. I make more than enough.'

Mina moved closer, put her arm around his shoulders. 'I'm so sorry, darling.' She kissed his cheek.

He thought he might blub, managed to get a grip. 'Not your fault. All mine, not . . . '

'I'm a lot to blame for her going back to being a solicitor,' Mina said. 'Not the sort of job I'd want. She always wanted to be a lawyer like her Daddy, and she is good at it. No way would she pass up the chance of a partnership. She has to prove herself, twice over perhaps. Think about it.'

'Tess is right I was too far up my own arse to think . . . How are you to blame for her going back?'

'That time I hung around for an age, and you too easy-going to ask when I might be going home. I was so worried about her, made her see her GP. She put her on anti-depressants. I told Tess she had to stir herself. Going back to her old firm was, I'm afraid, one of the options I suggested.'

He sat up, turned to look at her. 'Tess on anti-depressants?'

'She never told you?'

'She used to be the most together person. I admire her, the way she manages to pull everything in, the job, the kids, the house. Lately, though, she's been flaky. Totally pissed off with me. Simple as that.' *He'd probably got it wrong, wasn't Tom she hadn't wanted, it was him. Immediately after Tom was born he supposed she needed him to be around to provide for them. And now she could manage on her own. Whatever Mina might say, unless Tess wanted him, she certainly no longer needed him.*

'I've never liked Burroughs, always sniffing around even after Tess had the kids. What does she see in him? Lanky ginger streak with that precious accent.' Again he leant forward. 'I've begun to think they might be having an affair, making a fool of his wife as well as me.'

'Darling, trust me. They're colleagues who get on well together. Surely you have female colleagues you have a rapport with.'

He felt his face flush, hoped Mina hadn't noticed.

'Tom was a demanding little bugger. I wouldn't have minded being woken up, getting Tess a cup of tea. I was banished to the study divan. I used to love lying beside her when she fed Fran. At least I got to hold my baby. During the week sometimes that was the only time I saw Fran awake. Tess denied me that with Tom.' He scoured his eye-lids with the heels of his hands. 'I don't want to lose her. I didn't accept the Amsterdam job because I want to leave her. I should've discussed it with her. Would've been professional suicide to turn it down.' He sighed.

He felt Mina's firm artist's hand rest on the nape of his neck. She stroked the length of his spine as she would have caressed a cat. He began to relax. She carried on stroking for a while. He arched his back, sat up, drew her arm through his. 'What shall I do, Mina?'

She gave his arm a squeeze. 'When you get her home . . .'

'She might refuse to come with me.'

'I think not. Once home, darling, don't pussyfoot. Make mad passionate love to her.'

He felt the heat in his face. 'Don't think she wants me like that anymore.'

With her free hand, Mina cupped his face, making him look at her. 'Ironic then, Tess believes you don't want her. There've been rebuffs?' - His cheeks felt as though they were on fire. - 'Don't be bashful. You can tell me.'

He released Mina's arm, and again sat hunched forward so that he didn't have to look her in the face. He felt his cool down.

'What did Tess say?'

'For a while now, you've not made love, even when she tried to encourage you.'

One icy Friday night way back, he'd been away almost two weeks. Fran and Tom in bed asleep, Tess had lit a log fire, put on one of his old CDs, Pulp probably. He had showered, was relaxing in his bathrobe on the chesterfield. Tess knelt in front of him. Remembering Tess's caresses, her enveloping lips, her soft mouth, her tongue, he felt his face heat up yet again. Tess had failed to arouse him. He was mortified. She got to her feet, 'You must be tired,' she said. 'We'd better go to bed.' She kissed him on the forehead. 'To sleep.'

'She has no proof,' Mina was saying, 'she feels sure she knows the reason why. Specializing in divorce cases, one must be quick to jump to certain conclusions, I suppose. When it boils down to what women find irresistible in a man, you're quite a lethal combination, Mike. Status, no mean bankroll, charming with it, I'm sure men in a similar position far less personable get offers. And, if Tess is giving you a hard time . . .'

By the time Mina had finished he felt his face must spontaneously combust. He remained hunched forward. Silence, except for a background buzz from groups of strangers.

'Believe me, Mina,' his voice soft, 'when I wasn't able to get it up for Tess, I'm sure I couldn't have for any other woman.'

A heartbeat, then he felt her hand on his shoulder. 'Darling, you're not? You can't be. Have you seen your doctor?'

He sat up. Recalling and wanting to forget the folly of that Amsterdam June afternoon, 'No, I'm not, not any more. At my annual checkup, the company MO could find nothing wrong. He put it down to stress – the job on top of realizing Tess was pissed off with me. He told me I needed to spend more quality time with her. I'm not a drinker, few glasses of wine, or a pint. I've never smoked, not even grass at Oxford. Pretty bloody boring. No wonder Tess is fed up with me.'

'Never been exactly wild herself. As far as I know, she didn't bother much with boys, till you came along. At Oxford she had this cosy set-up with Calista Blake. I like Cal a lot. Have to say, I did used to wonder.'

'They were known as the Sapphic Ice Maidens. They still have something special. Cal's been a good friend to both of us.'

'They do make a stunning pair. I imagine lots of men at Oxford had this fantasy of making a threesome.' Mina chortled. For the umpteenth time, he felt his face flush. 'Took someone really special to carry one of them off.' Mina squeezed his knee.

'I knew Tess was the one, couldn't believe my luck when she joined a Nottingham firm. Thought she would want to be based down here. I said let's do something unconventional. Let's get married, she said let's. I don't want a divorce, Mina.'

'Then you have to convince her. If I were you, I'd deny everything.'

'Mina, it was just . . .'

'Darling, I don't want to know.' She got to her feet.

He and the whippets also stood ready to move. For the first time that morning he was aware of the panorama. 'Impressive,' he said.

'Don't you miss it?' Mina said. 'I can't imagine ever wanting to live anywhere else.'

'Never think about it. Home is where Tess is. If I lose her I'm wrecked.'

'Tess suffered when her beloved Daddy had little or no option but to fulfil his duties. He left us when she was seven. We shouldn't have had her.' She sighed. 'She's our love child. I so wish she wasn't suffering now.'

The early morning joggers and dog walkers had long gone replaced by a noisy babble of tourists jockeying for position around the plaque indicating the landmarks. Mina reigned in the dogs, and took his arm. 'I do wonder if you and Tess ever talk to each other.'

'We used to, before . . .' *Unfair to blame Tom. He should have seen how depressed she had been.*

'Come on,' Mina said. 'Let's get a move on. I could murder a mug of builder's tea, and toast oozing butter and jam.'

As soon as Mike walked in, Esther felt that familiar frisson of longing. She sat at her mother's kitchen table drinking tea, and wondering if she would lose face if she caught an afternoon train to Nottingham. She didn't have to get back, that time of year, no appointments all week.

He sat down opposite, reached across, took her hands in his. His like hers, were cool and dry yet they made her feel as though hers were on fire.

'Tess, I've come to take you home,' he said.

CHAPTER TWENTY TWO

Sunday Night - Ithaca

Calista and Adam sat at their usual table. The inscrutable waters of the night-sea lapped the harbour wall. A star-filled sky stretched to infinity. They talked very little whilst they ate, and soon sank their first bottle of wine. Adam ordered a second. The snapper fish was excellent but she hardly touched hers. The body in the sea could be PJ's. The thought sickened her. PJ, all on his own could have fallen overboard, *Thelma Jane* drifting. She wondered who would be the first to miss him. His half-brother or whoever PJ lived with in Vathy. On their Cephalonia trip she looked for the sloop in Fiskardo, in Sami, and again in Argostoli to no avail.

'Penny for them.' Leaning over, Adam stroked her cheek.

She gathered her wits. 'A bit insensitive to be revelling in earthly delights, like food and drink.' He raised his eyebrows. 'When you think about it, post-funeral do's often turn into a bit of a knees-up. We never drink two bottles of wine. The drowned man's given us intimations of mortality.'

'You make him sound like the Tarot's Hanged Man.'

'A shock. Death. Here in paradise.'

'People do die here. Look at the notices stuck on lamp-posts.'

They sat in silence. Neither seemed willing to be the first to make the move to take them into the shadows of the walk to the Erato. Adam looked round.

'Time to go.'

Cloths were already cleared and chairs upended on to the tables behind them. They had been oblivious. They manoeuvred through the tables edging the harbour and crossed the thoroughfare, barely a pick-up's width, which ran the gauntlet of more tables fronting the taverna. As they reached the threshold, Marcos appeared.

'May I offer you a Metaxa?'

'That would be lovely,' Calista replied before Adam could get a word in and sat at the table she had shared with PJ. Adam drew up a chair. Marcos joined them with three generously filled balloon glasses.

'How was Cephalonia?'

All the taverna lights were off except for one over the bar. They sat conspiratorially in shadow.

'Interesting, we liked it,' Adam said, 'but we're very pleased to be back, despite . . .'

'We saw your Mafia men and the Nephititi,' she said.

'Really.' Marcos didn't sound all that interested.

All along the front, brief concentrated bustle. In the space of minutes, lights were extinguished and shutters came down on the handful of other bars and tavernas circling the harbour. 'Goodnight,' the patrons called on their way home, as, one by one, they zipped past on mopeds, their whirr finally stifled by distance and darkness.

'Where had they got to?' Marcos took a sip of brandy.

'On Thursday, The harbour at Argostoli. There were three of them on the yacht that day. They seemed to be having a bit of a ding dong.'

Marcos excused himself for a moment. On the deck of the farthest sailing boat riding at anchor, a quartet, two men and two women caroused, their laughter echoing round the bay, competing with slap of water against wood, fibre-glass, stone. The only reflections left riding the wavelets were orangey-yellow from street lamps. Marcos returned bearing a bottle of five-star Metaxa, three-quarters full and placed it on the table.

'And was the third man, swarthy with dark curly hair in his late-twenties?'

'Do you know him?' Adam said.

'I think I told you, the older bloke, the Italian and his Albanian sidekick came to the taverna about a week ago, asking questions.'

'The younger chap's Albanian?' Adam didn't sound all that surprised.

'They said they were hoping to meet up with a young couple who, they'd been told, might be in Kioni,' Marcos said. 'They described the man as I have.'

'There was no young woman in evidence,' Calista said. She jumped when, with a pop, the nearest street lamp blanked out. They were in even deeper shadow now. The glow from the remaining light was completely dissipated by the time it reached their circle. The carousers had retired, everywhere silent, except for boats creaking. Spooky. As though on cue, they all took a gulp of brandy. Marcos broke the spell.

'That night Kristina and Yiorgos dropped in for a drink, I pointed them out to her. She knows better than me what goes on in her country. She told me to tell them nothing, which was easy because I knew nothing.'

'Your third man's a real smacker as Chloe, my pupil would say. Curious after what you said, I zoomed in and photographed them. As I say they were going at it hammer and tongues.'

'My wife is an avid reader of crime fiction, Marco. You must excuse her.'

Well past midnight, they ought to be getting back to the villa. 'We mustn't keep you, Marco,' she said. 'Your wife will be worrying.'

'She's taken the kids over to my sister-in-law's.' He made to pour the three of them more brandy. Calista covered the top of her glass with her hand.

Adam told Marcos about their horrible experience that afternoon.

'Somebody drowned near here?' Marcos sounded shocked. 'That's terrible. Haven't heard anything. Could be someone off one of those flotillas, I guess. The sergeant would be Pavlos Mastorantonakis,'

'Do you know him?' Adam asked.

'He's my brother-in-law's cousin's husband.'

'Here, everyone seems to be related, one way or another,' Calista said. 'Your brother-in-law's cousin's husband gave nothing away.'

'Tragedy like that, we'll hear something soon enough,' Marcos said.

Silence, except for water lapping the harbour wall, boats creaking.

'Lovely to see Kristina and Yiorgos so happy together,' Calista said.

'She's good for Yiorgos,' Marcos said.

'Last summer, we had this heart to heart,' Calista said. 'I found her sobbing over the washing up. Yiorgos had proposed to her. She was heartbroken.'

'What?' Marcos said.

'She told me she couldn't marry him. His parents had been good to her allowing her to live in her little house.'

'She helped them with the olives,' Marcos said. 'Bloody hard work that is. Don't know what they'd have done without her.'

'She didn't think they would want their only son to marry an Albanian. And she was no longer young. The decider, I gathered, was, she loved him too much to bring dishonour to his family. Some dodgy business her brother was involved in which operates between Italy and Albania, not here. I told her whatever her brother did, she couldn't be held responsible, wasn't her brother Yiorgos wanted to marry. If she was worried about that, she should confide in Yiorgos. She took my advice, and Yiorgos, well they seem made for each other, and delighted with their boy.'

Calista remembered the first time she saw Yiorgos, muscular, suntanned, in faded blue jeans and pristine white T-shirt. For someone so swarthy he had very light eyes, a striking looking man. She wondered how Kristina could resist him, except she knew Kristina hadn't. 'He says I must marry him.' Kristina had blushed. 'Because he burst open my rosebud.'

'Kristina's a hard grafter, and a clever woman.' Marcos chuckled. 'Don't see how she could not have married him. That baby was born only seven months after the wedding, a bouncing boy, not some mewling undersized thing. And okay she's what, thirty five-ish. What would Yiorgos do with a girl with painted nails, short skirts and skimpy tops like that sister-in-law of hers.'

'Where's the dodgy brother,' Adam said.

'Nobody knows, Marcos said, 'and if Ledia does, she's not letting on. She's been here since Easter. Yiorgos told me Kristina had this phone call, could Ledia come and stay for a while. Yiorgos took his fishing boat over to Fiskardo to pick her up. She's no sponger. Cleans my brother's villas and rooms like Kristina used to. Doesn't work here in the evening though. Helps out with the baby quite a bit. She loves that kid.'

Now the only smell was that of the sea mingled with a little tar. Soporific the slap of waves, the rhythmic creak of craft riding the ripples.

'Anyway, Kristina's half Greek.' Marcos's words stopped her nodding off. 'Her father was Greek, from Thessalonika. During the civil war, as a young lad, perhaps no more than twelve, he fought on the losing side.'

'A boy soldier in your civil war?' She knew a little bit about the War of Independence from the Ottomans in the 1820's because of Byron, quite the local hero.

'You've surely heard about the Civil War, Cal, immediately after World War II.' Adam gave her a resume of what he called first British and later American meddling.

'You mean Kristina's father was like Mandras in *Captain Corelli's Mandolin*.'

'I doubt it,' Adam said. 'That's fiction. Atrocities weren't confined to any one side. Let's drop the subject.'

'Terrible times,' Marcos said, 'When I was a kid you soon learnt not to get my grandfather talking about it. As teenagers, he and his brother went to Australia to find work. My father was born in Melbourne, like me and my brother.'

'So you're a couple of Aussies really,' Adam chuckled. 'Explains your command of the vernacular.'

'We think of ourselves as Greek, me and my brother. My grandfather used to long to come home.'

'Like Odysseus,' Calista said.

'Just like him, except he never got back. My great uncle and his family still live in Melbourne.' Marcos gestured towards the mainland, telling them Kristina's father and some of his comrades were lucky to escape from the last battle on Mount Grammos, get over into Albania. 'If you could call that luck. The government-side had napalm from the Americans, so he escaped a horrible death. At least he lived to marry and have a family. Sadly, his wife died when Kristina's younger brother was born. She has an older brother and sister in Albania.'

The incessant wavelets seemed to pause, in the space of an intake of breath, then the most heartrending howl.

'Bloody cats.' Marcos muttered, told them Yiorgos had gone to a school for officers to learn seamanship, a tradition on Ithaca and Cephalonia, and been at least twelve years away, captain on an oil tanker for the last three.

'He came home to settle down. Trouble is, he was always shy with girls, but he strikes lucky. Comes home, finds Kristina, living in his father's olive grove. She's not the sort of woman you feel shy with. He told me he fell in love with her smile the first time he spoke to her.'

'A fairy tale, like Cinderella,' Calista said surprising herself, if not the men.

Time to leave.

'I nearly forgot. PJ sends his regards, Mrs Burgess. He was here on Friday night, came with his brother and his brother's friend.'

She wanted to laugh out loud, to sing and dance. The man in the sea wasn't PJ. Then dejection, she had missed him.

Marcos had closed up and extinguished the remaining light before they had covered a couple of hundred yards. Seeming remarkably in control despite the brandy, he gave them a cheery wave as he overtook them, his moped's engine rasping through the silent night.

'Who on earth's PJ?'

She told Adam how they met over a glass of wine the night he went fishing. He seemed satisfied, except he questioned her about how much she had to drink.

'A couple of glasses.'

'And the rest. No wonder I found you in the wrong bedroom.'

Back at the Erato, the scent of pine and hill-side herbs drifting through their window was like a sedative. Night soft as velvet enveloped them. She lay on her side, gazing at the stars through the open window.

'Imagine being able to stay here forever and ever.'

'You'd get bored.'

Perhaps, and nothing was forever. She thought of the lifeless thing bundled from the sea. No tomorrow for him. What if her muggers had knifed her, and her life's blood had drained away on to the gum-pocked pavement.

'Kristina would have been mad to come to England when she loved Yiorgos enough to marry him.'

'Glad you married me?' Adam sounded on the verge of sleep.

She pulled the sheet up over them, pondering.

CHAPTER
TWENTY THREE

Monday

She woke up, head throbbing, mouth parched. She should not have had the brandy..

'Morning, Cal.' Adam stood in the doorway.

'I think I want to die.' She closed her eyes. 'Doesn't your head ache? You had more brandy than me.' She closed her eyes, then opened one of them. Adam stood over her.

'Ledia's been here ages,' a throw-away line as he left her in recovery mode.

After showering, she felt a little better. Adam had disappeared by the time she went down to the terrace.

'Good morning,' Ledia said when she brought out her breakfast tray. 'Mr Burgess tells me you enjoyed your trip to Cephalonia very much.'

Unusually expansive, Calista thought. 'Yes, thank you, we did. Are you okay, Ledia? You're looking . . . tired.' In fact Ledia seemed tense, anxious.

'I am well, thank you.' Then she smiled. 'Dhionysius woke us in the middle of the night, poor baby. He was screaming with pain. Tina was starting to panic. Yiorgos's mama calmed her, told her it will not be too long before he gets his first tooth.'

'The joys of parenthood,' Calista said.

'But he is beautiful, Mrs Burgess, happy and contented, until now. I wash my hands and let him bite my finger. That helps him.'

The way Ledia spoke, a tragedy for her if she really was unable to conceive.
'I really must see him before he gets any older,' Calista said.

While she made herself eat bread, butter and cheese to soak up residual alcohol, Adam reappeared at the top of the steps to the beach.

'Ledia,' he called through, 'another coffee for me, there's a dear.' He sat down at the table, Calista felt his scrutiny. 'Have to say, you're not looking your best,.'

'Thanks a bunch.'

'What are your plans this morning?' he said.

'What are yours?'

'As you're so obviously hors de combat, I shall inspect the villa, make sure the builder's done as promised. I'm rather disappointed. You haven't shown much interest.'

'Tomorrow, perhaps. I can visit Kristina, admire her baby. Will you see if it's convenient while you're over there?'

Ledia brought out his coffee. 'Don't be too long,' Adam said to her. Calista noticed their exchange of smiles.

'I'm going round to the harbour in the boat and giving Ledia a lift. She's on foot today. It's quite a walk into the village to her next job. Thanks to your tardiness, she's running late.'

Calista held her tongue, took a sip of coffee.

'I'll go down to the beach,' she said. 'Try and shift this headache.'

When she collected her beach gear, Ledia had already done their room. She left Adam on the terrace. *What the hell.*

She lowered herself on to a recliner, raked at just the right angle, popped a couple of Paracetamol with a swig from her water bottle, and tilted her sun-hat over her eyes. No sooner settled, low-voiced conversation, Ledia and Adam descending the steps. She resisted disturbing herself to look at them. They stopped talking as soon as they hit the shingle, footsteps to her sunbed.

'You'll be okay, won't you Cal? Have you got your phone?'

'Go, just go.' She raised her hat, opened one eye. He loomed over her. He made a pantomime of tiptoeing away.

She took refuge once more under her straw hat. Not long after, she heard the outboard bounce into life. *Nothing like a trip twice round the bay with a young woman you've so obviously got the hots for.*

Ledia, settled among the cushions in the prow, rewarded him with one of her rare smiles.

'Look at you,' Adam said, 'like the Queen of Sheba.'

'You are very kind, Adam.'

'Least I could do since my wife caused you to run late.'

'Is she sick?'

'Too much wine last night.' He chuckled. 'Then we had a brandy with Marcos.'

'My husband would be angry if I drank too much alcohol.'

'Now's your chance to let your hair down.'

'Except for red wine, I do not really like the taste. When we lived in Italy, Nik used to allow me to have a glass.' She looked wistful. 'We were happy there.'

'Is that where he is? Italy.'

Her face froze. She shook her head. 'I do not know. I do not care where he is. I would divorce him if I could. I think he would sooner kill me.' She was so obviously not joking.

He remained silent - "*rugged nurse of* savage *men*" was how Byron had described Albania in 'Child Harolde'.

'Does Kristina know how you feel about her brother?'

'My husband is a jealous man, hot tempered. I have told Kristina what happened between us, why I feel the way I do. He did a terrible thing when I was expecting his baby. He did not believe it was his, and now I will never conceive another child. Tina feels much pain when she thinks of Nik. She remembers him when he was a boy, her little brother. She does not approve of what he did when he became a man, what he does now. He is still her brother and she worries.' Ledia sighed. 'Tina and Yiorgos are very kind. They say I can stay . . . but . . .'

'Pardon my curiosity, what business is your husband involved in? I'll understand, of course, if you don't want to tell me.'

'It is not a secret. Import-Export, but I do not know what is imported or exported.' She told him her husband's boss Signor Raffo and someone Nik and Raffo referred to as '*il Capo*' did business with the Minister in Tirana. 'My father is a government official. I attended a reception with him, and that is where I met Nik. I was twenty, at university. Nik is handsome and charming. He wore an Armani suit, and taught me to swim in the Rogner pool. The Rogner is a big hotel in Tirana. My father was angry, and disappointed when I did not complete my studies. I married Nik instead and went with him to live in Italy. He speaks Italian and English and Greek, Albanian naturally. He is very clever. *Il Capo* thought highly of him.'

'Your English is very good, Ledia.'

'I do my best. Tina and I practice together.'

They had reached the harbour, Adam pleased with himself for finding out more about Ledia, married to a man who wore Armani which explained her un-cleaner-like clothes.

When she was sure the boat had cleared the cove, Calista got up, opened the beach umbrella, took several satisfying slurps of water, and sank down on to her recliner again. She closed her eyes shaded by the hat. Through the umbrella, heat filtered on to her body. Sod Adam, sod Ledia. Shush of sea on stones. Peace. Tranquillity. Soporific the sound of the sea.

She woke to the sound of pebbles rattling against one another. Stretching her extremities to the limit, breathing in pine-scented air, she felt life surge through her. Ready to take on the world, she opened her eyes. Blinded by the force of the sun's glare, she groped for her sunglasses. Scanning the cove, the shimmering sea, she was alone, and starving. She found her watch. Half past two.

No boat. No Adam. Not another accident. She got up. Too quickly. Dizzy. Deep breaths. What should she do? No, she hadn't brought her phone to the beach. She was being absurd. She would go eat and wait. She had wolfed the cheese and tomato omelette she had made herself, was sitting on the terrace sipping iced Earl Grey tea, when Adam appeared at the top of the steps.

'Where the hell have you been? ' She said.

He put his arm around her shoulders and kissed her on the corner of the mouth. 'Miss me?'

'You've been drinking.' She wriggled free.

'A couple of beers with Yiorgos. We went for a bite at Marcos's. Bit of a celebration, the villa's come on in leaps and bounds. Don't know why you've been so lukewarm about it. You'll love it.'

She had never really seen the point of the villa when they could rent the Erato which she loved. No doubt Adam had a cunning plan.

He went and fetched himself a glass of water and sat down opposite her.

'I think I've found out why at times Ledia can be dour,' he said. 'She's trapped in an unhappy marriage. Her husband's got a temper and gets jealous.'

'I already know that. Kristina told me last year. We were discussing her resolve not to marry Yiorgos. She told me her brother Nik was some kind of crook, that he had a violent temper and was madly jealous if any other man paid too much attention to his wife. You'd better watch your step. He may turn up unexpectedly.'

'She intrigues me, that's all, an attractive, intelligent woman working as a cleaner. In any case, she says she hasn't a clue where he is. What's more doesn't care. And if he is a crook, he's a successful one in an Armani suit.'

She listened to what Ledia had told him about Nik Kavathi's business.

'*Il Capo*, sounds to me very *Cosa Nostra*,' she said. 'But what do I know.'

'That's exactly what I thought.' He got to his feet. 'Think I'll go down for a swim. Coming with me?'

She said she would like to try and finish 'The Girl who played with Fire', if she could remember where she had got to.

'A swim will liven you up. Must say, you've seemed rather withdrawn this holiday. Come on, darling, keep me company.'

In the end she relented, would have been mean not to.

'By the way,' he said as they descended the steps to the beach, 'Kristina is looking forward to seeing you. I have to say, the baby is somewhat cute. And wait till you see where her hovel used to be. As soon as we've had breakfast tomorrow, we'll take a stroll over.'

CHAPTER TWENTY FOUR

Tuesday Morning

No lingering over breakfast, and the anticipated stroll to the building site turned out to be more a brisk trot.

'I'll put money on your objections melting away,' Adam said.

'All I said was, what's wrong with the Erato?'

'Too small, if we want family or friends to join us.'

So that was what he had in mind all along. She resented his not being more communicative about his plans. Last August he had tootled round to the harbour in the boat - *'Been to sound out Marcos's local knowledge. Very productive.' Adam had told her. 'Wait till tomorrow when I show you Kristina's house.'* Plus a cryptic, *'What a bit of luck Yiorgos Vassilatos happened to be at the taverna.'*

She could see the attraction of inviting Tess and Co to come on holiday with them. The weekend they had stayed at the Old Rectory was a hoot. Adam's patronizing sister, Antonia, her cipher of a husband, their two supercilious brats were something else.

At the end of the paved road, on their right, they passed the Vassilatos's house. A dog they couldn't see barked, loud and furious. They started along the rough track through the olives. After a couple of hundred yards, a drive-way of polished stones set in concrete veered off to the left.

'This way, darling.' Adam steered her up the short stretch which ended in a platform constructed of the same material as the drive. On the right a low retaining stone wall at the end of which nearest the villa, a dozen or so steps down the hillside.

'Enough standing room for a modest four-by- four,' Adam said. – *When was a four-by-four ever modest?* - 'And these walls won't look so stark once they're broken up with climbing plants.' He gestured to a concrete wall keeping the olive grove at bay, and, at a right-angle, the blind, white-painted end wall of the house.

He made for three shallow steps up to the terrace. Calista started down those descending the hill.

'I want to have a look where Kristina's house used to be.' She sensed his hesitation to follow.

At the bottom a patio of polished stones instead of compacted earth and scrubby grass. A white, flat-roofed one-storey building bore no resemblance to the smaller by-a-third, one-roomed house of rough stone built into a grassy bank, its red-tiled roof overhung with gnarled olive trees, a fig screening the lean-to. No doubt the bathrooms would be an improvement on Kristina's hole-in-the-ground loo, stone sink and cold-water tap. Sliding shutters protected glass doors which would give light and access to each of the guest rooms. She stepped over the low stone wall the better to view the building from the track.

'See,' Adam said. 'Just as you asked, that part of the roof which ex-tends beyond the upper terrace will be green, eeko-staygi as they say in these parts, and planted with stonecrop, wild thyme. I can't remember what else.'

'No dust for the clucking chucks to scratch in.' Calista pointed to the patio. He looked nonplussed. 'Can just imagine the jet-hire company if you told them we'd be travelling with our pet hens.' Hallelujah, that raised a smile.

The building was surrounded by olives and nature, beneath the trees this time of year dried out straw-coloured grasses, seed-heads of wild flowers, bronze and gold. The silky white thistle heads she knew attracted goldfinches. She imagined sitting reading. Perhaps she and Adam could have one of these rooms. She had argued for no more than this, big enough for a bedroom, bathroom and open plan living area, an ideal holiday refuge for two.

Adam broke into her thoughts. 'Let's go back up.'

As she climbed the steps, she remembered their conversation last August. *'You think it's a good idea, then building a villa where Kristina's cottage stands?'* He had had it in mind to buy or build a villa since their first visit the previous year. 'A whole year you'd been thinking about it, and you never once thought to discuss it with me.' She should have said that at the time. And now, she wasn't just resentful, she was hurt, aggrieved. They hadn't been married that first visit, had sneaked away just for the week. Neither had been to Ithaca before. Like her, he was enchanted, and probably at the time had visions of building for Annabel and his girls.

'What did you say, darling?' He was already at the top of the steps.

'Talking to myself,' she said.

She had asked how Kristina would feel about losing her home. 'It's a hovel,' Adam said. When Calista saw it, she had thought of a Wendy House; she'd peeped inside, immaculate. 'And the loo.' He had held his nose. 'Besides, Yiorgos has plans for her.' Another overbearing male, she thought, except she now knew Yiorgos consulted Kristina every step of the way.

No Adam, I've never believed it that good an idea because I've never seen the point. But, right from the start, your agenda was obviously never mine. The time had come, she decided. Tell me, Adam, the real reason you divorced Annabel.

A sturdy pergola frame painted holly green was already in place on the upper terrace. 'Just imagine this covered in bougainvillea and jasmine,' Adam said. 'And behind those shutters, our bedroom.' – To their left, he pointed to louvered shutters the same green as the pergola which concealed French doors. A frosted-glass door further along 'the lobby' Adam took a key from the pocket of his shorts. 'Let's go in.'

At the far end, glass bricks letting in light, a sound enough notion, they brought to mind a public lavatory. She was tempted to share her observation.

'Tarrahh.' He showed her the bedroom, a square white box, their bathroom. 'Look. They got a move on especially for your visit.'

Her designer had chosen well and she couldn't fault the workmanship. Thank God windows of louvered glass, not bricks, let in light along the back wall.

'They've done a good job.' She said, noting his look of relief.

'The sitting room's an empty shell like our bedroom, but come look at the kitchen.' He led the way back to the door opposite their room. Three shallow steps from the sitting room led up to an arch. The kitchen, not over-large but adequate, was already equipped with the units and appliances she had little interest in. Again the designer had chosen well.

'Well, what do you think?' Adam said.

'Absolutely no need for your flap.'

'I so wanted us to stay here this year,' he said.

Well I didn't, and I'm glad we couldn't, she thought. If they had been here, Adam might have been so taken with the novelty, he wouldn't have become bored and gone fishing with Yiorgos, and she wouldn't have met PJ Wood. *PJ, PJ, where are you PJ?*

Adam unlocked the kitchen's sliding glass doors and shutters leading onto yet another pergola covered terrace. This one overlooked the sun-baked patio inset with an azure-tiled swimming pool.

'You might've had it filled with water so that I could have a swim.' She turned to look at him, his expression apprehensive till she gave an impish smile. *She believed she was beginning to know him at last, and wondered why it seemed so important she should come round to the idea of this villa. He was wealthy – she didn't know exactly how wealthy, wouldn't even hazard a guess at a ballpark figure. He was a big noise in his sphere of influence. Why be so anxious for her approval? After all, she was only his wife. He had already disposed of one . . .*

What Adam insisted on calling the west wing was staggered three steps higher into the hill from the patio, a third the width of the main block. Not in the least curious, she wandered past what should be a utility room, a wet room and loo, and Adam's office, and down the steps which brought her to the far end of the swimming pool. Here only a knee-high stone wall came between nature and the villa's man-made intrusion. She looked back, two staggered oblongs with sloping terracotta roofs.

Adam joined her. 'Aren't you just a tiny bit impressed, darling?'

'Your architect's to be congratulated,' she said. 'The way he has used the terraces where olives once grew.'

'In an earthquake zone, you don't have to dig quite so deep for single storeys,' he said.

She wondered about planning permission, how much silver had crossed palms, kept the thoughts to herself. 'Just out of interest, how many olive trees were uprooted?'

'I really don't know. Don't forget the idea is for our ground rent to provide income for Yiorgos's parents, so that they don't have to rely so much on the olive crop.

'Ummm.' She looked around. 'It's all so . . . so barren compared to when Kristina lived here.'

'Wait and see when the pergolas are covered with climbing plants.'

He sounded somewhat peeved.

'Is that wall high enough to stop the Hurray Henrys tumbling down?' She indicated the stone wall bordering the outer edge of the patio.

'Hurray Henrys?'

'Your nephews when they're drunk.'

'That's a bit harsh,' he said.

'Adam, they got absolutely bladdered on your Single Malt. I can see them now, standing at the edge of the ha-ha and peeing into the meadow.' *Took all her willpower not to push them over the edge.*

'You're right, about the wall. They could miss their footing.' - *So they were on his guest list.* – He glanced at his watch. 'I'll lock up. Kristina's expecting us any time soon. We can reach the track that way.' He pointed to the far corner of the patio where two walls failed to meet, and steps led down the slope.

At the bottom, 'I wanted you to see this, before you left.' The patio's retaining wall was of cyclopean proportions shoring up the bank from the top down to the track. 'Can't have the pool sliding down. Thought this would look good with Livingstone daisies cascading like you see in these parts.' He stepped off the track and looked up. 'And a decorative wrought iron rail along the top ought to dispel your Health and Safety concerns.'

She nodded. *Not just his nephews who might fall.*

'Don't you dare tell me you're unimpressed,' he said.

'I suppose what we have here barely a year on is impressive.'

'Cal, I've thought of a name. How about Villa Thalia, a homage to the Erato which is named after the muse of love poetry. Thalia is the muse of comedy and pastoral poetry.'

'Alternatively, how about . . . *Chez nous?*' she said poker-faced. His expression, then a fit of giggles bordering on hysteria she had difficulty in supressing. 'Sorry. Thalia seems about right.' *More tragi-comedy than anything*, she thought. *As for love.*

'Villa Thalia, it is then.' He sounded happy, and relieved.

Before they reached the dirt driveway alongside the Vassilitos house, the invisible dog warned of their approach. Yiorgos came to meet them, smiling. He shook their hands. 'Kristina and Dhionysius are waiting for you Mrs Burgess.'

'I'll say hello before we go down to the harbour,' Adam said. 'We're going to the kafeneon. Yiorgos is going to teach me to play backgammon.'

'Great.' She meant it.

On the vine-covered terrace overlooking a vegetable plot, Kristina and her mother-in-law were waiting. Kristina introduced her to Yiorgos's mother,˙ no taller than Kristina but plump, her heavy dark hair cut into a bob, a contrast to Kristina's mass of curls. Like Kristina, though, her face was beautiful when she smiled. As they shook hands, Calista noticed from where Yiorgos had got his unusual palest-of-blue eyes.

'Come,' Mamma beckoned. 'Baby.'

She and Kristina followed her to the coolest corner, overhung by a fig tree where Dhionysius dressed in a yellow all-in-one, lay on his back in what looked like an inflatable ring covered in light green cotton printed with pink pigs, black and white cows, white sheep, orange-tan ponies. Gurgling, he gazed up at a mobile, all-colours-of-the-rainbow, suspended above his head.

'He does look comfortable lying there on his whatsit,' Calista said.

'His Playnest,' Kristina said. 'We found it on the internet. He loves to lie and watch the leaves when the wind stirs them, and his mobile of course.' She set it twirling.

Hearing his mother's voice, Dhionysios looked in her direction and smiled, his arms and legs working.

'What big blue eyes,' Calista said

Mamma said something to Kristina in Greek. Kristina nodded

Mamma clapped her hands, held out her arms. Dhionysius became even more excited. She picked him up.

'Please.' Smiling, Mamma held him out for Calista to take.

'Oh dear, I can't remember the last time I held a baby,' she said.

'But it is easy.' Kristina laughed.

Careful, Calista took him, and held him against her, his bottom lodged on the crook of her right arm, her left hand light against his back keeping him in place. His head rested where her neck joined her shoulder. She felt his slobber as he gummed her bare flesh. She hoped she was hygienic.

'He smells lovely,' she said, taken by surprise.

'You would not have said that if you had been here when I changed his diaper.' Kristina laughed.

Mamma spoke again in Greek. This time at length. Kristina replied. Mamma shrugged, shook her head as though disbelieving, then turned to Calista, and smiled. 'Frappe? Orangeade? ' she said.

'Frappe, please,' she replied.

'Let us sit down.' Kristina indicated a table and chairs. 'Mamma will bring us iced coffee and walnut cake. She made it specially. We are lucky, we have a walnut tree.'

'What else was she saying?' Clutching Dhionysius firmly against her, with her free hand, Calista pulled out a chair. She seated herself sideways at the table, and sat Dhionysius on her knee. She was getting the hang of this baby lark.

'She asked if you had children. I told her no. She thought not. You were so nervous. She asked if you would be having a baby. Greeks like to know these things about people they meet. I told her probably not. You are a career woman. She cannot understand any woman who would not want a baby.'

'Quite right too,' Calista said, thinking *but you would have to be care-ful who you chose for its father*. 'Who wouldn't want one as cuddly as you, eh Dhionysius?' She clasped him with both hands, held him up over her head and blew raspberries at him. Gurgling, laughing, he reciprocated, at which point Mamma came out with their elevenses. Her face broke into the broadest smile. She unloaded the tray and left them to talk.

Kristina brought the Playnest over.

'Do you know, Dhionysius, the only time your Auntie Ledia smiles is when she talks about you; now I know why.' Calista kissed him on the top of his head before she placed him down. 'One day, maybe she will have a baby like you.' She sat down again and took a sip of frappe.

'Poor Ledi,' Kristina's brow furrowed. She looked upset. 'My heart grieves for her.'

Calista took a bite from her slice of cake. Delicious. 'Ledia told Adam she has no idea where your brother is at the moment.'

'And we hope he will not think of looking for her here.'

'He doesn't know where she is either?'

'Ledi ran away. If she had gone to her father, or any of her friends . . . I am Nik's sister. Ledi hoped, believed he would not think she would come to me.' Kristina's eyes glistened with tears. 'I no longer know my brother. I no longer want to know him. And now he has also killed the love Ledi had for him. But,' she gave the deepest sigh, 'he is my brother and I worry.'

'Does Ledia plan to stay here working for Mr Karapanos?' Calista said.

'Her heart is mending. She worries, but she is no longer in fear of her life. Now she is angry. She will never forgive what my brother did. I am sorry I cannot say what. I gave her my word. When Ledi is better, I think she will leave. This quiet place is not good for a beautiful and clever woman like her.'

'But your ambition was to go to England,' Calista said. 'You taught yourself English listening to tapes, watching English-speaking films on TV. You understand Greek, Italian, and *Shqip* of course. You're clever too Kristina. You stayed here.'

'Sixteen years I have been in Greece. When I was eighteen I came on the bus to Ioannina from my home in Korce to find work to feed myself and send money to my grandmother and my aunt. They cared for me, and my two brothers and my sister after our mother died. You have no idea how bad it was in my country in the '90s, and before even worse. My aunt worked hard. She tried to save money for my brother Nik to go to the university. He is four years younger than me. I found plenty of work in Greece, in the potato fields, picking fruit –peaches, oranges, the grapes, later the olives.'

'You were a labourer, a young girl on her own. Weren't you afraid of being . . .'

'Cal, look at me, even now I do not have womanly curves. I wore overalls, and boots, cut my hair short. The boys I worked with, two as young as twelve years, I looked after them. They thought of me as their big sister. They would have killed anyone who harmed me. One thing I have learnt in my life, to be beautiful and a woman is not always a blessing. I am not beautiful but look at me now, I am blessed.'

'With two gorgeous men in your life, I'd say so.'

'Two?' Kristina looked puzzled.

'Yiorgos, and him.' Calista pointed at Dhionysius. 'And you seem to get on fine with your mother-in-law.'

'I would not have been able stay in Kioni these past six years, would never have met Yiorgos if I had not helped Mamma and Babba with the olives, if they had not let me live in my small house. I was happy here. In winter I would have had to find work on the mainland.'

'Last year you were worried they wouldn't want you to marry their son. Now you call them Mamma and Babba.'

'They told Yiorgos I was a good, hardworking girl.' She gave a wry smile. 'Me, a girl. My father was Greek. That helped. Yiorgos told them we had both waited a long time to find each other. It was our fate to marry. And now they have their first grandson. Yiorgos's sister has three girls.'

The black German Shepherd-like dog chained beneath a tree at the end of the vegetable plot began to bark.

'This will be Babba coming home for something to eat.' Kristina pushed back her chair and got to her feet.

An archetypal late-middle-aged Greek, with iron-grey crinkly hair and luxuriant moustache, appeared on the terrace. Kristina introduced her to him. He took Calista's hand in his and kissed it, his face wreathed in smiles, his eyes warm with good-humour. Calista suspected Mr Vassilitos Senior was a bit of a joker in contrast to his sober-sides son. He squatted down beside Dhionysius and dangled his komboloi just out of reach. The baby smiled up at him, his arms and hands working to grab the beads, legs kicking.

'Dhionysius is named after Babba,' Kristina said.

'Of course, here the first born son is named after his paternal grand-father. Saves the hassle of having to think of a name, I suppose.' Calista too got to her feet. 'I'd better be going. It's your lunchtime.'

Mamma came out onto the terrace, was pleased when Calista compli-mented her on the delicious cake. She shook Mamma's hand, kissed her on each cheek. Babba stood, insisted on the same treatment. Laughing, she concurred.

Kristina went with her to the end of the drive. They arranged to meet on Calista's last day, Friday, for lunch down at the harbour. Kristina promised to bring Dhionysius in his buggy.

As she walked away, Calista wished she had visited sooner. For an hour she had experienced the vibes of a loving and cohesive family. 'Oy vey,' she said to the trees. She had made up her mind. Showdown with Adam loomed.

CHAPTER TWENTY FIVE

Tuesday Afternoon

Adam sat at the table, a loaf of bread, a bottle of wine already in place. Naked from the waist up, leaning back, hands behind his head, he was obviously deep in thought. Sun-bleached shock of hair, tanned, he was well-fit for a man in his late forties.

Far too hot for coherent thought even on the terrace shaded by overhanging jasmine, Bougainvillea and vine heavy with embryonic fruit. The din kicked up by the cicadas did not help. She must get a grip, Calista thought. As soon as they had got back, she discarded her sweaty shorts and sun-top in favour of a thin cotton pareo.

She set the bowl down with an unintentional thud. Tuna steaks seared in the griddle pan in no time at all. To her they looked inviting on a bed of shredded lettuce similar to Cos. She had bought them fresh off the back of the fish-vendor's pick-up. Crunchy cucumber, green pepper, red onion, green beans, black olives, the most perfect *salade nicoise*, a change from their usual lunch, and for a reason. A large metal spoon inexplicably leapt out of her hands to land with a clatter on an empty plate. A frantic moth battered against her stomach lining.

'Just can't get the staff,' Adam said.

She took a deep breath, then dressed the salad with the dark olive oil and wine vinegar. Fresh, savoury salad, the unmistakable tang of the sea from the fish, and sweet-sharp tomato and onion. Her mouth watered.

'Come to think of it, as we're in Greece, probably is Cos.'

'Because what?'

'The lettuce, a Cos.'

'Don't forget salt. We need it in this heat.'

There were the anchovies. She insisted he should be the first to dig in.

'A pity to spoil such a work of art,' he said vandalizing it immediately.

She pulled apart a piece of bread. The air had to be cleared, now, or not at all. First, let him know she knew Annabel had wanted the divorce. Second, suggest there should be a formal arrangement for Helena and Sasha to spend time with him at The Old Rectory.

'Where's your wine glass?'

'I'm sticking with mineral water.' She pressed her stomach. 'I think I'm hungry.'

'Tuck in then.' He smiled. 'This is delicious. You may yet become semi-domesticated.'

Except for the cacophony from the cicadas, they ate in silence until dessert. She felt better.

He quartered a nectarine, and once he had sucked the juice from his fingers, 'What did you think of young Dhionysius, then? Hope he didn't make you feel broody.'

'Don't be absurd,' she said. 'He seems an exceptionally happy baby, and so he should, surrounded by all those adoring adults. And it was good to catch up with Kristina. We're having lunch together on Friday, down on the harbour. Hope you don't mind.' *She could kick herself for that last bit.*

'Mind, why should I?'

Only because it will be the final day or our holiday, and you might want to spend all of it with me, she thought. The remains of lunch were attracting wasps and flies. She started to clear the pots. He made to help her.

'Stay where you are,' she said. 'Coffee?' She didn't want him to come indoors.

'I would prefer mineral water.'

Before she could stop him he had collected up everything she could not manage and brought it through to the kitchen. She began to wash up.

'Can't that wait, Cal?'

'The flies.'

Already they were homing in. He dried. When all was neat and tidy, 'Adam, can we talk?'

He stood in front of her. Placing his hands on her hips then sliding them round to her buttocks, he pulled her to him. She felt his sex against her.

'Wouldn't you rather . . . Been an age, and . . . '

'Please, Adam.'

'Whatever is it?' Taking her hand, he led her to the banquette in the living area, and sat her down in one corner, his lips compressed. His eyes were wary.

Cooler indoors, the cicadas' chorus more muted. Soft breaths of air drifted through the open patio door bringing, by turns, perfumed hints of pine, rosemary and jasmine.

'What is it?' He said.

'Well.' She made to get up. 'Maybe I will have one glass of wine.'

Adam sprang to attention, brought the bottle, three-quarters-full from lunchtime, and two glasses, and placed them on the dining-table. He handed her a glass of wine and returned to his corner.

'Now please tell me what's bothering you.'

She sat forward, taking a generous mouthful of wine. In the pause before her reply, the cicadas seemed to carol louder and stronger. She was getting hot and bothered, again, felt sweat trickling between her legs. She took another gulp of wine.

'It's about Annabel. You never said.' - Inscrutable, he held her gaze. - 'She had someone else. She asked for the divorce, not you her so that you could marry me.'

Adam leaned forward, took her almost empty glass away and placed it on the floor. He cupped her face in his hands, made her look him in the face.

'Do you regret marrying me?'

She swallowed, feeling a tell-tale flush creeping up her neck.

'What does it matter, who asked whom for a divorce? Who told you about Bradley Brown?' He leaned back in his corner. 'That bloody little stirrer, Sash, I bet. Next time I see her, she really will feel my hand across her backside, if not my belt.'

She went cold.

'No she won't. That's assault, and it wasn't Sash, it was Len.' She told him what Helena told her. 'You must've had some inkling Annabel had fallen in love with someone else. Felt something about it. But you never once thought of talking to me. We were supposedly in some sort of relationship Adam.'

Another silence filled only by the cicadas' saw. They were getting on her nerves. He got to his feet, with his back to her, he stood between the open patio doors.

'Don't know why she didn't just have a bit of a fling. I've given her everything, she ever wanted. Children. Her idea, children.' He paused. 'Built her a studio so that she could piddle about with her painting, her ceramics. She's the one who's given Len the idea of going to Art School.'

He walked over to the table where he had left his wine, he drained the glass, and emptied the remains of the bottle into it. He pulled out a chair, sat at the table, and took a sip. The heat had drained out of her body.

'Bradley Brown!' He snorted. 'Typical Yankee name.'

'You're jealous?'

'Bloody angry, always been fond of her.'

At one time, the barbs of the little green demon would have pierced. She had the impression his physical relationship with Annabel was non-existent. She had tried to find out, subtly, she hoped, but he saw through her. Humoured her, made clear, the subject was not one for discussion. 'You've no reason to be jealous', he had told her to trust him. For the most part, she had. Tess was right, when it came to people, she could be incredibly naïve.

'Perhaps Bradley makes Annabel happy.' She remembered Helena's words, couldn't forgo the dig.

'Annabel's trouble was promising more than she delivered.' He fiddled with the stem of his wine glass, not meeting her gaze. She sat all attention. 'Twenty eight when I met her. Never been in love. Bedded girls naturally. Sex for me was like a dry martini before dinner.'

She was not as naive as to imagine Annabel had been his first.

'Never pretended to be other than a normal, red-blooded male. Getting back to Annabel . . .'

He had met her at one of his parents' rather dire parties, for Annabel the equivalent of being grounded. A year off 'A' levels, she'd been expelled from boarding school for smoking dope. He dated her over that summer, and before he knew it, she was demanding a shag, her terminology.

'Claimed she'd never done it before. I refused to oblige.'

Calista began to feel sick. She got up, she kicked over her empty glass, barely registered its shattering on the tiles, made for the open doorway, took in great gulps of hot, jasmine-scented air, turned to look at him, leaning her back against the jamb.

'How noble of you to hang fire.'

'Her parents were friends of my parents. I hung fire, as you so charmingly put it, until our wedding night. True, she was a virgin.'

He sat with his arms resting on the table, both hands pinning the base of his glass to its surface. He was looking into the glass, not at her. She was sure her head would burst, the heat, the nausea. She closed her eyes. She willed her breath to moderate, listened. It was as though he were talking to a priest. Annabel's parents agreed to the marriage because they thought he would be a steadying influence. He miscalculated, big time. He was. Annabel morphed from fun-loving rebel into wife in the space of no time at all.

'I don't know why she imagined getting herself pregnant accidentally-on-purpose was a good idea. Little more than a child herself I was absolutely furious.'

A pause. She opened her eyes.

'Takes two to make a baby. You must have been f f f . . .'

'Once I knew she was pregnant, I didn't. Moved to a room of my own. A long, long time after Len was born, before I went near her again.'

She felt faint, and, despite the heat, shivery. Making for the nearest chair, she sat opposite him.

'How could you be so vile?' She was surprised he heard her.

'I was, wasn't I?' He looked across at her. 'Then Helena arrived, my absolutely perfect daughter. Once Annabel gave me Len, I forgave her everything.'

'Forgave her for having your child.'

'I decided we should make a go of it, and when I suggested we try for a second, Annabel was happier than she'd been for a long time.'

The silence thrumming to the cicadas beat was suffocating. She concentrated on her own hands resting on the table. She took a deep breath.

'If you didn't go near Annabel, what happened to your red-blooded masculinity?'

'You're worldly enough to know a man in my position has no trouble finding women to accommodate his needs.'

Her eyes met an expression of amused scepticism.

'You complete and utter shit.' The words almost choked her.

'Don't be so suburban.'

'You cold calculating bastard.'

'Not types you'd break up a marriage for.' - *Including me*, she thought.

- 'As long as Annabel was my wife, I never totally severed relations with her.'

His words slithered snake-like to coil inside her head. She had trusted him, believed him when he had hinted he and Annabel stayed together for their children's sake. Before she could think, act, he reached across, his cool dry hands gripping hers. He impaled her very soul with his gaze.

'And then you came along.'

'I . . . I . . . Cheat on me, Adam. We're finished.'

He leaned towards her. She could see the sweat droplets on his upper lip feel his breath in her face. 'I see. Your past misdemeanours are okay.'

'My . . . my . . . You swore I had no reason to be jealous of Annabel.'

'You had no reason. What I feel for you is . . . different.' His grip tightened, as though he wanted to break every bone in her fingers.

She doubted he knew the meaning of love. She was only just beginning to. She tried to free herself from his grip.

'Let go. You're hurting me.' Her body convulsed. 'Oh my God.'

He let her go. She rushed out and across the terrace to heave partially digested *salade nicoise* over the retaining wall into the oleander bushes. Leaning forward, hands clenched into fists, the rough stone capping of the wall grazed her knuckles. Arms braced, she waited for the paroxysms to abate. Flinching, she felt his hand stroking her back.

'Here darling, drink this.' Taking her by the hair, he pulled her head back and put the glass to her lips. She gulped down cool water.

Physically, emotionally drained, she was conscious of pain in her right foot. Looking down, she saw blood. He picked her up - she hadn't the strength to break away - carrying her like a baby into the house and up the stairs.

'You've trodden on the glass you broke.'

He swabbed the gash in her foot with antiseptic and bandaged it.

Before she took to her bed, he made her take a salt tablet, drink more water.

'You've a touch of heat stroke. Try and sleep.'

Dark when she roused. Adam lay with his back towards her. Half awake, she snuggled against him.

'I'm forgiven then?'

She turned away, remembering.

'I trusted you.'

He pulled her on to her back, pegging her down. 'What I told you was all B.C.'

'B.C?'

'Before Cal.'

'If I ever suspect . . .'

He loomed over her, put his hand over her mouth, and forced open her legs, a rough game he used to like to play. She was stupid ever to have colluded. She bit into his hand, hard.

'Bitch.'

He rolled off, and swung himself out of bed, took himself to the other bedroom. Her eyes filled with tears. She was infuriated with herself, and if he thought he was punishing her by leaving her alone . . .

CHAPTER TWENTY SIX

Wednesday

Adam was up early and almost finished breakfast by the time she went down.

'Feeling better?' He smiled across the table as though nothing had happened between them, announced that morning he was off with Yiorgos in his boat. He was curious to see the property near Fiskardo on Cephalonia Yiorgos's maternal grandparents had left him. Yiorgos had plans for its development.

Thank you, God. She would have almost a whole day to herself.

The sound of a vehicle on the track, the toot of a horn, Yiorgos come to take Adam down to the harbour in his pick-up. As he was leaving, 'By the way,' his tone disparaging, 'I met your acquaintance, PJ last night. He drinks rose.'

She and PJ were destined never to meet again. Desolate, she went down to the beach to lose herself in nature. Only three more days, she wanted to be alive to the sounds and smells of Ithaca, sea on shingle, those unrelenting cicadas, the scent of herbs and pine, feeling the sun's warmth on her body. She loved to register the sea's ever-changing hue, that morning jade dappled with turquoise, and where sea met sky, rich lapis lazuli. Blue and green the colours of healing, heart's unease her disease. 'Time's a great healer,' her grandmother used to say. Trite but true.

She had been gullible. Tess used to try to make her see it didn't add up, Annabel's complacency. Another old saying, 'You've made your bed

. . .' but Gran would never have gone along with that. She would have remade it.

Taking off her sunglasses, she put them away, and leaning back, closed eyes swollen from weeping. As always the sea's schurr, schurr on shingle began to lull her to sleep. She roused herself, sat up, annoyed. She would not spend this glorious day asleep.

'Bloody cheek.' she said out loud. Some yachties had anchored just off her cove, and one of them was rowing an inflatable towards her beach. The oarsman turned to look over his shoulder.

PJ. Her heart raced, stomach churned, she had difficulty drawing breath. She leapt up. Waving with both hands, she ran into the water to meet him. Too late, she remembered. She was topless. She covered her breasts with her hands, sensing her chest, her neck, her cheeks become even hotter, as he turned to face her, his eyes impenetrable behind Ray-Bans.

'An unexpected bonus. My very own Page Three Girl.'

PJ jumped out of the dinghy and beached it, chuckling. He wore surfers' shorts, his chest and stomach as lean and spare as she remembered. He stood for a moment, hands on hips, that sardonic smile on his face. Although his eyes were hidden, she sensed in daylight she passed muster.

'Cal, come on.' He gestured her to join him on land. Laughing, but still embarrassed, she took his hand, offered to help her from the water. His touch was like an electric shock.

'What are you doing here?'

'Well, Hi there, P.J., how nice to see you again.' Falsetto, then in his own baritone, 'Hi Cal! I've dropped in to say Good-bye cos every time I think I'll catch up with you, you're like Macavity. Not there.'

They made their way towards the sun-beds, PJ not letting go her hand till they arrived. She immediately draped a pareo around her to conceal her naked top-half.

That smile. 'They're really nothing to be ashamed of.'

'Just in case, someone might . . .'

She sat sideways on her sunbed. He pushed the other out of the way to sit crossed-ankles in front of her. He removed his shades. She looked into his eyes, for a moment she stopped breathing, a tingling sensation an inner warmth matching that of the sun's on her body. She struggled to maintain some semblance of sangfroid.

'Thanks for comparing me to a depraved ginger tom cat. Where are you going? Back to Vathi?'

'To spend a couple of days with Ma before my next assignment.'

'Your mother lives in Vathi?'

'Thought I told you, we have a house to the south.'

He lived with his mum. She resisted the temptation to laugh.

'Ma lives here most of the year. She only goes back to England for monitoring, and treatment.' She hadn't seen him look sad before. 'Cancer. She says if she's going to die, she wants to do it where she feels at home.'

'I'm so sorry PJ.' She stretched forward, touched his hands.

'In remission at the moment.' He smiled, shyly for him. 'You must come and see her next year, fingers crossed, the gods willing, and all that.'

'I'd like that.' How sweet of him to want her to meet his mother. 'Always assuming I come back.'

'But Burgess has built a villa, a biggish one, so that he can bring his daughters.' - She had to suppress a smile at his intonation of Burgess. - 'He told me last night.'

'Hell or high water, whatever happens, I don't think anything, or anyone, could keep me away from this beautiful island,' she said.

'A date, then.'

'A date.'

'Burgess said you weren't well.' PJ looked concerned.

'Touch of heat-stroke.' She longed to confide in him. Tell him, how disillusioned, how unhappy she was. 'Why do you call my husband Burgess, not Adam?'

'Cos when we were introduced, he never suggested I should. I sure as hell ain't gonna refer to him as Mister Burgess.' He knuckled his forelock.

'He's gone to Fiskardo with Yiorgos.'

'I know. I watched them set sail. Are you sure you're okay? Your eyes look puffy.'

She told him she was feeling much better. She didn't add, how much seeing him again lifted her spirits.

'You've been crying,' clipped statement of fact. The intensity of those deep-blue eyes pierced her very being.

'About nothing.' No use protesting she hadn't. 'Since the mugging, the slightest thing . . .' She could see he was not convinced. 'And alcoholic remorse.' She told him about witnessing the body being brought out of the sea on Sunday, then drinking too much wine that evening, plus a Metaxa with Marcos.'

'The police are questioning everybody who sails in the area.'

'I was terrified it might be you.' She blurted it out.

He looked shocked.

'I imagined you all alone, an accident, you hit your head fell overboard, *Thelma Jane* drifting away. I was so relieved when Marcos told me he'd seen you with Brian and his partner.'

'Calista Blake, what's to become of you?' He shook his head. 'I've been in far more dangerous places than sailing the Ionian Sea. You spend too much time on your own.'

'Being alone never used to bother me.' She told him how, before she married, she chose to live on her own, never finding it a drag.

'There's being sufficient unto one's self, and there's being lonely, not that I've ever really felt that till . . .' a disturbing intimation of longing clouded his face before he gave one of his smiles. 'Anyway, right now Ma needs me to be there for her, which reminds me . . .' Glancing at his watch before putting on his Ray-Bans, he stood in one smooth movement. 'She'll be expecting me.'

She too got to her feet, wanted to say please stay just a little longer. Next year was so far away

'Before I go.' He fumbled under the flap of a pocket in his shorts, producing a card. 'My Vathy address, my London address, my E-mail address, my mobile number. Send me a postcard, or a message from time to time, just to say you're okay. Promise?'

'I promise.' She clasped the card, her most valuable possession, and placed it in the zipped compartment of her beach bag.

'And, Cal . . . remember this. If you're ever in trouble, if for some reason, any reason you need me, I promise I'll come running. Okay?'

She nodded. She was choked.

'Good girl.'

They made their way slowly toward the inflatable.

'Next year I'll teach you to sail' PJ said as she helped him float the tender off the beach.

She wanted to say, take me with you, let me meet your mother. Next year may be too late. She couldn't say any such thing for fear of upsetting him. She couldn't tell PJ how content, how secure she felt, at the same time all of a tingle when she was with him.

'Eh, that melancholy face again. Like that night we met.' He kissed her cheek. She longed for him to kiss her lips. She understood why he didn't.

Near to tears, she managed to smile. 'How I hate Good-byes.'

He climbed in the inflatable and set up the oars.

'Not Good-bye, Cal, *Au revoir*. And don't forget, once in a while, let your inner rebel escape.'

He began to pull away. She took a few steps further till she was up to her knees.

'PJ, are you an archaeologist?'

'God, no.' He rested the oars. 'That was my father.' He began rowing again.

She waded in deeper. 'What do you do?'

'I take photographs. Tell stories with them. True ones.' He was pulling farther and farther away.

'Where do you take them?' Her pareo, unfurled, floated around her. Immersed in seawater up to her midriff, she was naked above the waist.

'Where-ever there's trouble.' He rested once more on his oars. '*Twins of a gazelle*,' he called. 'What memory to carry with me. *Twins of a gazelle*.' He gave a deep throated chuckle before carrying on.

Twins of a gazelle? What was he talking about? He had gone too far to ask. She watched him haul up the tender, weigh anchor. He was using the engine. He waved. She waved. She waited till the *Thelma Jane* disappeared round the headland.

Feeling profound sadness relieved by only a smidgeon of joy, she waded back trailing the pareo. A whole year before they would meet again, but he wanted them to keep in touch. He had made her promise.

Almost seven in the evening when Adam returned carrying shopping bags. She had showered and changed ready for dinner, and was sitting reading on the terrace. He put his bags down on the table and, with a flourish, unpacked a packet of smoked ham, some *mortadella*, a tub of aubergine salad and one of stuffed olives – 'Antipasti' he said. Then he produced a packet of fusilli, tinned tomatoes, and finally onions, courgettes, okra, and a lump of hard cheese.

'I thought we might have dinner by candlelight here on the terrace. I'll make a pasta dish, like I used to in the flat. All you need do is prepare a bit of salad.'

A candlelit dinner sounded ominous. She would much prefer to go to Marcos's.

'Hope you don't mind staying in,' he said. 'Been quite a long day. I could do with an early night.'

An early night, even more ominous.

He gathered up his purchases. 'Better shower and change before I start cooking.'

'That's okay,' she said. 'I can wait. I might even finish my book.' *And tomorrow, if left to her own devices, immersed in Ithaca's magic, she could alternate between reading, daydreaming, remembering every gesture made, every word spoken by Mr PJ Wood. On Friday, a farewell lunch with Kristina and cute Dhionysius. Saturday, back to same old, same old.*

Once upon a time she would have delighted in dinner on the terrace in the stillness of an evening perfumed by jasmine. And would now with the love of her life. In the event she and Adam both mucked in to produce an acceptable meal. Adam brought out a bottle of chilled rose.

'Seeing that chap drinking it reminded me how much you like it.'

After Sunday night she had vowed to lay off alcohol for a few days. One glass wouldn't hurt. Each sip would remind her of PJ.

'How was your day?' Adam said. They started on their antipasti. 'Quiet?'

Bittersweet, truth to tell, she thought. 'Were you impressed with Yiorgos's plans,' she said.

'He's certainly studied his market when it comes to providing well-kitted out studios and bungalows for Greek island fans.' Adam looked thoughtful as he cut into a slice of smoked ham. 'Beneath that ingenuous, honest exterior lurks a shrewd business man.'

'Don't know why you're surprised about his commercial acumen.' She took a sip of wine. *Wish you were here, PJ.* 'Yiorgos has travelled the world, and been in charge of an oil tanker.'

'And ends up marrying Kristina, a migrant worker. Nice enough woman, but no looker.' He made a show of tasting the wine. 'Not bad, maybe you're friend's right about drinking rose in this climate.'

'Kristina has had the sort of life we have no concept of.' Calista felt the heat creep up her neck into her face. 'We read about deprivation and hardship. To people like us it's just words.' She drank more wine. *Must make it last*, she told herself. *Just the one glass, remember.* 'And you've overlooked the obvious. Yiorgos and Kristina are devoted to each other. What's more, his parents have taken to her. They're a real close-knit family. I know. I've seen how they behave first hand.'

'That's me well and truly told.' He gave a rueful smile. 'Time to dish up the pasta.'

'Talking of family . . .' he said as they began to eat. 'When Len and Sash came to stay, you got on okay with them, didn't you? In fact, you seem to have quite a rapport with Len.'

'They were really no trouble,' she said. 'They're your daughters, Adam. Perhaps you should come to some sort of semi-formal arrangement with Annabel.'

'We can do better than that. How do you feel about their making their home with us? They shouldn't be too intrusive. Term-time they'll be away at school, for part of the holidays visiting Annabel.'

'Is there a problem with Annabel and Bradley?' She imagined Sasha playing up.

'Only if you count their being dragged over to Boston to live.'

'Lincolnshire, surely that's no big deal?'

'For heaven's sake, Cal, Boston, Massachusetts. That's where they're on holiday.' He explained Bradley Brown, a visiting academic at Loughborough University, was returning to the Institute of Technology there. Brown was happy to take the girls on. 'But, I'll not have them Americanized. I told Annabel, if necessary, I'd take her to Court to prevent it. Married to you, I can provide the girls with a settled environment. Any judge would look on that favourably. In the event, Annabel and I have come to an amicable agreement.'

Maybe, no more than a couple of heartbeats before she replied. 'So that's why you married me. There was I thinking you couldn't bear to live without me.' She was surprised she wasn't more hurt, angrier. In any case, she could not be more disillusioned than she was already.

'Don't be silly, darling.' Leaning across the table, he stroked her cheek. She was tempted to bite his hand, again. 'I show you how much I love you as often as you allow.'

'When will the girls be moving in?'

Adam told her the August Bank Holiday weekend. 'We'll have a week to prepare for them. Most of their stuff will have already arrived when we get back. Don't frown. Before we left, I told Pam to expect it.'

'How long have you known Annabel and Bradley might take them to the States?'

'Soon as they rushed to get married.'

'And you wait till ten or so days before the girls are due to move in to tell me. Did it not occur to you to discuss this with me right from the start?'

His culinary efforts, the wine were all about manipulation, not because he was trying to make amends for yesterday. No wonder Annabel upped sticks. When was a marriage, or a relationship for that matter, not one in any meaning of the words? Adam Burgess didn't believe in mutual decision-making. He was used to riding rough shod over all lesser beings. *I've news for you, Adam. I'm not one of them.* She did not speak the words out loud.

'I didn't want to spoil your holiday,' he said.

He bloody well knew she meant before he sweet-talked her into marrying him. Then he would have had to tell her about the real reason for his divorce, and . . . She should be raging mad.

I'm not naïve, Tess. I'm a gullible eejit.

Let it go, Calista Blake.

Okay, but only for now, she told herself.

CHAPTER
TWENTY SEVEN

Homecoming Day One

She and Adam arrived home late Saturday evening. To Adam's annoyance, Beppo fussed round her, wagging his tail, jumped up, pawing. She fondled his ears, kissed the top of his muzzle. 'I've missed you too, old boy,' Calista said.

'He'll be an absolutely useless gun dog,' Adam said, 'thanks to you.'

After a light supper, Adam went straight to bed. She and Beppo took a stroll, she wishing PJ were with them to gaze at the stars. '. . . *A couple of days with Ma before my next assignment,*' he said. *Where are you P.J? Where are you?* 'Where-ever there's trouble,' he told her. Before turning in, she sent him an Email. – *Back at the Old Rectory,* gave her address, and mobile number, then added *I'm good. Hope you and your mother are too. Your turn, Cal xx.* She couldn't think what else to say.

Around nine on Sunday evening she took refuge in her study, made herself comfortable in one of the Club chairs, only her desk lamp giving light. With Beppo on the window seat for company, she called Esther. 'How are things? Can you talk?'

Esther could. Calista heard her say, 'Mike, Cal. I'll take this in the kitchen.' The sound of a door closing, 'I've so much to tell you,' Esther said. Then the scrape of chair legs on a slate floor, Calista pictured Esther making herself comfortable in one of the carvers, a cushion under her bottom and at her back.

'Me too, you go first,' Calista said. 'Your two weeks on Corfu delivered?'

'Sort of. We all loved Sidari. Warm, starlit nights on the terrace sitting over a good bottle of wine, the scent of herbs. Not the place to nurture animosity.'

'What about sex, making love?'

'We were affectionate. It was as though we were getting to know each other all over again. And we've made up for months of abstinence this past week.' Esther told her about her and Mike's god awful row which concluded with her kicking him in the genitals.

'Tess.'

'Wasn't on purpose. Don't laugh. Next day, I went home to mother.' Calista heard her sigh into the phone. 'Lucky for me Mike and my mum adore each other . . . and . . . We've a few more days on our own. Kath's not bringing Tom and Fran back until Saturday.' Another heartfelt sigh. 'When we got home we talked, without rancour this time. He told me the company doctor thought his inability to perform was because Mike believed I didn't want him, didn't need him. And the stress of the job contributed, of course. Anyways, no problem now. We still love each other, Cal.'

'Course you do.'

'Next week I'm going with him to Amsterdam,' Esther said. 'First of the month, there's some reception for bigwigs, the launch of his company's offshoot. Be a chance to check out this swish apartment he's rented.' Esther told her about Mike's being based there.

'A whole year. That's worse than Adam's London sorties.' Not that I now care how long he stays away, she thought.

'Mike says he'll be back most weekends.' Esther sounded doubtful. 'The alternative is, we all go with him. I could possibly wangle some sort of sabbatical. I'm not committing myself. Wouldn't be until the New Year. If at all.'

'Go for it Tess. You and Mike, you're . . .' Calista heard the catch in her voice.

'Don't worry darling. No way are we going back to the way we've been lately. Your turn. Was Ithaca just as romantic third time round? Do you feel less lonely?'

Her turn for a heartfelt sigh. 'I'm . . . I'm like one of Adam's trout lured by an iridescent fly. I succumbed to temptation, took a nibble. Too late. Adam reeled me in. Now I'm floundering in his net.'

'Umm, almost poetic,' Esther said. 'Except, "fly", "nibble", nudge, wink . . .'

Calista giggled. Hearing the click of the door latch, 'Hang on a minute, Tess.'

Adam poked his head round the door. 'Are you two still gossiping? I'm whacked, off to bed. Night, night.'

Calista wished him Good night, then glanced at her watch. She and Esther had been talking for over an hour.

'Okay, Adam's gone to bed. Where's Mike?'

'Happily reading some thriller. You were saying. Have you tackled Adam yet, about Annabel wanting the divorce?'

'While we were away. Thought now or never.' Then remembered what Adam had told her that afternoon had made her physically sick, Calista shuddered. 'He's the most devious, manipulative, cold-hearted . . .' She related all that Adam had said about his first marriage.

'And he actually told you, sex for him was like a dry martini before dinner?' Esther's tone resonated disapproval.

'I warned him, cheat on me . . . With his track record don't doubt he already has.' Another deep sigh. 'You know Stevie Smith's poem, *Not waving, but drowning* . . .'

'Silly, you've just said you're a trout. Make a hole in that net, swim free. You can do it, Cal.'

'Tess, I'm being submerged by Adam's schemes, his fancy villa, un-necessarily desecrating part of an old olive grove. And why? So that he can invite his bloody sister and brother-in-law, and God knows who. I'll be the last to know. Can understand he might want Len and Sash to have a holiday with us, but . . . And that's another sneaky fait accompli, they're going to make their home here, not with their mother.' She told Esther why. 'Poor kids. Obvious now why Adam didn't want us to carry on living in sin, why he insisted we move out of my flat to somewhere bigger. What came over me, Tess?'

'You were duped by his charm, darling. Even Mike was impressed. And Adam's well fit for a man of his vintage. Also, he is very rich.'

'You're saying I married him for his money?' She had believed she knew him – they'd been lovers for a good two years for God's sake - the life-style he offered maybe had been just too tempting to resist. She knew better now.

'Cal, you know I don't for one minute think you . . . '

'May surprise you, allegedly me such a clever clogs, I don't exactly know how much he's worth.'

'I said you were naïve. Thank God I talked you into a pre-nup.'

'And thank God, in the event of the marriage breaking down, neither of us has any claim on the other's assets, such as mine are compared with his.'

'Little wonder he snapped your hand off. But, what if there are children, Cal? I did say.'

'Trust me. There won't be any.' She took a deep breath. 'I've something to confess.' She told Esther about PJ Wood.

'Oh, My, God,' Esther said.

'Promise you won't tell anyone else, Tess. Not even Mike.'

Before ending the call, they also promised each other after Esther returned from Amsterdam they would make a date and catch up with developments.

Beppo asleep, Calista sat for a while relishing the stillness. Talking about PJ she had relived their precious, all-too-brief time together. She had not spelt out what she believed. She had found the love of her life, although all she knew about PJ was: he was thirty three, he sailed, part of the time he lived with his mother on Ithaca, and, from a couple of throw-away lines, she thought he must be a photo-journalist. Less than twenty four hours spent with him, and it was as though she had known him all her life. No doubt Esther would have told her not to be daft. To an observer, she and PJ had just had a helluva steamy one-night-stand. But, he had sought her out to say Good-bye, told her to keep in touch, and promised he would come running if she needed him. That had been less than a week ago. Her sigh was so loud, she woke the dog. He jumped down and rested his muzzle on her knee. She caressed his head.

'Darling loyal Beppo,' she said. 'You'll help me endure won't you, the days, the weeks, the months ahead?'

CHAPTER TWENTY EIGHT

Homecoming Day Two

Next day, Monday, when she woke up she was nauseous. Nerves, Calista imagined, having to come back to same old, same old. A fasting breakfast, hot water with a slice of lemon, a round of dry toast allayed the feeling. As soon as she thought he would be there, she called her Chambers Clerk. She would welcome something above and beyond the couple or so briefs she had well in hand, something new and demanding to keep her mind occupied, anything providing an excuse to take her out of the house. She was not optimistic, too much to expect in August.

'Quiet at the moment, Miss Blake, as per. I'll let you know as soon as something tasty comes in.'

Nothing for it but to make sure the Old Rectory was ready for the onslaught of two teenage girls. She wondered what they would expect, what they would need. They were Adam's daughters, for God's sake. He should be dealing with this. Just for once he was making use of his office in the old stable block, connecting online to his City HQ, and beyond. She was amazed he had managed the technology without the help of the young-smartarses he surrounded himself with.

In the undercroft, Pam had stored crates of Helena's and Sasha's belongings which had arrived whilst she and Adam were away. Best leave them for the girls to sort, she decided. She wandered upstairs to inspect their rooms. Both were, pro tem, minimally furnished, and no use second guessing what else they might want. They could choose. Her feeling of wanting to be sick had passed – *had to be nerves* she told herself, *like earlier on in the year feeling sick at the thought of food and not eating.* A sunny late-August morning, pleasantly warm, a long leisurely walk across the fields with Beppo beckoned. They could return via the next village and a pub lunch.

The Old Rectory was the last house at the top of the village. She walked up the lane until on her right she came to a five-barred gate into a meadow, beside it a stile onto a footpath leading to the top of a steep hill. She let Beppo off his leash. Blackberries were almost ripe in the hedge. 'Next time we come,' she said, 'we'll pick some.'

A long way from the sea, about as far as you could be in England, she wondered if rambling over the countryside was the sort of landlubber's activity PJ might enjoy. She imagined him by her side like they had walked together along the track through the olive trees that unforgettable night. Adam seemed only to like walking if he had a golf club in his hand, or touting a shotgun in pursuit of some hapless game bird. Those pursuits were networking, not for pleasure. She arrived at the top of the hill, climbed another stile, and before edging along the side of a huge expanse of stubble, she paused. A good vantage point to view the rolling verdant landscape, unspectacular but easy on the eye. PJ might enjoy it too, except his English address was in London E1. Perhaps he liked the contrast, London's buzz, tranquil Ithaca – '. . . *nothing quite like scudding along through the swell, the sound of the wind in her sails*'.

Living in the country had certainly grown on her. Pam was right. Walking was better than going to the gym for chasing the blues away, but for Beppo, something she might not have bothered to do. 'I'm sure he would like you, Beppo – I'm talking PJ now – I don't see how he couldn't, and you would have to like him, of course.'

PJ had not yet acknowledged her email. Perhaps he had not received it. Tomorrow, or maybe wait till Wednesday, if she still hadn't heard, she would send another. *Where are you, PJ? Where are you?* Fragments surfaced - '*I take photographs. Tell stories with them. True ones.*' – '*Wherever there's trouble.*' He probably had far more pressing preoccupations than to email her. ¬– '*I've been in far more dangerous places than sailing the Ionian Sea.*' She stood still.

'I couldn't bear anything bad happening to him, Beppo. But how would I know?'

Silly cow, you have his Ithaca address. You could send a snail-mail letter there, and if . . . if . . . even if his mother was . . . surely someone would write back, let me know if . . . She continued walking. *What if he hadn't replied because he'd changed his mind about keeping in touch? Get a grip Calista Blake, it's only thirty six hours since you sent the message, and if he's travelling in the back-o'-beyond . . . If he had changed his mind about keeping in touch, she knew him. PJ would have the decency to say.*

'No use, Beppo, I'll have to try and be patient, just a few more days.'

Over another stile, the footpath joined a bridleway, one side bordered by hawthorn interspersed with elder already bearing luscious berries, and every so often dotted with the occasional oak or ash, on the other a wire fence enclosing grazing sheep. She called Beppo to heel. They descended the slope, farther down another meadow partitioned off containing horses.

A conversation with Adam over dinner at Marcos's, the last night of their holiday. She had been curious.

'Where did Annabel meet Bradley?'

'At the stables where she kept her horse.' He gave a derisive equine snort. 'They're both enthusiastic riders.'

She had tried to think of what she and Adam liked doing together, apart from eating, drinking, and sex. She had completely gone off the latter. With him anyway. They both liked music, their tastes overlapping a little. Adam liked to go fishing. She liked the theatre, going to the cinema. He preferred staying in with a DVD. Since being married, they were to be seen together at all important social functions. After Adam had split up with Annabel, she supposed she had saved his face. She and Adam were little different from many couples who managed to rub along. She wanted, had expected better.

Adam had told her, in July Brown moved back to the States, taking Annabel with him. 'No wonder she was putting on weight,' he said. 'She's pregnant, and they were determined it'd be born over there. Due early October.'

'Are they pleased to be having a baby?'

'She took great delight in telling me. They plan to have another as soon as they can, in which case she'll have to get a move on. No problem for him. He's six years younger.' It rankled. She heard it in his voice. 'Won't last. Not with that age difference.'

'Less than between you and me.'

'That's the more usual way round,' he said

She smiled at the memory of feeling smug when she discovered she was five months older than PJ, choking on her food at his reaction – '*I've a weakness for older women.*'

'He was such a tease, Beppo, doing his best to wind me up. Later, something he said, he was really only trying to cheer me up. To begin with, I was irritated and fascinated by him. He has this sardonic smile, but he's not really mocking you. It's just the way his face arranges itself when he's in a good humour. And do you know, despite a whole night spent together, I still don't know what PJ stands for.' She had to see him again, if only to find out that. Who was she kidding, her body, her very soul ached to be with him again, and again, and again.

She and Beppo had got to the top of a second ridge where the bridleway made a T with the remnants of an old Roman road. She felt her iPhone vibrate in the pocket of her jeans, took it out to check, and wished she had left it at home. Adam. Nevertheless she answered.

'Where are you, Cal? I've been looking for you all over. Wondered if you'd like a lunchtime bite at the pub.'

'Beppo and I are out walking,' she said. 'The plan is to call in for lunch on our way home.'

'Great, I'll meet you there. How far away are you?'

'From the pub, say twenty, minutes, half an hour max. We're in no hurry.'

'I'll bring the car.'

'For heaven's sake, Adam. If you set out now, dawdling you'll get there about the same time as us.'

'Then we'll have to hoof it all the way back.'

'Yeah, all of a mile and a bit. See you.' She ended the call and continued walking Beppo and her thoughts for company.

With Len and Sash at boarding school, if Annabel felt as lonely as she had since marrying Adam, little wonder she fell for someone else. She wondered if there was anything to be said in Adam's favour. 'I don't know why she didn't just have a bit of a fling,' he had said about Annabel's affair. Somehow she didn't see him as a complaisant husband. He had been determined to keep control of his daughters. Short-term, having them around might relieve the monotony of life with him. Long-term . . . Right now, she didn't want to think further ahead than next week.

When they arrived at the pub, Adam was waiting outside. He had not driven. 'Quite pleasant walking here, and really not all that far.'

After her Spartan breakfast, and the walk she was hungry. Ale-batter fish and chips hit the spot, though, while Adam drank a pint of local beer, she opted for carbonated mineral water. She had really gone off alcohol since that Sunday night.

On their way home, Adam told her next day he would have to go up to London. 'Unavoidable, I'm afraid, darling.'

'Just for the day?' she said, testing.

'A couple, back on Thursday in time for dinner.'

'Don't you get tired of staying in that huge impersonal hotel?'

'Odd you should say that. Actually, I think it would make sense if I invested in a pied-a-terre.'

Wouldn't it just, she thought.

No more conversation, they had arrived home. Adam elected to go for a swim, she to the sitting room. She planned to start *The Girl Who Kicked the Hornet's Nest*, the last of the trilogy. 'Thank you, Matt for lending me them,' she said to the silence. 'Lisbeth Salander, my kind of girl.'

CHAPTER TWENTY NINE

Step-daughters

On Saturday Adam disturbed her as he got up before dawn complaining of only having had four hours sleep. He was to drive to Heathrow to pick up Helena and Sasha. *They're your daughters*, she muttered half asleep herself.

She was grateful to Pam volunteering to come in until lunchtime to help, and, as soon as she heard the cattle grid's rattle, Pam began to prepare breakfast which, Calista said, they would eat in the kitchen.

'What's wrong with the dining room?' Adam said, while the girls were freshening up.

'We always breakfast in the kitchen,' Calista said.

'Just thought, their first day . . .' Adam sounded put out, no more than she was by his absurd idea.

'Len and Sash aren't visitors,' she said.

Adam and Helena sat on one side of the antique pine table, she and Sasha on the other, she keeping them company with a bowl of easily digested, porridge drizzled with honey, Pam's suggestion for soothing her stomach which had rebelled at the idea of a Full English despite her hot-water, dry-toast palliative first thing.

'What no waffles? No maple syrup?' Sasha, affecting an American drawl, surveyed the bacon rashers, sausages, scrambled egg, grilled tomatoes, mushrooms, hot buttered toast.

Both girls were red-eyed and pasty with travel fatigue. Nevertheless they managed to polish off large helpings of everything. After they had finished eating, since for them it was still the middle of the night, Calista suggested they might like a nap.

'Is it okay if we unpack some of our stuff from home?' Helena said.

'You'd better check if there's anything you need before you go back to St Mary's,' Adam said. 'Let Cal know.' He smiled across the table. 'You'll sort it, won't you darling?'

Resentment followed amazement. She was on the verge of snapping, they're your daughters. Helena got in first.

'We won't need to bother Cal,' she said, 'so long as you pay up, like handing us over your credit card.'

How mean-spirited that made her feel, Sasha and Helena were her step-daughters. She anticipated tension enough without her having a hissy. When she was a teenager, she and her mother used to have humdingers of rows, about her clothes, staying out, not studying. No matter how much she and Mum shouted, they always made up. No such unconditional bond between step-mother and step-daughter.

He was on his feet. 'Whatever you want.' He sounded offhand. 'If you'll excuse me, I'm meeting Dando and a couple of other chaps for a round of golf.'

'Did it not cross your mind, Len and Sash might've liked you to be around this morning?' Calista said.

'You don't need me, surely. See you all later.' He paused at the door. 'By the way Len, who do you think has been coughing up for the two of you all these years? Your mother was good at spending money, not making it.' He shut the door behind him none too quietly.

Helena grinned across the table at Sasha. 'Same old Dad.'

Calista and the girls had carried most of their treasures from the under-croft to their rooms. They started off meaning to take only essentials, leaving the rest for the odd-job man. They got carried away by a collective frenzy which, Calista presumed, judging by the way she felt herself, was symptomatic of underlying anxiety.

Calista surveyed the mess of boxes in Helena's room. 'If you don't particularly like the furniture, or the calico coloured walls, we could . . .'

'But the colour, the furniture suits the house. I know it's not real Victorian wrought iron but I love my bed with its white applique linen.' Helena took a deep breath in. 'Everywhere smells of lavender. And I love this old wardrobe.'

'A Biedemeier, circa eighteen-twenty, I was really pleased when I found it,' Calista said.

On the surface, as always, Helena was equable, self-contained. Calista could not be sure, maybe she was already beginning to settle in. She left her filling the wardrobe with clothes.

Next door Sasha's room, similarly decorated, similarly disordered, boxes containing books, DVDs, one of distressed cuddly toys, one of old stones which turned out to be fossils. Clothes were piled on the bed which was the same style as Helena's, a laptop on the bedside table.

Calista walked over to the window and gazed out over fields of rotting stubble, of desiccated grasses, at tired trees and hedgerows, their leaves, their berries yet to be transformed into autumnal reds and gold. She always found the fag end of August depressing, more so than ever that year. A week near as dammit since she sent her email, and still no word from PJ She had taken to combing TV news channels for bulletins about current trouble spots, Afghanistan, Libya . . . No specific mention of a British photo-journalist among the casualties. She became conscious of Sasha standing at her elbow.

'Cal, don't be sad. I'll try not to annoy you.'

She turned to face her.

'I'm not unhappy because of you.' She gestured toward the view. 'Summer, with all its promises, has gone.' Sultry, an over-cast sky was not helping her mood.

'Could be that time of the month.' Blushing, Sasha sounded sympathetic. 'Your period coming on.'

'Maybe.' *If only,* she thought, and patted Sasha's arm. 'Just be yourself, Sash. I daresay you will exasperate me, but I was a teenager myself not all that long ago.'

'Not as long ago as Dad, that's for sure.'

'And he was a boy, perhaps even more of a handicap.' Calista spoke her thoughts aloud.

'What was he like?' Sasha threw back her head and laughed. 'Imagine, covered in acne, wet dreams.'

'Sash' She felt her mouth twitch.

'You won't tell him.' Sasha had the grace to blush.

'As long as you promise not to be put out if I lose my cool, and scream at you.'

'Mum does that all the time.'

Whilst Calista surveyed the room assessing what extra furniture was required, Sasha began arranging the soft toys on the Lloyd Loom chair. She buried her face in a threadbare yellow teddy. Calista heard a muffled sob. She put a tentative arm around the girl's shoulders. Sasha didn't shake her off. She hugged her and the teddy to her, holding her till Sasha's tears subsided.

'I shall miss Mum, Cal.'

'I know I miss mine.'

Sasha pulled away. 'Is she dead?'

'No.' Calista smiled at Sasha's look of relief. 'My parents live in Southern Spain so I don't see them that often. The climate helps keep them going. Dad's over eighty and Mum's seventy four.'

'I'm okay now.' Giving a wan smile, Sasha put her bear down on the chair.

Calista hoped she would soon feel at home and if she didn't like the Victorian pine chest-o'-drawers, she could have something else.

'Cool,' Sasha said. 'I like it.'

'Is it full?' Calista said.

'Haven't looked.' Sasha went over and opened a couple of drawers. 'Shall I put what I can away?' She gestured toward the jumble of clothes.

'Only if you're thinking of staying.'

They both laughed.

Adam arrived home around half past four.

'We could have done with your muscles,' Calista said, 'to carry the boxes upstairs.'

'What do you think I employ a handy-man for?' he said.

'Len and Sash need familiar things around them now, not next week.'

That evening, all longing for an early night, at six they ate comforting lasagne pre-prepared by Pam, plus a salad Calista made herself.

'And tomorrow I shall cook a Sunday roast,' Adam said, 'like I always used to.'

Later in bed, turning on her side, back towards Adam, 'The girls' rooms need more furniture,' she said, though that was not the worry that gnawed.

'That's your department, darling.' A noisy yawn, 'Night, night. That round of golf was exhausting.'

She resisted the urge to leap up and punch him in the face, her last conscious thought as she too, tired out, drifted into sleep.

CHAPTER THIRTY

Respite

On the Friday before the girls had arrived, Mr Swingler, the Chambers' Clerk had come up trumps with a new brief. The following Wednesday, she spent most of the day in Chambers, with few colleagues around a haven of tranquillity. She immersed herself in the must of leather-bound law treatises, the fust of papers. Tackling problems, however serpentine, with every expectation of resolution was an enormous relief.

A short break for lunch, she also visited the antiseptic cool of Boots' pharmacy. Purchases accomplished, outside in sunshine pedestrians-only Gallowtree Gate was thronged with mothers and buggies, children of school age, gangs of teenagers mobbing up and down, Senior Citizens resting on benches, all ethnicities and creeds, a microcosm of multi-cultural Leicester.

On her way back to Chambers, she popped into Tourist Information and bought postcards with views of the city, her intention, a light-hearted message, one to PJ's Ithaca address, one to his London address. If for some reason he had not received her emails, she hoped the cards would, in time, provoke a response. She was still confident if, God forbid, he had changed his mind about her, he would tell her. Feeling better for having a pro-active strategy in place, as she strolled along, she wondered how Esther was getting on in Amsterdam, whether she would feel tempted to live there for a while. Tomorrow, the first of September, was the day of the reception where she would meet Mike's Dutch colleagues.

Resisting the temptation to work late, Calista went home in time to join Helena and Sasha by the pool. No sign of Adam. They assured her he had spent time with them. The three of them, plus Beppo had walked the back lane to the next village. They had lunch at the pub.

After dinner eaten cosily in the kitchen, they all, including Adam, spent a pleasant enough evening in the sitting room watching a DVD, 'The Bourne Identity'. Calista was surprised to learn the girls had not seen any of the Jason Bourne films. She had all three. She enjoyed them so much every so often when all the twists and turns had slipped her mind, she liked to escape into Bourne's hocus-pocus world.

As she and Adam were preparing for bed, 'Cal, I've had an idea.' He suggested she got her interior designer to finish off the girls' rooms. 'She'd easily pull it in with the job she's doing on the villa, wouldn't she?' He sounded hesitant, and in only his boxers, looked vulnerable.

'Not that bad an idea, except tomorrow, I'm taking Len and Sash to look for one or two essential items. Might mean scouring the antique furniture shops in this county and the next. They're anxious everything should be in keeping with what's already in place.'

His face lit up. 'You are getting on well with each other.'

Once in bed, she lay back towards him, as she had ever since they returned home. Snuggling up, he put his arm round her, cupped her breast. 'Your period must be long over now. Do I get a reward for being a good boy?'

She wondered if, as promised, he was referring to spending time with his daughters, or the answer to her waspish enquiry when she assured her he would not be going up to London, not until sometime the following week.

'I really am very tired, Adam.' She held her breath. He had not attempted to make love to her since she had rebuffed him that night on holiday. He let her go, sighed and turned over.

For better, for worse, for richer and everything else, Adam was her husband. Except, she had promised to have him on no such conditions. All she did was take a breath in the wrong place, and call upon those persons present to witness her taking him as her awful wedded husband, an embarrassingly unoriginal slip of the tongue, quite inexcusable in someone used to holding forth in court.

'Truth will out.' Esther teased as, following the ceremony, the four of them, herself, Adam, their two witnesses, Esther and Taylor Dando, celebrated with afternoon tea at what used to be the Grand Hotel.

Beneath their warm coats, essential for the walk from Town Hall Square to the hotel on that sleety February afternoon, she and Esther were soignee in Paul Smith ensembles, her own predominantly midnight blue, Esther's plum. Smith's trademark classic tailored shape with an up-to-date edge, they agreed, was versatile enough to wear on other occasions. Under their topcoats, Adam and Taylor were handsomely dapper in business-like clerical grey.

'We should've had the forethought to order a wedding cake,' Taylor said, lounging back in a squishy chair. 'Smoked salmon sandwiches okay, but scones with jam and cream don't quite . . .'

'Drink up your Earl Grey.' Adam said. 'Their best champagne will arrive any minute.'

'A celebration, sir? Someone's birthday, perhaps?' the waiter said as the cork popped.

'I've just married the most gorgeous woman,' Adam said.

The waiter gave a nervous smile, poured the wine, and left.

'He thought you were having him on,' Taylor guffawed.

'Because we're not wearing buttonholes,' Esther said.

'Not that kind of wedding, was it?' Calista said.

Nor was it one at which one actually promised to forsake all others. She knew that was taken as read, but after his disclosures at the Erato her doubts about Adam were even stronger. And now, she was no better. Maybe Adam did love her, as far as he was capable of loving any woman. In eighteen months, she had acquired a husband, a ready-made family, and had met and yearned to be with another man. Two weeks to the day since they were together on the beach, she and PJ, another forty seven weeks to go. That is, if they ever did meet again. She ached to see him, would be devastated if he changed his mind about keeping in touch. *PJ, PJ, where are you?* Tomorrow she would send her postcards.

A fine mess you've got yourself into, Calista Blake. Just walk away. If only it were that easy.

CHAPTER THIRTY ONE

Thursday, 1 September – Amsterdam

The Baroque grandeur of the reception room with its gilded mirrors and painted ceiling of mythological scenes provided an ornate backdrop to the hum of urbane conversation, the group playing classics from musicals. All in all an entertaining enough schmooze fest, Esther decided, especially since, not being obliged to make her mark, she was quite relaxed. The speeches over, she was amused to observe who had real clout by the number and quality of those dancing attendance on them. She could not help but make a discreet scan of the assembly, one more time, wonder who was the one Mike might have forsaken her for, albeit temporarily. Not that he had confessed to any such lapse, and he was hardly likely to introduce her – *Tess, meet Catheline Klompen, my one-time bit-of-Dutch on the side.*

A medley from Gershwin's Porgy and Bess underway, *Summertime* began to soar above the hubbub. Mike and Willem Langmeijer excused themselves and sashayed in the direction of Charles and Eleanor Pennington, leaving her with Willem's wife, Marieke.

'That'll please, Mike,' Esther spoke her thought in a tone indicating it would not.

Marieke looked surprised. 'But Willem says Mike likes and admires Sir Charles very much.'

'Oh, no.' Esther put her hand to her mouth. 'I was talking about the music. Carmen Macrae sings this on one of my jazz compilations.' She sang softly lingering over the first couple of phrases. 'One of my all-time favourites.'

'And Michael doesn't like it?' Marieke sounded surprised. 'It's one of my favourites, too.'

Esther warmed to her even more' 'He wasn't in a very good mood at the time.'

'If you like jazz, Esther, perhaps the four of us could go to a club some time.'

'Love to. Mike and Willem get on well.' *Considering they were rivals for the top job*, Esther thought. 'I love what I've seen of Amsterdam these past couple of days. So many people speak English. I feel ashamed by my lack of fluency in any other language.'

'Willem tells me Michael is doing well with his Dutch lessons. He has a good teacher perhaps.'

Mike learning Dutch, is his teacher the one, Esther wondered. She looked in Mike's direction. In his tux, he looked distinguished, at ease. Despite what he had said, she did not for one moment believe he needed her to be there. Mike looked across, gave one of his smiles.

'The people I've met so far are so friendly and helpful,' Esther said

Marieke looked pleased. 'I am glad you like us and Amsterdam. Willem says you have two children, a girl and a boy already at school. Perhaps that is why you don't wish to live here.'

'I'm sure Fran and Tom would love living here for a while.' Not wanting to sound self-important, smiling Esther shrugged. 'I'm a partner in a firm of solicitors.'

'I have taken a break from my career,' Marieke said. 'Our older boy, Andries is four and a half, and Ivo is three.' She sighed. 'I loved my job. Perhaps if Ivo had been a girl, we might have stopped at two and . . .' Marieke gave a shy smile. 'I do hope to go back to teaching English once my children go to school.'

'No wonder you speak it so well. You're not teaching Mike Dutch, are you?'

Laughing, Marieke shook her head. 'No.'

Another blue-eyed blonde in a company of blondes natural and otherwise, Marieke's hair was a genuine honey colour, her face pretty rather than beautiful. Healthily pregnant, her complexion glowed, her ubiquitous little black number failing to conceal her bump.

'When's your baby due?' Esther asked.

'The fifteenth of October.'

'Is it a girl?'

'We want a surprise, though a little girl would be nice this time.'

'If you keep trying without success, you might end up with a football team.'

'I think we'd stick at five-a-side.'

They both laughed. Esther did like her. She had taken to Willem too. Half a head shorter than she was, and stocky, he had the most expressive face and good-humoured tobacco-brown eyes. If she and Mike could be friends with Marieke and Willem, Amsterdam became more attractive by the minute. She had already mooted the possibility of taking a sabbatical with Chris Burroughs. Chris told her, with planning, he couldn't see why she shouldn't, 'Be like taking extended maternity leave,' he had said. She told Chris she would have to make sure Mike wanted her and the children to join him. 'Of course he'll want you,' Chris said. *I wish I felt as positive about that,* she thought.

Not far from where she and Marieke were standing, a flurry in the double doorway separating the outer grand lobby from the even grander inner salon attracted their attention. *Three of Amsterdam's loveliest gutted to discover they've missed the speeches,* Esther thought. Cal would say the two tall young men in their tuxedos were well fit, one fresh faced, his close-cropped red hair like velvet, the other a Mediterranean dish with designer stubble and curly blue-black hair. They flanked a young woman with golden bouncy curls, ear-lobe short, who screamed celebrity. Her candy-pink, figure-skimming slip of a silk dress terminated mid- thigh to reveal long bare legs, and shoulders and arms, tantalizing suggestion of an all-over tan. She was balanced on slender heeled candy-pink sandals.

'Who's the girl?' Esther said. 'A model?'

'But of course, you won't have seen her before. She's Louise van de Velde, a consultant with the PR Company responsible, among other things, for this reception,' Marieke said. 'Michael has probably spoken of her.'

Mike had mentioned no such person. She was about to quiz Marieke when they were interrupted by Willem. So taken with the vision in pink, they had not noticed him approach with Charles and Eleanor Pennington who wished to be introduced to Marieke.

Then, smiling, Sir Charles turned to her, 'So pleased you could come after all, Esther.' – *What had Mike said?* She wondered. – Charles patted her hand. 'Now you'll appreciate what Michael has been up to these past months.'

Too right, she thought. While the Penningtons chatted to the Langmeijers, she returned her attention to Ms van de Velde. Waiters at every turn, Ms V. was unnecessarily despatching her escorts in search of drinks. Once they had left her side, she gave the assembly a quick appraisal, then made a beeline to a quartet of men, one of them Mike. She tapped him on his right shoulder, then dodged to his left. Esther had no time to register his expression when he realized who it was. Ms van de Velde, obviously delighted to see Mike, hugged him, kissed him on each cheek, plus a third kiss to one side of his mouth. *What happened to Mwah, Mwah?* The other three men warranted the briefest handshake.

Esther felt a touch on her arm. 'Are you all right?' Eleanor Pennington sounded concerned. 'The room has become rather stuffy.'

She had felt the warmth drain from her face, though doubted she could look pale. She strained a smile. 'Yes, it has rather.'

'Come.' Eleanor pointed to a couple of unoccupied gilded chairs either side of a small table by one of the open windows. 'Let's go and sit over there. The others won't miss us.'

True, the Langmeijers and the others who had joined their group were too busy hanging on Sir Charles's every word to notice them as they slipped away. They sat down. Eleanor signalled a passing waiter, and ordered two glasses of cool, still mineral water with a slice of lime and no ice.

'You look absolutely stunning, Esther. So stylish.' This from Eleanor, in her early-seventies, with sleek silver-blonde hair cut in an elegant bob, her tall, fine-boned figure draped in a long-sleeved, mid-calf-length sheath of midnight-blue, a fortune in pearls at her throat.

'Thank you.' Esther felt heat in her face. Her mother had persuaded her to go for the glitzy purple-plum, V-neck figured-silk, short enough to show off her legs, the deeper plum velvet jacket – *'Forget a little black frock. You can't compete with all those blondes,* Mum had said. *And no way can I compete with Ms van de Velde,* but her mother was not to know.

Eleanor must have followed her gaze. 'The young woman talking to Michael is exceptionally striking. But, I have seen the way he looks at you Esther. Be assured, no contest, as they say.'

Esther would like to believe her. Their water had arrived. They each took a refreshing mouthful.

'I feel better already,' Eleanor said. 'Now tell me, what have Fran and

Tom been up to since I saw them? Must be more than a year now.'

Esther knew she was not just being polite. The Pennington's only child had died of leukaemia thirty years ago. Esther could not begin to imagine what that must have been like. Eleanor involved herself in several children's charities, was genuinely interested to hear about children she knew personally, and Esther, despite being aware of their imperfections, was never reluctant to talk about Fran and Tom.

A light touch on her shoulder. 'Spotted where you were in a mirror.' Mike, and behind him, Ms Vision-in-Pink looking nonplussed. 'Lady Eleanor, Tess, meet Louise van de Velde, our PR guru.'

Esther and Eleanor got to their feet. Eleanor shook hands with Ms V-in-P first. Louise gushed, delighted to meet the illustrious Chairman's wife. She hoped Lady Eleanor was enjoying the reception, and her visit to Amsterdam.

Then it was Esther's turn. 'Louise, my wife Esther.'

A fleeting look of consternation on Louise's face. - *Now was that because of the word 'wife', or because I'm me*, Esther wondered. *Probably both*. Louise took her hand. 'This is a surprise,' she said. 'Last time we spoke, Michael told me you would not be here.'

'As well as everything else,' Mike said, 'Louise has done her best to teach me Dutch.'

'With some success apparently,' Esther said smiling. 'Willem Lang-meijer thinks Mike's doing really well.' *I can do PR too Ms Louise van de Velde.*

'I do my best,' Louise said. Again she shook their hands. 'Lovely to meet you, Lady Eleanor, Esther. Now I really must go and find my friends.'

She had no sooner disappeared in the crush, than Sir Charles, Marieke and Willem joined them.

'We've done our duty,' Charles said. 'Let's all go and find some proper food.'

'Remember, Esther,' Eleanor whispered as they made their way out, 'no contest.'

I'll find that out soon enough, she thought. The remainder of the evening she strove, and succeeded Esther believed, not to show how despondent she had become.

CHAPTER THIRTY TWO

At the Old Rectory

Still half anaesthetized by blessed sleep, Calista squinted at her clock-radio, just gone seven, and Sunday. Adam, she sensed, was almost on the point of waking. She slithered out of bed, made for their bathroom. Minutes elapsed, the door handle rattled.

'Darling, I need a pee.' Invariably sleeping in the buff, Adam stood naked in front of her. Since the girls' arrival, she had taken to wearing a strappy, silk nightdress. 'You're not getting up, are you?' Through sleep-filled eyes, he gave her a dreamy smile. 'In that nightie, you fill me with lust.'

She was in desperate need of her hot water drink and dry toast. 'I'll bring you up some tea.' She put on her bathrobe.

Adam put down his mug. She was half sitting, half lying on top of the duvet comforted by the lavender scent of her pillows. Adam turned to her. He slid one arm under her shoulders and the other round her waist, pulled her close. A pang of nostalgia, his mouth on hers was soft and sensuous. Then the taste of Assam tea on his lips made her want to retch.

A rat-a-tat tat at their bedroom door. 'Dad? Cal?' Sasha called. 'Are you awake?'

Calista eased herself away, swung off the bed.

'Tell her to bugger off,' Adam said.

Calista opened the door just wide enough to speak to Sasha, and glanced at her watch. Not yet eight o'clock, and Sasha already up and dressed in jog pants and T-shirt.

'Sorry.' Sasha blushed. 'Beppo's whining to go out. Shall I let him?'

'Be an angel. Take him up to the orchard for whatever.'

'See what happens when you have kids.' Adam was out of bed and in his bathrobe. He went over to the window and looked out. She joined him, managing to stifle *you were the one who wanted them here*. Soon the girls would go back to school. The house would become a morgue again. 'What if we'd been in the middle of coitus,' he said.

'It would've interrupt us,' she said smiling.

She was conscious of his turning to look at her. 'You're so centred on your career, brilliant at what you do. Everyone says so. Terrible if you lost focus.'

Her eyes, unwavering, concentrated on the horizon. 'What on earth makes you think I'm losing focus?'

'You've been so distrait since we came home, even while we were away you were . . . distant.' He sighed. 'Once you've got children, they're forever and ever.'

She went cold. 'Sash and Len are really no bother. They're good company.' Then her stomach's protest was loud enough for them both to hear. 'I think I'll go and make some porridge.'

'Let me,' he said. 'I'll call you down when it's ready.'

Sunday, *en famille* was a taste of an unquiet future - a note from Sasha on the kitchen table - *Cal, Dad, gone for a bike ride to the Eye Brook with Jason, cheers, Sash. P.S. Okay if he comes back for lunch?*

'Who the hell's Jason? ' Adam said.

'She met him in the pub garden on Wednesday, while you were at the bar chatting up that woman.' Helena put Adam straight assuring him Jason could be no older than fifteen, ginger hair, glasses. 'They're both under age. She did mention him a few times on the way back. He's a twitcher, her type. 'Spect she wants to show him her fossils.' Helena snickered.

'Reassuring that she feels she can invite him home,' Calista said.

'S'pose,' Adam conceded.

To get into art school, Helena needed to add to her portfolio. Calista had seen no harm in agreeing to pose for her nude. 'Never done one before.

You'll be a real challenge, Cal. Promise I won't let on my model was my step-mother.'

Helena had used oils, and had now set up the finished canvas on an easel in the drawing room. They stood back to view it. Reflected in the cheval glass in their dressing room lolling like an odalisque on the chaise longue, her skin still glowing from her holiday, Calista believed Helena had flattered her.

'You're curvier now. I remember at half term, you were a bit bony. You would have been more German Expressionist than Rokeby Venus then.' Helena gave a nervous laugh. 'Not that I have pretensions to be a Mueller or a Velazquez. Just have to show I can do figures.'

'I thought your preliminary sketches were excellent,' Calista said.

'They all go into my portfolio. Next up, Sash, I think, in acrylic. Now she is nervy and angular.' For a few moments they contemplated Helena's work in silence. 'What were you thinking, Cal? You look positively euphoric.'

Calista felt her face flush. She had made a conscious effort to suppress all ongoing anxieties including whether PJ had changed his mind about keeping in touch – he still had not acknowledged her email. She had concentrated on re-living her time with him.

'Just remembering Ithaca,' she said, 'It really is magic.'

'Dad says we could all go for half-term, if you got a move on deciding on the furniture.'

First I've heard, Calista thought. 'Just might be possible,' she said, *and, if I'm lucky, maybe I'll see PJ sooner than I ever could imagine.*

'Might ask Dad to pose,' Helena said. 'A male figure would be yet another challenge.'

'You'd be pushing your luck there.' Calista smiled at the thought.

'Not completely nude, obviously.' Helena pulled a face. 'Painting your father when he's naked, that'd be gross. In his trunks by the pool perhaps. I could take photos of him, about to jump in, mid-crawl like David Hockney's done, climbing out dripping wet, then base a series of acrylics on them. Not original but you're allowed to allude to other artists' work. It's what you make of the allusion that counts.'

Sasha burst in to summon them to Adam's traditional Sunday roast. 'Dad gave Jase a test. He had to set the dining room table. They seem to be getting on okay.' Sasha came further into the room to view the painting. 'Wow, Len, you've made Cal look mega cool,' which made Helena and Calista splutter with laughter. 'What?' Sasha said.

After Jason had left, Helena's artistic endeavours provoked a showdown, the Oxford versus art school controversy not yet having been resolved.

'Appointment with destiny half past six, Dad's office.' Helena came to tell her.

Despite the sunshine, that afternoon Calista had excused herself from joining the others by the pool, seeking respite in her study. 'Is he serious?' she said.

'S'okay, over there at least you won't hear the row. I've no intention of applying for his poxy Oxford College' If he won't support me, fine. I'm eighteen in January. I'll get a part-time job. Escort agencies pay well.'

In their bed on Sunday night, atmosphere heavy with Adam's hostility, 'Be a travesty if Len didn't go to art school.' Calista's tone was soft.

'I know.' Silence. 'I so wanted her to go to my old college.'

'Perhaps Sash will,' she said.

Adam gave a dismissive snort. 'She's not as bright as Len.'

'She's different, that's all. Don't underestimate her,' Calista said.

'Since when have you become a child expert?'

'I know people. Len's a young woman, and Sash is almost there. You can't make decisions for them or dictate to them like you did when they were little. If you try, you'll lose them. Presumably that's the last thing you want, or you wouldn't have talked me into being here with you now.'

Adam pummelled his pillows, put out his bedside light, then lay with his back towards her. *Suits me,* Calista thought as she too put out her light, and turned her back on him.

On Monday, Adam and Helena were still not speaking to each other. Helena spent the evening in her room door wide open so even with the sitting room door shut Calista and Sasha got the benefit of her choice of music played full belt. Jessie J's entire *Who You Are* album, Sasha told Calista when she asked. Wasted if she wanted to annoy her father. After eating, Adam went back to his office, where Sasha said he had spent most of the day.

Slumped up one corner of the sofa, 'Len's not going to give in,' Sasha said.

Calista sat beside her. 'Your dad will come round.'

Sasha said he came round when he realized how much their mother wanted a divorce. Calista wondered how he would react if, when she wanted one.

'Dad says Jason's okay.'

'Don't let that put you off him,' Calista said, 'He doesn't have acne, freckles but no acne,' which succeeded in making Sasha laugh.

They decided to watch a DVD, the second Jason Bourne film, volume turned up to drown Helena's music.

'Just as well we don't live in an apartment block, or semi-detached house,' Calista said.

Almost eleven o'clock when Adam came into the house quiet now. Sasha and Helena had gone to bed. He seemed subdued.

'Would you like me to bring you up some hot chocolate?' he said.

Sitting among their pillows, they must have looked like Darby and Joan. Adam had dug out a pair of pyjamas.

'I'll have to give Len her head, won't I? Not because of her silly threats about earning money . . .' He put down his empty mug, leaned back against his pillows. 'That beautiful water colour of the lane and the church she did at half-term, I had it framed and hung in my office in town.'

She had no idea. 'You must tell her tomorrow, she has your blessing to apply for art school.'

'I will but not tomorrow. Unavoidable I'm afraid I have to go up to London.'

She had turned off her bedside light, made herself comfortable among her pillows. She asked if he would be staying over.

'Not sure,' he said. 'Cal?'

'Adam?'

'I've been thinking about your brother.'

'Stephen, what on earth for?'

'Just that he seems seriously weird, a complete geek. I remember your father telling me he was an impossible child.'

She felt cold inside. *Where was this conversation leading?* 'In his own way, my brother's something of a genius. He's lived quite normally since he married Louanne, and he absolutely adores their daughter. He lives in California, remember, where, you maintain, they're all coots. Stephen must blend in nicely.'

'I didn't mean . . . And not all Californians.'

She turned on her side, her back towards him. Sighing, he put out his light and turned his back to her.

CHAPTER THIRTY THREE

PJ Wood

PJ prickled and itched under his fatigues and flak jacket, the heat made more intense by being squashed between two comrades as they juddered along in the Humvee. For the past couple of weeks, like them, living and sleeping in the same dirt-encrusted clothes, he was inured to the reek of foetid sweat, was used to breathing dust, eating grit. He adjusted the keffiyeh shielding his nose and mouth. He, Jim the American on his right, and on his left, Ahmed, a local journalist from Lashkar Gan, were in distinguished company, a reporter and his cameraman from al-Jazeera were in the front.

'PJ, where have you been?' He and Ahmed had embraced before going out with the patrol.

'Haven't seen you since . . .' Ahmed said.

'End of last year, and U.S. casualties were the worst ever,' PJ cut in, then realized how that must sound. Ahmed's baby daughter was one year old now, and any day she could be fatherless. Local journalists daily confronted corrupt officials, or drug barons, plus odds-on they could be caught in NATO friendly fire. Taliban ambushes were just one more hazard.

'PJ, don't give up on us.'

'I haven't, just been on assignments closer to home, is all, Egypt then Libya.' PJ gave a deep sigh. 'Does anybody really care? Politicians have agendas all their own. The mendacious hypocrites don't seem to give a toss about what people who gave them the power want.'

'My friend, all the more reason for you to show what's happening in the world.'

'Twenty-first Century Joe Public realizes he or she has no influence.' PJ said. 'In my country techie toys - PCs, iPhones, iPads, digital TV with a myriad of crap channels – are the new opiate of the people.' His friend had looked perplexed. 'Sorry to be so negative, deep down, I know you're right. Maybe there's been shock-horror-image overload. I guess we just have to plod on.'

'So, my Pashto lessons aren't wasted. You'll be coming back?'

'Let you know when, if we manage to survive this latest jaunt,' PJ said.

They had, and were on their way to Kabul, and, he hoped, at last a chance to reply to Cal's emails – *Dear Cal, Got away with it one more time, so right now I'm fine,* he would say. Again, his luck had held bar a few cuts and scratches. On this particular sortie, so far the material he had managed to send over the net had been well-received, though he doubted it was enough. Wikileaks had certainly stirred things up. The dead, the maimed, whether babies, children, women, or old men, their bloodied bodies riddled with bullets, guts spilling out, lying on village streets, in bombed houses, were still dead or maimed whoever was responsible. Soldiers were trained to kill, simple as that. No point in being outraged when they became trigger happy. And dropping bombs from planes, as for drones, virtual reality games. What did he know? *You're a wuss of a photographer, PJ, no killer instinct, unless getting in a good shot with your camera counts.*

Jim was asleep, lucky Jim, his head resting on PJ's shoulder, on his other side, he sensed the silent Ahmed's unease. For now, their destiny lay in the hands of their driver and Fate. A chance to think about Cal, not that she had ever been far from his thoughts, not since that first evening. *'Lately been a tad preoccupied, my love, is all,'* he murmured into his keffiyah.

He took a breath in, an attempt to replace present stench with the memory of her scent. He ran his parched tongue along cracked lips longing for the taste of her. He closed his eyes picturing her smile, her habit of tucking her hair behind her ears. As much as his companions allowed, he shifted in his seat imagining her body pressed against his. *She's married, remember. So! She's not happy. As old Solon said, "Call no man happy before he dies, he is at best but fortunate".* Cal had been adamant about being privileged in her own right, not because she had married a wealthy man.

When you went back to Marcos's those couple of times and she wasn't there, you did her no favours going out of your way to see her again. Except when he did, obvious what she felt about him. If they were to take that to its ultimate . . . From what he had seen of Burgess . . . Wouldn't be a breeze, as my old pa used to say. As for Ma, like mother like son. 'At last I've found my significant other, Ma. Guess what, she's already married, just like my father was when you met him.'

The Humvee juddered to a standstill. On a rutted dirt track between rocky banks, nothing except a few scrubby bushes, and for the moment, no other human beings in sight but them.

'Houston we have a problem.' Their Afghan driver, a member of Afghan Special Operations spoke pretty good American, not that that meant anything out here, not when it came to green on blue.

Fuck it, seems like my luck is about to run out, PJ thought. *Retribution from a jealous god? Insouciant Fate, more like, and I'm about to find out if Solon was right.*

CHAPTER THIRTY FOUR

Tuesday, 6 September
Calista Blake

Calista got up early, but not as early as Adam. She examined herself in the mirror above the vanity unit. She was pale, hollow-eyed. Yesterday had been a long day with an early start, like today. No use lying in bed fretting, she had to keep her mind occupied, and last evening, home failing to beckon, she had stayed in Chambers till gone six. Still no word from PJ, neither a response to her two emails, nor to her two postcards posted last Thursday. They had not been light-hearted after all, *I am assuming you haven't changed your mind about our keeping in touch, and give below my address and mobile number.* She imagined he would not yet be at his London address, and probably too soon to expect anything back from Ithaca, even though she had enclosed the card in an envelope and sent it airmail. God forbid he would think her neurotic. She was.

The doorknob's rattle disturbed the cauldron of her thoughts.

'Cal, going soon if I'm to make my train.'

She unlocked the door. Just after seven, Adam had been up for an hour and all set for London, immaculate in his double-breasted Gieves & Hawkes charcoal grey with the chalk stripe. At home, he only ever wore jeans and a sloppy shirt. His hands were cool and smooth resting on her shoulders. As he kissed her on the forehead, she could smell him, fresh and early-morning clean, the subtlest whiff of Guerlain *Vetiver*.

'Bye darling, see you later.'

Maybe that meant he would set about redeeming himself. Not stay over.

Mid-morning, while she was engaged with a client and his solicitor, Adam sent a text. He would be staying in London overnight.

Almost noon, and no further need for her to remain in Chambers, she came to a decision. No more pussyfooting, she would allay or confirm her suspicions.

Back at the Old Rectory, 'I'm having to pop up to London this afternoon. Need to consult a colleague in Lincoln's Inn.' She lied to Helena and Sasha over a lunchtime snack. 'Pam says she'll stay here overnight, in case I don't get back.' She was leaving the girls and Beppo in reliable hands.

She changed from her legal black into a natural linen skirt and jacket and low-heeled, comfortable shoes, packed toiletries, pyjamas, clean knickers into her favourite Louis Vuitton like an oversized handbag, a present from Adam. She arrived at the Tower Hotel reception just after six thirty. The hotel was massive. One she would not dream of using, impersonal, anonymous.

'Mr Burgess hasn't yet checked in, madam. If you'd like to leave your name, and wait over there.'

'Not to worry, if I have time, maybe I'll come back.' The whole point was to catch Adam unawares.

Outside, she made her way to a large nautical-looking instrument by the Thames footpath. Equinoctial Sundial, the plaque said, explaining how it worked, too complicated, too scientific for her. A pleasant September evening, she was wired with anticipation. She had reason to explore this area of London she was unfamiliar with. A fair few tourists, foreign and home-grown, and to her right Tower Bridge loomed. In an attempt to achieve equanimity, first off, she decided to stroll in that direction, take a look at the outer ramparts of the Tower. She had not been there since she was a little girl.

She approached a fountain. A sculpted athletic girl, back arched, with outstretched arms dived through the air towards a dolphin spouting water. Just beyond, a young woman, who could be Tess's younger sister, if she had one, stood looking out over the river. The resemblance was uncanny. Unable to resist taking the woman's photo to show Tess, Calista took her iPhone from her bag and held it as though capturing the fountain. Then she saw Adam hurrying, his laptop case over his shoulder, overnight bag in his hand. *All along he had planned to stay over.*

He stopped beside Tess's lookalike, said something. She turned towards him. Calista, phone still in her hand took a photo of them together. They talked. The woman took Adam's free hand, drew it to her mouth, then punctuated by a couple of words, a knowing look, sucked each finger in turn, starting with his pinkie, finally lingering on his thumb. Ice-cold now, Calista made a determined effort to control her shaking hand, record the scene. Adam pulled the woman's arm through his. *Just one more take for luck. Hadn't he lived up to expectation, hadn't he just.*

Suspicions confirmed she was numb more than anything, not angry, although she knew that would come, and soon, cold, prolonged, lethal. Screened as she was by a group of people admiring the fountain, Adam was unlikely to notice her. He had eyes only for the woman. Above the chatter of the group, she heard the sound of her heartbeat. She hesitated, not her style to run over to the two of them. Make a scene. Humiliating enough, the woman carried a Louis Vuitton identical to her own.

Adam and his companion, arm in arm, made their way towards the hotel entrance. If they had come towards her, she would have had no option but to confront them. The people around her began to move, she, separating their progress like a boulder in a stream, except she turned, following in the wake of the crowd. She could not spend the evening like a statue. She had her confirmation, and now something else she needed to see.

She followed the crowd to the metal footbridge over a lock. Leaning on the guard rail, she breathed in, taking in the foetid smell of oil and river water. Letting her breath out slowly through her mouth, she gazed into the ink-black bottom of the cutting. Well and truly dusk, she still had her phone in her hand. Before putting it away, she brought up a map of the area, made her way along the path past the original Dock Master's House and into St Katharine's Haven, the quays lively with people and lights. She passed down one side of the Dickens Inn, a tourist trap if ever there was one. She had to focus on things inconsequential. Round into a mews and a row of small houses, mock early nineteenth century labourer's cottages, dwarfed by surrounding apartment blocks. The cottages were a surprise, stopping in front of one of them, 'twee' didn't equate with a photo-journalist sailing the Ionian Sea alone in his sloop. Three steps led up to a dark green door, over the bell in the wall, a plaque proclaiming *Woodbine Cottage*, beneath that, no question, inset behind a small glass panel, a name, *PJ Wood.*

PJ's cottage looked forlorn, no lights, no sign of life whatever, no more than she had expected. Nevertheless she leaned on the bell, a prolonged and strident note. The front door remained closed. She would have to think about going home. Home. She was consumed by a feeling of despondency, dispossession. The Old Rectory was her home. If anyone should leave, it was Adam.

CHAPTER THIRTY FIVE

Adam Burgess

As always, he arranged to meet Sheena Jardine by the Girl with the Dolphin Fountain. Concealed by a concrete pillar, Adam watched. She arrived around a quarter to seven, the black cab dropped her off behind a coach decanting enthusiastic passengers chattering in a language he did not recognize. She crossed the walk-way toward the fountain. That evening she was dramatic in black, skinny jeans showing off her long legs, stilettoes, bomber jacket, her hair scraped severely back from the perfect oval of her face and coiled into the nape of her neck. *What would she do if he kept her waiting?*

In fading light, a still figure in a turning world, she stood gazing into the Thames. *Penny for them, Sheena.* He had met her at one of Sonja's euphemistic soirees. An acquaintance in the City had introduced him to the Sonja-scene a while ago. *Discreet and business-like, old boy. Plenty of thrills without the risks involved trawling the streets. And far better than jeopardizing family-life with some seccie who cuts up rough when you tire of her. Do you like'em young? I do. Sonja does the kids a favour, taking them off the streets. Runaways. Junkettes. They get a roof, medical care. And from the punter's point of view, soon as they become too old, they're pensioned off.*

Not that he had ever felt the necessity of picking up prostitutes, appalling thought. Most of the fun was in getting a girl into bed, the less experienced the better. Just turned forty when his acquaintance had approached him, he had been ready for something different. Sonja's set-up was a revelation, all eccentricities catered for. No recriminations.

No repercussions. He loved playing rough, but before Sonja's, never went beyond spanking, or pinning the girl down, taking her as she struggled. Just as well he had an outlet. Like Annie, Cal would balk at anything bordering on BDSM. Sonja's set-up and Sheena in particular provided release. Her accent had intrigued. She had not long arrived from Liverpool.

'Hope you haven't been waiting long,' he said, at Sheena's elbow. He had hurried over from his vantage point as though arriving late.

She started, turned to look at him. 'Ten minutes, I guess.'

'I've been cooped up all day. Shall we take a walk around the quays?'

'Did your day not go according to plan?'

'It went very well. Would you like to go to the Brasserie for dinner?'

'Room service, later, will be fine.'

She took him by the hand, drew it to her mouth, a couple or so words punctuating each suck of each finger in turn. 'I know . . . what you . . . would like . . . Come, let's go . . . to your room.'

He doubted anyone who knew him was nearby, a quick glance around. Passers-by intent on where they were heading, a gaggle of tourists admiring the fountain, or busy taking photos. He drew her arm through his and led her towards the hotel entrance.

'May I ask you something personal,' he said.

'You can ask.' - Nowadays only minor modulations hinted at her Liverpudlian origins.

'How old were you, that first time?'

'Seventeen, you were my very first at Sonja's. Why do you ask?'

'Just curious. Sonja maintains none of her girls are younger than sixteen.'

'She asks, you are sixteen, aren't you? As long as you say yes she takes you on. The more waif-like you look, the better, obviously,' her voice matter-of-fact. 'My colour was my selling point. I really was seventeen. Seventeen and two months. You taught me what I needed to know. Sonja said you would.'

Sonja had asked if he would mind breaking in the new girl, not so streetwise as most of the kids. She meant Sheena was not already too degraded.

They had reached the hotel entrance.

'You go and hide behind a magazine,' Adam said, 'while I check in.' He had a proposition for her.

Supported by pillows, Adam took sips from a balloon glass containing a surprisingly good Armagnac. He delighted in observing the nuances of Sheena's movements, felt himself aroused again by her undulating, accommodating arse. Enveloped in a white towelling bathrobe, she pushed the debris of their midnight feast, now confined to the trolley, out into the corridor. She dropped the robe to reveal small, firm breasts, a thin, perhaps too thin body. He knew her coke habit kept her going, chasing the dragon to bring her down. Sonja had told him. Her smoking heroin, rather than injecting was some consolation.

She climbed on to the bed, lay down on her stomach, chin resting on folded arms. He finished his drink. He propped himself on one elbow, lay on his side, and ran the tips of his fingers over the welts on her back and buttocks that evening imprinted by the birch. She flinched.

'Shall I bathe them for you?'

She turned her face towards him, looked surprised.

'I was heavier handed than usual.' He was ashamed, taking out his frustration with Cal on Sheena. 'There's something I want to put to you.' In return for paying her rent and living expenses, plus an allowance, he wanted her exclusive services, expecting her to be available maybe a couple of times a week. He ran the palm of his hand gently across her buttocks. 'And I promise no beatings, though I may want to manacle you sometimes.' Cal's angry, disgusted words echoed when he had threatened to take his belt to Sash, *That's assault.*

All the while Sheena's huge dark disdainful eyes were on him, assessing.

'Maybe you'll decide to try and break your habit. I'd be more than happy to pay for a clinic.'

'You're very generous, Mr Burgess.' She sounded suspicious.

'No catch, Sheena. In between our appointments, your time's your own. What do you say?'

'You really, really mean it.'

He thought she was going to cry. Amenable to satisfying his predilections, he would not admit to himself, let alone to her, he was attached to her.

'Yes.'

'I accept.'

'Come, let me bathe you.' He touched her shoulder then she could relieve his now quite pressing need.

'May I ask you something personal?' she said afterwards, as again she lay on her stomach. 'My turn.'

'Try me.'

'Don't you get any sex at home?'

'She hasn't told me, but I know my wife's pregnant.' He realized he sounded annoyed.

Her customary impassivity slipped. 'How do you know, if she hasn't said?'

'Sunday morning, I happened to notice a discarded pregnancy test in our bathroom waste bin. My wife had left the lid up. Distracted I suppose by my knocking on the door. It registered positive.'

'Aren't you over the moon?'

'Best she has a termination.' He spoke his thoughts aloud.

Sheena rolled off the bed, stood up straight.

'Make her do that, she'll hate you for the rest of her life.' For the blink of an eye, he waited for the slap across his face. 'And herself.'

She disappeared into the bathroom, slammed the door giving him no chance to say he doubted he could make his wife do anything she didn't want to do.

CHAPTER THIRTY SIX

Thursday, 8 September

When Calista first settled in Leicester, she had been seduced by Casa Romana's trattoria buzz. She breathed in the aroma of fresh-made coffee and, from the kitchen, wafts of garlic turning golden in good olive oil. Her mouth watered. Once her early morning nausea had passed . . . *Hurry up Tess, I'm ravenous.* On Monday evening Esther had phoned, I'll pop over to Leicester on the train, Esther had said. 'We can have lunch at your favourite Italian restaurant.' A lot to catch up with, they both agreed.

Calista sat facing the door, alternating between nibbling on *grissini* and sipping fresh orange juice. At last, Esther waved from the entrance. Calista got to her feet, the easier for them to mwah, mwah.

'Am I glad to see you,' they said in unison, then giggling sat down opposite each other.

'Orange juice, Cal?'

'S'pose one glass of Orvieto *abboccato* can do no harm.' Calista beckoned the waiter.

'I'll have the same,' Esther said.

Calista was convinced she would explode if she did not confide in Esther, and soon. She held back. Esther's turn first. Esther had taken the trouble to come over. Choices made, 'So tell me about Amsterdam,' she said.

'Liked it. Helps I suppose that so many Dutch people speak English. Mike's pad is fabulous. Fantastic communal garden, not big obviously, formal, shrubs and small trees in huge decorative pots, and sculptures. You'd never know it was there from the front of the building. And Wilhelm and Marieka Langmeijer are so friendly. They really made me feel at home.'

'So you will be moving over there with Fran and Tom.'

Esther shrugged. The waiter brought their wine, and a bottle of carbonated mineral water.

'Tess, you said things between you and Mike were sorted.'

Esther held up her glass, 'Cheers.' They clinked glasses, both took an appreciative sip of wine.

'Bet Mike was pleased about your wangling a sabbatical.'

'Haven't told him yet. Not sure he really wants us there'

'What?'

Esther told her, back at the apartment after the reception, she decided to sound Mike out. Before she could continue the waiter brought their starters. Melon and Parma ham for Esther, Calista had ordered a starter portion of cannelloni *magri*.

'Glad to see you've got your appetite back,' Esther said. 'What's in the parcels?'

'Mushrooms and spinach. Try one.' Calista indicated.

'Yummy.' Esther took a sip of wine before beginning to eat. 'And this ham is the best.'

'Tess?'

'Okay, I'll tell you Mike's reaction.'

'You don't mind if I carry on eating while you talk, do you?' Calista said.

Mike re-set the security system before he followed her into the kitchen. All evening she had longed for a cup of her favourite Earl Grey. He came over to her, arm around her, stroked her hip in that solicitous way of his.

'I'll make it,' he said. 'You get ready for bed.'

Instead, she went through to the salon. No way could she talk to him in the multi-mirrored bedroom. The past two sensuous nights they had taken full advantage of the erotic propensity of those mirrors. She heard him go to the bedroom. Before he tracked her down, she moved from the squeaky leather sofa to sit to attention on an elegant Louis XV open armchair.

'There you are. Thought you were still in the bathroom. Aren't you tired? I'm all in.'

How sexy he looked without his jacket, dress-shirt undone. He placed the tray he was carrying on the coffee table and sat down at the end of the sofa nearest her chair. Leaning forward, he poured tea from a silver teapot into white china cups. She held her saucer firmly and focussed on the contents of her cup.

'Mike, how would you feel about all of us, me and Fran and Tom, all coming over here?'

'But you are doing, remember, half-term. We agreed. The kids want to see where I'll be staying. And Amsterdam. Will it be as good as going to London to stay with Nana Mina? Are Ajax better than Arsenal?'

She looked up so that she could watch his expression. 'Not just for a visit, I meant to live here as long as you're here.'

As soon as he had finished speaking he had taken a mouthful of tea. She watched the movement of his Adam's apple as he drank. Still not answering, he placed his cup on its saucer. His eyes were warm and loving, his mouth, as always, threatening to break into a smile.

'Mike?'

'Needs a lot of thinking about.'

'You said the Netherlands would be an interesting experience for Fran and Tom.'

'Tess, sweetheart, you'd be giving up so much.'

She could not suppress a flash of anger. 'You don't want us. This way you can live like a carefree singleton, then come home to be pampered at weekends. Except you'll probably be getting plenty of pampering here . . .'

'That's not it at all,' he said, his voice soft. 'How were you when you were stuck at home before? I didn't realize the extent of it till Mina told me. All I'm saying is, we must consider all the angles.'

She felt her eyes fill with tears. Damn it, she could not wipe her eyes because she had to make sure she did not spill the blasted tea. 'You wish I wasn't here, don't you? You only asked me because Charles Pennington told me about it.'

He moved to squat in front of her just as he had done the night of their row, only this time he held her ankles so that she could not kick out.

'We weren't exactly on the best of terms, hadn't been for some time had we, Tess?' He stood up, took her cup and saucer from her and placed it on the table, then pulled her to her feet and held her close, stroking her hair. 'Been a long day, time for bed. Okay?' But they had not gone to sleep without first making love.

'Tess?' Mike sounded as sleepy as she felt.

'Mike?'

'If you're really serious about coming over to live with me, we'll talk about it properly first weekend I'm home.'

Calista was conscious of Esther's scrutiny as, with a chunk of bread, she mopped up the sauce from her cannelloni. 'Sorry, just too more-ish.' She wiped her fingers on her napkin. 'I really don't see what you've told me equates with Mike not really wanting you and his children to be with him. Strikes me, he's thinking more about you than himself.'

'But I haven't yet told you about Louise van de Velde.'

'Tess, eat up, then tell me.'

'Think I'd better.' Esther smiled. 'Before you finish it for me.'

The waiter came to collect their empty plates.

'You were saying, Louise Who-d'ya-flop?'

Esther described Louise van de Velde, how she made a beeline for Mike.

'Just because she was all over Mike like the proverbial, doesn't mean they're having an affair. She may want him to, but . . . Sounds as though she was gobsmacked when he introduced you. He would've warned her if . . .'

'S'pose.'

The waiter tantalized them with a glimpse of their main courses. They were both having grilled sea bass. 'Would you like me to fillet them,' he said, and whisked them away.

'But, Mike didn't come home with me on the Saturday, said he had one or two things to finalize, so last weekend was out as far as discussions went. And look at the way Adam strung his wife along while you and he were having an affair.'

'Esther Mahoney, don't you dare compare my lovely mate, Mike to my cheating manipulative shit of a husband.'

'Ooo-er, Missis.' Esther sat back in her chair feigning shock.

The waiter placed their fileted main course in front of them.

'Thank-you,' they said in unison.

'Enjoy your meal.' He gave them a quizzical smile.

'Do you think he overheard?' Esther said.

'Don't care if he did.' Calista cut herself a morsel of fish and ate. 'This bass . . .' Her fingers and thumb tips together, she placed them to her lips to show her appreciation, then pointed to the two serving bowls, one full of chips, one of salad. 'You dib in first.'

'You've certainly got your appetite back, and then some.' Esther helped herself.

'Well, seems I now have to eat for two.' Calista looked across the table and smiled. Esther's mouth fell open. Obvious this time her shock was for real.

CHAPTER THIRTY SEVEN

Breaking News

While Calista waited for Esther to say something, she too helped herself to a generous helping of salad and chips.

'I knew it, just knew it.' Esther pointed with her knife.

'Are you going to stab me?'

Esther put her knife down. 'You sound upbeat.'

'No point in not being,' Calista said. 'And what could you possibly know?'

'Thirty four next month, the clock ticking and all that. If you hadn't married . . .' Esther prised a bite-sized piece from her filleted fish. 'Umm, grilled to perfection . . .'

'Utter pants, Tess. You know me well enough to realize that procreation has never ever been high, if at all, on my agenda. And, if you must know, waiting for a father for my child, if that's what I was doing, well, it's been like waiting ages for a bus. Two came along at the same time.' Calista handed Esther, who looked as though she was about to choke, a glass of water.

After taking a sip 'When's it due?' Esther said.

'Haven't worked it out properly. Early next May? My period was due the Saturday we got back from Ithaca. No show.' Calista shrugged. 'Didn't think too much of it. Not after my emotional seesaw of a holiday. Then, no sooner home and I began to feel queasy first thing. Nerves, despondency about being back.'

'Surely you are, were on the Pill?' Esther said.

'Ahhh, slight hiccup.' Calista gestured towards Esther's plate. 'Let's tuck in before it goes cold.' She took a mouthful of wine.

'If you are pregnant,' Esther said, 'you should go easy on the booze.'

'Don't you just love the hint of honeyed aftertaste, and surely just the occasional glass . . . Good food, good wine, good company,' Calista held up her glass. 'Here's to us Tess. Bloody men, who needs 'em?'

They jinked glasses. 'May all our troubles be little ones,' Esther said with a mischievous smile.

They concentrated on clearing their plates.

'As you agreed to come over to give me the benefit of your expert advice,' Calista said, 'unless you would like a sweet, I suggest we adjourn to my chambers.'

'No pudding for me thank you. You?'

'I'm stuffed.' Calista patted her stomach. 'Whoops.' They exchanged smiles.

'Why me? You've got Family Law specialists in the same building,' Esther said.

'Because you're my best mate, and I can tell you anything and everything.'

A short walk from the restaurant on a sunny and warm September afternoon. 'I love the way you can work out the timeline of a city's development by the names of its streets.' Calista said. 'We turned into Chatham from Albion, and crossed Wellington, all redolent of the late-Eighteenth early-Nineteenth Centuries. And, behold, the Dominican church of Holy Cross, built in 1819 beside leafy New Walk, laid out in 1785 for the prosperous citizens of Leicester to promenade and show off their finery.'

Esther, hand to her mouth, exaggerated a yawn. 'Thanks for the history lesson. Think you may have the date wrong for the church. Has a pure 1950s air.'

They crossed in front and onto New Walk making for Calista's chambers.

'This part wasn't consecrated till 1958.' Calista pointed. 'Look there. An older redbrick, building is tacked onto the other end, or rather vice versa.'

'How come you know so much?'

'There's a plaque inside.'

'Jesus, Cal, when did you feel the need to turn to religion?'

'Heathen though I am, when I find I need to think through some personal problem, I slip across and sit in a pew. Usually works a treat. Just got it wrong when it came to marrying Adam.' Calista took Esther's arm. 'Come on, True Confession Time.'

Her first ever visit, Esther looked around Calista's office on the top floor at the back of the three-storied, late-Georgian terrace. Two light-oak desks, fronts abutting, filled most of the space, on one a laptop, desk lamp and notepad, a container of pencils on the other a lamp, a couple of reference books, a file of papers, box of tissues. At each desk, a swivel, executive chair, and next to the wall behind the desk with the laptop, a bookcase with two shelves containing the Concise Oxford Dictionary, and reference books on Trusts, Company and Commercial Law, and on the wall above a framed charcoal drawing of what Esther suspected was Beppo, Calista's spaniel.

'Don't know what I expected,' Esther said, 'but . . .' she gestured around the room.

'This is where Chloe, my pupil and I work,' Calista said, 'not where I see clients. As I'm your client, I thought we could talk here.' She gestured to the chair behind the desk with the laptop. 'You sit at my desk, and I'll sit at Chloe's. Earl Grey, I presume.' She went over to the small table by the window, underneath a mini fridge, and busied herself with an electric kettle and mugs. 'Cosy don't you think?'

Esther took a notepad and her Mont Blanc pen out of her handbag, placed them on Calista's desk, and settled herself in her chair

Tea made, the two of them each leaned back and sipped their drink.

'First of all, Cal, you're sure you are pregnant?'

'Ninety nine percent certain if the Clear Blue blurb's to be believed. I bought three kits, used the last one Sunday morning, all three tests, positive. Being mugged threw me more than I let on. I did what I always do when I'm upset, focussed on work, then I realized, once or twice, I was forgetting to take my contraceptive. No harm done, takes an age to become pregnant after you've stopped, especially at my age. That's what I'd heard. In any case for a while now, Adam's attentions haven't exactly been overwhelming.'

'Being married isn't quite as . . . I don't know, Cal, exciting, I suppose, as being in the throes of a clandestine affair.'

'Clearly not for Adam,' Calista said. 'And as far as I'm concerned, if I never have sex with him again, it'll be too soon.'

'Seems on holiday he must have . . .'

'Saturday evening, soon as we arrived . . . I really don't want to think about that. The rest of the three weeks, forget it. I really wasn't in the mood. You know why. Maybe he sensed my vibes. Certainly seems to have since we got back.'

'You could've been in the early stages of pregnancy before you went.'

'No, last day of period the Thursday before that Saturday. Numpty, I'd only gone and left my pack of pills at home. No worries, condoms are available in Greece. Then on the sixth day, the following Thursday that is, I go and meet Mr PJ Wood.'

'So prospective fathers being like buses is for real.'

'Go on, say what you really think. Over-educated, well-heeled, competent women don't get themselves into this sort of mess.'

'Cal, you'd be surprised, if not astonished, I can tell you. Don't you remember a few years back, that high-profile politician who was convinced the child of his ex-lover was his. He insisted the poor kid had a DNA test. The tabloids were full of it. I can't recall the outcome, wasn't that interested. What I do remember was, politician's upper class ex and her husband closed ranks soon as . . .'

Straightening her back, Calista sat forward in her chair. 'I've no intention of closing ranks with Adam. He'd love it, wouldn't he? Something to beat me over the head with. No way, Tess. I intend to divorce him.'

Calista drained her mug and put it down.

CHAPTER THIRTY EIGHT

Grounds for Divorce

Esther too put her empty mug to one side, and leant forward, hands clasped on the desk. So far she had seen no need to make notes.

'Getting a divorce, Cal, is not that easy particularly if PJ Wood turns out to be the father of your child. Adam would have grounds, not you, because you've had sex with someone else and Adam can claim he can no longer bear to live with you. And if Adam's the Dad, which he could just be, then . . .' She noticed Calista's eyes fill with tears which she knuckled away, Esther didn't finish her sentence. 'You have managed to contact P.J?'

'I've sent emails. No reply, but if he's in danger somewhere . . .' Calista shuddered. 'I did try Googling him. Doesn't seem to have a website, not under PJ Wood. He works through an agency but I don't know the name. Last week I sent a postcard in an airmail envelope to Vathi, my name and address on the back. Someone might get round to letting me know if . . .'

Calista looked so miserable, Esther pushed back her chair, scooted round the two desks and enfolded her friend in her arms. Calista looked up, eyes again filling with tears which she brushed aside with her fingertips. 'Oh Tess, I just can't bear the thought of never ever seeing him again. I don't even know what PJ stands for.'

Esther leaned her bottom against the desk's edge and held Calista's hands and gaze. 'You've been back barely three weeks. Early days, darling, if he's up to his eyes in ordure somewhere inaccessible.'

'That's what I keep telling myself but . . . I did send a second card to his London address. I actually went there on Tuesday evening. Seemed deserted, but it's for real.'

'You must've been feeling desperate to do that.' *Message to self, stop burdening Cal. Own troubles nothing compared to hers.*

'I was in the vicinity confirming something I've suspected for ages, and now I'm pregnant, I wanted to know for sure.' Calista wriggled her hands free, pushed her chair back, and got to her feet. 'Come, let me show you.' She went round to her own desk. Esther followed. Calista leaned over, switched on her laptop. Once it was up and running, she clicked on the Photo Gallery icon. 'I'd like to show you a few photos I sent from my iPhone.' She opened a folder.

Esther too bent over the desk the better to see the screen. She recognized immediately the location of the first shot. 'I know that fountain,' she said, 'just down river from Tower Bridge.'

'And near the enormous hotel Adam always stays in,' Calista said. 'But not for much longer, I suspect. He's hinted he's looking for somewhere less impersonal – a pied-a-terre.'

'Who's the girl? Or is she someone who just happened to be standing there.'

'By the look of her, your younger sister,' Calista said. 'That what made me photograph her in the first place.'

'Oh we mulattoes all look alike.' A smile in her voice, Esther elbowed Calista in the ribs.

'That would be beautiful then.' Calista turned to her. 'Wait till you see the next couple or so.' She clicked on a second photo

Esther saw Adam speaking to the woman who was smiling. A rendezvous? Another click, an indignant intake of breath on Calista's behalf. Adam and the woman gazing into each other's eyes, the woman holding his hand to her mouth, she sucked on his thumb. In the next photo, a back view of them arm-in-arm.

'That's all.' Calista straightened up.

Esther too straightened her back and turned to face her. 'Oh my God, Cal. Lucky he didn't once look in your direction.'

'I was mingling with a posse of tourists.' Calista gave a rueful smile. 'Besides, he only had eyes for her.'

'And you've no idea who she is?'

'Someone he's been seeing for a while by the look of it. Do you know what got to me more than anything? You'll laugh. Her Louis Vuitton's exactly the same as one he gave me Christmas before last, which if you recall was a couple of months before we were married. What's the betting he bought her one at the same time? Probably got a job lot for all his women.'

'I'm so not laughing, Cal. For God's sake don't be more upset than you already are. And, this doesn't mean I'm judging her. I doubt she's much more than twenty. But, I know what I think she is.'

'No need to spell it out.' Calista shrugged. 'I thought the same. According to his skewed moral compass when it comes to indulging his red-blooded masculinity, probably thinks this sort of thing doesn't count. Whatever his excuse . . . damn him, damn him. She's young enough to be his daughter. That's beside the point. Now don't tell me I've no grounds for divorce. I just need more concrete evidence for a pre-emptive strike. Okay?'

'I'd better make a few notes,' Esther said. 'You sit down.' She picked up her notebook and pen and went to sit at Chloe's desk. 'First, please email me copies of those photos. We need to identify the woman, make enquiries, try and discover how long Adam's had this arrangement with her, how he met her. When I say 'we', I mean the firm of private investigators we use. They're discreet, get results. They'll come up with the goods for your pre-emptive strike, and don't even begin to think getting them on the case is in any way scuzzy. Needs must as Shakespeare probably said.' Whilst she wrote, Calista forwarded copies of the photos to her email address.

Tasks completed, they looked across at each other and smiled. 'I'll drop you off at the station,' Calista said. 'I'm all done here for today. The girls are still with us and Adam won't be back till tomorrow evening. Marries me so there's no argument about his getting joint custody, then buggers off to London for days on end. Now we know why. He's taking them back to school on Monday. Thank God, I'll probably not see him again after that till the following Friday.'

Before they left, Esther had a closer look at the charcoal drawing. 'That is Beppo, isn't it?'

'Len drew him for me,' Calista said.

'Even I can see, she's caught the essence of him. That's some talent. I'm sure Mum would be happy to talk to her about a career as an artist, if Len would like her to, that is.'

'Bet she'd jump at the chance. Between us, we'll cook up something so they meet.' Calista sighed. 'You wouldn't believe how attached I've become to Len and Sash. Because I was lonely, I suppose. Whatever happens, they can come and stay with me whenever they like.'

'Don't think you'd get joint custody though.' Esther chuckled.

'But I shall tell them that when the time comes,' Calista said as they made their way down to the car park. 'Shan't want them to feel my divorcing their father's anything to do with them. And I shall certainly claim sole custody of Beppo.'

As Esther put on her seatbelt, she made up her mind. Calista was her dearest friend and she could and would say what had been at the back of her mind. 'Before you drive off, I feel I must say something. I hate to see you in such a mess, emotionally I mean. You haven't seen your GP yet . . .'

'Before you start, I've an appointment with her tomorrow afternoon. And I'm already taking folic acid. I do have access to information and advice on the internet, Tess.'

She placed a placatory hand on Calista's knee. 'Course you have darling. What I was going to say is, if you had a mind to be practical, have you considered having a termination? Wipe the slate clean. There, I've said it, and you'll hate me, especially as I don't think it's something I could contemplate myself.'

Calista twisted in her seat to look at her, met her gaze. 'Don't you think it crossed my mind? Foolish, maybe, but I just can't bring myself to do that. You must realize why. And, even if . . . though I don't quite see how . . . Adam's girls are lovely, and if I have a boy, then I'll do my best to make sure he's not messed up like . . . I can afford to bring up a child on my own.'

Esther leaned across and hugged her. 'Course you can, darling. And you know me and Mike, we'll support you all the way.'

Calista started the engine, 'Must say, I feel a whole lot better now I've got things moving, and I've something to say to you Mrs Mahoney. This weekend, no agonizing discussion, just tell Mike you've arranged a sabbatical and you and the children will be moving over to Amsterdam during the Christmas holidays. I know Mikey. He'll do cartwheels, whatever. And, don't even dream of bringing up the subject of Louise Thingy Once you've told him you're all going over there, she'll be toast. All that's needed now is for me to have news of Mr PJ Wood, good news that is.'

CHAPTER THIRTY NINE

Leicestershire – Thursday, 6 October, early morning

Calista stretched, pushed herself into a sitting position, reached over to take her secret Semikolon notebook with gilt-edged pages from the drawer of the bedside table. She removed two half sheets of A4 paper, folded, from the expandable pocket at the back, opened them up, on both, printouts of emails from PJ Wood, dated Sunday, 25 September 2011. The first read: *Cal, so sorry not to have replied sooner. You're not forgotten. How could I forget you? In quiet moments wherever I am, whatever I'm doing, I think of you. Hope you're still fine. I'm good, thanks for asking. Be in touch again soon as. PJ.*

She replied straightaway, sounding, she hoped, more laid back than she felt. *Not to worry, PJ. Just glad to hear from you at last, also that you're okay. You're unforgettable too. 'Unforgettable' that's an old song, surely? Schmaltzy! What I mean is, I think about you in my quiet moments, especially when I'm walking my dog. When, if we manage to catch up, I have lots to tell you. Love, Cal.*

He had not said where he was, but he came back immediately with, *"lots to tell me", sounds ominous. Have you let your inner rebel escape at last? And, this dog, he looks like me is what you're saying? Have to go now. Love and lots of kisses, PJ.*

He knew damn well that was not what she meant, imagined his smile as he teased.

'Well, PJ, your messages arrived five whole weeks after I sent you my first one.' She spoke her thoughts into the stillness of the room. 'So

221

much for telling me to let you know if I ever needed you. Not that I'm complaining. I do understand, I think.' If he was in the middle of an assignment somewhere . . . she ran through all the places he could be in danger, Libya, Syria, fingers crossed not Afghanistan. Wherever, he would have no time for her. Her own fault she was in this mess, up to her to sort herself out. She re-folded the messages, put them back in the notebook, returned that to the drawer, then, threw back the duvet and swung her feet to the floor. Time for a shower. Before making for the bathroom, she padded to the window to look out over the valley. The early morning mist was already clearing especially for her.

She luxuriated in the warm-silk spray of the shower playing over her body, the subtle scent of coconut-butter body wash. She was relieved that early morning nausea, the unproductive retching seemed to have abated. Almost a week since she last experienced that. Lucky you to get off so lightly, Esther said. She was also fortunate to be able to work at home whenever she wished, barring attending Court or advising clients, which should mean taking minimal maternity leave. A single mother needed to maximise her income. As from Monday, her pregnancy had been official, but for the time being only as far as Head of Chambers. He was delighted she wanted to carry on with as little disruption as possible. Life was never all bad, and today she was going to spoil herself. First, she and Beppo would go for a ramble, returning in time to spend a couple of hours on her latest brief before her lunchtime guests arrived.

She pulled on dark blue jeans – her waist couldn't be thickening already - topped them with a white T-shirt – uhh, uhh, she should be thinking of buying new bras. She slipped on a pair of loafers and went down to breakfast. The kitchen was welcoming, on the table near her place setting in a silver specimen vase, one perfect scarlet cactus dahlia picked from the flowerbed.

'Happy Birthday!' Smiling, Pam placed the bowl of creamy porridge in front of her.

'Thank you.' Calista returned her smile.

'Forecast's good,' Pam said. 'How are you feeling this morning?'

'Good. I'm good.' She trickled runny amber honey over the bowl's contents. Loyal, discreet, reliable Pam had sussed she was pregnant before she had herself, and did not question her request, please don't mention it to Adam, not yet. I'll let you know when it's okay.

Pam went over to the radio. As usual she was listening to Radio 2.

'Please don't turn it off,' Calista said, the music banal but more cheerful than the talk on *Today*, Adam's preference when he was home.

Whilst she ate, Pam sat at the table having a cup of tea and the two of them confirmed the lunch menu. A starter of roasted and sliced red, yellow and green peppers made into a salad, followed by trout meuniere with parsley and butter-tossed boiled potatoes, runner beans, the fishes, Adam's catch. Blackberry and apple Tarte Tatin with crème fraiche for pudding, the fruit and vegetables home grown. Matt Wakeham, and Chloe, approaching completion of her second six-month pupillage, were coming, part birthday celebration part discussion of current cases.

'Sure you'll be okay with the peppers?' Pam said.

'I'll be fine. Besides, Matt loves them.'

Adam so obviously peeved when he discovered she had invited Matt on her birthday, only at the last minute did she tell him Chloe would be there too. Terribly sorry I shan't be back till Friday evening Adam had told her. Her day was going to be so much more relaxing without him.

Beppo at heel, she made for the lane via the coppice, which would bring her out much lower down the hill than their main gate. Soggy underfoot, moisture dripping from foliage, she was glad of her new wellies, Hunters no less, the warmth of her primrose cashmere sweater, and her Barbour gilet, also new. 'If you could only see me, PJ, quite the country woman. I may even be in danger of joining the local WI.' She spoke her thoughts aloud as she breathed in the scent of damp earth, the decay of autumn, and there they were, growing through the humus beneath a hornbeam, pink, perfectly sculpted cyclamen. If only PJ were here to share her small pleasures. After lunch she would show Matt and Chloe. Careful to shut the gate with its unequivocal notice – PRIVATE KEEP OUT – in hazy sunshine she turned up the hill, pretending as she often did walking Beppo that PJ was a silent presence by her side. On their left, they passed the church, walked between high hedges decked with clusters of scarlet haws among leaves turning from green to gold.

'To paraphrase Dylan, – Dylan Thomas that is, not Bob – this is my thirty fourth year to heaven. The poet's birthday was in October, but toward the end. He was Scorpio. I'm Libra, in perfect balance, ha, ha. Can you hear that blackbird singing in the bushes? Or maybe it's a robin.' Again she spoke what went through her head. Beppo gave her a nervous sidelong glance. Rooks called overhead, not seagulls, and here no heron-priested shore. She had a sudden yen for the Norfolk coast where her parents used to take her and her brother. At this time of year on the marshes around Blakeney Point, there would be a cacophony of migrating birds.

Beppo had already slid under the five-bar gate into the field, she climbed over the stile to take their usual footpath up the grassy hill. The last week in October, the girls' half-term, Adam had chartered a plane so the four of them could spend it at the now completed and furnished Villa Thalia. She had not objected. Len and Sash had been so excited, and she had thought maybe if she had not heard from PJ by then, she might somehow glean news of him from Marcos.

These past weeks Adam had been affable yet subdued. He had made no attempt to make love to her, not that he needed her sexual favours. She sensed he suspected something was not right. Only another couple of weeks before they were due to go to Ithaca. She doubted she could keep her pregnancy from him much longer. What would she say, *Adam I'm expecting, but I very much doubt my baby's yours.* She would rather tell PJ first, in the hope he would be willing to take a confirmatory paternity test. The necessity of being fully briefed was essential when she confronted Adam and told him she intended suing for divorce. 'So you surely can see, PJ why I really, really do need you, right here, and right now,' she said, this time ignored by Beppo already way ahead intent on following a scent.

At the top of the steep slope, over another stile and a short stretch along the ridge, away from banked hedges and overhanging trees, she stopped, breathed in golden autumn air, and admired overhead an impasto of all shades of white clouds on a duck-egg blue canvas. Her GP told her she must keep active to prevent pre-eclampsia. Regular walks with the dog were ideal. According to her own calculation, and confirmed, she was coming to the end of her ninth week. Last Friday an ultrasound scan had also confirmed the first of May as her due date. 'May Day, m'aidez,' she had said, but her GP either did not get it, or being the consummate professional, ignored her feeble joke. Not that she felt light-hearted. Lately, without warning she would be overcome by such a sadness she would weep.

Despite Esther's and Pam's interest in every nuance of her condition, and though accident he or she may be, this was her first and probably only baby. As the weeks passed and each milestone reached – tender breasts, her new-found aversion to coffee, all meat except chicken - the worry of all sorts of blood tests - Sickle Cell Anaemia, Rhesus disease, STDs, HIV – she could go on – the relief when she was clear – how she longed to share all this with, and count on the love and support of her baby's father. She held her hand up to being more emotional than she had ever been in her life, but that lack above all else was what reduced her to tears. *You've made your bed*, Granny's aphorism rang in her ears. Caressing her stomach, she said, 'Don't worry little one, we'll manage okay on our own.'

Somewhere along the hedgerow a cock pheasant screeched. Starting, she wondered how long she had been standing gazing unseeing over the rolling ochre and umber-tinted terrain. She took her iPhone from her jeans' pocket to find out the time, and sighed. 'Better start back, Beppo, if I'm to do any work this morning. At least going home's all downhill.'

Almost there, she heard a motorbike engine rev, then the cattle grid's rattle. She began to hurry but was only in time to see the back of a large and powerful machine, on it a black-leather-clad figure, disappearing down the lane towards the main road.

'See what's waiting for you on the dining room table,' Pam said smiling, when, having taken off her wellies in the side lobby, she checked in.

'Come and show me,' she said.

In the dining room, courtesy of Inter Flora, an arty-minimalist arrangement of coral, orange and bronze flowers and foliage, which, except for three exotic orchids, she did not recognize. The message read: *To darling Cal, Happy Birthday! With love from Adam.* Attractive, unusual, and chosen by one of his smart-arse assistants, no doubt. Alongside, a stunning arrangement of shaggy, deep rose-pink chrysanthemums, pale mauve and white Michaelmas daisies intermingled, and a card saying: *To our dearest daughter, Calista, a very Happy Birthday! With love from Mummy and Daddy.*

'And you just missed the young man who brought these,' Pam said.

'I caught a glimpse of a motorcyclist,' Calista said. 'He brought these on a motorbike?'

In the most generous crystal vase she must have been able to find, Pam had arranged a mass of the most perfect translucent roses, a subtle shade of pale creamy-yellow not in too-tight bud, not so far out they were in danger of becoming blowsy. In front of the vase, a birthday-card sized envelope, simply addressed to Calista Blake. As she slit it open with her thumb, Pam said, 'There are thirty four of them, one for every year since you were born.'

With trembling hands as she took the card out of the now ragged envelope, she paid no attention to the picture on the front. Inside in bold, cursive script, *Happy Birthday, Cal! With love from PJ Wood.* So like him not to send her predictable old red roses. Blinking back tears, she buried her face in the flowers. Sprays of fragile Baby's Breath relieving their austere beauty caressed her cheek.

CHAPTER FORTY

Roses have thorns
[Shakespeare, Sonnet 35]

Eyes closed, Calista gripped the edge of the table. She sensed movement. A chair seat touched the back of her knees, a light hand stroked her back. 'Cal, please sit down before you fall down,' Pam's voice soft. Calista lowered herself into the chair, rested her forearms on the table, leaned her head on them, and wept.

'There, there,' Pam said as though to a child, 'let it all come out,' and continued to rub her back. Calista had no idea how long she cried, except, soothed by Pam's gentle touch, she got a grip, wiped her eyes with her fingertips, her nose with the back of her hand, and sat up.

'Better now?' Pam said.

Calista rested her cheek against Pam's hand which she had placed on her shoulder.

'Dear Pam, you do look after me . . . And the house . . . And Beppo.'

'As far as the house is concerned, just doing my job, and that old dog's no trouble.'

'Yes, but what would I do without you?' Calista turned her head to look at her and managed to smile.

Pam gave her shoulder a squeeze, 'You're a successful woman, but you've no side. You spend days in this huge house on your own. I sense how lonely you are. My heart goes out to you. I've two sons, both good to me, and their wives, but after my husband died I learnt what loneliness is.'

Calista gave the deepest of sighs. 'Pam, I've got myself into one helluva mess.'

'Why don't I make us both a hot chocolate?' Pam said. 'And while we're drinking it you can tell me all about it, if you want to, that is. You must know me by now. I don't gossip.'

'I do know. Give me a minute. I'll follow you.'

Calista picked up her precious birthday card. She was drawn into the picture's middle distance by a white fishing boat banded red with characteristic bright blue engine house anchored on a tranquil opalescent sea. In the foreground the waters shaded to inky blue-grey ripples reflecting a rocky promontory overhung with Mediterranean pine. On the distant horizon, a violet headland beneath the palest magenta sky. She turned the card over to look at the back for confirmation: *Photograph of boat in gulf in Ithaca, Greece at dusk*. Not a white-sailed sloop like the *Thelma Jane*. That would be asking too much, but a photograph which had the look, the feel of an oil painting. How she longed to return to Ithaca, keep PJ to his promise to teach her to sail.

She opened her card once more and with her fingertips traced the words *Happy Birthday, Cal! With love from PJ Wood*, his formality deliberate she supposed. But, thirty four perfect roses, hardly restrained.

She and Pam sat facing each other across the table. Beppo sat upright in his basket as soon as she had entered the kitchen. He looked as though he was, like Pam, waiting for her to tell her story.

'Before I begin,' Calista said, leaning back in her chair, 'tell me about the biker who brought those beautiful roses. Some sort of courier?' *No way could it be him. No way*. She took a sip of her chocolate drink, then another, and smiled. 'This really hits the spot, Pam. Thank you.'

Pam put her mug down. 'I'd opened the dining room window to air it a bit. That's when I heard a motorbike. You know that sound they make when they're not going very fast. Then the cattle grid rattled so I went to the front door. He didn't get a chance to ring the bell.

'Big powerful machine it was, not one of them scooter things delivery boys ride.'

'Yes, I just caught a glimpse,' Calista said.

'Well, he'd had the sense to take off his helmet. Hate it when I can't see their faces. His was really tanned, thought at first he might be . . . then I noticed his eyes, couldn't help but notice them, such a deep blue . . .'

Calista almost stopped breathing. 'And his smile. He did smile. Was it sort of mocking?'

'S'pose, but not what I'd call snide.'

No, not sneering, just the way his cheeks creased and the corners of his mouth turned down rather than up. An inherited thing perhaps. Calista was conscious of her heart's beat, her uneven breath. *Fate is cruel. I was within a hairsbreadth of seeing him. Pam wouldn't think to ask him to wait.* She tuned back into what Pam was saying.

'For Calista Blake. He was holding a cardboard box. Please keep it this way up. I asked him if he minded telling me what it was. Roses, he said. She loves roses, I said and he smiled. My favourites, despite their thorns. Then I asked if he was a friend of yours. He told me, kind of.'

Kind of, kind of! Calista wondered what Pam would say when she told her what kind of friend he was.

'I told him you were out walking the dog, and should be back any minute. That shook him, I could tell. He took a few steps back. S'pose he imagined you'd be out at work. I took a couple of steps towards him onto the drive. I asked if he'd like to come in and wait, then he could give them to you himself.'

'You thought to ask him to wait?'

'I liked the look of him, and he said he was a friend.'

Why hadn't he waited? Before she could ask, Pam answered.

'Looked all around him. Peered beyond me into the house as though he was making up his mind to go in. Then, better I don't he said, and thrust the box at me, plus the card.'

Didn't he want to see her as much as she longed to see him? 'I don't understand.' Calista heard the catch in her voice. 'You said I'd be back any minute.'

'Oh dear, Cal, I forgot to tell you –He said, be sure to say to Cal, beware Greeks bearing gifts. I'm sorry. And I should've let you open the roses, but I thought they might need water. They were wrapped in sturdy cellophane and standing in a reservoir. Oh dear, I'm so sorry, I spoilt it for you. Please don't get upset again.'

Calista knew her face must show she was once more on the verge of tears. Beppo too must have sensed her distress. He came to her and with a sympathetic whimper rested his muzzle on her knee.

'I'm not upset about that.' Swallowing, she managed to get a grip, for the time being anyway. 'I'm desperate to see him. Once you hear what I . . . Oh Pam, what was so bloody pressing he . . .' Then, she could no longer contain herself. She heard herself wail as though in agonizing pain.

So much for quixotic gestures. PJ Wood manoeuvred his Yamaha down the narrow lane wishing he could give it full throttle, put distance between himself and the Old Rectory, make it easier for him to resist going back. At the bottom of this slope what could be simpler than a U-turn at the T-junction with what in these parts passed as a main road. Cal's postcard waiting for him in London had sounded like a reproof. He would not and could not ever forget her, nor had he changed his mind about their keeping in touch. He would have done all in his power not to hurt her *–sorry my love, I was unavoidably detained by . . . well you don't really need to know, but I do have the photos to prove I wasn't skiving. And, I survived to tell the tale, a little Pashto goes a long way.*

Now he had crossed the main road onto a pot-holed, crumbling strip of asphalt no wider than a hay wain. No U-turns possible.

The roses he had chosen with such care were meant to make up for his five weeks' silence, a birthday surprise. He could have, should have sent them by courier, and mailed her card. On the postcard she had sent him she had spelt out her Leicestershire address. Curious, and with a day to himself, he decided to check it out, a nightmare to find once he had left the A6 near Market Harborough. He had expected a comfortable Victorian vicarage in the heart of a village, hopefully with a pub, not an impressive, late-Eighteenth Century house with a Tuscan-columned portico standing aloof from a mere hamlet. The Old Rectory, nestling on the side of a hill, was surrounded by oodles of ground. Burgess's choice, PJ suspected, rather than Cal's. That, and the shock of discovering Cal wasn't out somewhere laying down the law made him decide not to wait. He guessed the late-middle-aged woman who had invited him in was the housekeeper, was glad someone who seemed motherly and kind was looking after Cal.

Wood, you're a spineless dipstick. Cal isn't happy. He should have waited, then took her in his arms, said *we're out of here*, strapped her and her dog on the pillion and ridden off into the sunset like some Twenty First Century Lochinvar. Burgess, no 'dastard in war' he suspected, if he had to, he was more than willing to fight him for Cal. He, PJ Wood was by no means poor. Even so his bijou London residence would probably fit into a couple of the Old Rectory's larger rooms, and Cal would spend weeks rather than days on her own never knowing when, if, he would be back, or in what state he would be when he did return. Cal had a career. She couldn't drop everything and visit Ma like he did at the end of an assignment, and he couldn't ask Ma to re-settle in England. Ithaca and their villa with its memories of his father meant too much to her.

At last the traffic roundabout which would take him onto the A6 where he could give the bike some welly, experience the elation of taking every curve at speed, the buzz of just making it overtaking one HGV with another ploughing towards him. On the A14, if traffic were slow, he could weave in and out, and once he hit the M11 . . . No one with any sense would prefer a car over a motorbike if they wanted to get anywhere fast. He whizzed round only to exit where he had entered. Sod it, he longed to see her. She would think him an absolute shit not to have waited. He had to go back, explain. Put his misgivings to her straight.

CHAPTER FORTY ONE

Temptation

This time Calista felt Pam's arms around her shoulders, Pam's head barely touching hers. 'Cal, dear, whatever is it with you and that young man?'

'I . . . I . . . love . . . love . . . him.' Three sobbed out heartfelt words.

Pam gave her a hug. 'I have a suspicion he loves you.' Calista became aware of her tearing off a few sheets of kitchen roll. 'Now dry your eyes and wipe your nose. Then tell Auntie Pam all about it.' She pulled up a chair to sit closer.

Clasped hands resting on the table, Calista concentrated on her thumbs. 'Please don't think I'm irresponsible. Or unprincipled even though . . . I know I shouldn't have caved in, become Adam's . . . He was a married man.'

'Mr Burgess can be very persuasive, I'm sure. He's a fine looking man, quite charming, and very generous.'

'All those, but . . . You may think I'm a success but when it comes to . . . Tess says I'm incredibly naïve. I agree, but PJ, that's the young man. PJ Wood, I believe in him.' She told Pam how they had met. 'Adam had gone off on an all-night fishing trip.'

'He even left you on your own on holiday.' Pam made disapproving noises, tongue against teeth.

'I think PJ sensed I was feeling down, said things to provoke me. He can be such a tease. We ended up being the last to leave. He insisted on walking me back to the villa. I was grateful. After the mugging . . . More than grateful. I didn't want our time together to end.' Calista took a deep breath. 'Oh Pam, one thing led to another. Oh dear, that's sounds so . . . so . . . Please don't think I'm a slag.'

'I spoke to him only briefly but I can see why you might be smitten. More to the point, a man like him doesn't take trouble to deliver thirty four roses to a woman he thinks a slag.'

Calista looked up, met Pam's gaze.

'I'd not planned to have a baby. Never crossed my mind. Now I am and . . .'

'PJ might be the father.' Pam finished.

Calista closed her eyes, shook her head. 'Now tell me how competent and clever I am.'

'Cal dear, happens in the best of families. Trust me. Thing is what now?'

She opened her eyes. Then the doorbell chimed. Pam pushed back her chair, glanced at the kitchen clock. 'Who can that be?' She didn't seem in any hurry to answer the door.

Calista too got up. Beppo emerged from under the table where he had been lying by her feet. She rinsed her face over the sink, dried it with kitchen roll. 'Stay Beppo, stay,' then stepped into the passage leading to the main hall. 'Surely it's not Chloe and Matt. They're not due till one o'clock,' she said, loud enough for Pam to hear.

'The young man on the motorbike seems to have changed his mind.' Pam called to her. Then Calista heard her say, 'You'd better come in. Cal was disappointed to have missed you, and I'm sure you'd like coffee.'

Pam passed her as, heart pounding, she ran into the hall. No mistaking Mr Sardonic, she rushed him, threw her arms around his neck and buried her face into his leather-clad shoulder. He was here. His arms around her, his body firm against hers, she trembled against him. No she was not dreaming. She felt his lips brush her hair. Neither spoke, until he whispered, 'So what's this lots you've got to tell me. And, by the way, that's not a gun in my pocket. Okay.'

She pushed away from him just far enough to look into his eyes. Hers were brimming with tears, tears of happiness this time. He blinked a couple of times, she noticed. She smiled.

'PJ Wood, you're such a tease.'

'Me?' Exaggerating, he gave a furtive look around. 'Burgess won't suddenly appear with a shotgun . . .'

'He won't be back till tomorrow. But . . .'

PJ placed his forefinger under her chin, kissed her lightly on the lips, then held her at arms' length, 'My love, this is Burgess's house, also I have very little time, and we need to talk.'

'Yes, we do.' Frantic moths battering her stomach, she had difficulty taking deep enough breaths to slow the agitated beat of her heart. She took PJ's hand and led him across the hall to the sitting room door.

He drew back. 'Cal, point me in the direction of the john. Three times over that potholed track . . .'

'John?'

'Getting into U.S. of A. mode, I guess.'

He was going to the States. So many questions, when, for how long. He could have no idea how much she needed him here in England. She took a deep breath. *If necessary, you can and will do this on your own, Calista Blake.* She had no right to expect him to turn his life upside down just because she was pregnant and likely he was responsible.

'Come.' She beckoned. 'I'll tell Pam we'll be in the sitting room. Hope you like homemade gingerbread.'

An unspoken pact, they sat either end of the squishy sofa half turned so that they could look but not touch. She longed to breath in his scent, stroke his bare skin with her fingertips, shower intimate kisses where she knew he particularly liked to be caressed. His face was as tanned as in August, eyes as blue as she remembered, his brown hair clipped closer than before. He had taken off his biker's jacket, unwound a black and white keffiyeh to reveal a battleship-grey, thick-woven shirt over a black T-shirt, his leather trousers a second skin. She longed for him to take her in his arms. He was right, they should talk. His need for the loo had given her time to get herself together, to think. This was only their third meeting. Agonizing though it may be, for now she would hold herself in check, respond to what he had to say, rather than provoke a response she might have reason to regret. *Okay, Tess, so when it comes to lovers I can be gullible, but I'm also a barrister. I know when and how to argue my case.*

'Pam makes a mean cup of coffee.' PJ refilled his mug from the cafetiere. 'Are you not having any?'

'I'm awash with hot chocolate, thanks.'

'And this gingerbread . . .' He licked his thumb.

'Pam makes it for me specially. I've had quite a yen since . . . You were hungry.'

'Early start.' He sat back in his corner, gave her a searching look. 'Cal, it's your birthday and you've been crying. Something Burgess has done, like not coming home today.'

She shook her head. 'Not him.'

'Oh my love, me?'

'When I discovered I'd missed you by minutes . . .'

'Never dreamt you'd be around. Flashed through my mind, I shouldn't disturb your peace. Come here.' He opened his arms. 'Okay for us to just have a cuddle, do you think?'

She hotched over to PJ, nestled against him, breathed in his musk. With Adam, she now realized, any demonstration of affection was merely a preliminary to sex.

'Peace? The nearest I get, is when I'm out with Beppo.'

'Before I turned back, I had this fantasy, I should've waited, hoisted you and the mutt on my pillion, and ridden off with you like a modern-day Lochinvar. Trouble is Cal, reality ain't that easy.'

'When do you go to the States?'

'Tomorrow.'

She sat up. *Deep breath.* Then was able to turn her head to look at him. 'PJ Wood, are you never still?' And managed to smile.

He returned a wistful grin. 'Only when I'm alone aboard the *Thelma Jane.*'

'Sailing's not being still. If you were going to be in Ithaca the last week of this month, you might be able to teach me to sail.'

'Is that what you wanted to tell me?'

'There are a couple of other things. For now, they'll keep.'

'You're only saying that so I'll come back.' He leaned forward, cupped her face in his hands. 'I shall return. And . . .' She longed for him to kiss her. Instead, abrupt, he got to his feet, and wandered over to the French window. 'Jesus, Cal, you've quite some garden.'

She joined him, undid the bolts, turned the key, and opened the glass door. They stepped outside to stand side-by-side. Almost noon, on the south-facing terrace in full sun the air was balmy. He nudged against her. 'You'd be giving up an awful lot if . . .'

'Nothing I need, though it has its compensations. I'll show you after I've collected "the mutt".'

Enthusing, she took him to the coppice to see the cyclamen, Beppo ahead following some scent trail. He and PJ had paid each other only cursory attention. That was okay. Neither had shown antipathy.

'In spring, there are early purple orchids as well as bluebells, in summer, honeysuckle, foxgloves, red Campion.'

'You're a real country girl.'

'Wuzz the orchids what did it. And I never used to be keen on dogs. Beppo gets me through.'

'Dogs can be useful. Sniffing out landmines, roadside bombs.'

That brought her up sharp. She would have thought of dogs to help blind people. And sheep dogs. 'Beppo's supposed to be Adam's gun dog. 'Fraid he no longer tends to do what Adam commands.'

They had been standing side by side admiring the cyclamen. Before they began to retrace their steps, PJ drew her arm through his, pressed hers against his side. 'Can't imagine you doing what Burgess or anybody commands.'

'With his women, Adam's more subtle than that. If they're ingenuous, trusting, he charms them into submission. Others, I suspect, he pays well.' Impossible to keep the bitterness out of her voice. She sensed PJ scrutinizing her profile as now hand-in-hand they strolled back to the garden. 'While you're here might as well show you the rest of my domain.'

They had skirted the ha-ha, and on through the gate in the flower-border wall to the sheltered swimming-pool terrace where they paused. He turned to face her, pulled her to him, kissed her on the lips, long, lingering, sensuous. She closed her eyes. Her body ached for his, as, she could feel, his did for hers. Then, he took a step back, again holding her at arms' length, 'Happy birthday, Cal my love.' His eyes, his expression a reflection of her own longing. He let go of her, gave a rueful smile. 'Better we keep moving.'

'The orchard next,' she said.

Across the courtyard out to the front of the house and up the steps through the rockery. They were followed by Beppo who set about obliterating any trace of foxes which might have left their mark on his territory.

'In May, the fruit blossom was spectacular.' She remembered sitting on the bench under the crab apple that late-May morning repenting the day she ever got involved with Adam Burgess. And now PJ was here.

Surreal. She touched his arm. No dream, he was real. She reached up and plucked an apple, wiped it on the front of her T-shirt.

'Try a James Grieve. They're special, a very old variety our gardener tells me. Supermarkets have no time for them.'

Solemn, he took the red apple, held it to his nose, breathed in. 'Woman, how you tempt me.' He bit into it. 'I've never eaten an apple straight from the tree.'

As he ate, she watched him look around. The sunlight played on leaves beginning to turn golden, on ripened fruit, red, mellow yellow, apple-green. In dappled shade, pools of light and dark, the grass had given its final sigh before winter. She made for the bench and sat down, PJ following, the only sound the rustle of leaves in the October breeze.

'A world away from the apple orchards around Nerkh.' PJ threw his core into the rough under the Hawthorne bright with berries, then sat beside her, leaning forward his forearms resting on his knees.

'Where's Nerkh?'

'Just west of Kabul, where I've been these past few weeks.'

'Thank God I didn't know.'

PJ sat up, turned to look at her, then he stroked her cheek. 'Cal, that's something you need to think about. Often, when I'm away on an assignment, I never know for sure when I'll be back. This last sortie, I was scheduled to be in the south, based in Lashkar Gan. Three weeks at most should've been long enough. In fact I managed to file enough material in two. Then I was asked to pop up to Kabul, and . . . well, let's just say, though ultimately we did hit pay-dirt, we were unavoidably delayed. That's why I took so long to answer you. There's lots more we need to talk about, to consider. One step at a time, eh?'

She nodded her agreement. A step too far on this short, unscheduled visit to blurt out, *PJ I'm expecting a baby. Would you mind undergoing a paternity test so I know for sure you're the Dad?*

An all too brief but reassuring kiss on her lips. 'While I'm in the States, no reason why we shouldn't exchange emails every day.'

'Ooh, yes please.'

He stood, and smiling pulled her to her feet. 'Now, my love, I really have to go.' He stroked her nose with his forefinger.

She took hold his hands, held them tight. 'PJ?'

'Cal?' They looked into each other's eyes, intent.

'You keep saying "my love". Do you mean it?'

'Cal, I would never say it if I didn't.'

'And if I was in trouble you would come running if I really needed you. That is if you could?'

'What I said.'

'PJ, please come back to me soon.'

He pulled her to him, his kiss firm. 'Soon as I can. Promise.'

CHAPTER FORTY TWO

Satellite Man

For the time being PJ was content to tootle along the now familiar lanes. Although wretched because he had to leave her, he could whoop and holler and sing. Calista Blake loved him. But, no celebration yet. Too many hurdles, one not to be discounted Cal might never be able to live with what he did.

She already had a foretaste, five weeks incommunicado. He remembered her response to where he had been - *Thank God I didn't know*. A truism, circumstances alter cases, if she were his wife – *his wife! Right now she's married to someone else, dipstick* – he would tell his wife where he was going. Also, channels of communication were available in out-of-the-way places, except in Nerkh district, not to him anyway, where they ended up after they were hi-jacked. Nerkh, where the orchards and mud-walled compounds now and evermore were nursery and safe-haven for mujahedeen factions including Taliban. Ahmed had convinced their leader he, PJ could be useful just doing his job. *He shows it how it is,* Ahmed said. *Maybe one day the Americans will understand they cannot win.*

Don't hold your breath, PJ thought, but, instead of being taken hostage, and, if he were really lucky, held till a ransom was paid, he, in collaboration with Jim had a scoop. Once the article was out, he would show Cal.

I am what I do, my love. I can only hope you'll understand.

More to the point, he was certain sure, Cal was keeping something back. She held onto his hands so tight she was in danger of restricting his circulation, then her need for reassurance, he would come to her if she were in trouble. *Lots to tell you,* she had emailed. Going to Ithaca the last week of the month was not 'lots'. Burgess would be there too. He bet the *Thelma Jane,* if Cal anticipated trouble, Burgess would be at the bottom of it. In PJ's opinion, despite his veneer of charm, he lacked warmth. *But I would think that.* To be fair, he had reason.

That evening Burgess turned up at Marcos's without Cal, allegedly ill, he asked should she be left on her own. He replied he had dosed her with salt tablets, and codeine. *Out for the count when I left,* he said. *She won't miss me.* He certainly showed no sign of missing her. Yiorgos's stunning sister-in-law was with him. He explained to Marcos, *I dropped by to discuss tomorrow's arrangements with Yiorgos, and lucky me Ledia agreed to keep me company.*

He showed scant curiosity despite Marcos introducing him as one of Cal's acquaintances – *arrogant, self-satisfied tosser,* PJ thought. *If she were my wife, I'd want to know how we'd met.* Burgess had wasted little time on him, except to tell him about his villa project, his hope he would be able to bring his daughters there soon. The daughters were his not Cal's, PJ gathered. Then hand placed on her behind, he ushered Ledia over to his usual table on the harbour front.

Eating alone, he was free to observe a master-class in seduction, Burgess's engaging smile, amusing banter, his eyes locked on hers when she spoke, laughter, Ledia's wine glass regularly topped up, he more circumspect about how much he drank. Later, mood change, serious, sympathy, concern, his hand reaching across the table covering hers. Wine glasses drained, the bill requested and paid.

As they passed his table, Burgess had the courtesy to nod and wish him 'good night'. He had reciprocated, adding *please give my regards to your wife.* He smiled at the memory. Cool.

Later, he and Marcos, the only ones left sat drinking a nightcap, Burgess had no option but to pass in front of them on his way back to the Erato. Again they exchanged 'Kali nichta'. Marcos and he looked at each other, eyebrows raised, then when he was out of earshot, Marcos said, 'Nearly two bloody hours to walk her back to the Vassilitos's.'

PJ had heard the gossip about the wife of Kristina Vassilitos's brother, how she had turned up with one huge expensive suitcase and one designer holdall, distressed and pleading sanctuary. Rumour had it, her husband had needed to disappear without trace.

'To a man like him, an attractive woman's a challenge,' PJ said, 'He just has to have her.'

'There speaks the voice of experience.'

He felt his face flush. 'Not really, Marco. I like women too much to use them. Blame my mother.' *Not the whole truth, but near enough.* He could never do what he suspected Burgess had just done.

'Can't say Ledia hasn't earned her keep since she's been here,' Marcos said. 'Cleans my brother's properties, helps with the baby. That said, Kioni's no place for her. She's used to the high life. Astute that one, believe me. Who's to say she and Mr Burgess aren't using each other.'

'And where does that leave Mrs Burgess?'

'Too good for him. But you've already sussed that, haven't you?' Marcos gave him a playful punch on his upper arm.

If he had any qualms about the night he spent with Cal, they would have melted away that evening. Not that he had. He suspected neither did Cal. He remembered her bitter words apropos her husband and women - *If they're ingenuous, trusting, he charms them into submission. Others, I suspect, he pays well.* She had no illusions. Little wonder she was unhappy.

Without really noticing he had reached the island which would take him onto the A6. From now on he would need to concentrate, give himself up to the thrill of the open road. Back at Woodbine Cottage in no time, he would text Cal, let her know, fingers crossed, he was not in A&E – *Go carefully*, she said before she kissed him good-bye – He would ask her to email him details of her Ithaca trip. He doubted he would touch down in England long enough to see her beforehand, but with luck, he would be checking up on Ma by then. He would do his utmost to see Cal, and the devil take Burgess.

Calista watched PJ rattle over the cattle grid. He did not look back, only a minimalist wave of his hand as he turned left. She was relieved to hear his Yamaha putter rather than roar down the narrow lane, though, she suspected, that would soon change. *Be safe, my darling,* she whispered. Safe, a man whose mission was to photograph the truth, in his own words, 'wherever there's trouble', in war zones no less. As if that was not enough, he chose just about the riskiest means of transport, was on his way to that accident hotspot on the A14. *The love of my life seems driven to live his life on the edge,* she thought. *Oy veh, as Granny used to say, no use trying to change him. I love him. I shall learn to live with him as he is.* She imagined all the long weeks PJ might be away, satellite their only means of contact. *My Satellite Man, oy veh.*

CHAPTER FORTY THREE

Happy Birthday

Voices in the hall, Pam must have opened the door before they got to ring the bell. Beppo, stretched, jumped down from his window seat. After PJ left, a quick turn-around, just time to change into her new shift dress, one size up, midnight-blue, flattering she hoped with heels, brush her hair, a touch of make-up and ready to go. PJ had seen her face in all its tear-wrecked glory. He did not seem put off but Chloe and Matt were fellow professionals. She had her pride. And, with a few minutes to spare, she waited in the study as though she had been there all morning working on her latest brief. A tap, tap on the door. She took a deep breath and stood. Then Matt hugging her so hard, he lifted her off her feet, his kiss firm on her mouth. A growl rumbled in Beppo's throat. Matt put her down, laughing.

'How's my birthday girl?'

'I'm good.' *Yes*, she thought, *today I'm blessed. I've seen, touched, kissed PJ Wood, and now I'm having lunch with friends.* She felt her face light up with the broadest smile.

Chloe hung back, a rosy-complexioned girl with auburn bouncy curls, wearing fashionable wide-legged charcoal pants and a pearl-grey sweater emphasizing neat breasts. She held a bouquet of white Madonna lilies, and an envelope.

'Happy Birthday, Cal.' Hannah passed the flowers for Matt to hand to her.

'For my Lily Woman.'

'Thank you.' Her turn to kiss him, on the cheek. 'They're beautiful.'

'He says I'm a snapdragon.' Hannah did not sound too fazed. The three of them laughed. She handed her the envelope. 'Book token, so don't get excited.' She looked around the room. 'You've enough books already, I see.' She wandered over to the side-table. 'What fantabulous roses, and so many. Are they from your husband?'

'A friend.' Calista sensed Matt's scrutiny, felt her face flush. 'I'll go and put these in water. There's a bottle of Veuve Cliquot in a cooler in the dining room, if you'd like to do the honours, Matt.'

Chloe, her first time at the Old Rectory, the dining room was 'Fab', the view from the window 'Amazing' and Adam's flowers, now the table centrepiece 'Chic'. Lunch was convivial even though she and Chloe, who was Matt's chauffeur that day, stuck to one glass of champagne each, and her thoughts kept straying to PJ zooming up the M11 doing a ton, and the rest.

For Chloe, each course was scrummy, and Mat had seconds of tarte tatin. 'Glad to see your appetite's back, Cal. Looking good, you've put on a bit of weight.'

He was another friend she could, should confide in. He would be hurt if he heard of her predicament from someone else. She, Matt, Chloe got on so well together, work did not seem like work. Chloe was committed and was quick to comprehend the essence of a brief. Before her guests left, at their request she gave them a tour of the grounds.

'The kitchen garden first to show you where the vegetables we've just eaten were grown. Organically, naturally.'

'That's tautology.' Matt grinned.

Calista shook her head. 'If you're going to be like that I shan't show you the very tree the apples came from for pudding, nor the blackberry brambles.'

'Ignore him,' Chloe said. 'He just likes to tease.'

Ah yes, I remember it well, Calista thought.

Not long after the mugging, Matt insisted on taking her to lunch at Casa Romana. 'I'm worried you're not eating properly.'

Easy-to-talk-to Matt, she found herself pouring out her sense of loneliness, her unhappiness. Matt asked what she intended doing about it. She told him she hoped their Ithacan holiday might revitalize her and Adam's relationship. Then feeling guilty, 'I shouldn't have told you, Matt.

It's disloyal.'

On their walk back to Chambers, Matt drew her arm through his. 'Get it into your head, you're not disloyal.' Matt squeezed her arm against his side. 'Have you ever told Burgess about us? I often detect a touch of suppressed antagonism.'

'God no, though he does think you're in love with me.'

'We stayed good mates, Cal. Say in the first flush of enthusiasm, we'd got married. By now we'd probably be divorced, and at daggers drawn.' Matt halted in front of the main doors of Holy Cross. Disentangling their arms, he pulled her round to face him. 'We were too young to settle down, weren't we?'

'Too young, too ambitious, too competitive, at least I was.'

'Cal, I'm here for you always,' his kiss soft on her cheek. 'You're one of my best mates.'

'Cal, wake up.' Matt clicked his fingers in front of her eyes. 'Can we try an apple?' He pointed to the James Grieve. 'They're shouting "eat me".'

'Sorry. Of course.'

But it was Chloe who reached up and pulled one from the tree. She held it out to Matt.

'The Eternal Eve.' Matt's voice soft, his eyes dreamy. Chloe's smile epitomized mischief as, gazing at each other, they each in turn took a bite.

'Ahem, excuse me you two, gooseberries are out of season, and I'm not as green as I am cabbage-looking.'

'That obvious?' Matt pulled a rueful face.

By the swimming pool, Calista felt guilty. She should have invited friends and colleagues to a pool party, too late now. She said as much.

'There's always next year,' Chloe said.

By no means hard up, nevertheless Calista wondered if she could afford to buy Adam out.

And finally, her spinney.

'Thank God you seem more settled, Cal,' She and Matt stood on the front step while Chloe turned round her Mini Cooper. A gentle nudge in the ribs from him. 'So the text you sneaked a look at during lunch was the one you were expecting. You positively glowed.' She turned to look at him feeling her face colour. 'Like now.' He gave a cheeky grin. 'From PJ Wood by any chance?'

'How the hell . . .'

'You might want to stash that card next to your roses away. Sorry. Curiosity got the better of me.'

'S'okay. Thanks.' She was not prepared for a showdown with Adam just yet.

Engine raring to go, Matt pressed down the passenger window. 'We'll catch up maybe tomorrow, eh?'

She nodded. As the Mini rattled over the grid, he and Chloe stuck their arms out of their respective windows and gave a final wave.

'Well Beppo, that's my birthday celebrations over. Would've been bittersweet if all I'd had was an hour of PJ's time. Matt and Chloe, eh? Had my chance with Matt, and blew it. Oy vey. But then I might never have met PJ. Wonder where I'll be next year? We, I should say. You'll be there too old boy, no worries. We'll have a baby by then, God willing, five months old.' Beppo had stayed close by her throughout the day. She stepped out of her heels relishing the contact of cool stone beneath her aching feet. 'Time to change into joggers and sweatshirt. All this emoting, thinking, talking and walking, I'm fair worn out. We'll get ourselves comfy in the sitting room. We may even have a nap.'

Beppo jumping down from the other end of the sofa woke her. She had snuggled down face into the cushions where PJ had leaned. She did not open her eyes immediately using her sense of smell to try and detect his musk. When she opened them, Adam was hovering.

'Are you not well, Cal?'

'Adam, what a surprise.' She took her time swinging her legs off the sofa and sitting up. 'Whatever time is it?'

'5.30ish. Shall I ask Pam to make you an Earl Grey? I was hoping we could go out this evening. I've got a table at the Lake Isle.'

'You said you couldn't be home today.'

'Slight change of plan. Talk to you over dinner. Do you feel well enough to go over to Uppingham?' He looked and sounded edgy. She wondered what he had to tell her that he preferred to say in a public rather than a private place. Beppo had the sense to slope off while they were talking so avoiding being ordered out of the room.

'I'm not ill. I was tired. Dinner at the Lake Isle, what a surprise. Better shower and change.'

He looked relieved, but before he left the room he went over to her parents' mammoth bouquet of chrysanthemums standing in front of the empty hearth. 'Well, bang goes his bonus, they're for a pensioner, not a beautiful and sophisticated woman, which was his brief.'

'What are you talking about? Mummy and Daddy always send flowers appropriate to the season. Yours are elegant, exotic, thank you, Adam, or whoever was responsible. They're the centrepiece on the dining room table.'

He had the grace to look embarrassed. 'I'll take a look before I get ready.'

He was out of the shower and in the dressing room by the time she got upstairs. His idea of a cup of tea had been a good one. 'I noticed a spray of Madonna lilies on the sideboard. From Wakeham, I'm guessing,' he said, a sneer in his voice.

'Matt always brings lilies, because, he says, like them I'm pellucid and straight as a die.' *Which is more than can be said of you,* she thought.

'Umm.' Adam looked sceptical. She had almost shut the bathroom door. 'Not entirely true.' He muttered, but she heard. Maybe for now it would be wise to hide PJ's card.

CHAPTER FORTY FOUR

Dinner for Two

When she joined him downstairs, he was wearing his black Burberry jeans, lightweight French-navy blazer over a pale blue, button-down shirt- and appeared to be more his usual suave self. He sat at the kitchen table drinking tea, and discussing Pam's grandchildren. He was good at that sort of thing. He got to his feet.

'New dress?' She had changed back into her one-size-up shift. He came over, took her hands in his, and gave her a light kiss on the lips. For Pam's benefit more than hers, she guessed. 'Really suits you.' He held the sleeve of his jacket against her frock. 'Look, we're both in blue.' Perhaps he was trying to be nice. Presumably he had rearranged his busy schedule especially to take her out.

He drove them in his Jaguar saloon, though she had offered the use of her new Audi TT, a not very sensible buy as it turned out. She had ordered it before going on holiday. He had not replaced his stolen convertible – *I really don't need two cars, especially if I'm to stay in town all week*. His second Jag was eventually traced, torched, on waste ground near Northampton.

On the way to Uppingham, her phone signalled a text. Not PJ, who had promised to call during the evening. While she was alone she had texted about Adam's change of plan. From Esther Mahoney: *Hope your birthday's better than expected. Trust you got my card. Can you talk?*

'Who is it?' Adam sounded suspicious.

'Tess, she hopes I'm enjoying my birthday. If you don't mind, I'll reply.'

'If you must' with his usual implication, such behaviour was lacking in good manners. Then, 'Give her my love.'

Right now. With Adam. Lots to tell, 2morrow, then turned off her phone and put it away.

'I gather everything's A-OK now between Tess and Mike. What about the "other woman"?'

'Mike's not a bit like you.'

'Come off it, Cal. What other explanation was there?'

Maybe the reason Adam had made no move to make love to her since they got back was not because she had given him the cold shoulder, because he exhausted himself with that young woman, She conjectured how he would respond to a counter-question, *come to think of it, Adam, how's Sheena Jardine?* Thanks to Esther's private eye, she now had a name. She was not proud of herself, stooping so low, but as Esther said, needs must – *the merde you're in, you can't afford to be picky.* For the time being, though, she had drawn the line at using underhand means to garner samples of Adam's DNA for paternity testing, a necessary process of elimination, Tess said.

The Lake Isle's warm but subdued lighting was welcoming, intimate, and ideal for a romantic tete-a-tete. If only . . . Calista anticipated drinks might be tricky. In truth, the whole evening might be a bit of an ordeal.

'Am I to understand, for whatever reason, you're still being cautious about your alcohol intake?' Avuncular in his half-moon reading glasses, he peered over the wine list, an enigmatic smile on his lips. Not for the first time he reminded her of the "mighty civil and handsome" fox in Beatrix Potter's 'Jemima Puddle-duck'.

'Yes, well, yes. I had a whole champagne flute at lunchtime.'

'One whole glass. You would tell me if there was something wrong, wouldn't you Cal?'

'Wary of hangovers, that's all.'

'I suggest we just have the half a bottle of house champagne, then.'

'Lovely.' She would do her best to make sure he drank the lion's share. 'And a bottle of fizzy mineral water, please.'

Adam ordered their drinks. She studied the menu. So many tasty things to avoid, salami, blue cheese, Parma ham so probably pancetta as well. Soup seemed safest, and to follow veggie Butternut steak. Then Adam would ask if she was giving up meat as well as alcohol. Fillet of steak should be tender and palatable with chestnut mushrooms and baby leeks. Pam nagged her about eating the occasional piece of red meat, but you had to be wary. Once you were pregnant, seemed your body was no longer your own. She could so identify with Jemima Puddle-duck, an impatient sitter when it came to hatching eggs.

'I'll join you in having the steak. Pity you're not drinking, they do a very acceptable Nuits-St-Georges, ideal with our main. But soup when there's tempura red mullet?'

'Soup please.' She smiled at their waiter.

Adam leaned back and surveyed fellow diners. The rise and fall of their conversations, civilized, mannered, pervaded the room, then he looked at her. 'This is nice. We haven't eaten out since we got back from Ithaca. You will be okay to fly in a couple of weeks' time?'

'Why shouldn't I be? I'm looking forward to catching up with Kristina, and little Dhionysius.'

'Ah yes, the baby.' Looking thoughtful, he compressed his lips. 'I seem to remember you were quite taken with him.' Calista felt her stomach knot.

Their champagne arrived. 'A celebration, sir?' The waiter popped the cork, and poured a little for Adam to try. Adam nodded his approval. The waiter, careful, filled their champagne flutes.

'My wife's birthday. Many happy returns, darling.' Adam held up his glass.

She tapped hers against his. 'Chin, chin.' She took not too large a sip. Adam did not touch his.

'My mother used to say that, an Italian thing. I was always in awe of my mama. She too was a blonde, but more volatile than you.' He regarded her again for what seemed like minutes that enigmatic smile on his lips. She felt her face become hotter. Only when she was probably as red as one of their apples did he look away and take a sip of his drink.

The waiter arrived with their starters. Adam had ordered a cured salmon dish with scrambled duck egg – *Oh dear, devious Mr Fox and Jemima the impetuous duck again came to mind. She would have done well to have taken more notice of that cautionary tale, her favourite Beatrix Potter as it happened.*

'Did I mention, Tess is taking Fran and Tom to Amsterdam at half term? While she's there, she's planning on looking for a house to rent.' Between mouthfuls of satisfying seasonal vegetable soup, she told Adam Esther was hoping to persuade Mike she really would be content to take a sabbatical. Then she and the children could go and live with him till his stint in The Netherlands came to an end. '31st of August next year. Save him trekking home every weekend.'

'And bang goes his bit on the side.' He chuckled. 'Or rather he'll no longer be able to bang her.' Despite her disapproving huff, he still seemed to find it funny.

'I thought he'd rented some grand apartment,' Adam said.

'Full of antiques and expensive furniture,' she said. 'Not at all child-friendly.'

Adam did not respond until the waiter had cleared away their plates.

'Ah, one's children, the bane of one's life.' He gave a deep sigh. 'You'd do well to take note of that, Cal.'

Again her stomach tightened. 'But you adore Len and Sash.' She might remind him on their account he had married her.

'They share my genes. I try to do my best by them, steer them in the right direction. What thanks do I get? Len goes all Bohemian on me, and this term, more than ever, Sash is playing silly buggers.' He drained his glass, and refilled it, she was relieved to see.

'I'm so sorry, Adam. About Sash, I mean. Why didn't you say?'

When the waiter brought their main course, it looked and smelt delicious. She ought to manage to eat it, but wondered how anyone ever had a serious conversation in a restaurant with assiduous waiters about.

Adam continued. 'Sash is my daughter, my responsibility, but that's not to say I wouldn't value your input. You were right about Len.' He took a sip from his re-filled wine glass. 'Hey, this is your birthday treat. Let's not talk about Sash. She'll give us indigestion. Drink your champagne.' To please him, she did drink a little more. He smiled. 'Can't thank you enough for putting Len in touch with Tess's mama.'

While they ate, he explained the reason for changing his schedule. Next day, Len was travelling up to London. 'She and Tess's mother Ms Purslow-Onajole emailed each other, and Len attached photos of some of her work. Ms P. was encouraging, suggested they meet, and Len brings her portfolio.'

'For heaven's sake, Adam, call her Mina, not Ms Purslow-Onajole.'

'I've only spoken to her on the phone. She didn't say call her Mina.'

'Where's Len meeting her?'

'The art college where she teaches, Central St Martins.'

'Fantastic. I am pleased.'

'Don't tell Len. I've checked it out. I'm impressed. She would do well to get in there. This meeting's just a feeler. Ms P. - Nina will be able to give her some idea of her chances, also point her to other alternatives, just in case. Least that's what she said when I called her.'

'Not that you're an anxious dad, or anything.' Smiling, she shook her head. He was a lousy husband, but he did try to be a good father, over-bearing perhaps, controlling. Nevertheless, his daughters, and Annabel, seemed to manage to bring him round to their way of thinking. She wondered how he would have related, might relate to a son, if he should have one that is. Alpha-male lions, any testosterone-fuelled older males of species and their aggression toward younger males came to mind.

While he was telling her his news, her tender steak with its vegetables and rich gravy, not that it was called "gravy", was a pleasure to eat. She had cleared her plate. Although Adam had not quite finished, he put down his knife and fork.

'Thing is, Cal. I have to go back to town first thing tomorrow. I've booked me and Len into the St Pancras Hotel to stay over tomorrow night. The art college's in a restored granary behind King's Cross.' He told her first thing Saturday, he would drive Len back to Dorset in a hire car. 'I've a meeting with the Head. It's about Sash.'

'Sounds ominous.'

A discreet, 'Have you finished, sir?' Adam indicated he had. The waiter cleared their table, asked if they would like the dessert menu. She asked for 'just a mango sorbet, please', Adam the cheese platter.

'Now, where were we?' Adam said.

'Saturday you're up before the beak, or rather Sasha's head teacher.'

'Sash has always been what my nanny used to call highly strung. Or put another way, an attention-seeking, bloody nuisance from the day she was born. Len may be the artistic one, but Sash is a lot like her mother. Annie was expelled, have I told you?'

'And you love Sash and worry about her, Annabel too, I think, even though you were a horrendous husband. '

He looked taken aback, then his face reddened. 'Annie's fine, about to give birth any day now. We keep in touch.'

She would have thought even less of him, if he had not.

'Sash misses her mum,' she said. 'She believes Annabel won't want to bother with her once she's got her new baby boy. Poor kid was so upset. I had to give her a cuddle, told her it was nonsense. I said I suspected parents loved all their children equally, though maybe differently, because each child was an individual.'

'When did this happen?'

'The night before you took them back to school. I don't think she wanted to go. Why did they have to go to boarding school, one so far from home? And now she's miles and miles away from her mum.'

'It's an excellent school, forward-looking, based on the principles of Mary Ward. Len has done well there. Boarding school never did me any harm.'

'A Catholic boarding school? Or is that Annabel's doing?'

'Annie's not RC, neither did she want them to go away. I went to Ampleforth, a Benedictine foundation.'

She felt her jaw slacken. She must have looked quite gormless as the waiter put the sorbet in front of her. Adam cut into a piece of cheese.

'I never knew you were a Roman Catholic.'

'Well and truly lapsed, shouldn't you think?' He looked up, raised his eyebrows and gave a mischievous grin. 'Now eat and drink up. I've an early start tomorrow.'

Maybe he was preoccupied. He said nothing about her leaving a half full glass of flat champagne.

On the drive home, he said he was glad she still intended to go with him and the girls to Ithaca. 'They really like you, and tell you things they'd never tell me.'

An unsettling evening, at least it had helped make her mind up. By whatever means, she had to know for sure her baby was PJ's.

CHAPTER FORTY FIVE

Saturday Night, the loneliest night of the week

In fading light, Calista paced the lawn, oppressed by a sense of foreboding. She was learning each season had its own aura. Autumn evenings drifted into silence, colours faded, and a smell of damp portended decay. Beppo raced around glad to be unleashed and on familiar territory. They had just returned from a sleepover at the Mahoneys where her dog had been the best behaved pooch ever. A quick call to Esther first thing yesterday, Esther had invited her to a girls' night in. With Adam away, and Mike not expected home till Saturday morning, 'our chance to catch-up,' Esther said. She told her she wanted to know every last detail of PJ's flying visit, 'When will you see him again?' *Good question.*

She had arrived in Edwalton in time for high tea, Tom and Fran excited to discover Beppo was with her.

'We're having birthday cake,' Tom said, 'But mum says you can't have candles cos there'd be so many they'd set fire to the cake.'

Calista laughed. 'Your mum's turn to be this old next April, Tom.'

She thought she might cry when Tom held up a hand-made card. 'Me and Fran made you this. That's Beppo with a balloon. I drew him, and inside there's another balloon with 'Happy Birthday Yesterday'. Fran drew that, and it says with love to Cal from Tom and Fran, kiss, kiss.'

'Thank you, Tom. Thank you Fran.' She held out her arms. 'Big hugs, you two.'

She turned to Esther. 'No way you've baked me a cake?'

'The whole meal, including the cake's courtesy of M & S.'

'What would we working girls do without M & S? Maybe I should rephrase that,' Sheena Jardine came to mind. Esther's seriously good detective had unearthed more than Calista really wanted to know about her and Mr Adam Burgess.

'Can't think who you might be thinking of.' Esther placed two large pizzas in the oven.

'I don't condemn Sheena Jardine for what she does,' Calista said. 'If anyone's culpable it's Adam, and men like him. The girl's only twenty, not that much older than Len. No wonder Adam threw in the sponge and agreed Len should apply for Art School. She's meeting Mina today, did you know?'

'Len'll have no problem getting a college place, Mum says.' Esther brought over two mugs of tea. 'But what has Ms Jardine's age got to do with Len studying art?'

'Len threatened to finance herself by registering with an escort agency. That might have been the clincher.'

'Do you think she knew something we didn't till now?'

'Nah, Len's so like Adam it's uncanny, amiable with an inner core of cast iron, charm with a streak of ruthlessness. As an "escort", she'd have kept a Taser in her handbag, just in case. They are both Capricorn.'

'No way do you believe that nonsense. Adam a Goat. If it weren't so bloody tragic it'd be funny.'

'Not tragic, Tess, farcical. That's what I tell myself. Surely the Burgess's, just like the Archers, are an everyday story of country folk. PJ's Aquarius, freedom-loving, individualistic, rebellious, and sympathetic, compassionate, the sting in the tail, the latter two only "when things go their own quirky way". Nothing nonsensical there, my gran would've said, "An all-round good egg".'

'Time will tell.' Esther sounded sceptical. 'And eggs are oval, not round.'

The smell of baking pizza, herby, garlicky, melting cheeses, permeated the kitchen. Mouth-watering and ready to eat.

Fran and Tom in bed, Beppo asleep in his basket in the utility room, the chance for girly confidences. The sitting room, restful, only two table lamps on in the alcoves either side of the hearth where Esther had lit a log fire – 'Cheerful once darkness falls, and primordial, tales round the camp fire and all that.' The logs crackled. They faced each other, Calista feet up on the sofa, a glass of elder flower cordial on the coffee table, poured ready for her, Esther lounging sideways in her favourite chair at right-angles to the sofa, her long legs draped over the chair arm. She sipped chilled Pinot Grigio. The unmistakable, velvet tones of "Old Blue Eyes" flowed from a Zeppelin Air, soothing, unobtrusive.

'I used to listen to Frank Sinatra with my Nan Purslow. She was mad about him, saw him in Vegas once,' Esther said. '"I've got you under my skin,".' She sang along. 'Thank God, or ought I to say Steve Jobs, for the iPod. You can download almost everything and anything.' She put her glass down on the floor, swung her legs round, and leaned back. 'We'll save the most interesting bit till last. So, do you think it was his guilty conscience that made Adam make a special trip to take you out?'

Before replying, Calista took a sip of cordial. Then, deliberate put down her glass. 'Guilt? Doubt he understands the meaning of the word even though the most startling thing about last night was discovering he was brought up a Catholic.' She told Esther Sasha had scuppered his original plans. 'Trouble at mill, or rather school, where he's going tomorrow.' She shrugged. 'He'll call me, he said, as soon as he has a better idea of when he'll be home.

'The creepiest thing was remarks he dropped out, as though he knows I'm pregnant.' She shuddered to make her point. 'I felt like a mouse must feel under a cat's paw, then the cat lets go, only to pounce later. I must know he's not the Dad, before . . .' Calista picked up her glass of cordial again and drank more than half in one go. She wished it had a slug of vodka in it, something, anything seventy per cent proof.

Esther sat to attention, 'All along you've given the impression it is PJ's. If you'd collected hair from Adam's brush, an unwashed cup or glass he'd drunk from, any of those, we'd be there.'

'He's committed no crime, Tess. If anything, I'm the one at fault. I'm his wife and I slept with a total stranger, except PJ didn't seem like a stranger.'

'No crime. Would've been if Sheena Jardine hadn't been over sixteen. He's just an all-round shit of the first order of shits. We've discovered he's been going to this Sonja Volkova's so called soirees for years now.' Esther picked up her glass and knocked back its remaining contents. 'Okay, to Adam's way of thinking, and lots of men I'm sure, this kind of contractual arrangement is less risky than affairs that become messy, and has the advantage of pandering to all kinds of kinkiness. Adds spice to their otherwise predictable sex lives. But, Adam was juggling Annabel, you when he finally charmed you into bed, and this poor kid Sheena, who actually pre-dates you by a couple of months.'

Calista swung her legs off the sofa, and sat up. 'To be fair, sounds as though Annabel and her Bradley were contemporaneous with Adam and me.'

'You're not having second thoughts, are you?'

'Course not. When he revealed what a shit he'd been to Annabel. . . She was only eighteen, dammit, a mixed up kid by the sound of it, a lot like Sash. For God's sake, Tess, he was twenty eight. He should've been kinder, more understanding. When she got pregnant, probably all she wanted was someone to love, someone who would love her in return.' She picked up her glass, put it down again. 'Adam never once tried to disabuse my belief I was the reason for his marriage break up. Made me feel I owed him. Devious, conniving . . . No, I haven't changed my mind. I want a divorce, but I do worry about Sash.'

'She is his responsibility.'

'This side of the pond, I'm the nearest she's got to a mother.'

'Cal, you confound me. All the years I've known you, just didn't have you down as a mother hen.' Esther picked up her empty glass and stood. 'I'll just get myself a refill. Would you like a top up, or something else?'

'What I'd really like is vodka or gin, lots of it, but a top up will be fine, thanks.'

When Esther sat down again, 'So, when Mr PJ Wood dropped by you told him you were going to be a mother and were, what, ninety nine point nine per cent sure he's father.'

'Yesterday wasn't the time. Today he flew to New York. I got a text not long after tea to say he'd arrived.' She told Esther the saga of PJ's visit including what he said about being in Afghanistan. 'You do see, don't you, I can't turn his life upside down just like that?'

Esther sighed with what sounded like exasperation. '"*Men are unwise and curiously planned.*' She sounded scathing. '*They have their dreams, and do not think of us*" us being us women.'

'That a quote?'

'James Elroy Flecker, *The Golden Journey to Samarkand*. Nan Purslow used to read it to me. Lovely voice. Welsh, you know.' Esther put on the

260

authentic accent. 'Hope you know what you're taking on, Cal. That is if he hangs around. Never mind turning his life upside down, trust me, your life will never be the same once you've got a child.'

'While he's in New York, we're going to email each other every day. And he's promised if I really need him, he'll come running.'

'Yeah, as long as he's not somewhere on the other side of the world. Don't just email, Cal. If he's not back pdq, Skype. Tell him face to face that way.'

'I will, if things get really desperate with Adam.'

'I have to say you missed an opportunity.'

'What opportunity?'

'PJ's coffee mug.'

'Tess, you're supposed to be Family Division, conciliatory, non-confrontational.'

'Enough,' Esther said. 'Or we'll not sleep for fretting. Come on now, dish the dirt on Matt Wakeham and your pupil Chloe. Then you can advise me on how I'm to convince Mike I'm more than happy to take a sabbatical. Methinks, you know him as well as I do.' Raising her eyebrows, Esther gave a wry smile.

She whistled Beppo to heel. 'Time to go in, old boy. Pam's left me homemade leek and potato soup. And a cooked chicken I'll save for tomorrow. We had fish and chips for lunch.' She patted her stomach. 'Filling.'

They entered the house through the sitting room's French window. Dusk, Calista locked it behind her. In the hall, her footsteps echoed, Beppo's claws tapped on the ornate tiled floor.

'You know, Beppo, much as I love our coppice, the orchard, our rambles, even if I could afford it, I don't want to live here with just we three, you, me and baby.'

Perhaps Adam was right when he had called her "suburban". Esther and Mike had pressed her to stay another night. 'Soon as you hear from Adam, you'll have plenty of time to get back,' Esther said.

'I don't like to think of you alone in that huge house,' Mike said. As it was, she stayed on till mid-afternoon.

'I really should go now,' she insisted. 'I'm pretty sure he'll be back this evening.'

Truth to tell, the Mahoneys seemed so happy together, the kids cock-a-hoop Dad was home, and Esther exuded contentment, Calista felt like an intruder. 'Suburbia, Adam, has more going for it than this . . .' Speaking her thoughts out loud, she held out her arms encompassing all around her. She could not imagine Adam and Len setting off to fetch fish and chips like Mike and Fran, a treat when Mike did not manage to get home till Saturday.

While she was heating some soup, one of Sinatra's numbers came into her head, 'Saturday night is the loneliest night of the week', she sang. 'You can say that again, Beppo. I know what we'll do. We'll watch that dance competition thing while I eat. Call me uncool. I prefer it to that talent contest one. The pelvic action of those sexy male dancers . . . Then early to bed. Three roller-coaster days, I'm whacked.'

She fell asleep on the sofa, waking with a start gone eleven. A quick check, no email from PJ, so not every day after all. Maybe tomorrow, maybe not. No way would she blink first. Then, let Beppo out long enough for a last pee. She had turned out all the lights except for the one in the hall, made sure everywhere was locked, and was about to set the alarm when she heard the cattle grid rattle. Adam? He had not called. Her mobile vibrated in her jeans' pocket. She answered.

'Cal, it's me. Let us in, please.'

Us? She opened the front door.

CHAPTER FORTY SIX

Sunday Morning

Calista did not immediately open her eyes. She breathed in and slowly out several times savouring the lavender scent of soft bed linen, then stretched her limbs into a four-point star. Her right foot kicked against someone's leg. The body next to hers made a noise similar to Beppo before he gave a full-throated growl. Then, a half-asleep mutter, 'Sorry, sorry.' The voice was not Adam but Sasha. A surprise if it had been Adam. Since the girls went back to school, on the few occasions he had been home, he had taken to sleeping in one of the spare rooms – 'I think I disturb you when I can't sleep' – an excuse. He must have sensed her disenchantment. Not his style to ask what upset her. He probably had a pretty good idea if he deigned to think about it, if he cared.

Calista eyes now wide open, careful, sat up. Sasha, back towards her, was curled in the foetal position, her long, honey-hued hair half covering her face. Her right hand, fingers curled toward the palm, rested on her pillow. Sasha half roused. Her mouth unerring found her thumb. Calista thought, if you were my little girl, fourteen going on four, no way would I have sent you away to boarding school, no matter how progressive.

When she opened the door the previous night, glowering, Adam had manhandled a tearful Sasha over the threshold before picking up a large suitcase in one hand, a hold-all with the other and entering himself. Calista closed and locked the door. He dumped the suitcase in the middle

263

of the hall.

'Be an angel and deal with this, will you Cal?' He gestured toward Sasha. 'I'm off to my bed.'

Shocked into silence, Calista watched him stomp up the stairs, hold-all in hand, then she turned to Sasha, whose face was contorted with anguish, her eyes brimming with tears.

'Sorry, Cal.' She sobbed. 'Dad's so angry.'

Calista put her arms around the trembling girl and held her close. 'Shush, shush, darling. He'll get over it.' Despite wearing a fleece-hoody and jog pants, Sasha felt cold. She rubbed her back, and eventually Sasha's tears seemed to abate. 'Have you had anything to eat?'

Sasha told her Adam had stopped at a service station, and fetched them both a burger to eat in the car. 'I didn't want it but . . . Then not long after we set off again, I was sick. He was driving so fast . . . and . . .' She had aimed for the floor between her feet, but splashed her trainers and the bottoms of her joggers. 'Look.'

'Soon get them clean,' Calista said.

'First thing tomorrow, Dad says I must clean out the car. He hates me. I know he does.'

'Darling, he's upset. He wouldn't be so angry if he hated you. Now let's go into the kitchen. Beppo will be pleased to see you and I'll make you some toast with honey. It'll settle your stomach.'

She made them both toast, and mint tea. Sasha managed to eat two rounds.

'You get ready for bed,' Calista said. 'I'll come and tuck you in.'

While she was preparing herself for the night, Calista wondered if Sasha, like Annabel, had been expelled. If so, no wonder Adam was incandescent. She went to Sasha's room where Sasha, looking woebegone, was sitting on the side of the bed.

'Will you stay, just a little while? Please, Cal.'

'Darling, I'm really tired . . .'

Sasha hung her head. 'Nobody wants me, not Mum, not Dad.'

Calista took hold her hands and pulled her to her feet. 'Come on. My bed's huge, room for one slender girl and a not quite so slim woman.'

'What about Dad?'

'Snoring already, in the room next door.'

They lay on their backs side by side.

'Thanks, Cal.' Sasha spoke in a small voice. 'When Dad wasn't there, if I had a bad dream, I used to creep in beside Mum. But Bradley's always . . .'

'Your mum and Bradley love each other, and when . . .'

'I know. Mum's ever so happy. I can really see why . . .' Sasha sighed. 'If only her and Dad could've been like that. Bradley's nice. We had fun when Len and I were there in the summer. I did tell him I was sorry for being horrid about him.'

She leaned over and stroked Sasha's cheek. 'That was sweet.'

'Bradley said not to worry. When his kid sister was my age, she was a brat too.'

Calista chuckled. 'I think that's what my brother used to think about me. Now, shall we try to go to sleep?'

Sasha turned on her side away from her, sucking her thumb. Calista put out her bedside lamp, and settled herself down.

'Cal?'

'Sash?'

'What if Mum dies, and I never see her again. It's dangerous giving birth when you're older.'

Calista rolled over onto her other side. 'Listen to me. When you last saw her, your mum must have had at most seven weeks to go. Was she showing any sign of distress?'

She sensed Sasha turning towards her.

'No, but . . . she was . . . well ginormous. I wondered how the baby would ever get out. Mum laughed, said I was a silly duck for someone who was so keen on biology, and lent me a book about having a baby.' Sasha made sick noises in her throat. 'Gross.'

'Well, there's something for you to look forward to when you're older. Look, this will be your mum's third baby. Besides, I should think Bradley's made sure she has the best medical attention possible.'

'When he saw us off at the airport, he told us not to worry, he'd take good care of her. And he does, I know he does but . . . He's really active.'

'Bradley?'

'No the baby, Llewelyn. They're going to call him Llewelyn after one of Bradley's granddads. Mum let me feel when he kicked. Awesome.'

'There you go. Mother and baby both good. Can we try and sleep now?'

They both turned to lie on their sides backs towards each other.

'I just wish I was with Mum to make sure . . . Sorry. Night, night, Cal.' Sasha sounded as though she already had her thumb in her mouth.

Bradley's granddad, Welsh perhaps, like Esther's Nan. They must be everywhere. Bizarre she should think that, the last thing she remembered before she fell asleep.

Coming up to half past eight, Calista eased herself out of bed. Sasha did not stir. She looked pale, but at peace. Taking care to be quiet, Calista gathered what she needed, and went to the family bathroom, wet towels on the floor, water in the shower tray, so Adam was somewhere about. Although the kettle was still warm, no sign of him in the kitchen, or Beppo. She went out into the courtyard, the morning chilly, dampness in the air, only a few leaves of crimson Virginia creeper clinging to the garage wall warmed the scene. Beppo appeared from around the front of the house. When he saw her he trotted over wagging his tail.

'Morning, old boy. Did Dad take you for a walk?'

'Good morning, Cal. For a start, I'm not the bloody dog's father.' Adam too appeared, workmanlike in a pair of faded jeans, the sleeves of an old sweater rolled up, carrying a plastic bucket of soapy water. He was wearing rubber gloves.

'Good morning, Adam, or should I say Mrs Mop.' She felt her face erupting into the broadest grin.

'Ha, bloody ha. Been cleaning out the hire car. Sash was sick.'

'She said you told her she had to clean it up first thing.'

'I was angry.'

'I said you'd get over it.'

'How is she this morning? I tip-toed in about half seven to collect some clothes. Saw she was with you. Hadn't the heart to wake either of you. You looked so angelic. Huh.' He gave a derisive snort. 'Trouble with two capital Ts.' He retrieved a scrubbing brush from his bucket, rang out a cloth, and poured the water down the kitchen drain.

'Come on in,' Calista said. 'I was about to make tea and toast.'

They sat either side of the kitchen table with their mugs of breakfast tea, buttered toast on a breadboard between them, a pot of homemade plum jam. Adam took a round and spread it with jam. Calista did too. They began to eat.

Adam licked his thumb. 'One culinary art you have mastered, Cal, making toast. When Sash puts in an appearance, I'll make us some brunch. Bloody burger gave me indigestion. No wonder Sash was sick.' He took another bite of toast.

Peckish, she concentrated on eating hers, waiting. He drank some of his tea.

'Sorry I left you with her last night. Bit abrupt. Been a long and tiring day.'

'I did understand, Adam. London to Dorset, then Dorset to Leicestershire, a marathon drive.'

'Not to mention the bit in between.' He gazed at her across the table an expression in his eyes like Beppo's when he had been reprimanded for some misdemeanour. She wondered if the Head had had a go at him.

'Has she been expelled, Adam?'

'No, thank God. Suspended, sort of.'

'Sort of?'

Adam told her after a full and frank discussion with someone from learning support, plus Sasha's personal mentor, and the Head, he and they had all come to the same conclusion. Sasha needed time away from school. 'She's been a pain in the arse ever since she got back —uncooperative, mouthy, hasn't applied herself to her work, the inference being she was beginning to infect a couple of her friends. Till now, the school's always been supportive. They know her personal circumstances. She's not the only one whose parents have divorced. Just Sash, as per, being bloody-minded. In her first year, she took a while to settle. She missed Annabel, but once she got interested in science . . . field trips, like collecting those fossils.'

'I Googled the school after what you said. I can see why you wanted the girls to go there, but . . .'

'All I've ever wanted is the best for them. I was appalled when Annie told me she was pregnant with Len. Then once she was born and I held her in my arms . . . Must admit, I was keen on their going to an all girls' school. Teenage boys can be so . . .' He shuddered. 'So predatory.' He took another drink of his tea.

'So unlike middle-aged men.' Calista could not help herself. She noticed he had the grace to blush.

'Sash is dyslexic you know.'

'I had no idea.' She took a sip of her tea, still just about warm enough, and at least wet.

'That school's really brought her on. And this term they've obviously tried their hardest with her. I'm sorry, Cal, to drop this on you. Can she stay here till we go to Ithaca? The Head's agreed she can go back after half term, but only if she seems ready.'

'This is her home. Where else would she stay? And for as long as it takes, as far as I'm concerned. Though you do realize I can't be here all day, every day. Only some days I'm able to work at home. I shall have to have a word with Pam.'

Adam looked relieved. 'She promised her mentor she won't give you grief. Apparently she thinks you're cool. They were impressed she doesn't look on you as a wicked stepmother. She's been given a study schedule for the next couple of weeks. All we have to do is make sure she sticks to it. And emails her assignments through on time.'

For 'we', read 'you', Calista guessed. She doubted Adam would hang around longer than he thought necessary.

'I shall do my best to help her,' Calista said. 'Last night she claimed no one wants her, not you, not Annabel.'

'What utter rubbish. Annie was set on taking both of them to the States. Just didn't make sense to disrupt their education, certainly not the stage Len's at, though Brown was more than willing.' Grudging, 'Decent enough chap, I suppose. And, I married you and bought this house to give her and Len a secure base. If I hadn't wanted . . .' He tailed off, probably noticing her raised eyebrows, sarcastic smile.

'Also,' Calista said. 'She's full of anxiety, an indication of being depressed, I think.'

'Anxiety about what?'

'She's worried Annabel will die giving birth.'

'Annie sailed through her pregnancies, and Brown assures me she's doing the same with their boy. As for actually giving birth, no problem. In any case, what's the date?' He glanced at his watch. 'The ninth, almost any hour we could hear.'

'Could hear what?' Sasha, in her pyjamas stood in the kitchen doorway.

Adam pushed back his chair, and got to his feet. He opened his arms.

'Come here, you. Sorry I was so angry yesterday.'

Sasha threw herself at him. 'I . . . don't . . . don't . . . know . . . what . . . to . . . do . . . with . . . myself,' she said between sobs.

'Shush, shush.' Adam stroked her hair. 'Me and Cal, we'll look after you.'

Oh, dear God, Calista thought, what do I do now?

CHAPTER FORTY SEVEN

What Calista Did Next

Sunday afternoon, she and Sasha laid out most of the contents of the large suitcase, and Sasha's laptop on the dining room table. 'You'll be able to spread out in here, and not be disturbed,' Calista said.

'I really like this room,' Sasha said. 'Especially now you've put up Len's pictures.'

Calista picked up a copy of Steinbeck's *Of Mice and Men*. 'You're reading this. That's great.'

The letter from the Head Teacher attached to Sasha's study schedule addressed to Mrs A. Burgess was no surprise. Mr A. Burgess must have explained his role in the City precluded his spending weekdays in Leicestershire supervising his wayward daughter. The Head expressed her gratitude in advance, and told her how she could contact her at any time, should she feel the need.

Sitting side by side, she and Sasha went through the work programme. 'You can't sit around all day feeling sorry for yourself, can you now? And your teachers seem to have put quite a bit of thought into what might motivate you, including a bird-watching trip to the Eyebrook reservoir.'

'We had to write about something we did in the holidays. Jason helped me, but don't tell. We email and text all the time. Can I invite him over, Cal?'

'Don't see why not. I'll square it with your dad.'

'He'll agree, if you say so. He takes far more notice of you than he did Mum. And I will work, Cal. Just . . . Mum will be okay, won't she?'

She put her arm around Sasha's shoulders and gave her a squeeze. 'Darling, strange as it may seem, sounds as though your dad and Bradley are in constant touch. And, I hope you will work when I'm not here. I don't want Pam being played up.'

'Promise. I like Pammy. She's cool.'

What better accolade could anyone ask for, Calista thought? She pushed back her chair. 'Time for tea and gingerbread.' When they were both on their feet, she chucked Sasha under the chin. 'Is this the same waif who stood sobbing in my hall less than twenty four hours ago?'

Sasha threw her arms around her, hugging her. 'When I'm with you, I feel all warm inside.'

Monday, Adam elected to work in his office above the garage. 'I can't leave you to it completely, Cal, though I will have to go up to London tomorrow.'

She told him she and Sasha had mapped out a programme for each week day, starting at 8.30 with a two-hour break 12.00 till 2.00, finishing at 4.00 p.m. She suggested Adam spend some time with her. 'But let her call the shots. You could take her and Beppo for a walk, say before lunch.' He said he would.

She made sure Sasha was settled in the dining room, and Pam fully briefed – elevenses for Sasha around 10 o'clock - then she set off planning to spend the whole day in Chambers. She had work to catch up with. Come lunchtime, Matt insisted he take her to Casa Romana. 'Just for a plate of pasta, and a glass of wine. I'm dying to hear all about the romantic Mr Wood.'

Over their plates of *tagliatelli ciociara,* always a favourite, she gave a somewhat bowdlerized account of her relationship with PJ. Just did not seem right that she should share her pregnancy with any more people till the father got to know.

'Does this mean, Burgess is for the old heave-ho?'

'You sound like Bertie Wooster. There are reasons, one good one in fact, other than what does or doesn't develop with PJ.'

Matt reached across and stroked her cheek. 'I never liked him, but I am sorry it hasn't worked out. Is this what's put you off wine?'

'God, no.' She could not help smile at his look of concern, for her disastrous marriage, or maybe because she was off wine. 'My own fault. I had doubts. But we did have fun, like discovering Ithaca together, and when he said he and Annabel were divorcing . . . And he was so persistent . . . I thought . . .' Then she told him all about Annabel and her American Bradley Brown.

Matt looked stunned. Then he grinned. 'Look on the bright side, Cal. If you'd not gone to Ithaca with Burgess, you'd never have met PJ Wood.'

'I hope I don't live to regret that too. He's in New York right now.' She did not mention, the one measly text from him so far. 'After talking to Tess, I was all psyched up to tackle Adam this coming weekend, regardless . . . but now Sasha's here.' She glanced at her watch. 'I'll tell you about her on the way back.'

As they approached Chambers, Matt said, 'You know your best bet for the next three weeks, just go with the flow. And, if you feel the need to sound off, find me.'

Go with the flow, she remembered that was exactly what Esther had advised when she told her how lonely and unhappy she was.

Monday evening Calista arrived home around six thirty in time for an early dinner. Pam had made boeuf Bourgignon which smelt so good, she was able to eat some. She was relieved to see Adam and Sasha getting on well together. Later, to her astonishment, father and daughter settled down to watch *Coronation Street*, followed by some crime series, in Calista's opinion, both beggaring belief. She would rather have listened to music. Some Mozart would have suited her mood. *Don Giovanni* would be appropriate, or with herself and Annabel in mind *Cosi fan tutte* maybe.

On the sofa, Adam had his arm around Sasha, her head on his chest, thumb in mouth. Calista sat in her favourite armchair, feet up on a stool, Beppo lying doggo beside her chair. An idyllic family scene, if only Adam wasn't Adam, and her thoughts did not keep straying to PJ Wood – *Where the hell are you? Still in New York? What are you doing? If you go there regularly . . . After a gruelling time in Afghanistan . . . Is there some obliging woman you see? Why had she been so sure of him? She really knew very little about him.*

As soon as the drama finished, Sasha kissed each of them 'night, night' and went up to bed. Calista planned on following. She pushed away her footstool.

'Cal.' Adam switched off the TV and sat forward, forearms resting on his knees. He looked at the floor. 'I just want to say, thank you. Sash seems more together already. But you were right, she's full of worries about Annie. I just mentioned her mother as though en passant, and she began to talk, really talk.' He told her Sasha had always bonded more strongly with Annabel than she had with him. 'With me, it was Len.' He gave a rueful smile. 'In some ways she is the easier option. Today, Sash said she knew Len was my favourite, and she could understand why. Len was more like me than she was. I was stunned. My little girl saying that.'

Adam said he hugged her, told her he certainly did not love her less than Helena. 'I told her, maybe I love you more. I certainly worry about you more. All I ever want is what's best for you. Then she cried. She said she was crying because I said I loved her, and I get so angry, and I used to hurt her when I smacked her. I explained I was one of those people on a short fuse.'

Adam looked up and met her gaze, 'I think we understand each other better now, me and Sash. She's given me a lot to think about.'

'You've probably done more good today, than a therapist could do in a month of Sundays.' She decided now was not the time to suggest he might take a course on anger management.

Then one of his beguiling smiles. 'One of your granny's sayings, "a month of Sundays".' Adam Burgess the archetypal Jekyll and Hyde.

Before turning in she checked. No email yet from PJ. His roses were beginning to wilt. Tomorrow, she would ask Pam to throw them out. In bed at last, lying on her back in the dark, 'Go with the flow. Go with the flow. Go with the flow' she chanted. She really was exhausted. She turned on her side settling herself for sleep. About to doze off, she heard the door latch turn, then, as on the previous night, someone climb into bed beside her. 'Night, night, Sash.'

'Night, night, Cal. Mind the bugs don't bite.'

Now when was the last time she heard that? PJ, you bastard, you've absconded.

Tuesday, she, Sasha and Pam were chatting in the kitchen. The mouth-watering aroma of Sasha's request, a veggie lasagne layered with auber-gines and courgettes drifted from the Aga. Beppo with a low growl was out of his basket before they heard the side-door open and close. Adam walked into the kitchen, beaming. 'I've some good news. First let me get a bottle of Veuve Cliquot from the cellar. Pam. you'll join us, won't you? Sash, four champagne flutes from the dining room, pdq. Back in a tick.'

'Do you think he's made another million or something?' Sasha said before she obeyed.

Adam took off his charcoal chalk-stripe jacket and hung it on the back of a chair. Adept as always, the cork gave a satisfying pop, he poured champagne into the glasses without wasting a drop. 'A soupçon surely won't hurt, Cal.' He handed her a half-filled flute.' She hardly registered what he said before, 'Raise your glasses to Sash's baby brother Llewelyn Reuben Brown, born today in the early hours, 7.30ish our time, weighing in at eight and a quarter pounds.'

Sasha, the colour drained from her face, put down her glass. 'He's here,' came out as a squeak.

'What I said, Sash.' Adam handed her the champagne again. 'Now let's wet the baby's head. Your mum is absolutely fine.'

They touched glasses. Adam intoned 'To Llewelyn Reuben. Also, of course, to his mother.' The four of them sipped their drinks.

Calista was pleased for Sasha's sake, Adam was making a celebration of the news. Yet there was a sense of the surreal. She had met Annabel only once, Pam never, and Annabel had dumped Adam for Bradley. She and Pam exchanged bemused glances.

Sasha pulled out a chair and sat down. 'Did Bradley phone you, Dad?'

He had sent Adam a text early on, then just before Adam left for the train, made a brief call to say Annabel was exhausted but well. Bradley had stayed with her throughout. Adam shuddered. 'Rather him than me. He's taking photos and will send copies. After dinner, we'll go over to my office and see if they've arrived.'

'And Mum's good, the baby's come out okay?' Sasha drained her glass.

'That's what babies have a habit of doing left to their own devices, planned or otherwise,' Adam said.

Adam's attention on Sasha, again Calista and Pam exchanged glances. Calista shook her head, and, although she should not, quaffed the rest of her champagne.

'May I have some more, please?' Sasha held up her empty flute. 'I . . . I . . . I wish I was there.' Then she burst into tears.

Adam drew her to her feet and hugged her to him. 'Eh, Mum's okay. You'll be seeing her for real in a couple of months.'

'I . . . think . . . I'm . . . crying . . . cos . . . I'm . . .'

'Relieved and pleased you've got a brother.' Adam stroked her hair.

Pam and Calista put down their glasses and left, Beppo following them.

'Think I'll take Beppo out into the garden,' Calista said.

Pam had her coat on. 'Before you do – I don't want to intrude – would you put the lasagne in the keep-warm oven, please, or it'll spoil.'

The unspoilt lasagne was delicious, and though Sasha was quiet, she ate a large helping, as did she and Adam. Adam assured Sasha he had told Helena about their new brother.

Sasha asked to be excused. 'I'm going to phone Len.'

When she had gone, 'I hope she's going to be okay,' Adam said. 'Len's always been quite protective of her. Sash relies on her, I think. When Len leaves school . . . '

'Good you broke the news the way you did,' Calista said. 'You seemed pleased and relieved yourself.'

'I'm still very fond of Annie. Always will be. She is my children's mother, after all. As you now know, she was the one who pushed for a divorce. I really didn't believe that was necessary.'

Adam in his bespoke blue and white-striped shirt sleeves sat facing her across the dirty dishes and remains of dinner. She was aware, head to one side, she had raised her eyebrows, set her mouth into a wry smile.

He held her gaze. His tone measured, 'Even if she had already been pregnant, I would've accepted Brown's child as my own.' - Calista felt her face heat up. - 'Should she just have been having a fling, wasn't worth disrupting our family over. We are intelligent civilized human beings, after all.'

She looked away. No doubt at all that was how he had viewed his affair with her, a fling, though she had never wanted his marriage to break up on her account. As for the rest . . . Abrupt, she got to her feet and began stacking the dirty pots. He pushed back his chair, got up, and sat down again. Elbows on the table, he cupped his face in his hands looking pensive. She stopped what she was doing and regarded him. He gave a deep sigh.

'I hate to admit it. Annie's far happier with Brown than she ever was with me.' He looked deflated.

She modulated her voice to sound gentler than it might otherwise have been. 'Being married to you, Adam, can be a very lonely place to find yourself.'

His forearms flopped on to the table top. He looked . . . The door opened. Sasha burst in smiling. 'Me and Len, we can hardly wait to see Llew. Dad, Len says at the weekend do you think we could Skype Mum and Bradley, set up a sort of three-way conference like you do in business?'

Getting to his feet, Adam returned her smile. 'Don't see why not, darling.' He took his jacket from the back of his chair. 'Let's go and see if those photos have arrived.'

They left without a backward glance.

Sasha and Adam had been in his office for over an hour which Calista took to be a good sign. She decided to take herself to bed with a novel. She needed distraction. Still no email from PJ Wood. Esther had lent her 'The Postmistress' by Sarah Blake. She had become just as hooked as the dinner party guests were in the first chapter, wanting to hear why the letter had never been delivered when there was a knock on her bedroom door. She hoped it was not Adam. Nevertheless she called, 'Come in.' Sasha entered, a shy smile on her face.

'Dad asked me to come and see if you're okay.'

'I'm absolutely fine, darling. Did he stay in his office to do something?'

'Not work. He's drinking whisky. Said he'd follow me later.' Sasha came nearer to the bed. She produced something the size of an over-large postcard she had been hiding behind her back. 'Would you like to look at this? Dad printed it out for me to keep.'

Smiling, Calista took it from her, a photo of Annabel against a bank of pillows, her short blonde curls framing the dreamy smile of contentment on her face. She wore a white broderie anglaise-trimmed nightgown, and gazed down at the baby she cradled in her arms. All that could be seen of Llewelyn was his small pink face with closed eyes, his cap of dark hair, and his perfect little hands protruding from a primrose yellow onesie.

'Isn't he cute?' Sasha said. 'And look at Mum. She's gorgeous.'

'My friend Tess wore an expression very much like that when she held her babies,' Calista said. 'I guess you can't help feeling pleased with yourself when you produce something as marvellous as that.'

'Dad says Mum looked just like that after she'd had me. And Len. Do you not want to have a baby Cal?'

'You said it was gross.'

'Yes, but . . . well . . . well, it is Nature with a capital 'N'.'

'Sometimes you can be so perceptive for a fourteen-year-old.'

'I may be dyslexic but I'm not stupid.'

'Not stupid at all.'

Another knock at the door, this time it was Adam. He did not venture far into the room.

'Time for you to get ready for bed, Sash. And do you think tonight you might stay in your own bed.'

'Think I'd better. I'm so excited I might disturb Cal. Night, night, Cal. See you in the morning.' Sasha kissed her on the cheek. 'Come and tuck me in, Dad,' she said as she left.

'If she carries on like this,' Adam said. 'Looks as though she might be ready to go back to school after the break. Long-term, who knows.' He gave a heartfelt sigh.

'Are you okay, Adam?' She got out of bed and went over to him, close enough to notice his eyes were red. Blinking he looked away.

'Bit emotional, that's all.' He sounded irritated. Then, softer, looking directly at her, 'Cal, tomorrow I have to go up to town again. I thought I might stay overnight. I'll come back on Thursday afternoon without fail.'

Smelling the whisky on his breath, she took a step back. 'That'll be fine.' She expected he would be seeking the release with Sheena Jardine she was no longer willing to give. She turned to go back to bed.

'Cal.' He caught hold her hand. 'Thank you. Thank you for everything.'

'Good night, Adam. Everything will work out. You'll see.'

'Maybe.' Again he sighed. 'God knows.' He let go her hand and left her room.

No longer in the mood to read, she settled herself with the intention of falling asleep. Eyes open, she lay on her back staring into darkness, thinking. If she had ever really loved him as she ought to have done, she would try to understand, to forgive him. As it was, when she saw he had probably been crying, she was tempted to put her arms around him, comfort him. Unwise, to paraphrase Esther, he was a physically attractive shit of the first order of shits. Even now, near him, she felt that certain frisson.

She turned over on her side. If PJ, the father of her child then turned out to be a man of straw, as seemed possible, when she told Adam, she wondered if he would offer to accept her child as his own.

Where the hell are you, PJ Wood? What are you doing, and who are you doing it with? I'm telling you now, I ain't gonna be the first one to blink. She rolled over onto her other side. Go with the flow, go with the flow, go with the flow, she incanted into the dark.

CHAPTER FORTY EIGHT

Going with the Flow

A whole week since Adam announced the news of Llewelyn's arrival, or Llew as Sasha and Helena were already calling him. Calista, eyes closed, lay alone in her bed. She was having difficulty getting to sleep. *Tomorrow, and tomorrow, and tomorrow* - bad luck to quote the Scottish play. Life, her life – *a tale told by an idiot, full of sound and fury, signifying nothing*. She turned onto her back, stroked her stomach. Too nihilistic, little one, and began to sing *pianissimo*, *Always look on the bright side of life*. She had watched 'Life of Brian' with her granny, who was in stitches all through. The memory always cheered her up. Gran said, *if you didn't laugh, you'd cry*. Not so much displacement activity, displacement thought. Anything rather than try to second guess how the weeks and months ahead might pan out.

One bit of relief, Sasha already seemed on a more even keel. How nautical, Calista gave a rueful snort. So far, the promised daily emails from her sailor lover had failed to materialize. Another song sprang to mind, Granny again, *pianissimo* as before, she didn't want to wake Adam next door -

All the nice girls love a sailor, All the nice girls love a tar, For there's something about a sailor – and not forgetting the punch line *He falls in love with Kate and Jane, then he's off to sea again.*

Her intense, but, to be candid, nebulous relationship with PJ seemed to have keeled over, run aground, sunk. That was pragmatism, not flippancy. In her present predicament to be other than hard-headed *O! That way madness lies, let me shun that.*

Until Calista learnt otherwise, she should give PJ Wood the benefit of the doubt, Pam had counselled; wasn't as though she knew the reason why, no sooner back from Afghanistan, he had to go to the States. Perhaps he had unearthed something the American authorities were interested in, 'Perhaps he's somewhere it's difficult to send emails from.'

A well-worn cliché, Calista felt her blood run cold. 'You think he's been taken to Guantanomo?'

Pam shook her head, a look of consternation on her face. 'Heavens above. Cal, where did that come from? In his line of business, he must be savvy. He would never have gone of his own free-will, if he suspected that's where he might end up.'

'Practically every day you read about rendition, arbitrary detentions, stuff like that,' Calista said. 'PJ hardly strikes me as being a member of the Establishment.' Whereas, Adam, she thought.

Pam said PJ seemed genuine, and why go to the trouble to deliver the roses personally. Calista shrugged. 'Curiosity, I checked out where he lives.'

'When he came back to see you.' Pam said, 'he behaved like a gentleman. Could've taken advantage, I daresay.' Calista had felt the heat in her face under Pam's quizzical gaze.

She turned on to her other side.

The past weekend was relaxing compared to the previous one. On Saturday morning, despite the threat of rain, Sasha and Jason had taken a packed lunch and cycled over to the Eyebrook Reservoir. She and Beppo went on their favourite ramble and, as on a previous occasion, met Adam at the pub in the nearest village. No snide comment on her abstention from alcohol, she noted. Over lunch they discussed his daughters. Helena had been encouraged by Mina to apply to Central St Martins – Helena's first choice - and as a failsafe a couple or so other colleges. And, of course, they discussed Sasha's apparent improvement.

'She felt abandoned.' Calista said. 'Between us we've managed to make her feel wanted and loved. For the time being anyway. I know so little about children, but, she strikes me as being rather naïve compared with many fourteen-year-olds these days.'

'Can't thank you enough, Cal. You've only known my girls a few months.' He sighed. 'I'm really worried about Sash. How she'll be once

Len's no longer at that school. Annie wanted her to go as a day-girl to a good local school in Loughborough. I over-ruled her. Len was doing so well. I thought they ought to have the same opportunities.' Unusual for him, he looked so unsure of himself, she had to resist reaching across the table to stroke his cheek.

'I can well imagine Len thriving in such an environment,' Calista said. 'Boarding school could only enhance her innate qualities.' *Look how she outflanked you when it came to going to Art School rather than Oxford*, she thought. 'Sash is a bright, clever girl full of self-doubt,' she went on to say. 'May seem totally irrational to us but I'm sure she was genuinely worried her mother might have life-threatening complications when she gave birth. Now she's on a high because Annabel's come through.'

'What are you saying, Sash is a manic-depressive, or whatever they call it now.'

'I'm not a psychiatrist, Adam. Probably like most of us, she just needs to know she's loved.'

'I believed I was doing what was best for both of them.' Another sigh. 'I've been too heavy-handed a father, haven't I?'

'Literally in Sash's case.'

'My idea was to toughen her up. Did me, though I never used a hairbrush embossed with silver initials like my nanny did. Sometimes the bitch broke the skin. Really hurt when I sat down. Antonia used to bathe my bottom and put soothing cream on it.'

Calista was horrified by the insouciant tone of his revelation, and bravo Antonia, she thought. From now on, she would view her insufferably supercilious sister-in-law with respect. This time she did reach across, and stroked his cheek.

'Adam, girls don't respond to corporal punishment in the same way as boys. Whatever you may think, it is child abuse. My understanding is girls turn in on themselves, and even self-harm. As for boys, in my opinion, it can only brutalize them, make them indifferent not only to their own suffering but also to the pain of others. I can't help thinking whole empires have been built on, and are still being built on such callous disregard.'

Adam's face coloured up. He looked crushed. 'I'm not indifferent, Cal.' He looked away, pushed his empty plate to one side, rested his hands, fingers intertwined on the table, and contemplated them. 'Neglectful perhaps. Especially when I'm preoccupied.' He paused, the silence heavy between them. Then, 'Or following some self-indulgent pursuit.'

She covered his hands with hers. 'On a good day, you can be great company, and thoughtful and kind. You've certainly shown that side of yourself this past week.'

He looked up, met her gaze. 'I was worried about my little girl. It's been good, hasn't it, the three of us together, a family. Next week, I will have to go up to town, perhaps on two or three days. I shan't stay overnight.'

'Certainly best you don't do that.' She let go his hands.

He nodded, his expression hangdog. 'Yes, I know. I do know that.' He seemed to brighten. 'Friday don't forget, I'll be driving down to fetch Len.' Then his face was lit by a smile of anticipation. 'This time next Saturday we'll be well on our way to Ithaca. Do you think the girls will like Villa Thalia?'

She returned his smile. 'Adam, how could they not.'

On the way home, the skies opened to a steady downpour. They were prepared for it. There was something primordial about striding through the rain. 'Hope the twitchers took waterproofs,' Adam said. 'Or they'll come home looking like a couple of drowned water voles.'

And Saturday night was far from lonely. The three of them were invited to supper by Jason's parents. Adam took the call. They were both medics, his mother a GP at a practice in Leicester, his father a consultant surgeon. They lived in a comfortable, late-Victorian house in a much larger village a couple of miles up the road.

'As our children are friends, I thought we ought to get to know each other,' Jason's mother said. Her name was Celia, ginger-haired, freckled like her son, and attractive with it.

'Thank you for inviting us,' Calista said. 'We moved into our house a year ago but haven't really got to know anyone round about. Adam spends most of the week up in London, and practising law keeps me off the streets.' Also keeps me sane, she thought, just about.

Supper was simple and satisfying, a penne pasta bake with a combination of vegetables – courgettes, Calabrese, mushrooms, leeks, red peppers, plus mozzarella cheese, all in a delicious home-made tomato sauce - accompanied by a green salad and warm French bread to mop up the sauce.

'Cal, the mozzarella is pasteurised.'

Calista felt her face flush. Although Celia was a GP surely she could not tell just by looking at her, and neither she nor Lawrence had questioned her preference for mineral water over Montepulciano D'Abruzzo.

Adam and Lawrence – dark-haired, with laughter lines round his eyes– had fly-fishing in common and were surprised not to have bumped into each other at the Eyebrook.

Then, 'I haven't ever met anyone involved in Hedge Fund management before. I'm not sure I know what that is exactly.'

'If you've got half a day, I could bore for England.' Adam laughed. 'To simplify, it's about taking a position and a punt, say, for example, on a particular currency, or shares in a bank about to fall in value. You hold your nerve, aren't tempted to cash in your chips. The currency or the shares hit rock bottom, have no place to go but up. You wait and wait. They take off, everyone believes they're the next best thing to sliced bread, and you get back a lot more than you bet in the first place. That's the theory.'

Lawrence gave a nervous laugh. 'Sounds risky, like gambling in a casino.'

'No risk, no gain.'

'Think I'll stick to cutting people up.'

After they had finished eating, Sasha and Jason disappeared to catalogue the day's sightings. Once they had gone, Celia, Lawrence and Adam voiced their misgivings about their friendship, Jason not being sixteen until March, Sasha fourteen, and a young fourteen at that.

'What do you think, Cal?' Celia said.

'They're just a couple of kids who get on because they've interests in common, bird-watching, fossils. Let them be. I am only Sasha's stepmother but . . . In my opinion, if you're confident you've brought up your children the best you can, you should trust them. They may get up to a bit of mischief, a bit of experimentation. It's what kids do, but I really don't see Sash and Jason becoming teenage parents, if that's what's worrying you. For a start Sash think's having a baby's gross, and, despite her naivety, I'm pretty sure she knows her biology.'

'My wife always makes perfect sense,' Adam said. 'That's why I married her.'

Why he married me, not why he loves me, she noted.

She had enjoyed Celia and Lawrence's company, and Adam had been on one of his natural charm offensives which seemed to have gone down well.

'We must do this again,' Lawrence said, as she, Adam and Sasha were about to leave.

'Our turn to host next time,' Adam said.

As she drove Adam and Sasha home Calista couldn't help thinking, if only the events of the past week had happened, say, ten months earlier, although if they had, she might not now be expecting a child of her own.

Sunday evening, at their three-way chat on Skype, Sasha and Helena had talked to their mother and watched her bathe their baby brother. Back from Adam's office, Sasha bounded into the sitting room.

'His testicles look a bit big compared to the rest of him, don't they Dad?'

'Sasha.' Adam shook his head.

'No doubt he'll grow into them,' Calista said.

'You should see him, Cal. He's really long, bit like a skinned rabbit, but gorgeous. Hope when I go over at Christmas Mum will let me cuddle him.'

'He'll have plumped up by then.'

'Time you were in bed, Sash,' Adam said.

'Thanks for a fab weekend both.' Sasha kissed her and Adam. 'Night, night.'

After Sasha had gone, Adam asked if she minded if he sat with her for a while. 'I heard singing just before Sash burst in. What was it?'

'*Songs from the Auvergne,* sung by Victoria de Los Angeles. I'd only just started listening. Daddy had an LP, still the best version he says. I downloaded them. You're welcome to stay and listen with me.'

He asked if he might fetch her a glass of cold milk. 'I shall have a whisky, if you don't mind, but I've noticed, last thing, you've taken to drinking milk. Would you like me to warm it?'

She shook her head. 'Uhhgg, no thanks.'

They sat at each corner of the sofa listening, and sipping their drinks. When the music came to an end, he gave a satisfied sigh. 'On that note I think I'll turn in. A perfect end to an enjoyable weekend.' He got his feet, and stood in front of her. She looked up, waiting. 'Cal, when we get back from Ithaca, hopefully Sash will be back at school, you and I, we . . . we need to talk.'

'Whenever you want.' She forced a smile though her heart was pounding.

'No hurry.' He bent down and kissed her forehead. 'Night, night.'

Would be so easy to reach up, put her arms around his neck and kiss him on the lips. What folly. She did no such thing.

She would never get to sleep. She rolled over onto her other side. When they returned, Adam would want to discuss Sasha for sure. Saturday evening, 'Tell me about Jason's school,' he said. 'You say, he boards during the week and comes home weekends. It's co-educational and just over ten miles away.' Easy to guess what he was thinking. She remembered his remark in the pub, *it's been good, hasn't it, the three of us together, a family.* And he had sounded almost contrite recognizing his neglect.

What if she never saw or heard from PJ Wood again – she was sure as hell not going to panic, email him. If the past week was anything to go by, would her life be so terrible after all if she and Adam were able to talk out their differences and come to a mutual decision not to divorce. Right now what she did not want to contemplate was Esther's reaction to that idea.

Say, when she confronted Adam, he promised to finish with Sheena Jardine. More to the point, he might promise never to cheat on her again, though she doubted he could break the habit of a life-time. Would Adam forgive her, if she confessed to her 'fling' with PJ and being pregnant by him? 'Most likely end up with just you and me babe,' she whispered stroking her stomach again. 'Okay, I can do that.'

Go with the flow, both Esther and Matt said. As far as her private life was concerned, exactly what she had been doing ever since she became involved with Adam Burgess. A fine mess she was in as a result, and these past days she had continued along the primrose way. That play again. She drifted off to sleep.

CHAPTER FORTY NINE

Have Ithaka always in your mind
Your arrival there is what you are destined for
[Constantine Cavafy]

Tuesday, her third full day on Ithaca, she was alone and driving down to Vathy in their hired 4x4. The steep slopes of Mount Neritus on her left, the sheer-drop to the sea on her right, Calista tried not to let her fevered sense of anticipation make her lose awareness of the road's twists and turns, the straying goats. Rounding a bend, one of the locals in his pick-up truck came towards her in the middle of the road. To her left, the drop, he veered to his right just in time. 'Whew, little one, might've been curtains for the two of us. Then all our troubles would've been over.'

The previous Thursday, after dinner, she shut herself in her study to call Esther. More than ten days since she told her of Sasha's little difficulty, and how, for the time being, it had thwarted her intention to confront Adam. She had chickened out of phoning her ever since. Contrite, she began by asking if Esther had managed to convince Mike she and the children should live with him in Amsterdam.

'I'm more than half-way there,' Esther said. 'He realizes I am serious about taking a sabbatical. Now it's whether Fran and Tom will take to the plan. We'll get some idea when we're all there next week. Poor love, says he doesn't dare think about it too much, the reason for his initial negativity he says. Nothing to do with Louse van de Velde, I guess. I'm not sure absolutely nothing happened with her, but, far as I'm concerned, whatever it was, it's irrelevant now.'

'Good for you. Mike was bereft. He though he was losing you.'

'As if. Now tell me, no news is good news, or what?'

She told her Sasha was not nearly such a lost soul as when she first arrived. 'She and I have bonded quite well. Even so, I can't help thinking, long-term, particularly once Len starts Art College, better for Sash if she went to live with her mother. That would make her feel she really belonged, especially now there's the new baby. From what she has said, I'm pretty certain Annabel and Bradley would have her, but I suspect Adam has other plans.' She told Esther of his searching questions about Jason's school.

'Oh my God, Cal, you'll have to kibosh that. Anyways once you tell him you want a divorce . . .'

'Tess, I've not heard from PJ since he sent me that text to say he'd arrived in New York.' She had replied, *Thanks for letting me know. I love you too. Cal*, but she didn't tell Esther that.

'Holy shit, the bastard. That's two weeks ago. You do pick'em Cal. And don't tell me you're now having second thoughts about a divorce?'

'Not exactly. For starters I'd have to tell Adam my baby isn't his, not that he'll need telling. But, say he forgave me PJ and he was willing to accept my baby as his own. And say he promised to finish with Sheena Jardine . . .'

'Have you not heard of spots and leopards?'

'I know. Even so, he has been rather sweet. Seems to have enjoyed having Sash here despite the reason why, and he's sort of acknowledged he's been neglectful. Last week he stayed overnight in town only once, and this week not at all so maybe . . .'

'Unless he's got some woman other than Ms Jardine on the go, that doesn't surprise me.'

'What makes you say that?'

'I didn't want to tell you till you got back from Ithaca. Last weekend she checked in for rehab at The Priory. No prize for guessing who's footing the bill. And there's more.'

'More?'

'She'll have a rather nice bijou one-bedroom flat to return to.'

'So? She has to live somewhere. Adam's in the middle of buying a pied-a-terre for himself on Wapping Wall. He showed me the details. From the balcony you look across the river towards Canary Wharf. From the photos, rather impressive at night, reminiscent of the New York skyline. And this has three bedrooms and a sauna, and there's a gym and indoor pool in the complex. He wants me to go and look at it after we get back.'

'Some pied-a-terre. Think you'll find Mr Burgess's name also on the deeds to Ms Jardine's apartment. Quite an investment in her, hasn't he? Guess he won't be ditching her any time soon.'

Calista could not honestly say the news floored her. She felt let down. Yet again. Duped. Adam continued to play her for a dork-head.

'Cal, are you still there? I'm sorry if I upset you.'

'No s'okay. I'm gobsmacked the things your gumshoe manages to find out.'

'She's good and her remit is to discover all she can about your husband's relationship with Sheena Jardine. Trust me, Cal. Divorces can be totally messy. We need all the ammunition we can muster. And, in the circumstances, despite looking as though you would probably end up a single mother, better your baby isn't Adam's. Judges can make the outcome, well, not exactly what you'd like. They tend to make decisions they believe in a child's best interest.'

'Thanks for telling me, Tess. I might've been tempted to cosy up to him if he continued to be Mr Nice-Guy. Can't say anything yet though. Don't want to spoil the girls' half-term.'

'Soon as they're back at school, my advice.'

'Yes Ma'am, agreed.' She gave a salute despite Esther not being able to see, and rang off, thinking, Calista Blake repeat after me one hundred times, when it comes to men you're nothing but a numpty

She crossed the narrow Aetos isthmus, and, beyond a tree-covered promontory the road curved following the deep bottomed gulf. Approaching the red-tiled roofs and white walls of Vathy her stomach tightened, her heartbeat quickened.

On Friday afternoon, home early, going through outstanding emails before she went away, the one she had given up all hope of receiving popped into her inbox, sender PJ Wood.

My darling Cal, Please forgive me. I guess my silence has upset you, but please, please don't think badly of me. I'll explain when I see you. Just arrived

back in Vathy from the States. At the end of the month, shall be travelling to England with my mother for her routine check-up at the Radcliffe. You said you would be in Kioni all next week, and, somehow, perhaps we could meet. Please text me when you arrive. You did say you'd lots to tell me, and going to Burgess's villa isn't 'lots'. Are you in trouble, my love? Next time we meet, you must tell me. And what I can do to help. Neither a day nor a night passes without my thinking of you, your scent, the touch of your silk soft skin, the taste of those secret parts of you. Please, please reply.

As ever, you're adoring, or should that be adorable, PJ Wood.

She steeled herself not to weep with relief and joy. Her reply was simple. *You're forgiven. Will text. As ever, Calista Blake.* And today she was to meet him on the quay by *Thelma Jane's* mooring. Within minutes she would hold him, kiss him.

In morning sunshine, the harbour had that laid-back, end-of-season, Greek *avrio* air. She brought the 4x4 to a halt not too far from the *Thelma Jane*. PJ was pacing away from her. Then he turned, her sailor, in light blue distressed jeans, short-sleeved white linen shirt, deck shoes, and waved, unsmiling, inscrutable behind Ray-Bans. Rushing to meet him, she flung her arms around his neck and kissed him, their sunglasses clanging.

'Steady on, Cal.' He held her a little away from him. At last he smiled. 'I've my reputation to consider.'

'Are we going sailing?' Remembering his description, 'scudding along in the swell, the sound of the wind in her sails', she was dressed similarly to him, just in case. She imagined anchoring in some secret cove where they would make love.

'Much as I'd love to, we're going somewhere quiet to do some serious talking. Let's go back to your jeep. I'll navigate you to Villa Petrinos.'

Frantic moths fluttered in her stomach. 'Will your mother be there?'

'Maybe later.'

Throat dry, she swallowed. 'Oh.' She started the engine.

PJ guided her to the outskirts of Vathy and along a narrow road through olive groves. While she drove she told him Adam and the girls had gone off with Yiorgos in his fishing smack. 'A trip out for the girls, and Adam's interested in seeing how Yiorgos's small Fiskardo development's progressing. He didn't object when I said I wanted a day to myself.'

PJ told her his mother was off on a jaunt on her friend Evangelos's cutter, making the most of Ionia before going to cold, rain-soaked England. 'Though at this time of year it tends to rain here. So far, you've been lucky.'

He seemed distant, as though making small talk to a casual acquaintance.

They came upon a parking place. PJ directed her to pull in behind an ancient Fiat Panda. 'My mother's,' he said. Once out of the 4x 4, they climbed earthen steps covered in dry grass to arrive at a flag-stoned terrace dotted with terracotta pots of geraniums. The tall, square Villa Petrinos, stone-built, stood to their right, the terrace extending along the sides of the house. The surrounding grove, branches heavy with olives, leaves shimmering silver-green in sunshine, was held at bay by oleander bushes. She brushed the leaves of a nearby geranium the better to breathe the pungent scent.

'What a fabulous old house. Like the olive trees, it seems rooted in the earth.'

PJ went up three stone steps and unlatched the main door painted dark green, a shuttered window either side. The entrance led directly into a cool, twilit open-plan living room with a surprisingly high ceiling. He stood back making a gesture of invitation for her to go in. Curiosity for the moment overcoming nerves, she pushed her sunglasses into her hair. To the left, an L-shaped area fitted out as a kitchen. Next, a dining table and chairs which stood in front of shuttered patio doors. PJ opened them letting in light and air. Rough-plastered walls, white painted, were the perfect backdrop for a couple of comfortable looking sofas and easy chairs covered with colourful throws. Towards the back of the room, steps from the dining space led up to a gallery and a closed door. Set back beneath the gallery another door, and to the right in the corner, the top of a spiral stair. In the middle of the wall on her right, standing proud of it a wood-burning stove and either side, shelves of books, CDs, and vinyl.

'No wonder you always want to come back here.' She stood for a moment taking in her surroundings.

'Would you like coffee?'

'A glass of water would hit the spot.' She longed for him to take her in his arms.

'You're an undemanding guest, Calista Blake.' Still wearing his shades, he took a glass from a cupboard and poured mineral water from a bottle he brought from the fridge. At arm's length he handed her the water. 'Would you like a piece of Ma's special walnut cake?'

She sipped some water then put the tumbler and her sunglasses down on the nearest surface. 'Right now I'm far too nervous to eat.'

He took off his Ray-Bans and placed them on the worktop, then turned to look at her. Her stomach in knots, the first time that day she glimpsed the intense blue of his eyes. 'That makes two of us.' He looked guarded.

She burst into tears.

CHAPTER FIFTY

Ithaka gave you the splendid journey
Without her you would not have set out
[Constantine Cavathy]

'Please don't cry.' Cupping her face, PJ wiped her cheeks with the ball of his thumbs. Then his arms were around her, his spare, firm body pressed against hers. She clung to him, breathing in his elusive sweet-sharp musk. 'I'm here. I'm here.' His lips brushed her hair as he spoke. 'I know I shouldn't've . . . Soon as I saw you . . . that cheesy old song, "*Zing! Went the strings of my heart*". . .' - She felt his whole body sigh. – 'I only wanted to cheer you up.'

She untwined her arms from around his neck, pressed the palms of her hands against his chest, pushed him just far enough away to hold his gaze. 'And succeeded big-time.' She managed a weak smile.

'And totally messed up your life. Soon as I saw you at your house with your dog. . . What have I to offer you other than worry and heartache when I'm away, and . . .' He held her at arms' length. 'I'm not a poor man, Cal, but I can't run to chartering a private plane, I'm surprised Burgess doesn't hire a helicopter to hop across here from Cephalonia.'

The love and worry in PJ's eyes, staunched her tears. 'He revels in the anticipation, the drive across Cephalonia, the ferry. Perhaps he sees himself as a latter-day Odysseus. At home he likes nothing better than cooking a traditional Sunday lunch. Adam's a paradox, PJ. Only now am I beginning to know him.'

'And love him?' Looking dejected, PJ let go of her. They stood facing each other not touching.

'I think now I understand him. It had been a while when he . . . I'm only human. He charmed the pants off me' She took a deep breath before carrying on. 'I thought you'd given up on me.'

'Jesus, Cal, no way. Working with Jim on our feature was intense. All I wanted was to get back for you, for Ma, pdq. We, Jim and I had been where no Westerners had come out alive. A certain U.S. agency you don't ignore was interested in hearing about it. A tightrope, I'm a photographer not a spook. I thought you'd be okay. Pam's hardly Mrs Danvers.' He touched her arm. 'Let's go downstairs and talk.' He took a bottle of water from the fridge, another glass from the cupboard, and pointed, 'Bring yours.' A glimmer of a smile. 'Before we're through, we might need a drink. I've a bottle of Ouzo stashed somewhere.'

Anxious, she followed him down the tight spiral of steps. At the bottom she could see through the half-opened door no gloomy cellar, a shuttered, furnished room. He pushed the door further open. '*Will you walk into my parlour?* Though the way in is down a winding stair not up.' He put down the bottle and his glass, took hers from her, and placed it beside his on a chest-o'-drawers near the door.

'I remember what happened to that fly.' Again he had worked his magic. '*She ne'er came out again!*'

He gave her the fiercest hug, her feet left the ground. 'That's my girl.' Then abrupt, he let go, opened the shuttered doors of a French window leading onto a terrace she assumed must be at the back of the house. The aromatic scent of herbs wafted in, light flooded the room. She was able to picture him working at his computer, reading, listening to music. A pang of jealousy, who had shared his bed, a double divan.

'What an impressive room.'

'Used to be a wine-press and store room.' He indicated a door to her right. 'Bathroom, if you need it.' He steered her towards the open doors and the comfy chair he moved to face inwards. He drew muslin curtains across the opening, fetched their water and tumblers and placed them on a small table nearby.

'Please sit down.'

Frenetic moths stirred in her stomach. She didn't sit.

'Actually, I do need the bathroom.'

'Be my guest.'

She took her time. When she emerged he was swinging from side to side on his computer chair facing the one she now sat down in.

'Your bath just begs you to luxuriate in it,' she said.

He wheeled himself closer, planting his legs either side of hers. She was trapped. She pressed herself into the chair back. He sat like a judge. Looking into those eyes, she was spellbound.

'Cal, no more prevaricating. Before you start, let's make a pact. There'll be no secrets between us, ever. Promise.'

'I promise.' Though she might lose him.

He poured water into their glasses, took a sip from his. 'Now tell PJ your troubles.'

Only a moment's hesitation, she took a deep breath. 'I'm pregnant. In all probability my baby's yours.'

Despite his tan, he visibly paled, his eyes widened, jaw slackened. She noticed the tremor in his hand. With care, he put his glass down.

'I'm so sorry, so sorry.' Her eyes filled with tears.

'Sorry? Why?' He frowned.

'Must be a terrible shock.'

'Not terrible. Mind-blowing. Give me a minute.' His hand still shook as he picked up his water, drained the glass, put it down. He took a deep breath. 'In all probability?'

'Yes, I really am sorry.' She heard the catch in her voice. 'I never even dreamed of having a child, too wrapped up in my career, and when I tested positive, my first thought was to take the easy way out, but . . . '

He leaned towards her, placed his forefinger on her lips. 'No, Cal, not that. Not ever.' Then he held her hands in his.

Eyes smarting with tears, she shook her head. 'I just couldn't. Especially when I realized it was more likely to be yours than . . . Even if I never saw or heard from you again . . . I earn more than enough to bring my little one up on my own.' She gave a wistful smile. 'I bragged along those lines that night at Marcos's, at least about not being financially dependent on Adam.'

'I remember.' He took a deep breath. 'I still haven't quite got my head around all this. Me, a father.' He let go her hands, caressed her cheek, 'How far gone are you my love?'

'Twelve weeks.'

'That long? Possible, then.' He sat back in his chair. 'I don't know what to say. Are you absolutely sure I'm . . .?'

'I need you to take a paternity test for peace of mind.' She attempted a smile.

'But not until after the baby's born, I guess?'

She swallowed, doing her utmost not to start crying, took a sip of water. 'Not really. Anytime now, if you're willing to give a simple blood sample.'

She noticed the colour return to his face. He poured himself more water, took a drink. 'Does Burgess have any inkling of this?'

'I've an idea he's puzzled as to how it's come about. That's why he hasn't said anything directly.'

'Cal, he's your husband, he must . . .' Looking despondent, he shook his head.

She moved to the edge of her seat, her turn to take his hands in hers, looked at him straight. 'I haven't had sex with Adam since we arrived here that first Saturday night in the summer. He was exceedingly careful . . .' She felt the heat in her face, looked away. 'He wasn't best pleased . . . Last thing Adam wants, another child. He has his hands full with the two he already has.' She bit her lip then told him how erratic and absent-minded she had been after being mugged. 'I'd forgotten my pills, so . . . He did buy condoms in Argostoli but . . . And then I'd met you, and . . .' She gave the deepest sigh, sat back, and lifted her head to meet his gaze. 'I really am sorry. I didn't think . . . I've known a couple of women younger than me who came off the pill. Took them ages to get pregnant.'

'To be honest, Cal, we were both carried away by the moment. Some would say, what bad luck. But . . .' Again he frowned, looked thought-ful, then smiled, a tender smile. 'No, let us say, Kismet.' His voice soft, caressing.

'You really mean that?' Again, she was near to tears.

He took hold her hands, kissed each palm in turn. 'Beats me. How could he not make love to you?'

'PJ, if you knew the half.' Clinging on to his hands, she took a deep breath. 'He'd succeeded in alienating me, and even he wasn't insensitive to the vibes.' She told him about realizing Adam had married her to provide a home for his daughters. Otherwise they would have gone to the States with their mother and her new husband. She swallowed, then moistened her lips. 'Perhaps you can see now why I need positive proof my baby's not his.'

PJ loosed his hands from hers, and gave her water. She took a drink, held onto the glass.

'Deep breath,' he said.

She breathed in. 'Talk about a spider's web. Becoming involved with the affable and charming Mr Burgess is tantamount to being enmeshed in a sticky web of devious duplicity.' She drank a little more water and put her glass down.

'Such long words, Cal.' At last, Mr Sardonic came smiling through.

'I am a lawyer.'

'Not to worry, I'm the feather duster who'll release you. Go on, tell me.'

Smiling, she shook her head. 'PJ Wood how could I not fall in love with you?'

'Difficult not to, I know. As you can see there's a queue of women at my door.'

'Perhaps there would be if you encouraged them. Adam's always made sure, there's been a queue at his. When we go back to England on Saturday, Ledia Kavathi's coming with us. She's going to attend some British Council Language Centre in London to improve her English. Good for her. Her abusive gangster husband's disappeared, and she wouldn't be content to stay here for ever. I doubt Adam's gone to so much trouble out of altruism, any more than Sheena Jardine's a charitable cause.' She needed to take another deep breath, another sip of water.

Serious, pensive, PJ did not once look away. 'And Sheena Jardine is?'

'A young woman he . . . His liaison with her was ongoing before he wormed his way into my bed.' She shuddered. 'The poor kid hadn't long turned seventeen. At least Ledia's what, twenty six, seven.' She told him of entertainments organized for men compelled to spice up their sex lives. 'God knows how Sheena got into it. But what does that matter to a man who says sex to him is like a dry martini before dinner.'

'Did he tell you this?' PJ sounded terse, looked thunderous.

'Not about Sheena.' She told him the whole depressing story from Adam's revelations about his marriage to Annabel to her discovery of his cheating on her. 'I wasn't too happy about setting a private eye on him. Tess said it was the only way to get concrete evidence. If I want a quick divorce, I need something that'll trump his ace of my being pregnant not by him. I was about to confront him, then Sash was suspended. He knows I've become attached to his girls. Bet he thinks now he's got me by the short and curlies.' She forced a derisive laugh. 'How's that for lawyer-speak?' Then she could no longer hold back tears. For better, for worse, now PJ knew all there was to know.

'Eh.' As he stood, the wheels of PJ's chair skittered across the marble floor. He pulled her to her feet. 'Please don't cry. Together we'll get through this.' Holding her close, he rocked her from side to side.

'How . . . could you . . . think . . . I'd ever . . . sleep with . . . Adam . . . when . . . it's you . . . I love . . .' She sobbed into his shirt front. 'I thought . . . I was . . . never . . . going to . . . see you . . . ever again. . . And you'd . . . never . . . told me . . . what . . . PJ . . . stands for.'

He stroked her hair. 'You never asked.' He manoeuvred her so that he could look at her, then smiled. 'J is for John after my dad. The P's not so common. At school, I was teased. One or two fights, I became PJ which, if you think about it, couldn't be better for a photo journalist.'

She stopped crying, tried to pull away, not succeeding.

'Tell me then. What's the P for?'

'P is for Peredur.'

'Peredur.' She repeated, listening to the sound. 'What does it mean?'

'Don't know. Peredur was the hero of a Welsh Arthurian romance, a seventh son of a seventh son who has magical adventures.' His smile was tender. 'I've had a fair few adventures, you're the only magical one I can remember.'

'Peredur Wood you're a Welsh sorcerer who's bewitched me.'

'Only a sixteenth Welsh on Ma's side.' He held her at arm's length. 'Now Calista Blake we know what we long to do more than anything. But . . .' He tilted his wrist without letting go of her, glanced at his watch. 'Don't know about you, I'm starving. Breakfast was too strong coffees. Thought I'd throw up, if I ate anything. That would've impressed you.' He gave one of his signature smiles.

'I made myself have yoghurt and honey.'

'Quite right, you have the little one to think of.' He let go of her, his forehead. 'When's your, our baby due?'

'May the first.'

'May Day, m'aidez!' He gave a nervous laugh. 'We'll both need help, I guess.'

'That's my joke,' she said. 'Though neither the nurse who did my scan nor my GP got it. Next Monday I've another scan scheduled, and yet another blood test. This time for Down's syndrome.' She gave a heartfelt sigh. 'Fingers crossed everything will be fine. Has been so far.'

'And I can't be there. I really wish I could be.' His regret sounded genuine. 'On Thursday, Ma and I are travelling to Athens, then on Friday we fly to Heathrow. Brian, my half-brother will meet us to take us to Oxford. Ma's check-up is on Tuesday, and I really should hang around until . . .'

'PJ, of course you must. We'll at least be in the same country. I don't anticipate snipers taking pot shots at you from Carfax Tower.'

He took her hand. 'Come on, I'll get us something to eat, and while I do, we must make plans for your escape. I'll fight Burgess for you, every way and any way I can.' He pulled her to him, a tender kiss. Bliss. Then tentative, he said, 'When we've eaten and planned, maybe we . . . are we allowed to . . . now you're pregnant . . . you know?'

'Peredur Wood, what are you trying to say?' She gave an impish grin. 'We're allowed to make love as long as we don't play rough.'

'Cal, I've witnessed too much of man's inhumanity, and always the women and children come off worst. I'm not into playing cruel games for the fun of it.' He gestured toward the stairs. 'You go up ahead. If you fall, I'll catch you.'

They laid their plans as best they could, while PJ prepared lunch, traditional Greek salad, and grilled chops marinated in olive oil and herbs.

'S'pose in your condition, a pre-lunch Ouzo's out of the question,' he said.

'Fraid so, but you go ahead.'

'Maybe help steady my nerves, if you don't mind.'

While they ate - after their angst-filled yet cathartic marathon, she was more than willing to eat the lamb, mop up juices with fresh bread – she brought him up to date on the progress of her pregnancy.

'I'm doing my best to keep healthy,' she said, 'though I don't know how I'd have coped without Tess and Pam, and Beppo of course.'

'Ah, yes, the mutt. I think I'm more jealous of him than I am of Burgess.'

'Now you're being silly.'

PJ washed up, she dried.

'This feels so good,' He rinsed their plates under the hot tap. 'Beats being hi-jacked by Taliban hands down.'

'I'd give you a week, maybe a month before you got restless.' She discarded the teacloth, put her hand on his shoulder and turned him to face her, then gripping his upper arms, looked him in the eyes. 'You must never stop doing what you do on my account. I've had a baptism of fire when it comes to loving PJ Wood, photographer of war zones. But, as long as he loves me . . .'

Her kiss on his lips was soft, caressing. He began to respond. She took a step back.

'For ever, and always, Cal. That much I know. While I'm able, I can't and won't say I'll give up what I do. But, loving you . . .' He placed his hand on her stomach where her bump would soon appear. 'And now this unbelievable . . . I'll need to make . . . adjustments . . . compromises. The next few months, I shan't go away for weeks on end. That's a promise. You'll need me around.' He gestured toward the dried pots. 'I'll just put these away.' His smile was dreamy. 'And then . . .'

The front door opened. A petite, late-middle-aged woman in navy linen slacks, short-sleeved white shirt, stood on the threshold. She gave a mischievous smile, and said, 'I do hope while this old moggy's been away, you mice have had a lovely play.'

'You could say that.' PJ said. 'Ma, this is Calista Blake. Cal meet my mother, Thelma Wood.'

She and Thelma Wood shook hands, smiling.

'Just popped by to say 'hello', and 'good-bye',' Thelma said. 'Evangelos is waiting for me on the track. 'Must dash. See you later PJ.' And she was gone.

'Just couldn't resist taking a look at the only woman I've ever brought here.' Mr Sardonic gave one of his smiles as the door closed behind her. 'Thank God Evangelos was waiting for her. We might not have seen the back of her.'

'I'm pleased I've met her, if only briefly,'

'You'll have plenty of time to get to know her. She's over-wintering in Oxford with Brian and Paul. Something they cooked up between them, the idea being in between assignments I can hang around London. They must've had a premonition.'

He took her by the hand, drew her to him, a tender kiss. 'And now my beautiful iridescent bluebottle . . .'

'Bluebottle.'

With a dreamy smile, he led her down the spiral stair, and into his parlour.

CHAPTER FIFTY ONE

D-day, 6 November

Sunday morning, Calista chose to work on her laptop at the kitchen table, the comforting warmth of the Aga nearby. An attempt to calm nerves. A curled up Beppo dozed in his basket. He sat up, cocked his head to one side and twitched his Spaniel ears. Then she heard the cattle-grid's rattle. She glanced at the time registered on her toolbar 10.04, saved her file, clicked on hibernate. Adam had called around 8.15 to say he was about to set out - 'I haven't woken you, have I?' He had sounded on edge. 'Not at all', her reply. Up early, she did not tell him, she and Beppo were ready for their morning ramble wreathed in mist, November, one of her less favourite months. Now, she got to her feet, told the dog to stay, and went out through the French doors to greet him.

'Cal, I'm really sorry, I just couldn't get back before now,' he said as he got out of his Jaguar saloon. Taking her by surprise, he kissed her on each cheek. She caught that familiar and alluring whiff of Vetiver. 'Been non-stop ever since I left.'

'I've been busy too.' She noticed he had on the smart-casual outfit he had worn the previous Sunday. Then, he had packed a large suitcase, plus a couple of business suits and shoes to take with him, intending to drive directly to London from Dorset, which made sense. No surprise, all he retrieved from the boot was an overnight bag.

'So, you've moved into your pied-a-terre. I hadn't realized you'd finalized.'

'Just over three weeks ago. Didn't I say? Moved in just before we went away. So much better than a hotel. You must come and see it.'

'Love to.' She gave a wry smile. The palaver of their landing at Stansted instead of their usual airport so that his minion could take Ledia to her accommodation in London, Adam's apartment according to Esther's private eye. They each had their own bedroom she was told. So what. Given half a chance, Adam preferred sleeping alone.

They went into the house the same way she had come out. Beppo, stood waiting, wagged his tail. Ignored, he went back to his basket.

'Poor you,' she said. 'No Sunday lie in. You made very good time from Wapping.'

'I thought if I got here early enough, I could make us brunch.'

'I should do that. You've just driven a hundred miles.'

He was insistent, which, as usual, meant all she had to do was make toast. Maybe his way of making amends. He had been away the entire week, called her only three times, the first to say he had arrived in London after delivering the girls, the second mid-week to check she was okay, and the third to say he would not be back till Sunday. Above all though, to soften her up for the showdown she sensed was imminent. Nevertheless, she had no difficulty eating eggs scrambled to perfection, crisp but not too crisp bacon, grilled mushrooms and tomatoes, potato hash browns. Her appetite had certainly picked up the past few weeks.

Whilst they ate, complicit, they were both content to reprise their Ithaca trip, the girls' first time in Greece.

'Ithaca's certainly worked her magic on Len and Sash, just as she did that first time with us,' Adam said.

'And you got the urge to build a villa for your family, even made enquiries to get it underway. Though you didn't tell me at the time, but, why would you? I wasn't family then.' She met his gaze across the table.

'You are now, Cal, don't forget.' His look quizzical.

'Easy to remember when Len and Sash are around. Otherwise . . .' Calista shrugged.

'You must know you have my undying gratitude. You've helped me, and the girls through a difficult patch. Thanks to your sound counsel, Len's looking forward to doing what she wants above all else. And with my blessing.' She saw sadness in his eyes. 'As for my little Sash . . .' a catch in his voice. 'She's become really attached to you.'

'As I have her. But . . .'

'You're not her mother.'

'You know in your heart, Sash should go and live with Annabel and Bradley,' her tone gentle. 'Especially once Len's left that school. Sash should never have gone there in the first place.'

'As always, I over-ruled Annie. No wonder . . .' He swallowed. 'Brown's a good sort of chap.' Adam-like he regained his composure. 'I have talked to them, and . . . he's going to look into suitable schools for Sash come the fall, as he calls it.'

'Well done you.' She smiled with relief for Sasha, and for herself. 'I believe sometimes you need to let go, no matter how much it hurts. Sash loves you. No way will she not want to visit, or not go back to Ithaca.'

Adam got to his feet. 'Why don't we go through to the siting room? I'll make a pot of Earl Grey and bring it in.'

Less nervous, she concurred, Beppo following her.

Beppo lay in front of the hearth. Just for once he hadn't been banished to the lobby. Adam sat back in his favourite armchair by the side of the ready-laid log fire she had set alight. He nursed his breakfast cup and saucer against his chest. Calista had made herself comfortable with cushions at the farther end of the sofa, the more easily to observe Adam, and he her come to that.

'This is cosy.' He smiled across the space between them.

'I've always loved this room,' she said. 'The house itself is far too big. More often than not, I'm here all on my own.'

'You soon won't be.' He sounded pleased with himself.

She could not begin to second guess what he would say next.

Deliberate, he put down his cup and saucer, got to his feet. 'We shouldn't be drinking tea. A celebratory glass of Veuve Cliquot, at the very least a Buck's Fizz perhaps. You've been so abstemious lately.'

'What are we celebrating, Adam? Your new apartment?'

He took a step forward. To her relief, instead of coming towards her, he went over to the French doors and looked out. 'When were you going to tell me you're pregnant, Cal?'

Her nervousness evaporated. No more cryptic remarks, hints that he knew. She took a few sips of tea, put her cup down before replying. 'How long have you suspected?'

He returned to his chair. 'You shouldn't discard test kits in the waste bin of our shared bathroom.' - He had known ever since that Sunday morning she'd just finished the test, then Sasha came knocking on their bedroom door. - 'I hoped you'd confide in me. All things considered, there's only the slightest chance your baby's mine.'

'I was going to . . .'

She could not now say 'confront'. 'I was going to talk to you the weekend you brought Sash home.'

'The way you looked after her was above and beyond.' He picked up his cup, drank some tea. 'Have you told Wakeham you're pregnant?'

'Matt, no, not yet. Why would I?'

'I assume he's . . .'

'Matt, good God, no. Not Matt.'

He could not have looked more stunned if she had punched him between the eyes. His cup rattled in its saucer as he put it down.

'Who the hell is it then?'

'I hope we can divorce without rancour,' she said.

'Who is it? Don't you think I've a right to know?' His face had become red.

'Please, Adam, first hear me out.'

An impatient gesture indicating she should carry on.

'I never knew loneliness till I married you and we moved here. I can't fault you for wanting what you thought best for Len and Sash. After all it was for them, not because you couldn't live without me.'

'I've never been fonder of any other woman. Not even Annie. My respect and my admiration for you is . . . I owe you. More than you know.'

'You respect me? I don't think so.' She heard the heat in her voice, felt it in her face. 'If you do, you have your own ineffable way of showing it.'

She stood, picked up her iPhone from the coffee table. 'I have something I think you should see.' She went over to him, held the screen so that he could look. He leaned forward as she flicked through the photos she had taken near the Girl and the Dolphin fountain. 'I make no apologies. I needed to know, were you playing me for a sucker like you did Annabel? I did warn you, Adam, cheat on me . . . How is this respecting me?'

'This is nothing. Only sex.' His expression impassive, his tone acid. He remained sitting forward, forearms resting on his knees, hands clasped.

'Your dry martini before dinner. I do remember.' She put the phone down. Thumbs folded into her palms, she made fists with her hands, and returned to her seat. If she had stayed too close, she might punch him, kick him. Anything to shatter his complacency.

'She's well-paid for her services. Would you rather I had an affair with someone who ends up a bunny-boiler?' He said.

'She? Why don't you give her a little of your worthless respect, call her by her name, Sheena Jardine?' You've been using, abusing her since she was no older than Len.'

His face became drained of all colour. 'How do you . . .?'

'Tess specializes in divorce, remember. Some petitions aren't always straightforward. And . . .'

'The Sapphic Ice Maidens.' To her surprise, he sounded crushed, bowed his head as though contemplating his hands. 'Mahoney told me what you were called. At Oxford. You don't mess with them, he said.'

A silence so dense it could be heard. Beppo, eyes closed, head on forepaws broke it emitting a low, contented growl.

'If we agree terms as Annie and I did, a quick and amicable divorce is no problem. One thing I can agree unconditionally.' He had mustered sarcasm. 'You can have sole custody of the bloody dog.'

'Adam. I don't hate you. I just don't and can't love you enough to overlook your . . . your peccadilloes. You're unbelievably generous. I know what you're doing for Sheena.'

His high colour returned. 'How the . . .?'

'I'm sorry, I wasn't happy about it.' She told him what Tess had advised about collecting evidence. 'Her private eye's been over zealous.'

'I'd like to know how he did it.'

'She, actually. Nothing unlawful was involved.'

He harrumphed as though unconvinced. 'The Monstrous Regiment of Women. I should be incandescent.' He looked pensive. 'I've been worried. You pregnant. Didn't see how it could be me. I could hardly censure you though . . . any more than I could Annie. I hoped you'd get rid of it. Carry on as though it never happened.'

'I can well imagine.'

Another silence.

'I . . . I just couldn't . . .' her voice soft, speaking for her own benefit rather than his.

'You never ever mentioned wanting a child, or we could've . . .' He sounded regretful.

'I didn't think I did.'

His gaze was intense. 'If there's a problem, we don't need to divorce.

I would treat her or him as my own.'

'That's . . . that's more than I deserve.'

'I owe you, I said. What I'm doing for Sheena, something else down to you, Cal. I'm trying to make amends.' He gave a contrite smile. 'A good Catholic boy's shot at redemption, I suppose.' He leaned back in his chair. 'Now, if I promise to try and not blow my top, will you tell me, who is the father?'

She told him. He looked dumbfounded, then bemused.

'If, for me personally, it wasn't so tragic, it'd be farcical. You're a clever professional, Cal, and hardly in the first flush of youth.'

'Thanks for reminding me.'

'PJ Wood, a man who drinks rose. I thought he was a p . . . I thought he was gay.'

She resisted the urge to laugh. 'He said if I were ever in trouble to let him know.'

'Has he done a runner?'

'No he has not.' Adam looked crestfallen.

'How did he take it?'

'He's almost your neighbour now.' She told him about PJ's mews cottage behind St Katharine's Dock. 'He's willing to meet you, talk to you . . .'

A derisive snort. 'To say what? Apologize for impregnating my wife, arrange for pistols at dawn.'

Again he got to his feet. Beppo moved out of his way as he threw a couple more logs on the fire.

'PJ did say it was Kismet.' She felt herself blush.

He turned to look at her. Her face became even hotter.

'Kismet, you could say that.' He strode over to the French window, this time opened it as though he needed to breathe the damp November air. His back towards her, 'I may not be good husband material. My guess, neither is Wood. What now, Cal?' His voice was tight.

308

CHAPTER FIFTY TWO

Ithaca, Twenty-One Months Later

French doors open, as Calista roused, the first hint of daylight was beginning to filter through mosquito screen and muslin curtains. The familiar scents of herbs and warm earth washed over her. She opened her eyes, lay still. The stone walls of the one-time wine press, and the gnarled old almond tree shading the terrace ensured the room was cool. Careful, she turned over on her side to contemplate her beloved PJ.

Sunday, August 4th, already a whole week spent in paradise, except the first few days, she was on tenterhooks. PJ in Lebanon, the more easily to sneak over the border into Syria and bear witness to the truth of the insurgency. This an update, he had already been there earlier in the year. His message was unequivocal, *No worries. Take up Adam's offer. Save you so much hassle. Will join you at Villa Petrinos.*

Despite the hurt they had caused each other, she and Adam had managed to remain friends – 'We don't hate each other,' Adam said. 'Let's behave like civilized human beings.' Adam, had invited her to join him and the girls on their customary flight to Cephalonia.

Ledia had long gone. She had not stayed in London much above six months, and Adam had revealed the reason for taking up her cause, apart from the obvious. He had used his contacts to help her make a fresh start in Seattle, far far away from the Eastern Med because, Adam confided, Ledia's husband had been executed, a revenge killing, *hak marje,* to take blood as the Albanians called it. He did not say why though she suspected Ledia had told him. Shocked, Calista relayed the news to PJ.

'I keep having to revise my opinion of him,' PJ said. 'He not only did Ledia a favour, Yiorgos and Katrina too.' All Katrina told her was, she had news of her brother's death, not the how, or the why. 'Kismet,' she said. 'It was his fate.'

Sunday, Monday, Tuesday, no PJ, no word.

Nearby, behind a bamboo screen, safe in her cot, their fifteen-month-old daughter was fast asleep. PJ had chosen her name, Hana, spelt H A N A, he told her, Arabic, meaning happiness. And, Miriam, Hebrew for star of the sea because she was conceived by it. 'Whatever we call her, she'll be a sentence, Hana Miriam Wood. As it is, she'll spend her life correcting the spelling of Hana. On the other hand . . .' He looked thoughtful. 'We could call her Holly.'

At breakfast on the Wednesday, Thelma suggested, with Calista's permission, she might take Hana to visit Evangelos. The three of them would probably go for a cruise on his motor yacht, find a beach for a picnic. 'Do you good, a few hours to yourself. Put your feet up. Read a book. Trust me, as far as PJ's concerned, no news is good news.'

From her baby seat in the back of Thelma's new Fiat Panda, Hana, smiling, excited, waved 'Bye-bye.' At least Beppo will be missing me, Calista thought, I must call Pam, and find out how they both are.

She descended the spiral staircase, instead of a book she searched for music, played it loud enough to hear as she lounged in the shade of the almond tree, eyes closed. Eva Cassidy's fragile rendering of 'Somewhere over the Rainbow' came to an end, silence, except for the cicadas. She opened her eyes. PJ sat crossed ankles on the ground nearby. He smiled. As always, he must have moved like a cat. Even with music playing, she would have heard anybody else's step.

'When did you . . .' She swung her legs round to sit sideways.

'No kiss. Or, I've missed you.' His grin broadened.

'Why didn't you call?' She heard her voice, querulous.

'Eh, I shan't be going back there, or anywhere like it till well after our son's born.' – They had not long learnt his sex, their second child conceived around Hana's first birthday on the 28th of April. – 'I couldn't resist taking you by surprise.' He looked at her, accusing. 'Where's my daughter, my mother? You're obviously expecting a lover.' He hotched closer, took her hands, kissed the heel of each in turn.

'Your poor face.' She pulled them away to stroke gashes where he had cut himself with a razor.

'The three of you would've hated me with a full beard.'

He stood, pulled her to her feet. 'How long have we got?'

'A few hours.'

She stretched, smiling, remembering. PJ opened his eyes, turned to face her, rubbed noses with her.

'Happy Anniversary, Mrs Wood.' He spoke in a whisper. 'Two years since we . . . Can you believe it?' His smile broadened into the cheekiest grin. 'How many new QCs are pregnant, I wonder.'

'You're a dangerous man. Two children in less than three years.' She too spoke in a whisper.

Now his smile was dreamy, gentle, he pushed her onto her back, kissed her on the lips, tender, caressing, then he stroked her cheek. 'Twins of a gazelle, Mrs Wood?' Their code, and his parting shot that time in the Erato cove. He had repeated it in this room, on the second occasion they made love. Between her legs, she felt a tingle of anticipation. He caressed the swell of her breasts with his lips, her nipples, whispered '*Your breasts are like two fawns, twins of a gazelle that feed among the lilies.*' He had told her the beautiful words were not his, but from the Song of Solomon. When she asked if they were his standard line in seduction, he said she was the only woman who had ever brought them to mind.

Unhurried, as always they explored every part of the other's body, savoured the taste of each other's skin, she tracing with her fingertips the scar left by a bullet's graze on his thigh. Gentle, not frantic, quiet so as not to wake Hana, they took their time, revelled in the pure pleasure of their connection, with a soft sigh of satisfaction climaxing together.

'Thank you for loving me, Calista Blake.'

'Thank you, Peredur Wood. The ecstasy's all mine.' And the agony, her unspoken thought.

The End

ACKNOWLEDGEMENTS

First heartfelt thanks to my select band of readers who, I was delighted to learn, enjoyed my debut novel *Last Bite of the Cherry*, and said they looked forward to my second. I hope they will not have been disappointed.

I am indebted to members of my Tuesday Writers' Workshop, Just Write: Brenda Belcher, Josie Bicker, Mary Byrne, Karen Clarke, Maime Henderson, Margaret Kaine, Sally Knight, the late Nick Leach, Cathy Mansell, Keith Morley, Biddy Nelson, Richard Pike, Jean Podlubny, Liz Ringrose, and Kate Ruse for their perceptive comments and criticism of what started out as an 'edit' but developed into a complete re-write of material many of them were already familiar with. Thank you, you were a great help, and, a special thank you to Keith for the chapter heading 'Satellite Man', a throw-away comment I couldn't resist using.

Edwin Cullingford has my eternal gratitude for his backroom contribution, not least for his advice on the credibility of plotline and characters, and for checking my spelling, grammar and punctuation.

I would also like to reiterate my thanks to editor, Eve Farr, whose appraisal of the original *Twins of a Gazelle* gave me the confidence to become a founder member of The New Romantics 4. Without the inspiration, support and encouragement provided by **June Kearns**, **Lizzie Lamb** and **Adrienne Vaughan** I would not have published my debut novel, *Last Bite of the Cherry*, let alone this version of *Twins of a Gazelle*, or be looking forward to finishing a yet untitled third novel. Thank you Ade, Lizzie and June. No one could have better literary mates.

Finally, thank you Jane Dixon Smith for the design of a beautifully evocative cover.

ABOUT THE AUTHOR

Margaret Cullingford, Mags to her friends, lives in Leicestershire, England with her partner and a temperamental tortoiseshell cat. Having made a timely escape from the rumpus of a renowned university department, Mags realized a long-term ambition to write fiction, and in the process discovered, to her delight, she could create uproar she was able to control.

Mags published her debut novel *Last Bite of the Cherry* (paperback and eBook) in 2012. *Twins of a Gazelle* is her second, and whilst she could not claim either novel is 'romantic', both have a similar theme – clever woman, emotionally naïve, initially makes disastrous choice of man (men) before meeting 'The One'. Not the conventional Girl-Meets-Boy love stories, but about love nevertheless,

Margaret Cullingford, along with June Kearns, Lizzie Lamb and Adrienne Vaughan, is a member of the **New Romantics 4**, and indie publishing collaboration, New Romantics Press.

Follow The New Romantics 4 on Twitter.

To learn more about Mags, go to her website www.magscullingford.com or follow her on Twitter @CullingfordMags. See also www.facebook.com/MagsCullingfordWriter

NOVELS PUBLISHED BY THE NEW ROMANTICS 4 – NEW ROMANTICS PRESS

Margaret Cullingford
- Last Bite of the Cherry
Twins of a Gazelle

June Kearns
- An English Woman's Guide to the Cowboy
The 20's Girl, the Ghost and All That Jazz

Lizzie Lamb
- Tall, Dark and Kilted
Boot Camp Bride

Adrienne Vaughan
- A Hollow Heart
A Change of Heart

If you have read and enjoyed our books, please leave a review on Amazon or Goodreads. Look out for new books from The New Romantics 4 in 2015.

www.ingramcontent.com/pod-product-compliance
Lightning Source LLC
Chambersburg PA
CBHW062110170626
46813CB00002B/387